Hopeful Hearts at Glendale Hall

Hopeful Hearts at Glendale Hall

Victoria Walters

hera

First published in the United Kingdom in 2020 by Hera Books

Hera Books
28b Cricketfield Road
London, E5 8NS
United Kingdom

A CIP catalogue record for this book is available from the British Library.

Print ISBN 978 1 80032 139 7
Ebook ISBN 978 1 912973 45 3

Printed and bound in Great Britain by Clays Ltd, Elcograf S.p.A.

To Keshini, for your guidance and enthusiasm.

Prologue

My boyfriend Rory and I returned to Fraser Farm just after midnight. We had celebrated Hogmanay at Glendale Hall, now an annual tradition for us.

Two years ago, after watching the firework display there, we became a couple. Now, we had a son about to turn one. And I still couldn't quite believe it.

'Happy Hogmanay,' Rory said as we sat down in the living room with two mugs of hot chocolate, the warmth welcome after the cold air in the grounds of Glendale Hall. Our son Harry slept peacefully in his carrycot, and the only lights on were the fairy lights on our Christmas tree in the corner. We clinked mugs side-by-side on the sofa.

'I can't believe Harry will be one this month, this year has flown by. It's all been such a whirlwind. Who would have thought we'd be sitting here right now, like this?' I got pregnant so soon into our relationship that I felt I'd hardly had time to breathe. I had moved onto Rory's farm and had Harry, and feet had barely touched the ground since. I had known Rory since we were teenagers but even so, the speed at which we had moved since that first night together had been lightning fast.

'Not me, that's for sure. I didn't think I could ever get you into a pair of wellies, let alone to live on a farm,' he said with a grin.

'I certainly never expected to be the girlfriend of a farmer,' I said, smiling back, but truthfully it was still something I was struggling to get a handle on. 'Alcohol really has a lot to answer for.'

Rory chuckled. 'I thought it was my good looks and charm that led you to my bed, not booze. But, hey, I'll take it either way.'

'A combination of all of the above, let's say.'

'Well, for me, it was definitely how amazing you are.' He turned to me. 'I know I'm hopeless at anything romantic, blame it on growing up more interested in cows than women...' He trailed off as I burst out laughing. 'I didn't mean it like that!' he protested. Once I had controlled my laughter a bit, he continued. 'But you know I love you, I hope. And I know I've mentioned it before but maybe you didn't think I was serious... how about we get married? Become a real family.'

'We are a real family,' I said, taken aback. He had mentioned it before, usually in a jokey way, and our friends and family often made subtle remarks questioning why we weren't married yet, but he hadn't actually proposed. Not for real. Now he was. And I had no idea what to say.

'You know what I mean.'

I looked away. I thought about my friend Emily asking me in the summer about why we hadn't got married, and the reason I had given her. 'I still can't imagine getting married without her,' I half-whispered. My beloved mother. The only person I wanted at my wedding, and the one who couldn't be there. I had told Rory how I felt before. I knew he understood. After all, both of his parents had died when he was just eighteen.

'I know.' Rory took my hand in his. 'When you're ready then… will you?'

I met his gaze. Even though the past year had been scary, I loved Rory and Harry, and the thought of life without them was terrifying. I didn't want to lose them. 'Yes,' I said, and he leaned in for a long kiss as guilt rested heavily on my chest that I couldn't give him what he wanted.

Not yet.

Chapter One

Glancing at the clock striking three p.m., I sighed. Despite getting up an hour earlier than usual at five a.m. in the chilly darkness of a December morning to try to get everything done, we were still running late for the wedding.

'Please let me put your shoes on,' I pleaded with Harry, kneeling on the floor in my long, red, silk dress as my son kicked his legs stubbornly out of my reach. 'Why are you making this so difficult?'

'Problems?' My dad came into the living room then, dressed smartly in his grey suit, his grey hair combed neatly. He was ready at least.

'Oh no, we're fine,' I said, through gritted teeth as I tried to hold Harry's legs still. 'It's just that wearing shoes isn't something we want to do today.' I tried to smile at my dad but frustration rose up inside as Harry kicked his feet again. He was wearing a kilt in the Fraser clan colours and looked adorably handsome in it with his tuft of auburn hair. He would be two years old next month, and I hoped that the terrible twos weren't rearing their head already.

'Heather!' Rory, my boyfriend, called out then, opening the front door. We could feel the draught instantly. 'I can't get Prince out of the paddock, it's a two-man job unfortunately.'

'I've got my hands full here,' I snapped back, my patience evaporating.

'Angus is busy, Heth,' Rory replied. 'If you ever want us to get to the church...'

I closed my eyes for a moment. Sometimes it felt like I was constantly holding back a scream.

'Let me do those shoes,' my dad said quickly, scooting down beside me. 'You go and help Rory, and then we'll get going,' he added gently. 'And don't worry, we have plenty of time.' Even though it was a lie, I appreciated the attempt to stop me from worrying. He knew me too well.

'Thanks, Dad, thank God you're here,' I said, standing up. 'Fine, I'm coming!' I called back to Rory. I walked out quickly, relieved that my dad had just come for his annual Christmas stay with us. There were just two weeks left until Christmas but there was a threat of snow and we didn't want either of us stranded from the other so he had come now. It was hard enough to manage a toddler without having to help run a farm in the Highlands in winter, and on top of all that we had to attend a Christmas wedding as well.

In the hallway, I pulled on my sparkly wellies, bought for me one Christmas by Rory to try to ease the pain of me not being able to wear my beloved high heels to work anymore – but I still missed those heels. I threw on my thick parka over my dress, pulling up the hood carefully over my shoulder-length curly light brown hair and stepped outside, immediately shivering.

The brisk cold air whipped around my face as I made my way to the horses' paddock at the side of our red-brick farmhouse. The light was already beginning to fade in the late afternoon. Fraser Farm was perched on a hill in the middle of the countryside, miles from anywhere, and as such was often weather-beaten. Rory bred Highland cows here – gorgeous, furry ginger beasts who were as gentle as they were big. I didn't really get involved in their care though. I'd lived on the farm for two years now but when I had arrived, I was a librarian in Glendale village, and it had been a sharp learning curve; one that I was very much still on.

Love really did have a lot to answer for.

'We're going to miss the ceremony at this rate,' I said when I walked into the paddock. Rory was waiting by the open gate, wearing a big coat and wellies like me, which hid the kilt I knew he had on under there.

'Plenty of time,' he said airily. That man was too laid-back for his own good.

'Let's just hurry this along,' I said. 'We can't let them down.'

'Okay, okay, come on then. We'll try to lure the idiot out with an apple,' he said, with a sigh. The horse in question, Prince, stood in the middle of his paddock looking at us stubbornly. Despite the fact it was freezing and sleet was on the cards later, he didn't seem at all inclined to let Rory take him to his stable. He reminded me of Harry when he didn't want to do something that I asked him to, even when it was for his own good.

I joined Rory in the paddock and took the apple from him.

'Okay. You hold the apple and try to coax him with it, while I pull on his lead, and between us hopefully we can shift him,' Rory said, making his way to Prince, the large, silver horse, who watched him warily. Rory was trying to get me more used to our two horses, even attempting to teach me to ride, but I was nervous. The one and only time I went horse-riding as a child, I fell straight off the horse, and since then have avoided them at all costs. Rory reasoned though that being on a farm it was useful to be able to ride in case we got snowed in or couldn't use the quad bike, plus he had so much to do, it would help him if I took over some of the horses' care. But reason didn't help when it came to fear I had found.

I followed Rory through the mud, gathering my dress up in one hand hoping it wouldn't crease too much, my wellies squelching as I walked. I held out my other hand, the apple perched on my palm, willing Prince not to bite me. 'Hi there, boy,' I said nervously, showing him the apple. 'Look what we have for you.'

Rory took hold of his halter. Prince snorted with annoyance. I stepped back instinctively. 'Come a bit closer,' Rory told me patiently.

I sometimes worried my presence here was more of a hindrance than a help, but Rory took it all in his stride. I envied his unflappable personality. Stepping forward, I held the apple higher so the horse could see it. He reached forward, and I quickly moved back.

'That's it, lead him out,' Rory said, giving Prince a little tug in encouragement. I stepped backwards quickly as Prince started moving more keenly now, evidently deciding the apple was indeed worth leaving the paddock for. My hood slipped down, the wind pushing my hair back.

'There we go,' Rory said as I slipped through the gate. He quickly locked it behind us and I let Prince have the apple.

'Good boy,' I told Prince, reaching up to pat him as he chewed on the apple. Prince looked at me, his mouth opened, and with a thud he dropped the apple core on the top of my head. 'Ow! That hurt!' I cried. I heard a chuckle behind me, and spun around to see Angus walking past, an amused grin on his face. Angus was in his late seventies and had worked on the farm with Rory's grandfather. He still lived in a cottage at the edge of the property, helping Rory manage the farm. His sister's son Cameron also helped out at busy times. Other than them, it was just me and Rory out here, and I didn't think Angus thought I was up to the job. At times like this, I had to agree with him. 'Not funny,' I said grumpily.

'Ignore him. I'll take Prince on through to the stables, you get everyone ready to go,' Rory said, looking as if he too was trying to smother a grin.

'That horse hates me,' I grumbled, picking a bit of apple out of my hair, wondering why I'd bothered to wash and style it earlier. I couldn't believe I shared a home with that animal.

'I think he likes you – he was trying to share his treat with you,' Rory said, a grin finally breaking out on his face as he walked off with the horse.

Tutting, I set off back to the farmhouse, thinking I really needed another woman around here for support sometimes. I tried to ignore the pang of missing my mother that followed that thought. Once inside, I took off my coat and hurried to the hall mirror to apply some lipstick. I sighed as I looked at my reflection, the wind having ruffled up my hair. I wouldn't look as put together as the rest of the wedding party, that was certain.

'Okay, let's get these off,' Rory said, hurrying in behind me, taking off his wellies. He noticed me then and when he stood up, he whistled. 'You're simply stunning. If only that dress was more practical to wear around here all the time,' he said rather wistfully. I couldn't help but wonder how quickly he might want to take it off me later.

I smiled, somewhat mollified after being dragged out to help with the horse. 'I wish it was, there are only so many combinations of jeans and jumpers I can try.' I sighed. I didn't think I'd ever fully accept farm 'fashion'. I turned around as he took off his coat, revealing his kilt in its full glory. My eyes couldn't help but fall to his muscly bare legs. There was at least one perk of being married to a farmer. 'You know, you really should wear that kilt more often,' I said as I slipped on my fur stole. Rory was taller than me even when I wore my heels, and he had strawberry-blonde messy hair and a rugged beard. I still couldn't believe that the boy who used to tease me mercilessly was now the man I slept next to every night. But somehow a spark had been ignited three years ago that had yet to dim even if lately we didn't have much time to appreciate it.

'I'd say the same but I'm not sure wellies go with that dress,' he said, giving me an appreciative look up and down. I took my wellies off, replacing them with my four-inch silver heels, and picked up my clutch bag.

'Well, I better enjoy getting to leave the wellies off for one day then,' I replied, stepping closer. There were two plus points about weddings – the chance to dress up and let your hair down. I hadn't done either in what felt like forever. Rory reached towards me, his lips coming closer, when suddenly footsteps came bounding around the corner. We drew apart with a rueful smile. Interruptions were constant around here. 'You all ready?' Rory asked Harry who was followed by my dad, and was thankfully now wearing shoes.

'We're ready, aren't we, Harry?' Dad said, grabbing his coat from the hook.

'Thanks Dad. Look at this handsome boy,' I said, scooping Harry up into my arms. He was a such a mini-me of Rory. 'How late are we?' I asked Rory over his head. Our life was happy but tiring, there was always something to fix, and we seemed to forever be playing catch up. I was almost always tired.

'Only ten minutes,' Rory replied, shrugging on his kilt jacket.

'Okay then, let's get out of here before we find another problem to deal with,' I replied. I'd had to use almost a whole tube of concealer to cover the black circles under my eyes but at least my lack of sleep meant we wouldn't miss our friend's wedding.

We hurried out of our farmhouse into our jeep, and drove down our gravel driveway and through the gates into the countryside. Our farm was in the middle of nowhere and a twenty-minute drive into Glendale village. I looked at Harry in his car seat behind me, smiling with excitement. It wasn't his first wedding; last year he had attended not one but two weddings – my best friend Beth had married Rory's younger brother Drew, and then her mother had married her long-time companion John. But this would be the first he could walk at.

This time, we were on our way to a Christmas wedding, one that the whole village of Glendale had been buzzing about for weeks, if not months. Partly because it meant that our handsome minister would be off the market, but mostly because both Brodie and his bride-to-be Emily were such lovely people, and everyone was really happy for them. I had seen their courtship from the very beginning after Emily came to stay in Glendale for Beth's wedding, and basically never left, and I knew they were meant for each other.

'Looks like the whole village has come out for this,' Rory said as we drove into the High Street, passing by not only the Glendale Hall shop run by Beth and her family, and Emily's bakery, but also our very own farm shop, which was another string to our very full bow. Even though it was a Saturday, all of the shops had been closed for the wedding as no one wanted to miss out on the celebrations. We headed for the church where Brodie was minister, and about to be married in himself, and managed to find a space near to the village green.

'This is the first wedding I've been to at this time of year,' I said as I climbed out of the car. 'And I have to say, I'm not looking forward to sitting in a cold church.'

'Just think of the party at the Hall afterwards,' Rory said as he helped Harry out of the car, not wanting me to wrinkle my dress, bless him. 'I can't wait for a beer, I'll be honest.'

'You two are supposed to be focusing on the union we're about to watch,' my dad scolded us as he got out in his smart suit, but his eyes twinkled. 'What would the minister say?'

'He'd probably say hold a beer for him,' Rory joked, lifting Harry up as we set off, joining the throngs walking into the church. We paused outside the church and I gave Harry a big kiss. 'Be good, you lot, I'll see you afterwards,' I called with a wave as I walked round the side of the church towards the vicarage where Emily was getting ready.

Emily had given me a pass on the morning's preparations what with having the farm and Harry to deal with, and when I walked in I saw with relief that she had more than enough help on hand. Boxes were still scattered throughout as she was only just moving in –

Brodie and Emily hadn't lived together before today. There was make-up and clothes strewn around the living room, champagne glasses perched on all the surfaces. 'Is this organised chaos or just chaos?' I asked the familiar faces in the room with a smile, from the doorway.

'Heather!' Beth Fraser cried out in greeting at the exact time as Emily, who was standing in the centre of the room while her mother straightened the tiara on her head.

'Wow, Emily...' I breathed. She looked gorgeous. As we were so close to Christmas, Emily had wanted to go all out for the season theming the wedding around red and gold. Her love of vintage led her to the ivory prom-style dress she was wearing today, which showed off her hour-glass figure. She was all curves and red lipstick, and her blonde hair was pinned up in a chic bun. 'You too Beth, actually all of you!' I added. Beth was wearing the same dress as me, the mother-of-the-bride was in a pencil skirt and blouse, Beth's mother Caroline wore a smart navy suit, and Izzy, Beth's daughter, who had just turned thirteen, wore a shorter red dress as the other bridesmaid. Brodie's mother and sister, Anna, who I had met at the hen afternoon tea were also there along with Sally, who was Emily's aunt and the former housekeeper at Glendale Hall, and finally there was baby Iona, curled up in her pram fast asleep. She was Emily's daughter from a previous relationship but Brodie loved her like his own, I knew.

'Are you sure I look okay?' Emily asked the room nervously. 'It all happened so fast, I thought the dress was okay but...'

I stepped fully into the room. 'It's perfect. You are perfect.'

She smiled. 'Really?'

'Really,' everyone told her, making her smile.

She and Brodie had only got engaged on her birthday eight weeks ago but they hadn't wanted to wait to get married so with the help of Beth and her mother, Caroline, who had organised her own wedding to husband John at short notice, pulled off arranging a wedding at the church, which would be followed by a reception at Beth's family estate in record time.

'Only you left now, Heather,' Caroline said then as she handed me my bouquet of red roses. My stomach plummeted. This was one of the reasons I had not been as excited about the wedding today as I wanted to be. I was the last of our group without a ring on my finger, and no one was unforthcoming about asking me when it might appear.

'Mum!' Beth admonished, giving me an apologetic look. Behind her, Emily smiled at me reassuringly. They both knew why I hesitated in making my own trip down the aisle – the fact that my mother wouldn't be there to help me get ready as Emily's was, and as Caroline had been at Beth's wedding. I also knew that both of them hoped I would come around, and have my own happy ending, like them. I felt like I was disappointing everyone I cared about by not accepting Rory's proposal.

'You know me, I'm still holding out for Mr Darcy,' I replied, going for a joke, which was my go-to response when anyone brought it up. Far easier than telling them the truth. Plus, I wanted to diffuse any possible tension between Beth and her mother. They had reconciled a couple of years ago after ten years of estrangement but sometimes their old personality clashes resurfaced.

'I prefer Mr Knightley,' Izzy piped up then. That girl was as much of a bookworm as I was. She was still disappointed that I had left my job at the Glendale library.

After trying to juggle it along with looking after Harry and helping more and more at the farm, something had had to give. I still missed it though, it really had been this bookworm's dream job. But I hadn't been coping with trying to do it all, not that I had ever admitted that. I just told everyone I needed to put my family first. I still felt like I was on the back foot most of the time but at least I wasn't being pulled in quite so many different directions now.

'Jane Austen wasn't very kind about vicars, was she?' Emily asked. 'Look at Mr Collins.'

'Well, you've proved her wrong by finding a perfect one to be your husband,' I told her, glad the heat was off me.

'Speaking of, we'd better get you up that aisle,' Beth said, checking the time. 'You are the most beautiful bride, Em. You deserve a lifetime of happiness with Brodie.'

'Oh God, don't make me cry,' Emily said with a laugh as she clasped her bouquet to her chest, her eyes shining with happiness. I followed them out of the vicarage ready for our procession inside the church and couldn't help but wonder if I would ever be ready to make the same walk myself.

Chapter Two

It is a truth universally acknowledged that a single woman approaching thirty *must* be desperate to get married.

I had been asked by no fewer than five people at Emily and Brodie's reception when it would be my turn. I tried to laugh it off but it quickly began to grate. You would have thought nowadays that asking personal questions was known to be impolite but nope, at a wedding all bets seemingly are off, and no one was shy about it. 'I'm going to scream if one more person asks when Rory is going to propose,' I hissed when I found Beth at the back of the marquee talking to one of the catering staff. I held Harry with one of my hands, the other gripped my glass of champagne, as I waited for her to finish and walk up to me. 'I mean, seriously, are we stuck in the 1950s or something? They've never heard of a couple having a child and not getting married? And when did it become okay to question people's life choices anyway? Can they even hear themselves?!'

After the beautiful, and emotional, church service, we had all set off for Glendale Hall for the reception. This was Beth's family home and a grand house set in acres of land just outside the village. I had spent many days at the Hall growing up as I had known Beth since primary school although we had lost touch for ten years after she fled to London pregnant at sixteen. Once she came back to

Glendale with her daughter Izzy though, our friendship had continued as if we had never been apart, and now that I was with her husband's brother, we were practically family; along with Emily, we all spent tonnes of time together.

The reception was in a marquee in the middle of the lush, green, landscaped lawn. The marquee was decorated with fairy lights and roses, the theme red and gold to match the season, everything sparkling and elegantly festive. I'd soon lost sight of Rory as he found his brother Drew and their friends, as well as that beer he had been longing for, no doubt. So, I was left to answer all the difficult questions from Glendale's nosiest residents by myself. What none of them understood was that I wasn't waiting for Rory to propose at all. He already had. Last Hogmanay. I just hadn't said yes. Yet.

Beth shook her head. 'Okay, first, breathe. Usually, I can keep up with how fast you talk, I'm used to it, but even I had trouble with that sentence. And you know what our village is like. People still ask me when Izzy is going to have a brother or sister,' she said with an eye roll. I knew she and Drew had no plans to expand their family, they loved it being the three of them too much to change it. 'They have no filter, you know that. But they don't mean any harm. They're just invested in you and Rory, they can see how great you are together. Everyone loves a happy ending. And I know you do too, right?'

I sighed. She had me there. My favourite books were love stories, and I had definitely encouraged Beth and Drew to realise their feelings for one another. But I just couldn't quite visualise my own happy ending. 'Fine, but if someone else asks me, you'd better step in because I can't be held responsible for my actions.'

'I'll keep an eye out for you. But, seriously, why are you letting them get to you so much today? Usually you just laugh it off?' she asked, grabbing a champagne glass off a passing tray and taking a sip.

I thought about walking up the aisle in the church earlier behind Emily. I had met Rory's eyes up there as we walked towards the groom, and I just knew he had been thinking of what it would be like if our roles were swapped – if I had been walking to meet him at the altar. I had pictured it too myself for a moment. But then the familiar ache hit me. The fact that Emily glanced at her parents just before she reached the altar. The fact that if I did that then my beloved mother wouldn't return my smile, wouldn't be dabbing her eyes filled with emotion, grasping my dad's hand tightly, the fact that she wouldn't be there at all, and the fantasy disappeared as abruptly as it had started.

My mum died eight years ago, when I was twenty-one. I had just taken my final exams at university when my dad called me home after she suddenly fell ill. I'd dropped everything, left university before graduation, and my boyfriend there to be with her. A few weeks later, she passed away, and the absence that she left was still wide, and had seemed to become even stronger the past couple of years after I fell in love with Rory and unexpectedly got pregnant so early on in our relationship. It hurt every day that she would never know our beautiful boy.

A lump rose in my throat. 'Because I'm at another wedding, I suppose. And Rory and me are the only two of our group not married now. And all these people asking me about it, just makes me feel even guiltier for holding out on him,' I said. Harry squirmed so I put him down. He spotted a gold balloon on the floor and hurried over to it. 'I feel like I'm letting everyone down, I guess,' I admitted. I felt guilty because I thought I should have the same surname as my son, and I knew that Rory really wanted us to get married, but I just wasn't ready.

'It doesn't matter what anyone else thinks,' Beth said firmly. She knew what it was like to be talked about, after all she had been a teenage single mother, and I admired how she seemed to be able to ignore the local gossip. 'Only what you think. It's your life, not theirs. And you know that Rory understands how you feel about your mum. He loves you and wants you to be happy, he won't push you,' she said with a reassuring smile. 'When the time is right, you'll know.'

'That makes me feel more guilty though, he's too good to me,' I said, swigging my glass of champagne dry. We didn't go to many events nowadays so the champagne was already starting to make me feel light-headed. I would pay for it tomorrow when I had to be up at dawn with a hangover but it felt like the best way to get through today.

'That's not true, he should be good to you,' Beth replied. 'Don't worry, it's not like he doesn't know you're committed to him. You two are meant for one another.'

I wondered how Beth could be that sure when I still felt so uncertain about the future. Before I could ask though, I saw Harry start running off after the balloon. 'Harry, come back!' I gave Beth an apologetic look but she just waved me off; she knew what life was like with a toddler.

Turning around, I frowned as I lost sight of him. 'Harry, where are you?' I hissed, trying not to be too loud and disrupt the reception. Panic began to rise as I rushed around, trying to see where he had gone. Rationally, I knew he couldn't have gone far and it wasn't as if this wasn't a safe space, but not being able to catch sight of him still made my heart begin to thud inside my chest. 'Harry!' I called louder this time. I reached the tables set up for the dinner and bent down, trying to see if he might be under one.

'Lost someone?'

I stood up hurriedly to see Rory behind me, Harry in his arms, holding the balloon triumphantly.

I clutched my chest in relief. 'He just ran off. I don't know what happened. I was right there then he just disappeared, and I couldn't see him anywhere—'

'Hey, it's okay,' Rory interrupted, frowning at my gabbled words. 'He was just on a balloon hunt, weren't you?' he said to Harry who was, of course, completely unruffled whereas my heart just wouldn't slow down. 'I think someone might be getting too excited.' He looked at me with concern. 'Why don't we go for a walk before the meal, tire him out a little? Get some fresh air, huh?'

I knew I could do with that so I nodded. 'Let's have a look at the trail,' I suggested. Every year, Glendale Hall put on a Christmas trail of lights in the grounds raising money to fund community projects and for the whole village to enjoy, and they had put it up earlier than usual because of the wedding. It was a magical trail – Beth and Drew had even got engaged walking down it one Christmas. Both Emily and Brodie had wanted guests to be able to take a walk down it after dinner so Beth had laid down a track of carpet to avoid anyone getting mud on their fancy shoes, or heels sinking into the grass.

Rory and I pulled on our coats and headed off to it together. It was already dark outside and the stars were shining brightly thanks to the clear sky. I had only left Glendale for three years when I went to university at St

Andrews and I had missed being able to see the stars like this. They always helped to calm me down.

Harry's eyes lit up as we passed by the banner I had designed for the trail in its first year hanging between two trees, an inflatable snowman and Santa standing at either side of the entrance. I loved designing things. I had taken adult classes at the local college after my love for it was reawakened by designing this banner. It was something I had enjoyed while growing up but it hadn't felt like a career path. Instead, I studied English Literature at university and ended up working at the Glendale library when I returned home, not wanting to leave my dad alone after my mum died. Then, when I moved onto the farm and had Harry, it became hard to juggle it all so I left the library. I wanted to do more design work like the logos I had made for Emily when she opened up her bakery in the village, but it was hard to fit it all in. I had an idea that when Harry went to school, I might start my own business. But I wasn't sure if it was possible, the farm and our farm shop in the High Street took up so much time.

'Feeling better?' Rory asked lightly, but I didn't miss his look of concern. I knew he found it hard to understand how much I worried about things, and I couldn't blame him. I found it hard to understand my anxiety a lot of the time myself too. I tried to shield him from it as much as I could, tried to keep a smile on my face, but I knew he saw through me. He always had.

'It was just worrying not being able to see him,' I said, looking down at Harry walking with his hand in his father's, dazzled by the lights. The world always seemed so much more special through his eyes. 'I shouldn't have taken my eyes off him.'

'You can't watch him every second. He's walking now, he needs to find his own way in the world and fall over sometimes. That's life, right?' Rory pointed. 'Look at those snowflakes,' he said, showing Harry the lights draped around a tree as we passed it.

I knew he was right but I still felt like I had to watch Harry all the time, especially at the farm where there were so many hazards for someone so small. 'It really is beautiful this year,' I said, attempting to change the subject. Beth and Glendale Hall's gardener, John, spent a lot of time on trying to improve the trail each year, I knew. 'Look at that, Harry!' A huge tree stood in front of us decorated in what looked like a thousand lights. We all looked up at it in awe. 'How pretty is that?'

'We can decorate our Christmas tree together this year,' Rory told Harry. 'Start an annual tradition.'

'That would be nice,' I said. 'He'll be aware of Christmas this year, we should make it special. I want him to love Christmas as much as I did growing up. My mum always made it so special for me.' I swallowed hard, thinking about how she had always gone all out celebrating, which was why I found it so hard at this time of year without her. She should have been here to celebrate with us. She would have spoilt Harry so much, I knew.

'It will be special,' Rory promised. 'I think we'll have early snow this year, it's already freezing. Let's go to the grotto, my legs are turning blue.'

'I hope you're wearing underwear,' I said with a grin. 'Otherwise they won't be the only thing turning blue!'

Rory snorted with laughter. I always enjoyed our banter when we got to spend time together. It felt as if we had been teasing each other forever. It had begun when he had just been Drew's annoying older brother, and now it was like a secret language just the two of us shared.

We walked towards the grotto, a tent at the end, the grand finale of the trail. I hoped the snow wouldn't be too heavy yet, sometimes we ended up getting stranded at the farm, which always worried me in case of emergencies. Rory was used to it though, having lived his whole life there, and as long as the animals were okay for food and water, he actually quite enjoyed it, which I just couldn't understand.

Harry let out a gasp as he saw the giant sleigh piled with presents inside the grotto. There was also a Santa and two reindeer figures that looked lifelike, alongside the fake fireplace hung with stockings. And a workshop table with crafting things for the kids to make and do. Harry ran over to the sleigh to touch the reindeers, not bothered in the least that they weren't the real thing. Rory stepped over to me and wrapped an arm around my waist as we watched our son. 'I can't believe he's almost two. Where has the time gone?'

'I know,' I agreed with a sigh. 'I still think of him as a baby but he's becoming a little person now. I love these moments when it's just us three.' We had such a big group of family and friends, and such a busy life on the farm, that I cherished these quieter times when it was just the three of us. I felt more able to relax somehow. I didn't have to put on any kind of front, I supposed.

'Me too,' Rory said. 'Soon he won't want to hang out with us so we'd better make the most of it. I guess that's why people have more than one child, to hang on to this for longer,' he said, gesturing to Harry talking animatedly to the fake Santa. About what I couldn't tell, he still sometimes just spoke what sounded like nonsense, in his adorable little Scottish accent.

I couldn't help but stiffen a little. I knew Rory dreamed of having a big family, and I did want to give Harry a sibling but the past two years had been such a whirlwind, it felt as if I was still playing catch up. 'That's still a long way off hopefully, he can't even put his own shoes on.'

'Is everything okay, Heth?' Rory turned to me then, his usual jokey tone turning a little more serious. 'I feel like the past few days you've been really quiet. I know it's been busy but we haven't really talked.'

Sometimes I loved that he called me out on things. I'd never been as honest with a man before Rory, but other times, like this, I wished he'd let me off the hook. 'I guess it's because Mum's birthday is coming up,' I admitted. The fifth anniversary of her death had come and gone in May, but it was her birthday that always hit me the hardest because it came during what had been our favourite time of year, and I missed the celebrations we used to have together. I could hardly believe she had been gone so long. Her absence still felt so large in my life.

'It's so hard,' he said, reaching to squeeze my hand. 'Do you want me to come to the church with you?' It was one thing we shared. Rory understood what it was like to lose your mother after tragically losing both his parents in the same car accident. He had only been eighteen at the time, and Drew just fourteen so Rory had not only taken on running the family farm, but responsibility for his younger brother as well. I had always admired how he had got on with running the farm, and helped Drew study medicine, afterwards. And now that I knew how hard it was to lose a parent, what he had done seemed even more impressive. I was certain I couldn't have done it.

'It's probably better I go alone with Dad. But thank you.' My father and I marked her birthday together every year. He found the day as difficult as I did. I was dreading it to be honest.

'And that's really it?' Rory checked. 'Nothing else is worrying you?'

'I guess it's this wedding too,' I admitted, glancing at him. 'Everyone talking about when we are going to get married… They make me feel guilty. And seeing Emily with her mother today, you know.' I swallowed hard. My mother had loved weddings. She used to buy *OK!* or *Hello* magazine whenever they had a celebrity or royal wedding in them, and we'd pore over the pages, dissecting what everyone had worn, and what we would have done differently. She always cried whenever she went to a wedding, and she and I had often discussed what kind of day I might have in the future. The thought of her not being able to plan it all with me made me feel like the task would just be impossible. 'It just all feels a bit much today, that's all. I worry I'm just not good enough.'

'Good enough for what?'

'Good enough for you, and Harry. As a mother… a partner… and working at the farm.' I shrugged, not wanting to meet his eyes in case I started to cry.

'Heather, of course you're good enough.' Rory came over and touched my arm. 'No one could love anyone more than how me and Harry love you.'

'I can't see what the future looks like.' It was hard to put my worries into words especially as I knew Rory rarely worried about anything other than practical things.

'Well, none of us know that.'

'But you're always so sure. Of everything. You want us to get married, have more children, expand the farm, and

I want all of that too but it scares me too.' It was so hard to explain how I felt as I wasn't even one hundred per cent certain myself.

Rory rubbed my arm. 'It's okay. I already said there's no pressure. You know I want to marry you, you're the only woman I could ever want by my side but I only want that if you do too.'

I did want it but I just couldn't seem to let myself have it. 'I love you, Rory.' He pulled me closer and then I felt a hand on my leg. I looked down to see Harry looking up at us. Rory scooped him up, and the three of us shared a group hug.

As we held each other, I silently promised the universe that I would do better for both of them.

Chapter Three

Back inside the reception after the delicious meal, Rory put Harry in his pushchair hoping he might have a nap, and I wandered to the edge of the dancefloor watching as the new bride and groom circled slowly in the centre, Emily's head resting on Brodie's shoulder.

'She looks so happy,' Beth said, appearing beside me then. 'Remember us talking about her and Brodie, how we worried they'd never tell each other how they really felt?' she asked me as she snapped a photo of the couple on her phone. They hadn't had the easiest beginnings for a relationship, that was for sure.

'They got there in the end,' I agreed with a smile. Emily's ex-boyfriend Greg, and Iona's father, had battled alcohol and gambling problems, and had cheated on Emily, resulting in her moving to Glendale and falling for Brodie. It had been a long journey for all of them but Greg was doing well, he lived nearby in Inverness and saw his daughter as much as he could, and he was happy for Emily and Brodie. No one could begrudge Emily happiness, she was so selfless and kind.

'I'm going to post this to the Glendale account,' Beth said, smiling at the photo.

'How's that going?' I asked her. She had decided Glendale needed social media accounts to promote our community and businesses – she was always thinking of ways to keep the village thriving.

'Really well, we have quite a few followers now. You haven't sent me any photos of the farm shop or farm yet. It could help.'

'I will,' I promised. I just hadn't had the time yet. I knew I needed to though. Business was okay in the farm shop but could be better, especially during winter when we only had locals to rely on. I watched Brodie spin Emily in a circle, making her laugh. I remembered the time she had asked me how I juggled working with Harry as she contemplated moving to Glendale to open her bakery while she was pregnant with Iona. I had realised that she needed encouragement and while I never lied to her, I also didn't tell her how some days I didn't know how to do everything that needed doing, how to keep all those juggling balls up in the air, how to keep everyone thriving. I told her that no one can have it all but that we can have everything we want. And sometimes it did feel like I had that. To the outside world, I'm sure it did. But there was something missing, as I had tried to explain to Rory. And what that was, I wasn't quite sure how to pinpoint.

Perhaps it was belief that I could live this life I had been thrust into, and live it well.

'Ugh, my feet are killing me in these shoes,' Beth said then with a grimace. 'I don't know how you can enjoy wearing them.'

'Well, for one, I'm much shorter than you so I like the extra height, and they've always given me an extra dose of confidence, which unlike you I need.'

Beth shook her head. 'Everyone needs extra confidence now and then.' She looked over at Sally who was watching Harry and Iona, both fallen asleep in their pushchairs. 'They're so close in age, they will grow up like siblings, won't they?'

'I hope so. We always said we missed out on siblings, didn't we?' I thought back to that first day at secondary school, seated next to Beth. We were asked to do a family tree and we immediately bonded over both being only children. Beth said she'd always wanted a sister to help gang up on her grandmother and mother, and I'd always wanted one as I was obsessed with the *Famous Five* books. Life just seemed more fun in books with siblings.

'I don't think we did though really,' she replied, nudging my hip with hers. 'After I met you, it felt like I had a sister.'

'It did,' I agreed. Beth was my best friend after that day even if we always had been different and liked different things. We had so much fun together and had always been able to rely on one another.

'I still regret missing out on ten years of your life,' she said, wistfully.

'Oh, don't, I'm emotional enough today!' I protested. 'You really didn't miss much, anyway.' Beth had run away to London aged sixteen, after falling pregnant, because her grandmother had tried to make her not have the baby. She had returned ten years later when her grandmother became gravely ill and had reunited not only with her family but also with Drew, Izzy's father, who hadn't known about the baby. Beth hadn't wanted to stop him from fulfilling his dreams of becoming a doctor. It had been a difficult time but I was so pleased she had come home, and everything had worked out for her and Drew and their daughter in the end.

'I missed you at uni, I could have stayed in your tiny room, and I could have met your university boyfriend, and got drunk at the student union with you. But I was raising Izzy.' She sighed. She had missed out on going to university and although she would never regret Izzy, I knew she sometimes felt she had missed out not having that experience.

'We got drunk together more than enough before you left, even though we were only sixteen.' We giggled, remembering our nights out at the local pub, the Glendale Arms, together.

'We never would have imagined we'd both end up with one of the Fraser brothers,' Beth said then with a smile.

'Well, I hope you both are glad you did!' I turned to see Rory approaching, grinning at us. 'What with our devilishly handsome good looks, our wit and charm, our—'

'Humble nature?' Beth interrupted, arching her eyebrow, making us laugh.

'Speaking of humble. How about I show you my moves on the dancefloor?' Rory said, turning to me.

'Can you promise not to step on my toes this time?'

'Oh my God, that happened one time…' I laughed as I took his hand.

'Where's my husband got to? He owes me a dance,' Beth said, looking around.

'Old Mrs Smith has cornered him to ask about her arthritis,' Rory told her with a grimace. 'The best part of my job is that no one needs my advice at weddings.' Drew was a doctor, and although he worked at Inverness Hospital, people were always trying to get medical advice from him at functions.

'I'd better go and save him,' Beth said with a laugh.

We made our way on to the dancefloor that was filling up with other couples beside the newlyweds.

'I can't believe Emily is now a minister's wife,' Rory joked, following my gaze. 'For someone who never used to go to church...'

I smiled. 'I think people would say the same about me. The girl who was happiest reading in her bedroom growing up, now living on a farm.' I had certainly never fantasised about being with a farmer. I was *so* not an outdoorsy person. And Rory was completely different to the only other man I'd had a serious relationship with.

But love wasn't something you planned, I supposed. I thought back to the first time we had kissed after coming home from the Hall. It had been such a crazy night...

–

'Are you okay?' Rory stood in the doorway to the spare bedroom of the farm. 'I brought you up a cuppa.' I sat up in bed and smiled as he came over and perched on the edge, handing me the mug.

'What a night,' I said, taking it gratefully. We had been celebrating Hogmanay at Glendale Hall but after the fireworks display at midnight Beth's grandmother had collapsed and been rushed off in an ambulance. She had terminal cancer and was the reason that Beth had returned to Glendale after ten years away. Beth had asked us to look after Izzy so Rory had brought the three of us back to the farm. 'I just checked on Izzy and she fell asleep reading. She was so worried, poor love.'

'Drew just texted to say he's on his way back. The family just want to be alone. She's still unconscious, I think. It doesn't look good.' Rory sighed and took a sip of his tea. 'Not the start to the New Year I was expecting.'

'Nor me.' I put the tea on the bedside table. 'Thanks for putting me up, I didn't want to drag my dad out at this time to pick me up.'

'It's no problem. Thanks for helping with Izzy. I'm still getting used to being an uncle.' None of us had known that Izzy was Drew's daughter, and everyone was still coming to terms with the news. 'I guess I should let you sleep.' He made to get up.

'I don't really want to be alone just yet,' I admitted. I still felt shocked by what had happened. 'Sit with me for a bit, please?'

Rory climbed onto the bed beside me, on top of the covers. We sat in silence for a minute. 'I didn't think you'd ever spend the night here,' he said then in a low voice. 'You know that you once told me you could never fancy a farmer.'

I turned to him. 'No, I didn't!' I protested.

He smiled. 'You did. You, Drew and Beth had been at the farm all day, and I found you guys out in the field. I told you all off for being lazy on your summer holidays when I'd been working hard all day. Beth said I needed to learn to relax more and that maybe if I had a girlfriend, I might chill out more. Then you said you could never fancy a farmer because they had rough hands and smelled of animals. I remember Beth couldn't stop laughing and Drew said he was relieved that girls fancied doctors to which Beth told him off as he shouldn't care about any other girls.'

I shook my head. 'I don't remember that but it does sound like me. To be fair, you were always teasing me back then. Your kid brother's friend wasn't someone you would fancy either.' I turned, leaning against the headboard as he met my gaze, our faces only inches apart. It was funny how our age gap had seemed so huge that summer when I was sixteen. Now, it was nothing.

'You did have very frizzy hair,' he said softly. Then he reached out to touch it. 'It's different now.'

'Better hair products,' I said lightly. 'What about your hands? Are they still rough?' I held out mine and he opened up his palm. I traced a fingertip over it and heard his breath hitch. I was relieved that I wasn't the only one affected by our closeness. His skin was warm and it was calloused but it didn't bother me anymore. 'You could use some hand cream.'

'Noted. What would your teenage self say about us being in the same bed, I wonder?' He took my hand and laced our fingers together.

My heart began to pound. 'She would be shocked. But then again, she was very innocent.' My university boyfriend, Stewart, had been the first man I had slept with – I had done no more than kiss boys at school. Rory had been a man to me then, I would have been terrified to have been in bed with him. Now, I felt a surprising thrill of attraction.

He cocked an eyebrow. 'But you're not innocent now?'

If I hadn't had so much wine, maybe I would have just laughed that comment off. But I had. 'Why don't you kiss me and find out?' I challenged instead.

He didn't need asking twice. His lips met mine, and when we kissed, desire rose up in me faster and hotter than I could have imagined.

–

'I'm glad I managed to entice you onto my farm,' Rory said in a low voice, pulling me back to the present. I looked up into his eyes as he pulled me close, twirling me on the dancefloor. Those hands I had once ridiculed were strong around my waist now. 'I just hope you don't wish you were still in the library reading books instead.'

'On a winter's morning, it's hard not to,' I replied. I saw his face fall a little. 'But maybe if you brought me more cups of coffee to bed...'

'Maybe I will, if there's a reward waiting for me there...' He leaned down and brushed my lips with his. I pulled him closer and deepened the kiss until we heard someone wolf whistle. We drew back with a self-conscious laugh. I was still surprised by the intensity of my attraction to Rory. After that first night together, I had been sure he would laugh it off, tell me it had been a mistake, but instead he had told me that he had fallen for me, and I'd realised that I was head over heels in love with him in return.

'I think your dad is still shocked to see you mucking in on the farm,' Rory said then. 'He likes coming to stay with us though, doesn't he?'

'I love having him with us,' I admitted. I didn't like him living alone in my childhood home in Glendale village, and selfishly, I found day-to-day life easier with him there to help with Harry, even if he did chuckle at me carrying out farm chores, remembering how adverse I was to anything like that when I was younger.

'Maybe we should think about making it permanent. If it's something you want.'

I looked up at him. 'Really?'

'Of course.' He shrugged. 'If it's what you want.'

I felt a rush of love for him. He'd obviously sensed that I was less stressed with my dad around. 'I'll talk to him about it,' I said.

34

'Good. You just stepped on my toe, by the way.'

'No, I didn't!' I cried indignantly.

Rory grinned. 'I could argue with you forever.'

'How romantic,' I said drily, but I knew what he meant. I smiled, glad we had been able to be together today away from our farm duties – it was a rare occurrence nowadays, and made me remember how and why we fell in love, which wasn't something at the top of my thoughts when carrying out farm chores at dawn in the bitter cold; I was more likely to be cursing him under my breath then.

A tapping of a wine glass drew our attention to the side of the dancefloor where Beth was trying to get the attention of the room. 'It's time to cut the cake. And Emily's old boss Molly made it, so we will all want a taste,' she called out. I looked across at the amazing three-tiered red velvet cake, and my mouth watered despite the five-course meal we'd eaten earlier.

'You don't need to say cake to me twice,' Brodie called back.

'Hey, are you saying you prefer cake to dancing with your bride?' Emily asked him.

'Don't pretend you wouldn't choose cake over me,' he replied, slipping an arm around her as they walked towards the cake. We all laughed because cake to us lot was like honey to bees.

'We'd better head off after the cake,' Rory said to me as we went over to the table. 'I'm knackered. And we've already walked the trail after all.'

I sighed, but agreed. In the summer it was easier to stay out late but when you had to be up in the dark and freezing cold morning for farm work, you didn't particularly fancy partying all night long. I did miss the days when I would have happily danced here until the early hours though.

'I can't wait for bed,' he added in a lower voice, his lips brushing my hair as he spoke, sending a little shiver through me.

And right then, neither could I.

Chapter Four

It was still dark as it always was this time of year when I got up. I woke up in bed alone, toasty warm, and not at all happy at the prospect of having to leave the comfortable bed. I closed my eyes briefly thinking back to last night, once we had gone to bed after the wedding. A wide smile came over my face. We often ended up falling straight to sleep after a long, hard day on the farm at this time of year so it had been a welcome change to feel Rory's touch and urgent kisses. I had slept better than I had in a while too.

I knew I couldn't stay here replaying last night unfortunately. Not for the first time, I let myself imagine that I was about to pull on a blouse and high heels and go off to a heated workplace as I had done at the library, instead of needing to wear countless layers and brave the elements outside.

A noise from Harry's room across the landing from ours finally pulled me out from under the duvet. I slipped on my dressing gown and shuffled into my slippers and went into his room. He was half standing in his cot, yawning sleepily. 'Mummy,' he said when he saw me and gave me that cheeky little smile of his. The one that always reminded me of Rory.

'Morning, love. What did you dream about last night then?' I scooped him up and he flopped against me as if he was putting his whole trust in me to keep him safe. Which still freaked me out, if I was honest. I walked us over to the window and drew back the curtains, which was pointless as it was still dark outside and there was nothing to light up the view. 'Shall we have a warm drink before we head outside? I think we're going to need it,' I said, brushing the hair back from his face.

When Harry was first born, I couldn't sleep. I kept a watch over his cot checking that he was still breathing. Perhaps it was something that all mothers did, I wasn't sure. I was too embarrassed to ask Beth or Emily, and it made me miss my own mother even more who I could have talked to about anything. I managed to ease myself out of the habit at least, but my fear hadn't really gone away.

I was terrified of not only losing Rory or Harry, but of them losing me. Like I had lost my own mother.

Holding Harry tightly, I carried him downstairs to the kitchen with me wishing that my mum could have known him. They had found her cancer far too late, and her demise had been far too quick. I had been helpless to stop it. And now I was unable to talk to her about everything I wanted to, to ask her questions I hadn't even thought of asking while she was still here. Especially about motherhood.

I thought back then to when I found out I was pregnant.

–

'Well, my stomach bug hasn't come back.' I walked out of the bathroom to where Rory was perched on the side of his bed, waiting. I held up the pregnancy test, feeling utter shock. A few weeks before I'd had a nasty tummy bug, which had clearly stopped the pill from working. I hadn't felt properly well since, getting tired more and more, falling asleep in the evenings, and generally not feeling myself. Finally, I'd realised that my period was also late so I'd taken a test, certain it would be negative. I had been very, very wrong.

'What are we going to do?' I asked, sitting down next to him numbly, the test falling into my lap. I loved Rory and I had always planned to be a mother one day. But we had hardly even been a couple for long, just four months. We weren't ready for this. I wasn't ready.

Rory took my hands in his. 'We are going to raise this baby together, that's what we're going to do, and you're going to come and live with me here. I love you, Heth. I have for too long to even say.'

'But it's too soon.' I felt a tear roll down my cheek. I felt sick… panicked… scared. I hadn't planned on falling in love with Rory and now I suddenly was going to have his baby. 'I can't live on a farm,' I said, as I dissolved into tears.

He pulled me to him. 'It's going to be okay. Don't think about the timing. Think about how you feel. Do you want this baby, Heth? I'd understand if…'

I looked up. 'Of course!' I said automatically. I touched my stomach. This was part of us. 'I'm just… terrified. And I want my mum to be honest.' I needed her to tell me that I could do this because I just wasn't sure.

'I'm scared too but we love each other, we can do this together. I promise you.'

And Rory held me close and made me believe that we could do this.

But there were still days, even now, when I questioned whether Rory had been right about that or not.

After I'd had a coffee and Harry had had some warm milk, we pulled on thick layers and wellies and headed outside ready for the morning chores. I used to strap Harry to my back but now I let him walk with me because if I tried to put him in his pushchair, he just got cranky. Seeing him scampering around the farm did make me smile, especially in his tiny wellies.

I was amazed that he was here even after all this time. I still felt a little lost as a mother. Maybe because I didn't have my own mum to guide me through it all. I wondered if I could ever be the kind of mother to Harry that she had been to me.

Sometimes, I felt like I was one step from losing my grip on it all. And I didn't want to say those words aloud to anyone, even to Rory.

It was why I held back from getting married and having another baby. What if I just couldn't cope? What if I ended up abandoning them and running away? Or worse? I squeezed my eyes shut. What if something happened to me like what had happened to my mother? What if I got sick and left Rory and Harry? Perhaps I was holding back to try to protect them from ever having to lose me.

'Chickens!' Harry said enthusiastically, as we weaved our way around to the chicken coop with a bucket of water.

'Chickens, that's right,' I told him. The chickens were free-range but in winter had to stay in the coop built by the side of the farmhouse, it was just too cold to be outside. 'Want to scatter some feed?' I bent down and poured some into Harry's little outstretched hand. He threw it inexpertly on to the floor far from the chickens but he looked so thrilled. 'Good job, they will love that,' I told him, watching the chickens rushing to their food, pushing one another out of the way. I looked at their water trough. It had frozen again despite the ball we kept on it to try to prevent it. I cracked the ice with my hand and re-filled it. Sometimes in winter, tasks like this felt unrelenting – we had to do the same things over and over. At least the winter hadn't gotten so cold yet that our electricity was affected, that was always hard for me to cope with. I was a townie after all.

We left the chickens then and headed to feed our goats and pigs. I had only taken on my own responsibilities on the farm over the past two years. When I first moved in, I was pregnant and working full-time at the library so I really hadn't been that involved. But then Rory opened the farm shop, and I had lots of ideas and wanted to help – I designed the logo and sign, I helped decide what would be stocked and to design the layout, and then I started to get involved with how the produce arrived in the shop from the farm, and other suppliers, too. Once I had Harry, I went part-time at the library and things got even busier at the farm so I stepped in to help. Then when I finally had to let my library job go, I found myself with plenty of my own responsibilities on the farm.

The main work I did was for our farm shop though. Rory's profits had been dwindling, the farm taking much of what he made from the cows, so when Beth had taken over the shops in Glendale, we had opened up a farm shop together in the High Street. We had a full-time manager, an older lady called Hattie who had lived in Glendale forever like us, and who the customers loved, but I visited the shop most days, and was always trying to come up with ideas for things we could sell. Rory took care of the meat, and we also sold milk and cheese, eggs of course, homemade chutneys and jams, and fresh vegetables and fruit grown on the farm. It wasn't easy though, and Beth had reminded me that I needed to do all I could to help keep our profits up. I had promised her a photo for social media.

'Right, what would people like to see of our farm?' I asked Harry, looking around. I watched as Angus let out the horses into the paddock before heading off to muck out the stables. Behind the paddock, the sun was just starting to rise, creating a pretty pastel light above the horses as they chewed on the grass. I quickly pulled out my phone from my pocket, and snapped a photo of it. It really was a beautiful scene and I stood for a moment to drink it in, grateful I could see it even if it had meant being up so early and out in such cold weather. A reminder that it could be beautiful out here. Something I forgot too often.

'Hungry,' Harry said from beside me, leaning against the fence with a sigh.

'Come on then, let's have some breakfast. I think we've done everything anyway,' I said, sending the photo to Beth and taking Harry's hand in mine. We set off back to the farmhouse for breakfast. I looked up to the hill fields and could see Rory making his way back down. He lifted his hand in a wave, and I waved back. It was nice that we lived and worked in the same place even if we didn't get to spend enough of that time together.

'Morning, Dad,' I said when we went into the kitchen through the back door. Dad was at the table with a cup of tea. 'It's freezing out there,' I told him as I removed our coats and boots.

'Had a good morning, Harry?' Dad asked, helping him into his highchair. 'Did you feed the chickens?'

'Chickens,' Harry agreed. 'Milk,' he added.

'Say please,' I reminded him, but when he said it, it came out sounding more like 'peas'.

Dad chuckled. 'Here we go,' he said, pouring some into his beaker.

'Right, let's get some food on,' I said, going to the fridge. Something brushed my legs. 'You hungry too, Tabby?' I asked the cat, who was meant to be the farm mouser but was too lazy to do a good job.

'Morning everyone,' Rory said cheerfully then, coming through the back door. Being outdoors always put him in a good mood even on a morning like this. He came over to give me a kiss then mussed Harry's hair as he joined him and Dad at the table, grabbing himself a coffee and pouring one out for me too.

I made scrambled eggs and toast for us all, joining them at the table with two big platefuls. I had eaten the best I ever had in my life moving out here. The eggs and milk were from the farm, the bread fresh from Emily's bakery, and it all tasted so much the better for being homegrown and homemade. We all tucked in eagerly.

I looked fondly at Harry. He loved his food. All the fresh air outside made us good eaters, and all our cheeks were rosy from the brisk weather. I hadn't had a cold in two years, and I was sure Harry would grow up just as resilient as his father, who was never ill. He would have a very different childhood to mine growing up in a three-bed semi-detached in the village, that was for sure. 'I need to head to the shop after breakfast and drop off some produce,' I said then.

'I need to sort things out before the auction next week, and repair that fence before the snow comes in,' Rory said with a grimace. There was always so much to do. Often

Rory and I were apart for most of the day, doing all the separate things that needed doing, which was a shame, but at least we had the evenings as a family.

'Will you be okay here for a bit by yourself?' I checked with dad.

'Of course. I can take Harry though, if you like?'

'It's fine, he'll enjoy the trip out,' I said. It wasn't that I didn't trust my dad to look after Harry, of course I did, but I just didn't like not being at the farm with him, keeping an eye on him.

'Oh, Drew invited us all to dinner by the way,' Rory added then.

Relief washed over me. We often had dinner at Glendale Hall, and it meant I didn't have to worry about cooking later. 'Great,' I said. The day sounded like a manageable one for once. 'Right, I'll go and have my shower then,' I said, draining my cup of coffee dry, hoping it would give me the burst of energy I needed. Rory teased me for putting on make-up out here and washing my hair every day but that was me, and I didn't want to change what I had always done.

I glanced out of the window and my heart sank when I realised it had started sleeting. 'I hope that doesn't turn into snow.'

'It'll be fine,' Rory said as he picked up Harry. 'You worry too much.'

I glanced at him bouncing our son on his knee and sighed a little. The problem was I did all the worrying for all of us whereas Rory didn't seem to ever really worry about anything.

-

Glendale always looked its best in the run up to Christmas. The High Street had a large Christmas tree right in the centre brightly lit up, there were fairy lights strung along either side of the road between the lampposts, and each of the shops were brightly decorated inside too. Even though I wasn't a fan, I had to admit that the sleet added to the festive feel of the village when I parked outside the Fraser Farm Shop. So much so, I jumped out and snapped a photo and sent that to Beth as well, hoping it might encourage a couple more customers to think of us when it came to their Christmas shopping.

'Right, let's bring the food in, shall we?' I said brightly to Harry when I went around to his side of the car. I pulled the hood of his coat up and put him in his pushchair as I wanted to get in and out of the shop quickly and letting him walk would not be conducive to that. Opening the boot, I pulled out the pots of chutneys and jams that we paid a local woman to make for us, and balanced the box on the pushchair, walking into the shop, glad to be in the warmth once I was through the door.

The shop was a small square space with a fresh food counter along one side where we sold beef and pork products as well as cheese and there was a fridge of goats' milk next to it; then there was a table in the middle with eggs, fresh veg and fruit, although there wasn't much at this time of the year, and the chutneys and jams. Then the other side of the shop had the till counter and the mugs and tea towels we had made with the farm logo I had designed printed on.

'Morning!' I said to Hattie, our manager, my heart sinking at seeing the shop empty. There weren't many people at this time of year about the village who didn't live here; the tourists only really came in the summer although there were a few more in winter now that the Glendale Hall festive trail was becoming more well known, but business was a generally lot slower in the colder months. 'Got a delivery for you! I'll pop it out the back, I'll just park Harry here a sec.'

I left the pushchair by the counter and carried the box of new produce out the back. When I returned, Hattie was talking to him.

'He's a bonnie lad,' she said when she saw me. She was about sixty-five and had actually retired from her lifelong teaching career, where she had worked with my mum, who had been a history teacher, but she had become bored at home so had been eager to come and work for us when the shop opened. We had a school-aged boy help her out on the weekends. During the summer, I also helped out but in December, she was capable on her own in here on a weekday. 'His eyes are just like your mother's. She would have doted on him, wouldn't she?'

'She would have,' I agreed, feeling wistful that she would never know how he was a mix of our families.

'And that Fraser hair,' she continued. I smiled, Hattie said the same thing pretty much every time I brought Harry in, bless her. 'Reminds me so much of his father when he was his age. He'll love growing up on that farm like Rory. Rory was almost feral running around that farm as a boy. Always struck me as a pretty great life for a kid.'

'He already wants to be out there with me as much as he can,' I said, trying not to think about him growing up and taking over the farm. It was a calling that was still hard for me to understand; Rory said the farm pumped through his veins like blood throughout his childhood, and I knew he wanted Harry to feel the same way. 'So, how's it been here this week?' I asked, a little reluctantly. Sometimes I didn't always want to hear the answer to my questions.

'Not too busy, but I think it'll pick up the closer we get to Christmas,' she replied – like Rory she was ever the optimist.

'Beth thinks I should do more promotion on social media to help.'

'Oh, you should. I'm on Twitter and Instagram now.'

'You are?' I stared at her, unable to contain my surprise.

'I have to keep up with all my friends and family. It's how I found out about the suits in the village.'

'Suits?' I asked, still taken aback at the thought of Hattie tweeting.

'Aye, two men in suits sniffing around the village. From Edinburgh, apparently, in a rather flash car, snooping around the village. Asking a lot of questions too apparently about the place. I'd warn Beth if I were you.'

Beth had already saved the village from a development company, she would be furious if someone else wanted to tear down the place. 'I'll give her a heads up, for sure. I wonder what they're doing here. We really don't need any more problems to deal with.'

'More problems?' she asked, sharply, looking at me.

'With the village,' I said, quickly. Hattie was lovely but definitely a gossip, I didn't want to let on that I was struggling with anything.

'Aye, we don't need anyone slowing the progress we've made reviving the place. It's getting back to how it was when I was just married, and I walked to the village every day for the bits I needed.'

'Let's hope we won't have a bad winter to put people off,' I said, biting my lip. I knew from last year that even though the community had rallied round to support the High Street shops when Beth re-opened them, a heavy snowfall kept people at home more.

'I'm sorry to say but I can feel a sharp front coming in. There will be snow up on your hills soon, make no mistake. Tell Rory from me.' When you lived in Glendale as long as Hattie had, you didn't even bother to watch a weather forecast.

I sighed at the thought of snow. 'He thought there might be, but I'll warn him it's coming sooner than forecast, thank you.' Highland cows were extremely hardy but if there was bad snow on its way then Rory would likely move them down a pasture lower where there was an open shelter made of stone for them to use at night. A customer came in then so I took that as my cue to head off. 'Nice to see you, Hattie. Say goodbye, Harry,' I said, smiling as he waved at Hattie obligingly.

Outside, sleet was still floating on the wind like small feathers. I glanced at the Glendale Hall shop and Emily's bakery. Usually I would pop into both but Emily was on a long weekend honeymoon with Brodie by Loch Ness, and Beth was finishing off the Christmas trail at the Hall ready for the grand opening, so instead I found myself wandering past the library where I used to work. I peeked in to see the new manager at the desk on the phone, and a couple of people reading at the tables by the window. I glanced at the spot where I used to have a large Harry Potter display but it had been changed and was now a cosy crime selection. It was strange seeing the place I had run for so long carrying on without me and I felt a little wistful at walking away from the cosy place filled with my favourite books to head back to the farm to prepare for snow.

Chapter Five

When we got back to the farm, it had turned bitterly cold outside, and I thought Hattie would be proved right, unfortunately, and there would be snow before tomorrow came. And the thought of being at the farm alone when it arrived, made me extremely nervous. What if there was a power cut when Rory was away at the cattle auction? I didn't think I'd cope by myself, but I knew we needed to make these sales so I would have to keep quiet.

Taking Harry inside, I found Rory still at the kitchen table doing paperwork before the auction, ready hopefully for the new owners of the cows. A cold cup of unfinished coffee sat in front of him. 'Hattie says snow is on the way,' I said as we came in, shaking the sleet off us. 'Told me to warn you.'

Rory looked out of the window. 'Hattie never fusses about a small drop. I'd better move the cows lower to be on the safe side. We have enough food in case we do get snowed in, don't we?' I nodded. We had done a big supermarket shop a couple of days ago. We had gas central heating, thank goodness, as his father had it installed when Rory was a boy, so that was okay if the electricity did go out, and the Aga would still work too. 'I'll get Angus to check we have some salt to grit the pathways actually. And I'll bring out the extra water troughs from the barn.' He stood up, always happy to spring into action. 'Fancy helping me move the cows this time? You could come out on Prince?' He saw me hesitate. 'If we do get stuck, you might need to ride somewhere.' He knew how much I worried about us being snowed in. If I knew I could get somewhere on horseback when travel by car or walking wasn't possible, then it would ease my mind a little.

'Okay,' I said, letting out a breath. I felt silly being so scared of the animals I lived with but every time I got on a horse, I thought back to the time I fell off, and was just waiting for it to happen again. 'Let me see if Dad is okay to watch this one.' I scooped Harry up and found my father in the living room in his slippers cleaning the coffee table with polish. He wasn't confident helping out with much of the farm, and to be honest wasn't in great physical health to do it, so when he was here he liked to help out around the house as much as possible. I winced though when I saw him because I knew I hadn't dusted in here for too long. Sometime it just felt impossible to keep up with household chores on top of everything else, but I knew I should do more.

'Hey there, you two,' he said with a smile. My mum always said my dad was never in a bad mood, and it was hard to remember seeing him in a temper growing up. They had rarely fought as he refused to fight back if she did raise her voice. When I was a stroppy teenager, he would just come and bring me a cup of tea and leave me alone until I felt better. I envied how he seemed to sense what people needed.

'Would you be okay to mind Harry for a bit? We think a bad snowfall is on the way tonight so we're going to move the cows lower down the hill where there's a stone shelter for them, and they'll be easier for us to get to. Rory wants me to come on Prince.' I took off Harry's coat and boots, and he hurried over to his toys in the corner.

'No problem at all. And I'll get some lunch ready for when you both come back. The sky certainly is grey,' he replied, finishing off the table. 'Be careful on the horse, won't you?' He smiled, no doubt remembering my childhood troubles.

'I think that's one thing you can always be sure of me being,' I told him, trying to laugh it off. 'Okay then, I'll be back soon.' I hovered in the doorway watching Harry sit on the floor, pulling out one of his toy trucks. Why did it always feel as though I was being pulled in different directions lately?

'We'll be fine,' my dad said firmly.

'I know,' I said but I still gave them another look before I finally walked out. Maybe it was different because I hadn't grown up on a farm but I was always on the lookout for things that could hurt Harry, whereas Rory's attitude was if that happened then Harry would learn what not to do, just like he had.

I stepped outside into the sleet again, thinking it was a good job I was happy to let my hair keep its natural curls because if I attempted to straighten it then as soon as I left the farmhouse, it would just be a frizzy mess. Rory was saddling up Prince outside the stables when I approached them, and I reached up to give Prince a tentative pat. 'Please be nice,' I whispered so Rory couldn't hear me.

'I'll walk with you,' Rory said, pulling the reins over. 'Need a leg up?'

'I'm fine,' I said, hoping I could manage. I didn't know how anyone managed to be dignified when climbing up onto a horse to be honest, but I certainly wasn't one of them. He held Prince steady while I lifted my foot into the stirrup and heaved myself up into the saddle. Rory checked my other foot was secure in the stirrup then took the reins and led Prince out of the stables and into the yard. I was still unsure about the feeling of being on a horse, up so high, the horse moving so much beneath me. I always felt wobbly, and like I was clinging on for dear life. My knuckles had already gone white, and my thighs were straining with how tightly I was pressing into his side. Rory led us into the field as we wound up the hill that rose up behind the farmhouse.

It was impossible for me to really relax but I couldn't deny the view up here was stunning. Prince was being good, which helped, and Rory led us at a steady pace. As we climbed higher, I could see the cows ahead in the very top field, their ginger coats at stark contrast to the green grass. It felt as if we were almost touching the grey sky. The temperature dropped even further when we reached them, and my cheeks felt raw from the wind.

'Here we are boys. Ready to go lower?' Rory called out when we reached them. I smiled – it was always amusing to hear him to talk to his beloved cows like they were people too. 'Here we go then.' He lifted the reins over Prince's head to hand them to me. 'Happy to go it alone?'

'Happy is the wrong word,' I said, gripping them nervously.

'You'll be fine,' he said confidently.

I watched as he went to the cows, humming a tune under his breath, and wished I had half his confidence. I gazed over the other side as he picked up some hay to help lure them down with us, and over the top of the hill, I looked down into the fields on the other side of our farm, that once had been used for sheep, but were now empty, and saw to my surprise two men walking there. It was a pathway used by a lot of walkers, walkers having been allowed through this land since records began, but we rarely saw anyone up here at this time of year. I squinted. They were wearing what looked like suits, which was also very unusual to see.

'Heth! Are you stuck?'

Hastily, I turned to see Rory already on the move, leading the cows downwards. 'Crap. Come on, Prince,' I said, tightening the reins. I urged him forward with my legs and thankfully, he started to walk down to the back of the file of cows. Rory was too far away for me to tell him about the men I had seen. I realised then that they could well have been the ones that had been spotted in the village that Hattie had told me about earlier.

But why were they up here? And just what had brought them to Glendale? I just hoped they were nothing to do with us, I really didn't want anything else to have to deal with right now.

My thoughts of them faded as I concentrated on walking the horse downhill; holding my balance was always harder when gravity came into play. Our cows were a good-natured bunch and they trusted Rory, following him easily, albeit slowly, down to the lower field where he gave them fresh hay and water as a reward. Their coats were beginning to become dusted with sleet and visibility was definitely becoming poorer now. 'I hope we can make it home from the Hall later,' I called out to Rory, anxiously, when I reached the field and watched the cows amble over to their supplies.

'We'll just make sure we come home early. We might not get there for a while otherwise. Let's hope there will be a good turnout for the auction if it does snow a lot,'

Rory said. 'Right then,' he added, pleased that a job had been well done. 'Want to try a trot?'

I looked at him in horror.

Chapter Six

That evening, we drove through the large iron gates of Glendale Hall ready for a family dinner. I always marvelled at seeing the grand house rise impressively in front of me. It reminded me of a house right out of a novel, rather like *Malory Towers*, the boarding school stories I had devoured as a girl. Rory yawned widely as he parked outside. 'Are you tired?'

'Exhausted.' After we'd moved the cows, all the other animals had needed to be moved to inside shelters with extra food and water. Angus had locked all the machinery away in the barn. He seemed to be in his element with bad weather on the horizon, waving us off cheerfully saying he'd see us in the morning if he could get out of his cottage door.

'Maybe we shouldn't have come...'

'Saves you cooking though,' Rory said with a shrug.

'I would have cooked,' I protested, once again feeling like I wasn't doing everything that I should have been doing.

'I didn't mean...' Rory trailed off with a weary sigh. 'It's just easier, isn't it? Come on, let's go in, the sooner we get inside, the earlier we can go to bed.' I watched him climb out and go around to the back to get Harry out, and I met my dad's gaze – he looked worried. I threw on a smile and climbed out. The problem with being so tired was it made us irritable with one another sometimes especially because I felt guilty that it was easier on me when we ate at the Hall. Rory put Harry in his pushchair as he was sleepy too, and we all filed up to the front door, which swung open as we walked up to it, flooding the driveway with bright light. 'There you are,' Beth said, her smile wide. 'Dinner's all ready.'

'You are a lifesaver, thank you for cooking,' I said, giving her a kiss on the cheek as we walked into the hall. She greeted the others behind me as I shrugged off my coat. A huge floor-to-ceiling Christmas tree greeted us then, the centrepiece of Christmas at Glendale Hall every year. It dazzled with twinkling white fairy lights and sparkling gold ornaments, and made me eager to get decorating at the farm.

'Everyone pitched in,' Beth said, waving off my compliment. I was in awe sometimes of how calm she was running this spectacular home, looking after the grounds along with gardener, and now her stepfather, John, as well as being a wife and mother, and being landlord of the shops in the High Street. She took things in her long-legged stride that I would just stumble over. 'Come on, let's get you all a drink. We're all in the kitchen.' We followed Beth into the vast open-plan kitchen where there was a huge long table looking out into the stunning grounds although it was too dark to see out there tonight. Soon the trail would be lit up and people would be walking through but tonight, it was just us.

'There you are,' Drew said, jumping up from table when we walked in. 'We were worried you'd decided the weather was too risky to come.'

'We'll have to leave early,' Rory told him as Drew gave him a hearty pat on the back in greeting. 'But all the animals are safely covered, and the cows are down lower, so nothing else to do but wait and see.'

'I bought a few things from the bakery on my way home,' Beth said. 'And picked you up a basket too in case you are stuck in,' she said, gesturing to the basket on the side full of bread and pasties. 'Let's hope Emily, Brodie and Sally can get back from the Loch okay tomorrow.'

'That's really kind of you,' I told her gratefully. Sometimes my friend's thoughtfulness pricked my conscience as I had so much going on, I didn't feel like I was there for her as much as she was for me.

'Right, sit down you lot, I'll get the drinks,' Drew said, walking into the kitchen. We joined Caroline, Beth's mother, and her husband John, and Beth's daughter Izzy at the table. It was a smaller party than usual with the honeymooners away along with Emily's aunt Sally who had gone with them to help with baby Iona. Although she was no longer the housekeeper here, she was thought of as family so now lived in the cottage in the garden for her retirement. Beth hadn't found a permanent replacement to move into the Hall. I think she couldn't quite let go of Sally running the house; she had had her here all of her life.

'Heather, I have to say those pictures you sent me are so beautiful – especially the sunrise,' Beth said from beside me. 'They've got twice as many likes as mine ever do.' She showed me on her phone. I couldn't help but smile at the lovely comments. 'You should set up your own account, or one for the farm. It could really get publicity for the business.'

'Hattie did say it's been quiet at the shop.'

'It has?' Rory asked, raising an eyebrow. 'And the weather won't help if it does snow and people just want to stay home.'

'I mean, I'm happy to try social media if you think it'll help,' I said quickly. I knew Rory had too much going on to do it, and I doubted he'd ever taken a photo in his life, too busy moving around to stand still and wonder at a sunrise. I was always trying to find ways I could help more with the farm, ways that didn't involve me either being terrified or messing up anyway.

'You've always had such a visual eye, I think you'd be great on Instagram,' Beth said, showing me her account. 'And everyone wants to live on a farm so you'll get loads of followers.'

I swallowed down the thought that sometimes I wasn't sure I enjoyed living on one, and told her I'd have a look at it later. It would be fun to use my visual brain again, and get a bit creative, there wasn't a lot of opportunities at the moment to do that.

'Are you enjoying your stay at the farm, Don?' Caroline asked my dad as he sat down opposite her. Caroline had always been a formidable woman, strict with Beth who rebelled against her mother, but she had softened in recent years since Beth and Izzy came back to live in Scotland, and since she'd admitted her feelings for John.

'Always,' he replied, making me smile. I thought again about Rory's suggestion we invite my dad to make his stay permanent, and wondered if he would accept it or not. 'We should think about decorating for Christmas, these guys have beaten us to it,' he added, looking down the table at me.

'We put ours up as we knew we wouldn't have time once the trail opens up on Monday. I can't believe it's less than two weeks to the big day, it seems like last Christmas happened yesterday!' Drew said, coming back with a glass of wine for me, and a beer for Rory and Dad. 'We can bring you a tree if you need one?'

'We'd love a Glendale tree,' Rory said, taking his drink from his brother. 'Harry can actually help decorate it this year.'

'He'll love it,' I agreed. I really needed to start sorting things out for Christmas. I needed to order a turkey from a neighbouring farm ASAP. Most of Harry's presents were bought but I hadn't wrapped anything, and to be honest the tree had slipped my mind. Dad had brought a box of decorations though from our family home. I remembered every year my mum and I would decorate our tree together. We always had a real one and we would try to fit on as many ornaments as we could. She would have loved the Glendale trail, she had been such a big fan of the festive season. I was too but with so much to think about, I hadn't got fully on board with it yet this year. I glanced at Harry who was starting to wake up with all the voices, and felt yet another prick of guilt. It would be the first Christmas he would be aware of what was happening, I had to try to make it as special as my mum had always made Christmas for me.

'Right, here we go – perfect food for this cold weather,' Beth said cheerfully, carrying over a large pot of steaming beef stew. Drew brought over mash and bowls of veg, and we all helped ourselves to large plates. All of us ate well in Glendale especially when the weather was like this. I carried Harry to the table and gave him a small plate of food.

'Izzy, stop reading to eat,' Beth told her daughter.

I looked along the table and smiled. Izzy was trying to hide her book on her lap. A girl after my own heart. 'What are you reading?' I asked her. She was thirteen now and becoming as tall and willowy as her mother, with the same wavy dark hair. Which was infuriating as they both ate like horses. Beth also drank copious amounts of coffee, like me, and I wondered if Izzy would start up the same habit.

'*Jane Eyre*. It's amazing just like you said.'

'That book... it steals your heart,' I agreed, pleased she was enjoying my recommendation. I started reading the classics at her age, on the advice of my mum, and it started a love that had so far lasted a lifetime.

'Not another handsome man none of us can live up to in real life,' Rory said with a roll of his eyes. He never understood how someone could fall in love with a character in a book. He was far too practical to do anything like that.

'Speak for yourself, big brother,' Drew said with a grin across the table.

'Ignore them, Iz,' I told her. 'A well-read woman is a dangerous creature.'

'You definitely are dangerous,' Rory agreed, nudging me with his elbow.

I flicked a few peas at him in response, making everyone laugh.

Then Harry flicked a pea at his father, making us laugh even harder.

'Your mother is a bad influence,' Rory told him as his son chuckled along with us.

After dinner, we were badgered into playing Monopoly, which Beth won as she always did, followed by a Harry Potter game, which Izzy won, and then she tried to do a puzzle with Harry but he kept trying to chew on the pieces so she read to him instead, looking archly at her mother who couldn't tell her off for being with a book this time. The rest of us sat around with coffee and mince pies, the fire crackling in the background.

'Will you still go to the auction on Monday?' Drew asked Rory.

'Unless the roads are unusable, I need to – we have two cows to sell.'

I bit my lip. I was always worried when Rory left the farm. I mean, I knew Angus was there, but still it felt like a big responsibility even if it was just for the day.

'So, have you heard about these strangers wandering around the village?' Beth asked, coming to sit with me, handing me a cup of coffee. We both definitely drank too much of the stuff, and had since we were studying together for our exams at school and needed as much caffeine as we could get our hands on.

'Yes, Hattie mentioned it,' I replied. I glanced at Rory but he and Drew were chatting about the auction still, oblivious to us. 'In fact, I was sure that I saw them near the farm too.'

Beth raised an eyebrow. 'That's interesting. It seems they're scoping us out for something. But, what?'

'It's not the council trying something funny again, is it?' Caroline asked, coming over. She didn't miss anything. The council had tried to sell off our High Street to a development company, which Beth's dad had been part of but had since stepped down from, but Caroline and Beth had saved it. 'Do I need to make a phone call?'

'No one seems to recognise them though,' I said. 'So, they can't be from the council. But, if not, I have no idea who they are or what they want.'

'Let's hope they go on their merry way again soon,' Beth said. 'Fingers crossed that the snow will put them off from sticking around, they certainly didn't look like hardy Glendale folk by all accounts.'

'Maybe I should wish for snow after all then,' I replied.

'Don't worry, we won't abandon you if you do get snowed in,' Beth promised. She knew that I got nervous about the bad weather. 'I just hope it passes enough for the trail opening night. You will set up that Instagram account, won't you? You could start with the two photos you gave me. I can share it on the Glendale account and on Facebook too.'

'For someone who avoided social media for ten years…'

She shrugged. 'I know but there was a reason for that. Now I'm on it, I'm addicted.' She glanced at Drew. She had avoided social media in case he worked out she'd had his daughter. I had a Facebook account but I didn't update it much. I wondered if some part of me avoided it in case my own ex-boyfriend saw my posts on there. Not that I'd tell Beth that in front of Rory. I knew he wasn't a fan of the fact I had loved someone before him. For him, there had only ever been me.

'We'd better be making a move, hadn't we?' Dad asked then, coming back from where he'd snuck off with John, no doubt to have a glass of Beth's family's whisky. 'The sleet is getting thicker out there.'

'I think you're right,' I agreed, draining my coffee cup. 'Thanks for this tonight, Beth, I always feel so relaxed here.'

'You need to relax more,' she said pointedly. 'As soon as the snow clears, we'll bring you that tree,' she added as we all got up and started to make our way into the hall. They had lots of Christmas trees on their land and sold some each year out of their shop.

I gave her a big hug as a thank you. Rory pushed Harry out, followed by my dad, and I waved at Beth and Drew in the doorway, the bright lights of home shining behind them. They were such a strong couple, they reminded me of my mum and dad sometimes, people you could count on, and who counted on each other. I wanted that to be Rory and me, but I worried too much about how to cope with life's ups and downs. He was the capable one, not me, I thought.

We drove off towards the farm – the roads were dark and twisty and sleet made the driving even more difficult so Rory went slowly and carefully. The car was quiet and when I looked behind me both Harry and my dad had fallen asleep. 'It's all right for some,' I said, turning back to Rory with a smile.

'You're not worried about me going to the auction, are you?' Rory asked a moment later in a low voice so he didn't wake the others up. He must have seen my face when Drew mentioned it.

'I just don't want the weather to get too bad.'

'It'll be fine. I'll be back before you know it.' I nodded, but I was still anxious about it. 'Hopefully Drew can get that tree to us soon, and we can decorate it together. We should make it an annual tradition. Like you said you did with your mum?'

I was touched that he remembered me talking about it. 'I can't wait,' I told him. I gazed out of the window but I couldn't see anything, there were no lampposts out here. I knew though that we were passing rolling fields on our way back to the farm. 'It'll be nice to create traditions for Harry like we had growing up.'

'I always begged my parents to tell me about their life before they had me. I wonder if Harry will ask us, and we'll have to come clean that we didn't get much time just us two before he came along. Although I bet he wonders why it took us so long to actually get together.'

I looked at him and smiled. 'I'll just tell him that his father really wasn't boyfriend material when I first knew him.'

'Oh, really? Perhaps it was you who wasn't girlfriend material.' He reached out to gently squeeze my thigh. I was relieved our earlier bickering had faded away after a lovely evening with our family. 'The best things are worth waiting for though, right?'

Rory and I had grown up teasing each other, and it was still surprising when he said something sweet or romantic to me. I treasured it, which I think he knew. 'True. But I'm still waiting for you to shave that beard off,' I replied, unable to resist.

'Over my dead body.' He swung the car though the gate and into the bumpy road that wound up towards the farm, lights from the top of the hill guiding the way. 'I'd get thrown out of the farmers' union if I didn't have a beard.'

I snorted. 'You mean you're too lazy to shave every day.' I was only joking really. I liked his beard, and his messy hair – he wouldn't be Rory without them.

'And it keeps me warm in winter, don't forget.' He stopped the car outside the farmhouse. 'Want to watch a rom com after we get Harry to bed?'

I smiled. 'Always.' I didn't believe my luck when I realised Rory loved rom coms as much as me. He blamed his mum, she loved watching them and when he lost her, he carried it on by himself, and now with me – on the condition I never revealed his love to Drew or any of the others, they would undoubtedly take the piss.

We woke the others up and went into the farmhouse. Harry started crying when I took him out of the pushchair. Rory went to make him some milk as I took him upstairs, saying goodnight to my dad on the landing. 'I think you're over-tired, just like your mum and dad,' I told Harry as I put him in his cot. He was already dressed for bed.

'Song,' he said when Rory appeared.

'Oh, so those tears were just a ploy, huh?'

'You soothed him too much when I was pregnant,' I said, sitting down beside the cot, remembering all the times he had sung to Harry inside of me, and how much our son had kicked in response. Rory leaned against the cot and obliged our boy, singing a Christmas carol in his lovely, deep, Scottish lilting voice. He nodded at me and I joined in with the chorus, smiling. I loved how our voices combined. The world faded away as we sung. We were in our bubble of three, and in that moment, everything felt like it would be okay.

Harry's eyes fluttered as he listened, fighting sleep to hear the rest of the song, but he soon gave in. We finished the song together, lowering our voices at the end as he drifted off to sleep.

When we had finished, Rory came over to me, leaned down, and whispered: '*You've Got Mail* or *While You Were Sleeping*?'

'As if I could choose between them, we'd better watch both,' I whispered back.

Chapter Seven

The alarm clock buzzed at six a.m., making both Rory and I groan. Sunday lie-ins were non-existent around here. I swatted it off with my hand and rolled over.

'It's snowed,' Rory said, sitting up.

'How can you tell?' I asked croakily, rubbing my eyes sleepily. Even though I had lived on the farm for two years, my body still protested at waking up at such an early hour especially when it was still pitch-black outside.

'The silence.'

I listened. It was extraordinarily quiet. 'I'll look,' I said, climbing out of the bed and sliding my feet into the slippers I kept beside the bed. Much of the winter was spent feeling cold so I did all I could to stay as warm as possible. I padded over to the window, which over-looked the farm, and gazed out at the fields to see they had indeed been blanketed in white. Soft, gentle flakes were still drifting down from the almost white sky. 'It has snowed.' I looked down at the fence. 'But not that much,' I said as I could still see most of it. Last January, the snow had reached right up to the top of it. 'We're not snowed in, at least,' I said over my shoulder, relieved.

'Good, means I can get to the auction after all,' Rory said, jumping up, eagerly. I sighed. Part of me had wished he would have to stay here but we needed these cows to sell to see us through the winter months, which were always tight money-wise as much more money was spent on looking after the animals, and keeping the farm warm plus Christmas was an added expense, and our shop wasn't as profitable. Rory had gone through everything with me once I had moved in so I knew it was a necessary trip for our finances. 'I'll check on the animals and make sure Angus is okay too,' he said, pulling on trousers and a jumper. 'You and Harry stay in the warm.'

'Are you sure?'

'We gave everyone extra food and water so there shouldn't be much to do,' he said with a nod. 'And I know you hate the snow.'

'I don't hate it. It's pretty to look at but it makes so much more work,' I said, trying not to be a Scrooge about the weather. I knew Harry would be excited to see it. I watched Rory go downstairs with a cheerful whistle, and marvelled at his good spirits.

I pulled on my dressing gown and then grabbed my phone and looked at the Instagram account I had created last night. @fraserfarmglendale. A little unoriginal but I wanted people to be able to find us easily. I added the sunrise photo first with the caption *Oh what a beautiful morning*, and then one of the shop with *Our farm shop is looking wonderfully festive.* Then I texted Beth to say it was up and running, and slipped across the landing. Dad's bedroom door was closed, clearly he was still asleep like most normal people on a Sunday. I peeped into Harry's room. He was used to us getting up early so his eyes were open, lit by his nightlight. 'Mummy,' he said sleepily when he saw me in the doorway.

'Come and look what happened in the night,' I said, going over to him. I picked him up and took him to the window, opening the curtains, and watching as his eyes widened at the sight of snow. 'It's snowed. Can you say "snow"?'

He reached out to touch the window as the flakes landed gently against it. 'Play,' he said, eagerly.

'After breakfast, when it's light, then yes. We'll go outside and play,' I promised. His face lit up and I thought that maybe snow had redeemed itself a little for me. Having kids reminded you of things that brought you joy when you were younger. Even I, who was averse to an outdoors life, had jumped around our garden when it snowed, and made angels in it, although I had been very eager to get inside for a hot chocolate afterwards.

I carried Harry downstairs into the kitchen, turning on the lights and then I let out a startled scream.

Right in the middle of the kitchen stood one of our pigs.

'Bloody hell,' I said, clutching my chest. Harry gasped at both the pig and me swearing probably. 'How did he get in?'

Harry pointed and I saw the back door had been left ajar. By Rory, no doubt. My mum would have asked if he had grown up in a barn, which he practically had.

'What's happened?' Dad appeared behind us then, flustered, hastily wrapping a dressing gown around him having evidently run down the stairs to see why I had screamed.

'A pig's got into the kitchen,' I told him, putting Harry down onto the floor.

'Not something I thought I'd ever hear, I've got to be honest.'

'Me neither. Okay, I need to try to get him out.' I set off, unsure how one removed pigs from the house to be honest. The pig grunted at me, looking a little stressed to find himself alone in our kitchen. 'Come on, boy, let's get you back outside,' I said in what I hoped was a calming voice. I pushed the back door open wide and the pig just looked at me hopelessly. 'Come on, let's go,' I said, waving my hands in the direction of the door. The pig just grunted in response. Did all the animals around here have to be so bloody stubborn?!

'Tempt him with some food maybe?' Dad suggested. I could tell he was trying not to laugh. Why was I always stuck right in the middle of something going wrong on the farm? I felt like an idiot once again.

'Fine.' I opened up the fridge and pulled out a carrot. 'Here we go.' I showed it to the pig who finally took notice, and set off towards me. I stepped back, holding out the carrot, as he shuffled after me, grunting loudly. Once outside, I threw the carrot into the yard and he hurried after it, munching on it greedily.

'Everything all right?'

I groaned inwardly as Angus came marching out of the barn and stopped short on seeing me in my dressing gown and slippers, standing in front of a pig eating a carrot, shivering as the snow fell on me. I always felt like he was there to witness all my disasters on the farm, and I was so embarrassed that he had to witness this one. 'Um... a pig got into the kitchen,' I said stupidly, stepping back, my cheeks flushing bright pink.

His lips twitched. 'I'll bring him in the barn,' he said, gruffly.

'Oh, great. Uh, thanks,' I said, quickly ducking back inside the kitchen, shutting the door behind me, sure he was out there laughing at me. 'Am I on a hidden camera show?' I asked no one in particular.

Late morning, Drew and Beth's Range Rover appeared on the drive.

The flakes had stopped falling, leaving a light covering everywhere, and I had brought Harry outside buttoned up in his coat, hat and mittens, to have his first playtime in the snow. Last time it snowed, he wasn't walking, so he was really excited to be out in it now. Rory had to bring the two cows he was taking to auction into the barn and make sure they looked as good as possible to potential buyers and Dad wanted to watch a film on TV, so I took Harry out by myself. I was a little sad that Rory wasn't here to watch how his son smiled as he gingerly stepped onto the field with me.

I turned around to see the car park behind us in front of the farmhouse and lifted my hand in a wave. 'Uncle Drew and Auntie Beth are here,' I told Harry as he jumped into the snow, which reached up to the top of his wellies. I could see the cows watching us interestedly in the distance, their coats dusted with snow like it was icing sugar.

'We brought the tree as the weather wasn't too bad after all,' Beth called as she made her way towards us, wrapped up as warmly as we were, her cheeks pink from the wind. 'I hope we're making snowballs,' she said, when she reached us.

'We were just about to. But do we need to help with the tree?'

She shrugged. 'Drew can get Rory to help him bring it in. Izzy isn't at all interested in the snow this year, teenagers apparently don't appreciate it. We left her reading with a hot chocolate so I need some snow fun.'

She shook her head, unable to understand why that was a preferable activity to Izzy than being outside here.

'I don't blame her, that sounds like a good time to me. But I'm happy to entertain you in the snow along with Harry,' I said, rubbing my gloved hands together. I watched as Beth gathered snow into a little ball and threw it for Harry to see. Then she made one for him, which he tried to throw but it just fell onto his shoes, making him crack up. I laughed along, delighted to see how happy this was making him. Perhaps I did need to get more on board with snow after all.

'I shared your Instagram by the way, you already have a few followers – I think people are going to love seeing things on the farm.'

'Really?' I pulled my phone out of my pocket – I had about a hundred followers on there. 'I'd better give them a snow scene then.' I snapped the hill covered with snow, one of the cows in the foreground, its coat tinged with white. Then I turned the phone on Beth and Harry. 'This one is just for us,' I said, smiling at them playing in the snow.

'He's going to have such an idyllic childhood out here,' Beth said, throwing another snowball. Harry tried to copy her again. 'I loved being out in the grounds of the Hall, I think he'll be just the same out here.'

'I remember you making me help you with that patch of land John gave you in the garden.'

'Oh, yes, and you were furious when you got mud on your new jeans,' she replied with a laugh. 'I made Sally ply you with lots of cake in case you didn't forgive me.'

'We were so different, it's a wonder we even became friends. Although, I think Rory and me are very much opposites attract too.'

'It's all about bringing the best out in each other. I made you more confident back then, and you made me less selfish and wild. You and Rory do the same for one another too, right?'

It was an interesting way to look at it. Rory definitely helped to calm me when I needed it, and I had brought him out of his shell, and made him much more sociable. Perhaps it was about balance. It wasn't always easy to remember that when you were firefighting problems all day though. I glanced behind us to see Drew and Rory trying to lift the tree off the roof of the car. 'I can't believe I'm a farmer's girlfriend. A bloody pig got into the kitchen today.'

Beth snorted. 'Never a dull moment here, that's for sure. But you enjoy it really, don't you?' She looked at me seriously then as if suddenly realising I might not be joking.

'It's harder work than I imagined,' I admitted. 'There's hardly a moment of peace.'

'Peace is overrated though when you have all this in your backyard. Maybe you and Rory need some quality time together. We can always look after Harry. Izzy would love to babysit.'

I wasn't sure I could cope with Harry staying away from the farm but I smiled. 'Maybe once this auction is out of the way, thank you.'

'Okay, well, make sure you take me up on the offer. Now then, I think what the three of us need to do now is make snow angels.'

'We'll freeze!' I protested.

'Come on, we always used to do that when you came to the Hall.' She got down in the snow, giving me a forceful look. One I remembered well from growing up.

There was something about Beth that made you end up doing whatever she wanted you to. The problem was it was always usually fun so she was often right, worse luck. With a sigh, I got down too and we lay in the snow, pushing out our arms and legs. Harry watched us, spellbound, and I couldn't help but laugh as I felt the cold snow pushing into my back.

'You just need to remember to have fun as well as work hard,' Beth said, looking across at me pointedly. 'You didn't used to find that difficult.'

'I know, you're right. Some days I'm just too tired to even think about having fun... God, I sound really old.' I thought back to my days at university, where there was always a night out or party to enjoy. Now though, I couldn't remember the last time I had stayed up past midnight.

'You sound like a mother. It's not easy, don't beat yourself up. Come on, Harry!'

I watched as Harry sat down on the snow beside me. I wanted to have fun with him, to be a fun mum, there were just so many things to do sometimes that fun took a back seat. Harry lay down beside us and tried to make his own angel. I smiled and showed him how to move his arms, spluttering when snow flew across the air over me.

'Harry will help you enjoy yourself when you need it,' Beth said, sitting up and smiling at us.

I wondered how I had reached the point of needing reminders from Beth and Harry to enjoy myself. I really needed to do something about that.

Chapter Eight

'Do you remember this?' Dad pulled a pink bauble out of the cardboard box on the coffee table, which he had brought back from our family home in the village. 'You were desperate for us to buy it at a Christmas fair even though it didn't match anything else we had.'

Dusk had fallen and we were in the living room with Rory and Harry, the large real tree that Beth and Drew had brought over, standing bare but proud in the corner. Beth and Drew had stayed for lunch then headed off to make sure the Glendale Hall festive trail was ready for the grand opening tomorrow, and to entice Izzy away from her book. Rory had finished his preparations for the auction and after we had sausages and mash for tea, which I couldn't help but relish after my run-in with the pig earlier, we had come in here to decorate for Christmas.

'I was obsessed with pink back then,' I said, taking it from him and smiling at it. I was cross-legged on the floor with Harry trying to unravel a set of lights. Rory was digging in another box trying to find something for the top of the tree. Christmas songs played out softly in the background, and our log fire was lit and crackling. It felt cosy and warm in here, and more like home than ever before. I supposed it was down to the act of getting ready for Christmas, something that couldn't fail to cheer both a room, and the people in it, up.

'Our ornaments don't have to be matching, we're not showing it to anyone but us,' Rory said, triumphantly pulling out a gold star from a box. 'Uh, Harry, don't eat that,' he added.

I turned in alarm to see Harry deciding one of the bulbs on the fairy lights looked edible. I snatched it away, relieved they weren't switched on. 'I think I'd better put these on the tree,' I said, carrying the lights hastily over to it. It didn't matter how carefully we packed them away each year, they were always tangled again when we brought them out the following year. The smell of the fresh tree floated around me as I started to drape the lights around it, standing on my tip-toes to reach up the top.

'Heather made this one,' my dad said then, holding up a wooden reindeer that I had made in secondary school. 'It has to go on the tree.'

'I almost sawed my finger off that day,' I said with a shudder, remembering. I had certainly not been good at any practical skills back then. Not that I was particularly great at them now. I tried to tell myself that each of us have our own skills in life. I went back to the box and pulled out the second string of lights. 'Oh, look,' I said in a half-whisper, seeing an ornament sticking out. It was a sparkling gold bauble. I pulled it out and let out a gasp when it dropped from the holder leaving just the string in my hand. I just managed to catch it before it smashed on the floor. 'Oh, no.'

'That was your mum's favourite,' Dad said, looking at it. 'She bought it as the first ornament for the tree in our house our first Christmas after we got married. She found it in a charity shop and hung it on the otherwise bare tree. It took a few Christmases to fill it up as we didn't have much money.'

'It's broken,' I said, looking at it, my eyes filling with tears as I pictured her all excited buying it for their first Christmas tree together.

'I can fix it,' Rory said, holding his hand out. I dropped the parts into his cupped hand. 'I'll be back.' He hurried off, always happy to try to fix something. I watched him go, and couldn't help but wonder whether he saw me as someone that needed fixing.

'It's always strange without her at this time of year, isn't it?' my dad said, going back to the box but not before I saw his own eyes had welled up too.

Harry reached for me then and I pulled him onto my lap, letting him grab hold of a bit of tinsel. I couldn't help but hold him tightly against me. 'She'll never know Harry, Dad. She should be here helping us dress the tree, she would have loved it.'

'Aye, she would.' He looked up. 'But she wouldn't want us all maudlin, would she? She would crank up the music, get out the mulled wine and tell us to enjoy ourselves.'

I smiled through my tears because that's exactly what she would have done.

'Sounds like a good idea to me,' Rory agreed, appearing behind us again. 'All fixed.'

'Thank you,' I said, giving him a quick hug as I took it from him. My dad smiled at us. 'Where's the fairy we put on the top last year, the one you had growing up?' Like me, Rory had only his memories of his mother during the festive period, but also his dad, and he needed something of theirs on this tree too.

He fished the fairy out of a box. 'We should make a wish when we put these up,' I told them firmly. These were special ornaments, and it was a special time of year, surely that equalled the possibility of some Christmas magic being available?

I picked a spot right in the centre of the tree and hung my mum's ornament on it, closing my eyes, and wishing that I could be as good a mother to Harry as she had been to me. I opened my eyes and watched Rory standing on his tip-toes to top the tree with the fairy, which had faded over the years. I wondered what he had wished for. Dad started to clap, which Harry joined in with enthusiastically.

I looked at the bauble as it sparkled back at me, and I took out my phone to snap a photo for our Instagram.

My mother's favourite ornament hanging on our tree in the farmhouse. I miss her the most at this time of year, but she was with us today, I'm sure of it.

–

It was five a.m. the following day when the alarm went off. Rory needed the extra early start so he could get the cows ready and set off for the auction, which was a four-hour drive away. I got up too, eager to spend as much time as possible with him before he headed off. I wanted to make him a good breakfast for the journey too.

The snow was patchy over the grass when I went outside to feed the chickens. It was freezing outside, but the weather had turned into a bitter wind, more snow seemingly fended off for the time being. I had left Harry inside with Dad so I could do the chores faster and then we could all have a family breakfast together. As I re-filled the water trough, Angus walked by.

'Cows are in the trailer ready,' he said, without saying hello. Rory had gone inside to shower and change.

'Great, thanks.' I turned to go then paused, feeling bad for not thinking he should be included in our breakfast. The thing was, he rarely came into the farmhouse. I had worried it was to avoid me when I came to live here, but Rory said he had rarely done it when his father was in charge either. That he preferred to keep to himself in the cottage. I thought he must be lonely there sometimes though. 'Do you want to join us for breakfast, Angus? We're making a cooked one for Rory.'

'No, I'm going to let the horses out. But thank you.' He tipped his hat and slouched off. I couldn't help but be curious about people, and I longed to ask him for his story. He wasn't married, and had no children either, had lived on the farm since he arrived aged twenty, and rarely left it. But I didn't feel like I could ask him. He didn't really invite conversation, even with Rory he only talked about the farm. I was relieved he would be here though with Rory gone – what he didn't know about farming wasn't worth knowing.

'Right, I think I'm all done for the morning,' I said when I walked in the back door. My dad was grilling sausages and the smell instantly made my stomach rumble. 'You didn't have to do that.'

'I keep telling you – I want to help as much as I can,' he replied sternly. 'Now, sit down and see to your son, I'm perfectly capable of cooking breakfast.' My mum had done the cooking all through their marriage but when she died, he tried to learn as I was out working all day, and he now was pretty good at a whole host of comforting dishes, especially a good old fry up. I did as I was told and sat down, getting a glass of milk for Harry and a cup of coffee for me.

'Daddy!' Harry said then as Rory came in washed and changed with a spring in his step — he loved going to auctions and seeing all the farmers and getting all the news from around the county.

'This smells great, Don, I'm starving,' he said, coming to sit with us. 'Everything okay, Heth?' He added then in a lower voice, noticing the frown on my face.

'Just been looking at the forecast, more snow is on the way,' I told him, looking up from my phone. We didn't always get a phone signal out here but the Wi-Fi worked well thank goodness. 'For here, and where you're going.'

'I need to go, it'll be fine,' Rory said, waving off my concern. 'After this, you'll have me for the whole winter, you'd think you'd be glad to see the back of me for a day,' he joked.

I managed to raise a smile in reply. I knew he was trying to cheer me up. But I just didn't feel confident with him gone even though I wasn't alone with my dad and Angus here, and Harry too, of course. I went on to Instagram and was surprised to see a bunch of likes, comments and new followers after my tree post. A few people had mentioned that they always thought of loved ones more at this time of year too, and how lovely it was to have my mother's ornament on the tree. 'Look at this,' I said, showing it to Rory. 'I didn't think people would be interested...'

'So many people have lost someone, haven't they?' he said quietly. He leaned over to give me a quick kiss. I often thought that was why nothing really fazed Rory; he had been through the worst when he'd lost his parents. 'I won't be gone long,' he added in a low voice, perhaps feeling bad about not taking my concerns seriously.

'I'll be fine,' I said, taking my phone back, hoping if I said the words then they would be true. I wasn't someone that shared how I felt with many people, I tried to keep my worries to myself as much as possible, although it was hard to fool my dad or Rory, or Beth a lot of the time, but I hated to make them worry about me, and sometimes I just felt embarrassed by my feelings. It was a lot easier to keep up a cheerful front, but opening up on that post, even in such a small way, had made me feel better, and it seemed like others felt better because of it too.

'Right, kids, eat up,' my dad said then, carrying over plates piled with eggs, bacon and sausages. He brought over a rack of toast too. 'Although if I keep eating like this every day, I won't fit into any of my trousers.'

'You'll have to come out to the cows, that uses up more than enough calories for the day,' Rory said.

'I don't know how you do it all, in this weather too. Puts my sitting behind a desk for my working years to shame. I still can't believe you've persuaded my daughter to this life,' my dad said, buttering his toast, throwing me a grin.

'What can I say? I was too charming for her to resist,' Rory replied. 'Isn't that right, Heth?'

'If you believe that, you'll believe anything,' I replied with a snort. Rory grinned at me, seeming pleased that I sounded more cheerful. I wished I didn't have to force it but I couldn't help but worry about Rory being gone all day, and having responsibility for the farm without him. I had hardly been here by myself so it was nerve-wracking. I really hoped nothing went wrong today. I glanced out of the window as a large snowflake drifted down, and bit my lip.

Chapter Nine

After Rory left, my dad suggested that he take Harry with him into Glendale. He had left a couple of Christmas presents at home, and offered to take the milk we had for the farm shop. 'It'll be too much for you,' I protested.

'No, it won't. Let me help you more, please,' he replied firmly, scooping Harry out of his highchair. 'You said yourself, you wanted time alone to wrap some presents now, didn't you?' I couldn't think of an argument to that so once they had put their coats on and walked out to the car, I found myself in the farmhouse alone. Something I didn't think had happened since I moved in.

Heading into the living room, I went to the chest in the corner and pulled out the presents I had bought for Harry, Rory and my dad and tried to enjoy the quiet as I pulled out the wrapping paper, and bows, and sat on the floor to wrap them. Tabby, the cat, soon found me, and tried to run off with the ribbon. 'That's not a toy!' I cried but she rolled on her back and began to wrestle with it, evidently thinking it was. I supposed at least a goat hadn't got in and chewed up the lot – a cat I could cope with. The only pet I'd had growing up was a hamster called Honey – after she died and I cried for two days, my mum had banned any others. Now I had a menagerie.

Tabby soon grew tired of playing with the ribbon, and curled up on a sheet of paper and fell asleep instead. I knew as I wrapped the gifts, I had bought far too much for Harry. He would likely be more interested in the paper I wrapped them with but it was far too easy to order things online. I still had this nagging feeling that I should be doing more as a mother, and this was one way I had tried to do so. Rory hadn't seen half of what I had got, and would no doubt tell me that I'd gone overboard. But I needed this Christmas to be a wonderful one for us all. If I could make it perfect then maybe I could stop feeling like I was failing here.

The doorbell rang out in the silence then, making me jump. I couldn't remember the last time the doorbell had rung – our family and friends usually just walked in the back door. I hoped it wasn't anyone official. The farm was regularly inspected without warning and I so did not need that today with Rory gone. I thought again about the two figures I had seen near to the farm, and hoped it wasn't anything to do with them. Reluctantly, I got up and made my way into the hall, leaving the mess on the floor and the cat curled up in the middle of it. So much for my stress-free morning.

I opened up the door to a man in a dark coat standing on the doorstep. 'Can I help you?' I asked, keeping my hand on the door warily.

He broke into a grin. 'What, you don't recognise me? It's only been a few years.'

My mouth fell open unattractively as I took him in properly. 'Stewart?' I squeaked. I stared at him in utter shock – my height, wearing dark jeans, a black jumper with a wool overcoat, his dark hair ruffled by the wind, his blue eyes bright. Just as handsome as he had always been. 'Oh my God! What are you doing here?' I asked my ex-boyfriend, reeling. I hadn't seen him since my abrupt exit from university when my mum had become ill.

'How about you ask me inside for a coffee, and I'll tell you?' he asked, his lips curving into a warm smile. 'It's pretty cold out here.'

I realised then that he was still on the doorstep, and hastily pulled the door wide open. 'Sorry, of course, come on in,' I said, watching him walk past me in wonder. I honestly hadn't expected to ever see him again. I touched my hair, wondering how messy it might look after the morning chores. I tried to smooth it down as I took in a steadying breath trying to calm down my shock at seeing him. I closed the door and faced him again, arranging what I hoped was a more collected expression on my face. 'Right, this way,' I said, leading him into the kitchen. I couldn't help but feel relieved to have the house to myself. Rory knew about Stewart, of course, but it would have been far too strange to see them in the same room together. 'Coffee then? Sit down, sit down,' I said, hurrying over to make us a drink. Stewart sat down at the table, looking around with open interest. I glanced over my shoulder to see him turn his gaze on me and smile. He looked the same. Older, of course, and thinner maybe, but the same. It was disconcerting. 'I can't believe you're sitting in my kitchen.'

'I've never seen someone look as shocked as you did when you realised it was me.'

'Well, can you blame me? It's been years. University feels like a lifetime ago,' I replied. We had been a couple for three years at St Andrews, and I hadn't seen or heard from him since.

'It's been too long, hasn't it?' He gazed into my eyes, and my cheeks grew hot under his scrutiny. I wondered what he was thinking. 'I want to know everything… What have you been doing for the past few years? And how am I finding you living on a farm, quite possibly the last place I expected to ever find you?'

I let out a little laugh. Stewart had always been direct. 'Well, I fell in love with a farmer, Rory – he owns the farm, so I live with him now and our son Harry, who's almost two.'

'Wow. You're a mother, and a farmer?! I've missed so much,' he said, shaking his head a little. 'Is Harry here? I'd love to meet him.'

'He's out with my dad in the village. And Rory is at an auction.' I showed him a picture of Harry on my phone. 'He has hair just like his father.'

'But he has your smile,' Stewart said, looking from the picture to me. I was pleased he had noticed. 'I know you always wanted children, I mean we always said…' he trailed off, coughing a little as if he was embarrassed. I put my phone down, knowing that he was remembering how we had talked about having a family together one day. It was strange to think how close we had once been, and now I had no idea what his life was like. 'But I must admit I'm surprised to find you doing something so outdoorsy. Whenever I thought about you over the years, I thought maybe you were doing something in publishing or illustrating, I don't know, but a farmer…'

I couldn't help but wonder how often he had thought about me. I thought back to our conversations about what we wanted to do with our lives. He was right, of course, I could never have imagined back then how my life would have turned out. 'I actually was a librarian first, after I came back to Glendale I got a job there and stayed until I had Harry. And then it got too difficult juggling everything so now I help out here, and also with our farm shop in the village. But what about you? Did you become an architect?'

'I did,' he said, sipping his coffee. 'Just how I like it. Always amazes me how few people can get coffee right. But you were the one who hooked me on to it,' he said, smiling down at his cup.

'God, yes, I can't believe you'd never even tried it until you met me,' I said, shaking my head. 'I think I drink even more now than I did during exams thanks to having to get up so early here.'

'I have to ask, now that you live and work on this farm... what's happened to your beloved heels?'

'I know, ugh. I miss them so much – I wore a pair to my friend's wedding the other day and that was the first time in like six months, I think. Felt like I was in heaven. But completely unpractical around here.' I nodded at him. 'What about you though, I thought you were always destined to wear a suit?'

Stewart chuckled. 'You're right, and I do wear one for work. I run my own development company now with... a partner. I do the designing, he does the building. It works well,' he said. 'So, yes, I followed through with my plan.'

'Was there any doubt?' I sipped my coffee. Stewart was always driven. He aced all his exams, and didn't even need to put in that much effort, whereas I'd had to spend days in the library to get my 2:1.

'Maybe a little after all the nights out you took me on,' he replied with a smirk I knew well.

'Me!' I spluttered my coffee. 'You were the one who always made me stay out all night at the Union bar, not to mention the times we went to that club in town. I think that's the only reason I didn't fall apart when I got no sleep after Harry was born. I had already had sleep-deprivation training.'

'We had some good times though, didn't we?' he asked with a grin. 'What about that party we had at Halls, they made us spend the whole next day cleaning up. Completely worth it though.'

'I still remember that hangover,' I said with a shudder.

'There are some great bars in Edinburgh, I went to one recently that was in a bookshop. You would have loved it.'

'I really would,' I agreed, a little wistfully. 'I don't get much time to go out nowadays especially not to fancy bars. The local village pub quiz night is the highlight of the month to be honest.'

'Well, you have a lot of responsibilities now. I still can't believe you're a mother. You're so grown up, Heather,' he said then in wonder.

'Harry really is wonderful. I had planned on waiting a few more years though...' I shrugged that thought off. 'Anyway, you still haven't told me how you're in Glendale right now. I didn't even think you knew where this place was,' I said, pointedly. He had never come to see me in Glendale, he was a city boy through and through, and in holidays from university, I had visited him at his parents' house in Edinburgh.

'I'm in Glendale on business, actually.' He glanced at me. 'I thought you might be still here but I wasn't sure. I'll be honest, I asked around about you, and was pretty stunned to find out you were living here. Right next to where I was the other day.'

So, the men I saw from the top of the hill – one of them had been Stewart. I was glad I hadn't alerted Rory to their presence after all. I thought about how I had begged Stewart to come here after my mother died and I had told him I couldn't leave my dad, but he had stayed in Edinburgh. It was utterly surreal to see him now in my kitchen.

'I wanted to get in touch through the years, I really did, but I wasn't sure you wanted me to, to be honest,' he said.

It was hard to know how to answer that. I didn't know if I would have wanted him to either. I had been head over heels in love with Stewart. And my heart had broken when we spilt up. I wasn't sure how you ever stayed in touch after that. 'So, why now?' I asked instead, swallowing hard. The smell of his musky aftershave hit me. It was the scent I had bought him. He still wore it. It was making me feel light-headed. Reminding me of all those years I had spent with him. It was so strange. How he had disappeared from my life as if our relationship had never happened. But now he was suddenly back in my life again. 'Why are you in Glendale?' I repeated my earlier question, confused as to why he had come to find me.

Years too late.

Chapter Ten

'How about you give me a tour of the farm, and I'll explain everything? I'd like to see where you've been hiding yourself these past few years,' Stewart replied. 'Please?' he added as I hesitated.

'Okay, I'll just grab a coat.' I walked out into the hall, glancing at the mirror as I went to the coat rack. My cheeks were bright pink. As I slipped on my parka, I couldn't stop myself from remembering the first time I met Stewart, eleven years ago now, when I was just eighteen.

-

I'd just said goodbye to my parents and was trying not to cry as I walked back to my tiny room in halls. 'Be careful, those are my favourite books,' I heard a male voice say. A couple of rooms away from mine, he stood in the doorway in a long, dark coat, arms folded as a younger boy carried a box in. I couldn't help but take a peek when I heard him mention books. 'When your younger brother has no respect for Fitzgerald,' he said when he caught my eye.

'I was furious when I found out we only got one shelf for books, took me a week to pick which books to bring, and then I realised I had forgotten to pack clothes until last night,' I replied, hovering in the doorway to my room.

'Luckily, my mum is as much of a bookworm as me so she understood why we left two hours late to get here,' I added with a chuckle. My dad had been less impressed but he'd always been the organised one of the family.

The boy strode over and stuck out his hand. 'Stewart. How about we go for a drink and you tell me which books you chose to bring? If we picked more than five the same, then we definitely belong together,' he said, his lips curling up into a smirk.

I laughed as I shook his hand, firm and warm, and took a quick look at him. 'I'm Heather.' He was incredibly good-looking, and I'd never met someone so confident. It was really attractive to me, someone who had never been confident. He was looking at me in a way that suggested he knew exactly what I was thinking. I felt myself blush annoyingly. 'Belong together? What are we swans, about to mate for life?'

'Let's have that drink and see, shall we, Heather?' he asked, still holding my hand in his. I had no power to resist, and he knew it.

We stayed out until the early hours talking about books and drinking, and it turned out we had chosen ten of the same books to bring with us.

When he kissed me goodnight, I found myself for the first time wondering if I might finally get a love story like the ones I enjoyed reading about so much.

–

'Ready?' Stewart said, startling me out of the past as he appeared behind me in the hall. I shrugged my coat on, slipped into my boots and nodded. I wondered if he was remembering our time at university together too as I led the way out of the farmhouse. We had been a couple from that first day until I had received that phone call from my father asking me to come home. I had just finished my final exam so I had rushed back to Glendale to be with my mother, who had been diagnosed with cancer at such a late stage, she had only lasted another six weeks. Stewart had still had exams to finish, his final one on the day of my mother's funeral so I'd had to face that alone, and when I had said I couldn't leave my dad alone, Stewart had chosen to follow through with the offer of an apprenticeship in Edinburgh without me, refusing to join me in Glendale. I had been gutted.

I showed him around the yard first, taking him to the horse's paddock, and into the stables, the chicken coop, the pig enclosure, and then around to where the goats were, glancing at Angus's cottage, hoping he wasn't looking out of the window. He usually retreated in there for tea and biscuits at this time. I didn't think I should feel guilty as I hadn't invited Stewart here, but it was strange showing him around without Rory knowing, as if my past and present were colliding. I planned, of course, to tell Rory about it but it was a lot easier not having to go through any awkward introductions.

'Mainly we are a cattle farm, the herd are in the lower field at the moment in case of snow, usually they are up on the hill,' I explained to Stewart as we reached the front of the farmhouse. I pointed up to the hill in the distance.

'I'd love to see up there,' he said, looking across at me as he put his hands in his pockets, a sharp wind blowing through the air. 'I still can't believe you live out here. Don't you miss civilisation?' he asked as we walked towards the fields where the cows were grazing.

'Sometimes. But we're not that far from the village, and my sister-in-law... well, Rory and I aren't married... anyway, she lives at Glendale Hall which is a short drive away. It does feel more isolated in winter especially if it snows, but it's really beautiful on a summer's day. I don't know. I'm getting used to it, I suppose. Still very much on a learning curve though. Rory has lived here all his life so it's instinctive for him, a way of life. But I'm a townie, after all.'

Stewart smiled. 'Well, I admire you for doing something so different. I couldn't live without my daily Starbucks fix, or eating out at my favourite restaurant in the city. And wandering around the bookshops, of course. You must miss bookshops?'

'Well, we have the library in the village, and it's pretty well-stocked, I made sure of that when I worked there. To be honest, I order pretty much everything online nowadays apart from trips to the supermarket, and we're not that far from Inverness if I do want to go shopping.' Although I hadn't been in months. I thought about how if I also lived in Edinburgh, I would enjoy exactly what Stewart enjoyed there, and I felt a little envious of him. But I breathed in the brisk fresh air as I opened the gate to the field and tried to focus on the wild beauty we were walking into. A very different world.

'And here are the cows,' I said rather lamely as we walked past the grazing Highlands. They looked at us with interest, a couple wandering over hoping we had brought food no doubt.

'Do you really help out with farming work then?' Stewart asked as we kept on walking up the hill. He sounded a little breathless from the steep climb. I was used to the incline now so I slowed my pace for him.

'I really do. I won't pretend it's easy or comes naturally though. Rory is trying to teach me to ride, and I'm no natural horsewoman, that's for sure.' I smiled, ruefully.

'So, what's this Rory like? I'm trying to picture the man who managed to get you living out here?' he asked with a chuckle. 'I assume he loves books as much as you do?'

'Actually, not really. If he reads anything, it's a farming book. I never knew there was that much to know about cows, but there is,' I replied, shaking my head. 'He's really practical. He can fix anything. He loves being outdoors. He's funny and kind, he'll help anyone who needs it, and he really looks after me and Harry.' My heart swelled a little at the thought of Rory, and how he managed to keep this farm running all on his own. I felt Stewart watching me intently. 'I actually knew him growing up but we didn't get close until my childhood friend Beth came back to Glendale. She's married to Rory's brother now.'

'But you haven't got married?' he asked, glancing at me quickly.

Of course that *had* to come up. 'No, I guess we haven't had the time, with Harry and all this…' I trailed off. I really didn't want to explain how I felt about marriage to Stewart. He just nodded thoughtfully. I wished I knew what was going through his head. My own was full of confusion about him being in Glendale after not having seen him for so long.

We reached the top of the hill then and fell silent as we stopped to take in the view. 'Well, I can't deny that this is stunning,' Stewart said. 'It's a special view.'

'It is,' I agreed. 'So, now you've seen the farm, are you going to finally tell me why you're here?'

Stewart turned to me. 'See that farmhouse over there?' He pointed down the other side of the hill to the abandoned building below us.

'Hilltop Farm,' I said with a nod. It had stood empty for two years after the farmer there, old Sam, died and passed it to his nephew, William, who lived in London. It had been up for sale ever since.

'I'm here to look over the land there. We are considering buying it and developing it into a hotel and golf course. It's been empty for a long time so they're willing to sell for a very good price.'

'Oh,' I said, taken aback. I looked down at the rolling fields and couldn't imagine a resort standing there instead. Alarm ran through me at how close it would be to our farm, how much the landscape could change. 'Would you get planning permission for something like that?' Surely land like this was protected?

Stewart turned to me and shrugged. 'We're waiting to see… We've put in a planning proposal to the council. So,' he said with a smile, 'we might be neighbours soon.'

I had no idea how to respond to that. Hilltop Farm had been in the same family for generations, like Rory's, but when old Sam died William hadn't wanted to take the farm over and had been trying to sell it ever since. Rory had said he wished we could afford to buy it and join up the two properties, but it was impossible financially. And now Stewart wanted to develop it all. I knew Rory would not like the idea. 'Is there enough land for such a resort?' The farm was slightly smaller than ours, which ran to five hundred acres of land, and I imagined you'd need a lot of space for a golf course.

'Just enough, we think. It would be our most ambitious project to date. There isn't a golf hotel for miles around so it would be a great spot,' Stewart said. His eyes were bright at the thought of it. 'We'd turn the farmhouse into the hotel, of course, and the golf course would need to run along this side,' he said, pointing. 'The other side has protected land because of the trees growing there. We'd never get permission to cut those down, but that would be a draw for guests too, I think.'

I followed his gaze and frowned. The golf course would be on the side closest to our farm. I wondered if it would disrupt our cows once they were back grazing up here. 'How far would the course come up to?'

Stewart pointed. 'Up to where that land rises there, I think.'

'But that's part of our lower field,' I said, shaking my head. 'Our land boundary runs up to that patch of heather down there,' I told him. Rory's father and grandfather before him had grazed sheep down there where the land was flatter, and more sheltered, but after foot and mouth reduced the herd, and harsh winters meant the sheep had to be grazed elsewhere, Rory's father decided to focus on Highland cattle and all sheep left Fraser Farm. Rory often talked now about re-introducing them in the future.

'Not according to the boundary map we have from William, Hilltop's owner, that clearly shows this area as belonging to Hilltop Farm.' He faced me. 'I can show you. I don't have the plans with me though…'

'I'm certain that is Fraser land as sheep used to be grazed there. I'd have to get our deeds out.' If I was wrong than the hotel and golf course would impact us at the farm, that was for sure, but if I was right then it would be at least further away, and might even mean they couldn't fit a full golf course there. Stewart had realised that too, I could see by the look on his face.

'If the land does belong to Rory then maybe he would sell it to us instead?' Stewart asked, unable to hide the hope in his voice.

I wasn't at all sure that he would. I knew that having hotel guests so close to our cows would concern him. 'We'd have a completely different view,' I said instead, thinking about how it would look up here once Stewart had built on this land. I was so used to us being alone out here, to seeing countryside in whichever direction I turned, but that would no longer be the case.

'I would want to fit in with the landscape as much as possible, you know that. I wouldn't want to harm your farm. Tell you what, why don't you find your deeds, and I'll gather the plans we have, and we can go over them together?' He stepped closer. 'Why don't we have dinner tonight? We can talk it all through when you've had a chance to think about everything. I'm staying in Glendale all week and really don't fancy eating alone every night.' He nudged me with his elbow. 'You know how I hate to eat by myself. And how long has it been since you've been out for a meal? Come on, my treat. Please, Heather?'

Why had he always been so hard for me to say no to? He was giving me a pleading look, and he was right that I rarely went out for dinner nowadays. I wasn't sure though. Rory wasn't due back until late but he wouldn't be particularly happy to know I was eating out with an ex. But then maybe it was a chance to sort the land issue out without me having to bother Rory about it. I was always looking for a chance to prove myself here after all. Him being at the auction would buy me some time to try to prove the land was ours. 'Okay,' I agreed. 'I have to go to Glendale Hall first, their festive trail is opening tonight and I promised my best friend I'd be there. But I could meet you about seven-thirty, I think?'

Stewart broke into a wide smile. 'Great, I'll book somewhere, and text you. What's your number now?' We exchanged numbers, and I tried not to feel like I was doing anything wrong, but I couldn't quite convince myself.

'Come on, it's getting too cold to stand around up here,' I said. I knew my dad could return with Harry at any moment. I didn't want him bumping into Stewart. Although Stewart had never visited Glendale, they had met a few times at university when my parents came to see me. I didn't want my dad to know he was here. Or anyone. Not until I knew what was happening with our land, and how this hotel might affect it. I didn't want to worry anyone else with this yet.

We walked down the hill and I shut the gate behind us. I looked down at Stewart's sleek, black car, which looked so out of place in our yard, as he did. I wondered if I looked out of place here to him or not. I was sure that I did.

'It really has been so good to see you again,' Stewart said as we stopped by his car. 'I'm looking forward to taking you out tonight.' He leaned in and kissed me on the cheek, startling me a little. I looked around worriedly but we were still alone. 'Heather Douglas,' he said, shaking his head. 'Back in my life again after all this time. I guess I should believe in fate now. What were the chances of me picking the land right next door for my hotel, huh?'

'Pretty crazy,' I said, my cheek still warm from the brush of lips against my skin. I couldn't deny that the attraction I had had that first day at university hadn't completely faded like I thought it would have. 'I still can't believe you're here.'

'See you tonight then,' he said with a grin, climbing into his car.

I lifted my hand in a wave as he set off out of the farm, watching him go in disbelief.

It was so strange to remember what we had once been to one another. To be reminded of the woman I had been when we were together.

A very different woman to who I was now, that was for sure.

Chapter Eleven

I was still standing there when my dad's car turned up the winding, gravel drive, towards the farmhouse. I pretended I had been waiting for them, breathing a sigh of relief that they had missed seeing Stewart here. Seeing them both made me feel strangely guilty for the time I'd just spent with Stewart. It had felt illicit somehow. And agreeing to have dinner with him too made me feel jittery. 'Did you have a nice time?' I asked when Harry skipped out of the car towards me. I lifted him in my arms. 'And what's this?' I asked as he almost hit me in the face with a cuddly toy.

'Lamb,' Harry said triumphantly, proud he had learned the word.

'Well, I'm pleased to see it's farm appropriate,' I said with a laugh.

'He saw it in the Hall shop and we just couldn't leave without it,' Dad explained, coming into the hall with a brown paper bag. 'I bought us some fresh bread to have with our dinner later,' he said, holding it up. 'Did you get all your wrapping done?'

I had completely forgotten about that. 'Almost. Pop the kettle on, and I'll be through in a couple of minutes. And it's time for an afternoon nap for this fella, I think.' I put Harry down. 'Do you want some warm milk first?'

'Please,' he said, trotting after my dad.

I hurried back into the living room, and hastily tidied the presents into the wooden chest. Tabby had since disappeared, the wrapping paper she'd been lying on all torn up. When the room was clear, I ducked into Rory's study. I pulled open the filing cabinet. His mother had been meticulous about recordkeeping at the farm, thank goodness, and everything was labelled in there. There was a folder labelled 'deeds', and I yanked out the paperwork, laying it on the desk to look at.

The deeds for the farm and the land boundaries were in there. The original ones were written in really old, formal language but I could make out that Rory's grandfather owned the property, and then there were transfers to Rory's father, and then himself. There was a map with the original deeds and I pulled it out, spreading it in front of me.

Leaning over, I traced my finger over the red pen-marked boundary line following it from the front where the farmhouse was along the edge where the hill fields were and then over the top into the land beyond, my heart sinking when the red line stopped far before the heather patch. I thought back to the first time Rory had shown me his land properly. I had visited the farm as a teenager accompanying Beth the summer she and Drew fell in love, and I had visited a few times since Beth returned to Glendale, and more when Rory and I had become a couple, but suddenly I was moving in, and I was nervous of how big the property was, amazed that I now lived in so many acres of land.

–

'It's not that far,' Rory laughed as I puffed behind him walking up to the top of the hill.

'I am pregnant,' I replied, giving him a furious look. I was still tired a lot of the time, and was holding him personally responsible for any suffering I felt. Plus, I wasn't an outdoors person at the best of times. Walking wasn't high on my list of enjoyable activities.

'I'm sorry, but look at this view.' We stood on top of the hill looking at the vast countryside around us. It did take my breath away.

'And all this belongs to you?'

'All the land that reaches up to that woodland there,' he said proudly, pointing to the far side of the farm. 'And right up to that heather patch down the other side of the hill over there,' he added, pointing towards Hilltop Farm. 'Maybe it's a sign that heather grows here?' He grinned at me.

I smiled back. 'Maybe it is.' I bit my lip though, still feeling nervous.

'The rest is the neighbouring farm's land although it's been empty for ages. I have no idea if it'll ever sell. So, what do you think? Can you see yourself living here?'

I turned to him. 'Are you sure you want me here? That it's not just because of this one...' I touched my stomach.

'Of course. You know, I wanted you to stay here before we found out about the baby, but now I want it even more. Don't you?'

'It's just that it's all happening so quickly. And I've lived in the village all my life. You had to buy me a pair of wellies! I just don't know how much use I'll be here.' I bit my lip. Being up here, it suddenly seemed real. I was about to move onto the farm. To live with my baby's father. Scared didn't even begin to cover it.

Rory put his arm over my shoulders and pulled me close. 'It's not about being useful. I want you here because

I love you and we're going to be a family. I want to look after you, and wake up with you every day.' He turned to me and brushed my hair back as it blew around my face in the breeze. As always when he looked at me, the world faded into the background and it was just the two of us, and it was so much easier to not feel as scared. 'Heth, it's scary but exciting. What do you think? Will you come and live here with me?'

How could I say no to him? I pushed my fears aside as far away as I could and took a deep breath. 'Okay,' I said. He grinned and picked me up, twisting me around in a circle as I laughed and gasped, 'put me down, you fool!'

The memory of that day faded as I stared at the boundary map now. Rory had been wrong about the boundary with Hilltop. We didn't own the lower field up to the heather patch after all. Which not only meant that we lost a good chunk of our land, but also meant that Stewart's golf course would start right at the edge of our farm. I wondered why Rory had got it so wrong, he must have always thought that land was his, but why?

I'd have to confess this to Stewart, but maybe I could talk him out of his plans for Hilltop, or at least persuade him to take our farm into account? I still couldn't believe that he had chosen the land right next to ours. What had Stewart said – something about fate bringing us back together? I wondered if fate had a sick sense of humour because as if I didn't have enough to worry about, now I had this on my mind too.

I put the documents away, feeling lower than I had for a while.

I really didn't want to have to tell Rory that our land was under threat, and from my ex-boyfriend too. It felt like it was my fault somehow.

Like it was yet another thing I was getting wrong around here.

–

'Welcome to the annual Glendale Hall Christmas trail!' Beth called out a warm greeting as the crowd around her fell silent. We had all gathered at Glendale Hall for the grand opening of the festive trail in the grounds. Most of the snow had gone now so there was a good turnout. I was there with Dad and Harry, who was bundled up in his pushchair protected from the cold night. It was strange not to have Rory beside us.

I kept checking the time on my phone. I had told my dad that I was meeting an ex-colleague from the library in the village for a quick meal afterwards. I felt so guilty for lying to him, and for not telling Rory what I was going to do. Underneath my long winter coat, I had put on a black dress and my heeled boots, an outfit I hadn't worn since last year. My hair and make-up were more carefully done than I would usually bother with for just coming to the Hall, and butterflies danced inside my stomach. I was going to go out with another man, and I shouldn't be feeling at all good about it. But I was excited.

I told myself it was just because I so rarely went out nowadays and surely Rory would understand that. But deep down, I knew I was just fooling myself on both counts. I had almost phoned him to tell him but I decided that it was best to find out more about Stewart's plans before telling Rory anything, and I doubted he would understand any reason I gave for having a meal out alone with my ex-boyfriend. I knew it was all above board, but he might not. I felt my cheeks flush. It was definitely all above board, I told myself firmly, wishing my pulse would slow down.

Maybe I just felt buzzed because it felt like for just one night I could be like my eighteen-year-old self again, with no responsibilities, and nothing to worry about.

'Enjoy!' Beth cried then as her mother cut the ribbon tied across the entrance to an enthusiastic round of applause from the villagers standing with us. I snapped a photo of the open trail for Instagram. I had two hundred followers on there now, and I was sure they'd appreciate the twinkling fairy lights with a clear, star-filled sky, above. I was pleased with my shot – Beth was right, it appealed to my visual brain. I was enjoying it more than I thought I would.

'Heather!'

I turned as people filed past us into the trail, and broke into a smile to see Emily and Brodie arm-in-arm walking across the grass towards me.

'Catch us up,' Dad said to me as he pushed Harry into the trail alongside John and Caroline.

'We missed you,' I said, pulling Emily into a warm hug.

'Us too! You look lovely tonight,' Emily said, beaming, looking at me as we pulled apart. 'I love that lipstick.'

'Oh, thanks. I'm meeting a friend afterwards... Anyway, how was the honeymoon?' I asked, brightly, turning to Brodie, trying to cover my guilty thoughts as I lied to my friend.

'We had a great time, didn't we, Em?'

'I love it there. I mean, it was freezing in that cabin, only we would choose Loch Ness in the snow, but it was magical too. It was just nice to have a few days away. We missed Glendale though.'

I nodded. I understood. They were such fixtures of our community. 'We missed you guys too.'

'Where's Rory?' Brodie asked, looking around.

'He's at an auction today, I'm expecting him back late. I thought he might have phoned me by now, but he's probably too busy talking to all the farmers there.' I rolled my eyes.

'That's what I'm like when I meet up with other ministers,' Brodie said, with a laugh.

'I swear men are worse gossips than we are,' Emily said, looking fondly at him. Her new gold wedding band sparkled under the starlight. If any couple was a good advertisement for marriage then Emily and Brodie were it.

Drew and Beth found us then and greeted Emily and Brodie.

'Where's Iona?' Beth asked, missing the baby.

'Sally has her at the cottage, they both needed a rest. We'll pick her up on the way home,' Emily explained. 'Shall we walk the trail or have a quick mulled wine first?'

We all looked at one another and laughed, heading off to the refreshment table and scooping out ladles of mulled wine from the steaming pot there.

'So, how does it feel to be a minister's wife?' Beth asked Emily, her gloved hands wrapped around her cup. In the distance behind her, the lights of the trail sparkled, and we could hear cries of delight from the children as they discovered this year's lights.

'So far so good,' Emily said. 'Although I'm dreading all the unpacking I have to do at the vicarage. I want to get it all done tomorrow as I need to be back at the bakery after that.' Emily made her busy life all look so easy.

Drew came to stand beside me so I took the opportunity to casually speak to him. 'I was wondering, Drew, how much you knew about the land of Fraser Farm? Have the boundaries always been the same?'

He considered. 'As far as I know, yes. Obviously, I wasn't born when my grandfather bought the farm from the landlord, but I believe he kept the same land as he'd had when he was just the tenant. Rory would know better than me though. He was always more interested in all that, I'm afraid,' he said ruefully. Unlike his brother, and father and grandfather before him, Drew hadn't felt the call to farming, and had instead pursued medicine, even living away for years in Boston to study and train.

I sipped my wine. It was warm and spicy and comforting, but I still felt cold. 'And the land over the hill, in the lower field, the one that borders Hilltop Farm?'

'Where we used to keep sheep?' I nodded. 'That's always been ours as far as I know. Why the interest in the boundary lines? Thinking of breeding sheep again?' He smiled but looked curious.

'We might do,' I replied, non-committedly.

'You could get a sheepdog,' Beth broke in then with excitement. 'I've always wanted a sheepdog.'

I smiled. 'I always wanted a dog growing up,' I remembered. It was actually not a bad idea. It might help make me feel safer out there when Rory wasn't around. 'Maybe I'll mention it to Rory.'

'Well, he'd let you have anything,' Beth said, slipping her arm through her husband's. 'He just wants you to be happy. Right, now we're fuelled up, shall we check out the trail?' The others agreed and set off eagerly, with me following more slowly behind. I knew she was right, Rory did want me to be happy.

Why was I finding it so hard to be then?

My phone buzzed in my pocket, and I was startled to see Rory's name appear on the screen. I paused, then answered it, telling myself there was no way he could know about me meeting Stewart. 'Hiya,' I greeted him, hoping I sounded just like I normally did.

'I'm really sorry, Heather, but there's a blizzard coming here.' He sighed down the line. 'It's already snowing, and laying thickly.'

'So you're waiting it out?'

'I'll have to stay overnight, it looks like.'

I gripped the phone. I'd never stayed overnight at the farmhouse without Rory. I knew I wasn't alone with my dad, Angus and Harry there but still... 'I told you there was snow on the way, I said you shouldn't go,' I burst out.

'They didn't predict it would be this bad tonight,' he replied wearily. 'Besides, we sold both cows. We needed that money, Heth, you know that.'

'I hate how everything ends up coming back to money, and how tight things always are,' I said, pushing back my hair in annoyance.

'I'm sorry, that's how farming is nowadays.' He sighed, sounding tired, and very far away from me. 'I can't do anything about the weather. I'll leave as soon as I can, I promise, okay?'

'Not much I can do about it, is there?' I snapped. I knew I was taking my anxiety about being alone out on him, but I couldn't help it. He didn't seem to understand how worried I was about being responsible for the farm without him.

'It'll be fine, it's just one night. And Angus will be there if you need anything,' he said.

'Okay,' I said unhappily. 'I need to go, Rory, the others are waiting for me at the trail. It's opening night, remember?' I said, looking back to see Beth giving me a worried look; no doubt she had heard my raised voice.

'Right then. Well, I'll talk to you tomorrow? Give Harry a big kiss from me.'

'Sure,' I said, hanging up with a sigh. I followed the others into the trail, putting on a smile for them, but I was worried. I hoped he'd be okay, that the blizzard wouldn't be too bad, and he would only need to stay away for one night. I also hated the thought of sleeping at the farm without him, something I'd never done before. Thank goodness I had dinner with Stewart to focus on. I couldn't help but look forward to my evening away from the farm, even if we had planned to be talking about it. It had been a long time since I'd gone to a restaurant for a meal, and I had always had a good time with Stewart.

There was nothing wrong with that surely? It was all perfectly innocent.

The problem was, there was a little voice in my head telling me I was lying to not only Rory, but also to myself.

Chapter Twelve

I slipped away from the Hall, trying to hold on to my anger with Rory and not let guilt overwhelm me as I waved goodbye to my family and friends and set off in my car to the pub Stewart had booked for dinner a few miles away. I was relieved he hadn't suggested eating at the Arms, where he was staying, as I knew there would be too many people there I recognised, and no doubt gossip would have spread around Glendale if I was seen eating with another man. Not that there would be any foundation to it, of course.

Finding the pub car park, I pulled in and spotted Stewart's car already there. I switched off the engine taking a few breaths. Then I glanced at my flushed reflection in the rear-view mirror. 'Too late to cancel now,' I whispered to myself.

Pushing open the pub door, warmth and laughter greeted me and I spotted Stewart at a table in the corner close to the log fire, so I weaved my way around the tables towards him. He was wearing a dark shirt and stood up when he saw me, his face breaking into a warm smile. He leaned in to kiss my cheek, his aftershave wafting over me again. 'You look lovely, Heather,' he said, reaching for my coat.

'Thank you,' I replied, pleased that he had noticed I'd made an effort. I let him slip the coat from my shoulders and drape it behind my chair, and then we sat down, close together thanks to the small table. I was more nervous than I cared to admit. Stewart was, after all, my first love and it was incredibly strange to be with him again. My leg bounced under the table. 'I haven't been here before,' I said, looking around so I wouldn't have to meet his piercing gaze. It was a small, cosy pub with low wooden beams across the ceiling. Fairy lights were draped over the beams in the centre lending a rather romantic atmosphere to the place. I shifted in my seat, drawing my eyes back to him.

'The landlord of the Glendale Arms recommended it,' he told me. 'I thought you'd appreciate a place that you don't need to wear wellies to.'

'Always,' I said with a smile.

'This place reminds me of that pub off campus, do you remember it? The Red Lion, I think, with the same kind of beams across the ceiling. I had to carry you out one night…'

'God, I do remember. You started a shot competition even though I had an early lecture the next day.' I remembered protesting I needed to go home but Stewart bought another round — he had always been good at persuading me to stay out later than I planned. 'I would be on the floor now if I had a shot, I don't know how I drank as much as I did at uni.'

'Don't tell me you're all old and boring now? Let's have one drink at least… for old times.' He waved over a waitress and ordered two glasses of wine, despite my weak protest. To be truthful, I needed a drink. 'I suppose you have to get up too early on the farm to go out much now.'

'Exactly. There are chores to do every morning and evening. Rory is stuck at an auction tonight, he got snowed in there, so I'll have to do them when I get back.

I mean, we have Angus who lives with us and helps but there is always so much to do. And we have the farm shop in the village to look after too.'

'And I don't suppose it's easy to make money nowadays in farming, and running a small business too. I mean, I know how hard that is with my own company. And Glendale is such a quiet area.'

'It is but the community is strong, and everyone likes to support each other. But that's why Rory had to go to this auction, winter is definitely harder all round on us.' The waitress came back with our drinks, and took our food orders. Stewart ordered steak, and I went for the shoulder of lamb.

When she had gone, Stewart held up his glass so I did too. 'Here's to good company and good times,' he said, clinking my glass with his. I took a long gulp. 'You seem so grown up to me with all your responsibilities,' he said then. 'It's hard to compute with the woman who used to be running around campus late to her lectures in those boots you had then.'

I laughed. 'Trust me, I'm still late everywhere. There are not enough hours in the day what with the farm and the shop, looking after Harry, and trying to find time to spend with Rory. I just run around in wellies instead now.'

'You sound a little frazzled, I hope you're not taking on too much. You need some time to relax too. Read all those books you always wanted to read.' He smiled. 'And what about your love of drawing and designing, did you ever do anything with that?'

'Well, I took some art classes at college while I was working at the library, and I've done some projects for friends. The trail I went to tonight, I designed the banner and marketing materials for that, and my friend Emily runs the bakery in the village so I helped with her logo and menus, and of course everything in the farm shop too. I really enjoy it. I did have an idea to start up a business when Harry goes to school maybe, but it really depends on what's happening with the farm then. If I can fit it all in or not, really.'

'I hope you can if it's something you love, you must miss being creative on the farm. I remember you were always reading or drawing or taking pictures.'

'Actually, I just started up an Instagram account to get back into that.' I told him all about it. 'It might help the business, but even if it doesn't, I'm really enjoying it.' It wasn't quite my own business but it was getting me back into something creative, and that was no small thing.

'But do you actually enjoy working on the farm, Heather?' Stewart asked then, leaning forward. 'It just seems too unlike you, I have to be honest. All the things we talked about that we wanted to do at university, I must admit I'm surprised to see where you ended up. Do you know what I mean?'

I nodded. I did. I hadn't planned any of it. Love had taken me to a really unexpected place in life, that was for sure. 'I do miss the library sometimes, usually on a cold, dark morning when I would much prefer to stay in bed, but I get to be with my son every day, and seeing the farm thrive under our care is rewarding even if I do think the animals gang up on me sometimes.' I chuckled. 'And I get to work with Rory, although we don't get as much time together as I would like. It's hard work but we're doing something that's been done for generations, and we are building something together. It's a way of life really, not a job.'

'Interesting. Well, it makes me wonder if I should still mention what I've been thinking about today, or not...' He tilted his head as he trailed off.

'What do you mean?'

'Well, to be honest, I wondered if you could be really happy doing something so unlike you. And it got me thinking about the past. We had such a good time together at university, didn't we? And we talked about the future so much. I can't deny I have wondered what would have happened if we had done what we said we would do. We were going to set up a company together, do you remember? A design company. Where we could both use our creative skills.' Our food arrived as I thought back to the late-night conversations with Stewart about what we could do when we left university. He had told me that he wanted me to join him in Edinburgh while he did an architect apprenticeship, and that we would set up a business together down the line where he would design buildings, and I could do graphic design work. I hadn't really known what I wanted to do, I just knew I enjoyed drawing and designing things, and I loved reading, of course, so I was happy to go along with his idea for our future.

'I haven't thought about that in years.' I looked down at my plate, a little sadly. It wasn't easy to think about that time. I had thought my whole future had been destroyed that year – my mum had died, and Stewart had gone to Edinburgh to follow through on his plans, plans that I was suddenly no longer part of. I felt a spark of bitterness, and lifted my eyes to meet his. 'None of that happened because you decided to do it without me.'

He looked stricken. 'It wasn't like that, things happened that we could never have foreseen. What happened to your mother was so tragic, we both had to make choices, hard choices back then, Heather. But I wish it hadn't turned out like it did. You have no idea how much I wish that.' He leaned forward. 'As soon as I saw you again, I couldn't stop thinking about what a good team we were back then. And I realised that we could be a good team again. I'm going to be in Glendale for a long time, working on this project, and it's the most ambitious thing that my company has done so far. I'll need some great talent by my side to work with me on it. And who is more talented than you?'

I stared at him. 'What do you mean?'

'I mean, I'd love you to come on board. Come and work for me. Put your designing skills to use again. Help me design the hotel, and everything we'll need for it – signs, logos, a website… all of it. We could do it together. And you're local, you can advise on how we can fit into the landscape, how we can keep the community on our side.' He reached out to touch my hand. I was too surprised to move it away. 'And you could make sure Rory's farm is protected too.'

'Are you serious?' I couldn't deny the idea had instant appeal. Working in design like I had always planned to do, and helping on such a big project, which would set me up perfectly if I did want to start my own company in the future. Plus, I could ensure the farm was kept at a safe distance from the hotel, and I could make sure it impacted us in the least way possible. But I would be working with Stewart. After all that happened between us, was that really a good idea? And what would Rory say about it?

Stewart cut into my confused thoughts. 'Do you really see yourself working full-time on the farm forever? What about your designing dreams? If you came on board with my company, you'd get to do what you love but wouldn't have the risk of setting up on your own, not just yet anyway. I know you, Heather. You would love it.' He smiled. 'And I mean, honestly, are you really happy working on the farm? You seem stressed out, and tired too. I know how anxious you can get, and if it's making you more anxious then maybe you should step back. You need to put yourself first sometimes. I'm sure Rory would understand. Surely, he wants you to be happy like I do? You said it's a way of life for him, it's all he's known, right? But that doesn't mean you feel the same way. And, if you don't mind me saying, it would be rather selfish if he didn't let you follow your dreams, wouldn't it?'

I didn't know what to say. Stewart was saying aloud all the dark thoughts I had sometimes. That I just wasn't cut out for the life I was living. That I wasn't good enough. That I didn't belong. Not in the way that Rory did. I was an outsider, and Stewart could see that. All I had done to make my family work seemed to crumble under his piercing gaze. Like he was tearing off the outer layer of my skin to reveal the troubled mess underneath. 'It's not like that, he doesn't *make* me work on the farm...' I said uncertainly.

'But you said that you had to leave the library so you could help him with the farm and the shop, didn't you? He could have hired help instead, couldn't he?'

I hesitated. We'd never really discussed it. I had just sort of slipped into life on the farm. Organically. But I supposed Rory hadn't checked it was what I wanted. 'Well, maybe. I mean if I was earning a salary then we could afford more help,' I mused. If I worked with Stewart then Rory could have a proper workforce on the farm. And Angus could retire too. It was an interesting thought.

But then I'd see even less of Rory than I did now. And what about Harry? I would hardly have time with him. 'It would be a huge change though, to family life, you know,' I said, gulping down another sip of my wine, my head starting to spin. 'Rory would support me whatever I wanted to do though,' I insisted then. But I knew he'd be heartbroken if I walked away from the farm.

Stewart beamed as if everything was settled. 'Well then, nothing to worry about. You just need to tell him what you want to do. You've fallen into this life, but it doesn't have to stay that way, does it?' I was unsure if he meant farming or more generally being with Rory. I thought it was best not to ask. I shifted my hand, and he finally moved it away. 'You need to think it all over, of course. I hoped you were still here, you know. When I heard there was a site available in Glendale, and that it might work for our hotel, all I could think about was whether it was a sign that I should find you again. After all these years. And it looks like I was right to.'

I lifted my head and met his eyes, feeling confused about everything suddenly. Was he right to? I thought about how much I worried about whether I was capable enough on the farm, perhaps Stewart's offer was a sign that it wasn't what I was meant to be doing. Did I really belong on the farm? 'What about your business partner? Would they be happy if I came on board?' I asked, taking a small bite of the food but I felt too churned up to really enjoy it.

'I've told him all about you,' Stewart replied with a smile. 'He likes us to have the best people around us, so he would be very much on board. Oh, and I have those plans...' He reached down and pulled out a folder. 'Here are the plans the council have for the land, you can see that Hilltop owns that lower field. I want to help, I really do, to not disrupt the farm if that's what you want, but I'll need your help to do that.' He slid the folder across the table to me. 'I suppose you just need to think about what's really important to you, Heather.'

I looked at the folder and wondered why it felt like it was a bomb threatening to explode in my face.

Chapter Thirteen

Why is it when you really need to sleep, your mind just won't let you?

I had no need of an alarm the following morning after barely sleeping all night, running over everything Stewart had said to me in my head. After spending two years worrying that farm life just wasn't for me, suddenly he was offering me a way out. My ex-boyfriend. It was beyond confusing, and on top of that, I felt so guilty about having seen him behind Rory's back.

When I had arrived home last night, I had gone to see Angus to tell him Rory was stuck at the auction, and he had gruffly told me he'd see to the horses, and the cows, if I sorted everything else in the morning, which I had agreed to, relieved that he was here to help out. I knew Rory thought he should have retired by now, and tended to do more things himself than he had in the past, and I kept suggesting we needed more help so we could spend more time together. But it wasn't easy when all the spare money we made had to go back into maintenance of the farm and keeping the animals happy. Especially during winter when we made less from farm produce in the shop.

And Rory was fiercely loyal. Angus had worked and lived here since Rory was born, he had become like a second father after Rory's parents died. I couldn't help thinking though, if I took Stewart up on his offer, we would have far less money worries, and could bring in extra help around here.

Working with my ex though would be strange. I had been so hurt when things ended between us but I supposed it had been my decision to stay in Glendale, breaking our plans to move to Edinburgh. Perhaps I couldn't still blame him for not joining me. We had been young, and he had been so ambitious.

And it had been nice to see him again. We had had fun together at uni. We'd had no responsibilities, and had gone out all the time, partying with our friends and staying up until dawn talking. It had been my first proper relationship, and I had been completely infatuated with him, not wanting to leave his side, and needing his opinion on everything. It was hard not to look back on those times with a certain nostalgia; it was so vastly different from my life now. No wonder Stewart had been so surprised to find me here.

But working with him would mean it was no longer just in the past. It would mean changing the life I had. It would mean letting him back into it. And I wasn't sure if that was something I wanted to do or not.

I climbed out of bed, realising that I wouldn't be able to go back to sleep, and went to the window, pulling back the curtains. It was still dark outside and I could see it had started snowing again. I sighed heavily. A dark, snowy morning made me want to stay in the house, crawl under a duvet by the fire with a good book and a hot chocolate, but you just couldn't do that on a farm. Rory never complained about having to go out in all weather. I supposed though it was all he had ever known.

I got dressed in my warmest clothes ready to brave the elements, thinking back to my first morning on the farm after I had moved in.

–

'So, these are the stables,' Rory said as I trailed after him as he did his morning chores. 'Angus usually lets the horses out into the paddock, if it's not too bad weather, and then mucks out the stables and gives them fresh hay and water and so on,' he said, gesturing to Angus who was leading Prince out of the stable.

'Morning, Angus,' I said as he walked past. He gave me a curt nod. 'I don't think he's happy about me moving in,' I confessed to Rory once we were alone again.

'Oh, he's always like that,' Rory said breezily, reaching up to pat Duke who I had just fed for the first time. 'He prefers animals to people, but if you need help, he'd be there like a shot.' I stood well back, nervous of the large animal.

'It's weird though to be living somewhere with someone who barely talks to me,' I said. I didn't feel comfortable around Angus. I felt like he knew I had no idea what I was doing here. I worried that he agreed that I didn't belong here.

'I'm used to it I suppose.' He saw my face and reached for me. 'He has no problem with you, I promise. And even if he did, it wouldn't matter to me. You make me so happy being here.'

'Even if I'm too scared of the animals, hate getting up early, am cold all the time, and burst into tears this morning when I dropped the cat food all over the kitchen floor?'

Rory grinned. 'Even then. Why do you always give yourself such a hard time? You don't need to worry about any of that. And you're pregnant. Doesn't that give you a free pass to be tired and emotional?' He pulled me to him and I relaxed a little in his embrace. 'How did I end up falling for such a worry wart, huh?'

'Worry wart? Are we living in the 1950s?' I smiled though, his jokes always cheered me up.

'Living here sometimes feels like that.' He dropped a kiss on my lips. 'Right, let's go and feed the cows. And I promise that I'll always be here so you don't have to feel scared or worried, okay? I'm looking after you from now on. If you would just bloody let me.'

'Okay, but I warn you now after Beth told me about the time a cow chased after her and Drew in the field, I'm not at all excited to be around those cows of yours.'

'The poor cow was terrified at the sight of two teenagers kissing in the middle of its field. Besides, Drew has zero affinity with animals, that's why he's a doctor, so don't listen to any of his stories. My dad once said he'd never met anyone less suited to living on a farm.' He held out his hand and I took it, letting him lead me out towards the field, all the time worrying that I'd turn out to be just like his brother, and any enthusiasm he had for me being here would soon disappear. I glanced back and saw Angus giving Duke more food, evidently thinking I hadn't filled up the trough enough. I suddenly wanted to re-pack all my bags and scurry back to the safety of my childhood home.

—

I had become more comfortable here than I would have thought possible back on that first morning but I still felt like I didn't really belong, and I still worried that both Angus and Rory thought the same thing sometimes. Stewart had given voice to those worries by being so surprised to see me working and living here. He thought I belonged in an office with him.

Was he right?

Rory had repeatedly told me that I did have talent for designing. And so had Beth and Emily when they asked me to design the festive trail banner, and the logo and menus in the bakery. I had taken some classes at college and done well at them. I always enjoyed that work, and had thought of pursuing it when Harry was older. Stewart was now offering me a chance to do it, and with much less risk than my starting up my own business would pose.

Failure scared me still. It had followed me to and from university. So, I had often followed the easy route in life. Taking the library job was an example, to be honest. It had been an easy job, but I had been grieving at the time. I didn't think I could handle anything that would challenge me.

Falling for Rory and moving on to his farm, having Harry — they had been the first risks I had ever taken in my life, and they both challenged and scared me still every day. I could tell Stewart found those life moves hard to process, and I didn't blame him. So did I, after all.

I wasn't particularly good at making decisions. I never had been. My mum once said I thought too much about everything, and she had been right. I always envied how carefree she was. Once I lost her influence in my life, I think it all got a bit worse. The worrying, the anxiety about making the wrong choice… And here I was, with a choice to make once again, and no clue what to do.

Leaving my dad and Harry asleep upstairs, I slipped into the kitchen and had a quick cup of strong, hot coffee, before pulling on my thick parka, covering my hair with the hood, and wellies, and walking out of the back door. As I walked around into the yard to collect the chicken feed, I heard a strange noise. It was a low groaning sound.

Frowning, I changed direction to follow the sound.

It was so dark, I could barely see but I was sure it was coming from the direction of the field. I walked over and the noise got louder. As I approached I could see the gate was open slightly and one of the cows was standing by it, making a pitiful noise.

I pulled out my phone and switched on the torch. I could see the cow's right leg was trapped in the opening. He must have seen that the gate was slightly ajar and tried to push it open but his leg had got stuck on some mud and he was now trapped, and clearly distressed because of it.

'Oh, bugger,' I muttered. I couldn't understand why the gate had even opened slightly for him. I thought back to walking up the hill with Stewart. I had definitely closed the gate behind us, hadn't I? 'It's okay, boy, don't worry, I'll get you out,' I promised him even though I had no idea how to deliver on it. The cattle were friendly but as he was distressed, I didn't fancy getting in there with him alone, and I wouldn't have the strength to pull him free by myself either, it didn't look like.

I needed help and I really didn't want to ask the only person around I could ask. I turned to see the lights were on in the cottage. 'Angus it is,' I said to the cow. 'Wish me luck, and don't go anywhere, okay? I'll be right back.' I tried to smile at my weak joke but I couldn't raise one. This was exactly what I worried about with

Rory away – something going wrong here. And I was worried I had let this happen by leaving the gate unlocked. The responsibility felt like a weight on my shoulders as I hurried to Angus's cottage and knocked loudly on the door.

'Where's the fire?' Angus asked grumpily, opening the door with a frown.

'Angus, one of the cows is trapped by the gate, stuck in some mud. Can you come and help?'

'Go and get a torch from the barn, I'll grab some rope,' he replied, closing the door abruptly on me.

I didn't have time to complain about his manners so I hurried off to find a torch, went back to the field and turned it on. The cow hadn't managed to free himself and some of the others had moved closer, drawn by his cries I assumed. 'It's okay, guys,' I called out soothingly. 'We're going to help him.'

Angus appeared, now in a coat and holding a thick rope. 'How did he get the gate open?' Angus asked, looking at me accusingly.

'I honestly thought it was locked,' I said, helpless, annoyed at myself. I hated that this was my fault. I bet he was thinking he'd been right all along about me.

He snorted instead of responding. 'Right, let's get this around him.' I helped him wrap the rope around the cow, who let out another moan. 'You go around that side of him, I'll take this side,' he said, climbing over the fence and getting into the field. I stayed near the gate and watched as he climbed in beside the cow. 'You got a good footing?'

'I think so,' I said, trying to sound more confident than I felt. I held tightly onto the rope with one hand, and with the other held the torch so we could see.

'Okay, you pull with the rope, and I'll push him, we just need to free that leg from the mud. Go gently so we don't hurt him.'

'Okay,' I said. 'On three,' I said, counting us down, and then tugging on the rope. Angus grunted as he pushed the cow's flank, and the cow whimpered as he tried to kick his legs. I felt him slip a little forward. 'Not that way,' I said, pulling harder. I put the torch down and pulled again using both hands. Angus was saying words of encouragement to the cow who scrambled in mud. 'Almost,' I cried, trying to hold him steady. 'God, he's heavy.'

'One more go,' Angus cried quickly. Heat rose up my face with the effort as I pulled again. Angus pushed the cow towards me and I felt his leg move. He shuffled backwards, freeing himself from the mud. I let go of the rope as he found his footing and climbed out of the mud back onto the grass. Angus quickly pulled the rope off him as the cow hurried off to find the others, letting out a snort that could either mean 'thank you' or 'about bloody time'.

Angus held the torch up to watch the cow re-join the herd. 'He isn't limping,' he said with relief as the cow let out one last grunt and disappeared into the darkness. Angus quickly slammed the gate shut and locked it.

I flopped against the fence. 'Thank goodness.' I wiped my sweaty brow and sucked in a breath. That cow weighed a bloody ton. I wondered if I should start lifting weights but that really seemed like too much work to be honest.

'Good job, Heather,' Angus said, throwing the rope over his shoulders.

I stared at him, startled by the praise. 'Oh, thanks. I really thought the gate was secure.'

'It could have been the cold not letting it shut properly, it has happened before, I'll check it when it's light.'

'I know it's such a basic thing...' I trailed off, feeling really cross with myself.

'All's well that ends well,' he said, surprising me by not giving me a lecture or anything. He looked at me. 'What were you doing up so early, mind?'

'Couldn't sleep for worrying,' I replied honestly. And this incident wasn't going to help stop that. It could have been really bad. The cow could have got injured or worse actually got out of the field and been hurt, or escaped. In fact, the whole herd could have gotten out. I shuddered at the very thought. What would Rory have said?

'A day of worry is more tiring than a week of work, as my Pa used to say,' he replied. 'We'll make a farmer of you yet,' he added, sloping off with a whistle.

I watched him go, amazed. I really thought he wished I wasn't around. Mind you, with Angus those words could have either been a promise or threat.

The sun was rising then, and I watched the cow munching on the grass, as if nothing had just happened. I pulled out my phone, wanting to capture this moment. I felt so satisfied with what I'd been able to do without Rory here.

I went over to the cow, and for the first time in my life I took a selfie with one. He lifted his head obligingly for the picture, chewing on the grass, and almost looked as if he was smiling along with me. I looked at the photo – my hair was a frizzy mess, my cheeks red from the cold, and the exertion of moving the cow, but my eyes were bright, and my smile was wide. I looked proud of myself – I *was* proud of myself. I sent it to Rory, telling him what had happened.

And then I opened up Instagram to post it on there. It was my first selfie but I wasn't as nervous as I might have been before. I thought about how connected people had been to the post about my mother so I decided to be honest in the caption again. Just writing it made me smile, reassuring me that I was doing the right thing.

I've lived on Fraser Farm for two years now but my boyfriend Rory has always dealt with our cattle, not me. This morning, he isn't here so when I saw this cow stuck in the mud, I had to step in. Along with Angus, who works with us, I managed to help free the cow and he's now happily back with the herd scoffing his face with grass. It's a small thing to everyone else but to me, it feels like the first time I've felt capable out here. For someone who used to work in a library, and has been nervous around the animals since I moved in, I feel like a superstar right now. And I'm going to try to hang on to this feeling, and not be so worried that I can't do this.

Because today, I've proved to myself that I can!

Chapter Fourteen

Rory didn't get back until the evening. I stood outside as he drove up in his van, a now empty trailer attached, and shivered in the cold wind, some snowflakes still floating around me.

I broke into a smile when he climbed out of the car. I really had missed him. 'You're back!' I cried cheerfully, hurrying towards him. Then I saw his face. He looked confused, even a little hurt, as he stopped by the van. 'Rory?' I said, stopping in front of him, nervous as I'd never seen him look at me like that before.

'I stopped off at the shop to drop off some marmalade I bought at the auction and a customer said they saw you last night in a pub with a man he'd never seen before, and you looked, I quote, "very cosy" together.' He lifted his hands to make the speech marks in the air.

'I can explain,' I said quickly, before I realised that sentence made it sound like I'd done something wrong. Which I suppose I had by not telling him that I was going for dinner with Stewart in the first place. I should have realised Glendale was too small a place for me to have not been seen by someone. 'Let's go in the warm and have a coffee, and I'll explain everything. Okay?'

'Fine,' he said, walking past me inside, shrugging off his coat and boots.

'I just took Harry up. Dad's watching a film,' I said quietly, leading him into the kitchen. Rory watched me pour two cups of coffee out and sat down at the table.

'What's going on?' He broke the silence finally as I sat down opposite him, passing over his coffee.

'I was having dinner with Stewart. My ex-boyfriend from university. He's in Glendale because he wants to buy Hilltop Farm. He wants to turn it into a hotel and golf course,' I said, all in a rush. 'I didn't want to worry anyone yet, that's why I didn't tell you.'

'Why would it worry me?' He frowned, trying to catch up.

I pulled out the folder Stewart had given me in the pub and opened it up on the kitchen table. 'It turns out the lower field, over the hill, the land we thought we owned, it actually belongs to Hilltop.' I showed him the boundary marked on the map he had given me. 'Which would mean the golf course would run right up to the edge of our farm. But Stewart has said he would be willing to work something out so the farm isn't impacted, if I come on board and help with the project.'

'Help how?' Rory asked, staring at the map between us. He traced the red marked line with his finger, shaking his head.

'Help Stewart design it all. I could make sure the farm isn't impacted by it...' I said, trailing off when he looked up at ne.

'And it wouldn't be impacted if you go off to work on this hotel?'

'Well, yes, I know but I just said I'd think about it, I didn't say yes or anything.'

'And that's what you want? To work with your ex-boyfriend?' He leaned back in his chair, watching me, his face unreadable.

'It's not about him,' I said uncertainly. 'I have always liked the idea of designing… and if I helped, I could make sure the farm is okay.' What had made sense when Stewart said it, felt awkward with Rory watching me silently. 'I said I'd think about it, that's all,' I added. 'He just sprung it on me last night.'

Rory looked at the plans again, not saying anything for a whole minute. Then he looked up. 'And why did he choose this spot for his hotel? Because you live next door?'

'No, he didn't know that. I mean, he assumed I was still in Glendale, but he didn't know I lived here until he asked about me in the village.'

'And you really believe that?'

'Why would he lie about it?'

Rory looked away. 'Why indeed?' He sighed. 'That land has always been ours, there must be a mistake.' He stood up abruptly. 'I'm really tired, Heather. I need to go to bed. We can talk again in the morning. I'll ring up our solicitor first thing.'

'Okay. I think it will be fine. I mean, Stewart is reasonable, I'm sure that he won't do anything to hurt us.'

'I don't know how you can say that when he's already hurt you. Didn't you tell me it broke your heart when he refused to come to Glendale to be with you?'

'Yes,' I whispered. 'That was a long time ago though…'

He walked to the door, shaking his head. Then he paused, and looked back. 'People don't change, Heth. And I don't doubt he wouldn't give a toss about hurting me or this farm. I'm not going to trust anything he says, and maybe you shouldn't either.' He left me alone then, the tiredness clear in his voice and his bowed head as he went slowly up to bed, the first time he had done so without asking me if I was going to join him.

It hadn't been an argument, not exactly, that was never Rory's style, but I knew he was disappointed. And not just in the situation we had found ourselves in, but with how I had handled it. Why did I keep on getting things so wrong?

I wrapped my hands around my coffee cup, hoping it might warm them up. I didn't know what I could do to fix things but I desperately wanted to. I couldn't stop thinking about Stewart's offer; if I worked with him then surely the farm would be okay, and Rory could get in help here with the money I would be making. Harry would have to go to nursery or if Dad moved in then he could look after him, I suppose. I put my head in my hands as I tried to think about how I could make it all work. And make everyone happy.

But I wasn't at all sure that would even be possible.

Chapter Fifteen

'Our solicitor can fit me in this morning,' Rory said when he came in through the back door, wiping his muddy boots on the mat. It was a rainy morning, dark and miserable, and we both had got wet and muddy doing the morning chores. Harry and my dad had stayed in the dry farmhouse, and were in the living room watching cartoons as I made breakfast for us all. 'So, I'll shower and head straight into Inverness. Do you need anything while I'm there?'

'I don't think so, I have everything for Christmas, just need to do a final food shop a couple of days before Christmas Eve,' I replied, glancing at him to see if he was still angry with me. 'I hope the solicitor can help.'

'So do I. This has been farming land for centuries, the thought of it being developed, of our way of life out here changing, I don't want that for Harry,' he replied quietly. 'You'll be okay having him this morning then?'

'Of course,' I said, thinking over what he had said as he walked upstairs to take a shower. I hadn't thought about the future but I supposed if the hotel did go ahead then it could potentially harm our way of life enough that we might not be able to continue farming here. Surely not. I turned back to the milk I was warming up for our son. Like Rory, I had assumed the farm would be around for years to come, that if Harry wanted to then he would take it over one day.

My phone vibrated with a message then. I picked it up and saw Stewart's name on the screen. I was relieved Rory had already left the room.

> I'm heading over to Hilltop to look around. Why don't you meet me there and see what you think of the place?

Instinctively, I felt I should say no but then again, it was an opportunity to understand better what he was planning to do there, and see how much of an impact it potentially would have on us. And if I was going to accept his job offer, I needed to know what I was letting myself in for. I glanced up at the ceiling, hearing the sounds of the shower running, and decided it was better to keep Rory in the dark until we both came back later. I fired a message back to say I'd meet Stewart at Hilltop at ten, and hoped I was doing the right thing.

'Everything okay?' my dad asked when I carried a tray of drinks and toast into the living room. The Christmas tree was lit up against the dark morning making the room feel cosy, and Harry was happily watching the TV in his snuggly jumper. I wanted to curl up beside him and forget everything that was happening but this was about his future. I needed to try to secure it for him. 'I have to run a couple of errands but I won't be long, will you two be okay for a little while?'

'Of course. I wish you would take it a bit easier, you look worn out,' Dad replied, looking at me with his typical insight. I hadn't realised that I looked as tired as I felt. I wanted to tell him about Stewart but I wanted to wait until I knew more.

'I'm fine,' I insisted, although I knew he was right. I hadn't slept well again. I leaned down to kiss Harry. 'Be a good boy for Grandpa. When I get back, we'll do something. Maybe we can bake some cookies?'

'Cookies!' he repeated happily. He had definitely spent a lot of time around Emily. He held out his hands for his milk and my heart was full of love for him as I watched him sip it, his attention back on the TV. He looked so much like Rory this morning with his auburn curls and his big blue eyes that it felt like a gut punch. I hated that I was lying to everyone I loved but I was trying to protect them.

That would have to be enough for now.

—

Hilltop Farm was a fifteen-minute drive away along twisting, narrow country lanes, and I went slowly through the unrelenting rain. Turning into the gravel road at the sign, I looked ahead and could make out the empty farm-house. Stewart's sleek car was outside already, looking as equally out of place here as it had done on our farm. Hilltop had been empty since I moved to Fraser Farm, a once thriving sheep farm it was now in disrepair, the nephew of the old farmer desperately trying to offload it. Stewart was probably in line to get it for a really good deal but it was a shame to think of all the years of farming there that would now fade to history.

Stewart appeared in the doorway as I parked, and I hurried inside, pulling my hood down once in the dark hall. 'Raining cats and dogs, isn't it,' he said, leaning in to kiss me on the cheek. He was wearing dark jeans and a thick jumper this morning, a line of stubble across his chin, and he smiled warmly at me. 'I'm glad you came.' He held out one of the coffee cups in his hand. 'I thought you'd need this.'

'Thanks,' I said, taking it. I sipped it and smiled – he remembered how I took it after all this time. 'Well, you've certainly got your work cut out for you,' I observed, looking around.

'You know I like a challenge,' he replied, leading me into the open-plan living area. It was similar to our farmhouse but older and smaller as well as freezing cold from not having been heated in years. I could see my breath on the air. 'We'd have to rip all this down and build from scratch obviously.'

I glanced at the open fireplace and stove. I wondered about the age of the farmhouse. All the original fixtures and fittings would be gone if Stewart's hotel got the go-ahead. It did seem a shame to lose it all. I loved the original fireplace in our living room. 'What kind of style are you thinking for the hotel?' We walked over to the kitchen where there was a wide window looking out over the land, rain streaking down the dirty glass.

'I think it has to be traditional, tourists love all that especially the golf crowd, lots of tartan covered furnishings and dark wood, that sort of thing. We can play on the history of the place… the suites would have four-poster beds. A bit like that place we stayed in for our anniversary, do you remember?' He turned to me. 'In Edinburgh.'

'They said it was haunted, didn't they? I remember the pipes creaking in the night and we thought it might be a ghost!' I smiled, thinking back. We had curled up together in that bed, not wanting to move in the morning for breakfast. I wondered what our past selves would say if they could see us now.

'I really want you to be part of this,' he said then. 'I know I took you by surprise with my offer but I think we could design something amazing here.' He gestured out at the land.

'Do you really think I'm the right person to help with all this?' I asked. I knew that I could do simple things like designing logos or menus, I'd done that for Beth and Emily, and for our farm shop, but this was on such a bigger scale, and I wasn't sure if I had the skills to design things like building layouts, or the interior of a hotel.

'Of course I do. I'm not sure why you don't.' He looked at me. 'You still have trouble believing in yourself, huh? We'd be working together, there would be nothing to worry about. I could teach you all I know.' He had a twinkle in his eyes then and I let out a laugh. 'This is just sitting here doing nothing, we could turn it into something that people fall in love with.'

'Rory has gone to see our solicitor today,' I said, looking at the rolling fields, and missing the sight of cows on them. 'About the land on the hill.'

'I meant what I said about not wanting to hurt your farm. I'd never want to hurt anything you cared about.'

I met his gaze then. I suddenly felt too hot in my parka. 'Even if it impacts your vision for this place?'

'Even if…' He stepped closer and reached out to tuck a stray hair of mine behind my ear. 'I can't stop thinking about us. How we had something special and then we let it slip through our fingers.'

'Don't, Stewart,' I gasped, stepping back in surprise.

'I'm sorry, I can't help myself. You were everything to me once, I can't just forget that. Surely, you can't either? Don't you remember what we had?'

'That was a long time ago. I was so upset when things between us ended, but I had to move on,' I said, avoiding his gaze. I was still attracted to him, that was hard to switch off, as was thinking back fondly to the good times we had but I had Rory, and Harry. 'Things are different now,' I said.

'They don't have to be though. I never found anyone I loved as much as I loved you and coming here and finding you right next door… Maybe the universe is trying to tell us something. Don't you miss how we were back then? Because I do. I was a fool, Heather, to let you go. I know that now.'

'It's too late,' I whispered, wishing I didn't feel this pull towards him, that he wasn't saying all the things I'd wished he'd said back then. 'I'm with Rory now. We have a son,' I repeated, trying to sound firmer than I felt.

'And you have to put your son first. If you came to work here, I could help secure his future. I would leave that land alone, I'd push back the hotel so it didn't affect the farm. You would have my word on that.' He reached out and touched my cheek as I tried not to think about his unsaid words – that if I didn't work with him, then our farm very much could be under threat. 'You deserve to have the life you want, Heather. So, what do you want?'

Chapter Sixteen

When I returned to the farm, the rain had slowed to a light drizzle. Dad and Harry came into the driveway as I pulled up, both wearing wellies and macs and waving cheerfully. I felt a little sick when I saw them knowing where I'd just been and what Stewart had said to me. I had left Stewart promising him that I would think over his proposal and let him know soon. It was clear that he was happy to help me protect our farm if I came on board with his project, but if I did that I would be leaving this place, and I would be working closely with him for months, and he had made it perfectly clear he wanted a whole lot more from me.

'This one was getting cabin fever,' Dad explained when I got out, throwing on a smile that I didn't feel inside. 'We thought we'd come and greet you.'

'Well, I'm glad you did,' I said, crouching down and holding out my hands. Harry waddled over and hugged me. *Don't cry*, I warned myself. 'It looks like the rain is stopping for now. Maybe we can do something outside and leave the cookies until later. What do you want to do, squirt?'

'If you need something to do...' a voice said from the yard. I looked up to see Angus walking towards us. 'The horses could do with some exercise. I was going to take them out into the field. You could ride Prince,' he said to me. 'I bet Harry would love to watch.'

I hesitated. I had only ever been on a horse with Rory looking out for me. If Angus was on our other horse Duke, I felt like I would be riding alone for the first time. And I wasn't sure I was confident enough.

'I won't let anything happen,' Angus added, seeing my face. 'We'll stay in the paddock. I'll saddle 'em up,' he said, striding towards the stables without waiting for me to agree.

'Why is Angus so blooming scary?' I said to my dad once he was out of earshot.

He chuckled. 'I reckon his bark is worse than his bite. Right, Harry, let's watch Mummy ride, shall we?' He took his hand.

'Swing!' Harry cried so I took his other hand and we swung him between us as we walked over to the paddock. I remembered doing the exact same thing with my mum and dad, and smiled to see how happy it made Harry to do it too. The rain had eased completely now but the grey clouds kept colder weather at bay so it wasn't too unpleasant to be outside. Harry and my dad stood at the fence as I went into the paddock and Angus led the two horses in.

Reaching for Prince, I patted his flank as Angus held him steady by the reins. I eased my foot into the stirrup and pulled myself up. Prince shifted a little as I lifted myself up and over, and steadied myself in the saddle, sliding my other foot into left stirrup. 'Please don't let me fall,' I whispered to him as I took the reins from Angus who gave me a nod before moving to Duke, and climbing up into the saddle of the brown horse. I glanced at my dad who waved and Harry who joined in when he prompted him. I took a calming breath.

'Let's go,' Angus said, urging his horse on. He started walking around the perimeter of the paddock, and after a little encouragement Prince duly followed. I breathed as we set off. As usual, it was an alien feeling for me to feel the movement of Prince beneath me, and to feel so high from the ground. I looked out to the hill where the cows were grazing. It was the picture of peace.

'Let's try a trot,' Angus called out, rising and up and down in the saddle ahead.

'Oh, Christ,' I muttered. 'Come on, Prince, we can't have Angus making us look bad.' I urged him on and he sped up.

'Keep your heels down!' Angus called as he rounded the corner and looked back at me. I pushed them down, and felt my balance improve. Seated better, I felt less like I might slip out of the saddle. I took another breath.

'Looking good,' Dad called out as I passed him and Harry. I found myself smiling for the first time on a horse. The breeze whipped my hair and I understood in that moment why people enjoyed this.

'Daddy!'

Turning at Harry's cry, I saw Rory step up to the fence, picking Harry up and sitting him on it, holding him tightly. When he smiled at me, it felt just like it always did.

Like I was home.

–

Rory and I didn't get a moment alone until late into the evening. Harry was in bed, and my dad went up to his room to read, leaving Rory and I on the sofa together in the living room. The fire was crackling, the fairy lights twinkling, and we both had a glass of wine, and *Serendipity*, one of my favourite festive films, was playing softly on the TV. I pulled the soft throw from the back of the sofa and draped it over our legs. 'What happened today?' I asked him.

He groaned, pushing his hair back. 'Andrew has the same plans as us and can't find any that give us that lower field. I just don't get it. My dad was certain that it belonged to us, I know it. Andrew said he'll talk to the council but he said if Stewart has submitted a planning application and it hasn't been rejected, they must have the same plans as we do.'

I knew I had to come clean. 'Listen, I talked to Stewart again,' I said. 'And he really doesn't want to affect the farm, he said he'd change his plans to avoid that field to help us. I really think he will.' I leaned against the sofa to look at him. 'He asked me again to come on board and work for him.' Obviously, I left out what else he had said to me. That would just hurt Rory, and I was still trying to get my head around it. After all this time, had Stewart really not stopped thinking about me?

Rory looked at me. 'Are you thinking that you might want to work with him then?' he asked.

'I don't know. It is appealing,' I admitted. 'I never expected to work on a farm, you know that.'

'I know that you don't feel the same about this place as I do—'

'It's not that,' I interrupted. 'I just always feel like I don't do quite the right thing. It's not that it's hard work, that doesn't scare me, but it's that I feel a lot of pressure not to let you down.'

Rory frowned. 'I hope I don't make you feel like that. You know I think you're amazing. I know this life isn't easy but I don't know, I thought you liked working and living together too?' He looked hurt but I knew I needed to be honest.

'I do. But sometimes we hardly spend time together, do we? And I could help protect the farm if I did work with Stewart.'

'We would sort it out, you know, I won't let him threaten our home or family, it's not all on you, Heth.' He reached out to take my hand. 'I keep telling you that I'm here to support you. We're a team. I mean, I hope we are.'

I smiled. 'Of course,' I replied but I felt like I was the weak component of the team, I couldn't help it. I didn't quite meet his eyes and he noticed.

'I know you feel like you don't get things right but that's not the case at all. I couldn't function without you, and all the things you do for me, and Harry.' He ran his fingers across my palm, making goose bumps appear along my arm. 'I want you to be happy though. I know you love designing, so if you want to do this, then we will work it out.'

'Thank you,' I said. That meant a lot to me.

My phone beeped with a message then, from Beth.

OMG have you checked your Instagram?

I hadn't, but I did. 'Oh, wow, look at this…' I showed my screen to Rory so he could see too. My post about saving the cow had gone a bit crazy. There were so many likes and comments, I couldn't believe it.

'See?' Rory said, grinning at me. 'Look at what you're doing to publicise the farm, I could never have done something like this. You have really struck a chord.' He read some of the comments aloud. From farmers and their partners saying how hard this life was, from people who generally felt worried they weren't living up to expectations, and people saying how I lucky I was to live on the farm. 'See? You didn't need me for this.'

I did feel proud of the post. 'I really didn't think people would respond like this. But maybe I'm not the only one who feels like they're struggling.'

'Of course you're not. Heth, we all feel like that sometimes. But look at what you're doing, not only with this but today, riding Prince on your own, you need to give yourself more credit.'

I smiled. 'It was satisfying being on Prince today, I must admit. I couldn't believe it that I did that all by myself.'

'I always told you you could do it. I wish you'd believe in yourself, like I believe in you.' He passed my phone back to me, brushing his fingers against my hand. 'Do you remember when you first moved in and we had that really bad snowstorm… I've never seen you so panicked. But that wouldn't happen now.'

I still remembered that night vividly.

–

'There's been another heavy fall,' Rory said when he came into the living room. 'Tabby got stuck outside. Can you take her while I check on the horses before I lock up?' Rory handed me the cat and hurried out again. It was the first time I had seen him look mildly stressed since I moved into the farm. It was December and I only had a month left until the baby was born so couldn't help him. I carried Tabby over to the log fire and stroked her fur. She looked as happy as I was about the weather.

And then suddenly, everything went black.

My breath came in heavy bursts as I sat in darkness save for the flickering flames in front of me. It was crazy to be scared but I'd never experienced a power cut in the middle of nowhere, snowed in. What if the baby came now? I'd be stuck at the farm, unable to get help. I put the cat down and tried to suck in some air to my lungs.

'Heather? What is it?'

I wasn't sure how much time had passed until Rory returned and wrapped his arms around me as I knelt on the floor struggling to stay calm. 'What if we're stuck here?' I gasped. 'The baby… there's no power… all the snow…'

'Shh, it's okay. Nothing bad will happen, I promise. This has happened a million times before. It will all be okay. I'm here.' He held me close and my pulse began to slow a little bit. 'When I was young and scared in a storm, my dad used to sing to me,' he said then, his voice low and deep and calming. And then he began to sing. I recognised the old folk song. My mum had sung it when I was growing up too. Both of us had lost so much. I was panicked we might lose more but gradually as Rory sung, his voice deep and reassuring, so strong in that silent, dark room, I got my breathing under control.

And then softly, I began to sing along. I felt the baby kicking so I took Rory's hand and held it over my stomach, my hand over his, and I could hear the smile in his voice.

–

As he had done so many times since we had fallen in love, Rory had calmed me, had pulled me back when I felt adrift. But he was right – yesterday, I had proved to myself that I could pull myself back, that I was capable, that I didn't always need him here to help. And I thought about how many people seemed to be inspired by my Instagram post. The likes were moving into the thousands. I couldn't believe that so many people had connected with it. Sometimes I felt alone in my anxiety but how could I now? And I knew deep down that Rory was right – I could do so much more than I thought I could.

But was it enough?

Rory reached for me then and brushed my lips with his. 'Do you know when I first realised I felt more for you than just the fact you're my brother's old friend from school?' he asked with a smile. I shook my head. 'When I came to your mother's funeral. I hadn't seen you for a while, you'd been at university and when I saw you in the church, you looked so broken... I just had this urge to hold you, to try to make it better for you somehow. And I don't think I've ever stopped wanting to hold you. Or to take care of you.'

A tear rolled down my cheek. Seeing Rory there had given me a boost. As had all our family and friends, and the village, they had all rallied around me and my dad, and tried to support us as much as they could. Which I really had needed especially as Stewart had been stuck at St Andrews finishing his exams. I'd had no idea Rory would become so important to my life then. 'I can't believe it's been over eight years since the funeral. And soon, it's her birthday. It's still so hard.'

'I know.' He wiped it away with his fingertip. 'I wish I could stop it hurting.'

'You help. Our family helps. More than you know.' My mum was all about family. She was fiercely loyal, and had loved me and my dad with all her heart. I knew I had been her whole life. I wanted to be like her. But I worried so much about whether I was good enough for my family. And I worried about the future.

I once again missed her so much it hurt. She would have known what I should do about Stewart, about all of it, she would have given me some great advice, but now I had to muddle somehow through without her.

'I love you. We can get through anything together.' Rory reached for me again, and we shared a long kiss. 'I promise you, Heth,' he whispered as he trailed kisses across my collarbone. I wanted to believe him more than anything. I pulled myself onto his lap and Rory lifted my arms to take my jumper off. Rory had always made me feel as though I was the most beautiful woman in the world, and I never wanted that to change.

When he eased my bra strap down, I pushed aside everything I was worried about and allowed myself to get lost in his touch.

Chapter Seventeen

'Heather!'

I turned in surprise to see Stewart behind me as I walked down Glendale High Street, pushing Harry in his pushchair after dropping in to the Hall shop to see Beth. The air was cold but clear and Christmas was in the air. Stewart was wearing a suit today with a dark coat over it, holding a takeaway coffee from Emily's bakery. It was still surreal to see him here. I wondered if Emily had served him and what she thought of him. I hadn't told anyone other than Rory that my ex-boyfriend was in the village, and had been putting it off as I didn't want to tell them about what he wanted me to do until I'd made a decision. It wasn't that I didn't trust Beth or Emily's opinions, but I knew they wouldn't understand me not wanting to be on the farm with Rory, and I felt bad for even considering what Stewart had suggested. I knew that Beth especially would be appalled at the idea of a hotel being built in our beloved countryside, and once she found out, would get involved in trying to stop it. I supposed I was trying to keep the peace for as long as I could, but I knew it wouldn't last much longer. Not here where news always spread like wildfire.

'Morning,' I said when Stewart reached us. 'Harry, this is Stewart, an old friend of Mummy's,' I said down to Harry who waved at him. I smiled. He loved waving.

Stewart waved back. 'Fancy a stroll with me? I realised I'd been stuck in the back room of the pub working for too long today.'

'Some fresh air sounds good to me too,' I agreed.

'I can wait if you want to grab a coffee?'

'I'm fine, I just had one,' I lied, not wanting to go in if Emily was there, she would want to chat and I'd have to explain why I couldn't. We set off towards the park at the end of the High Street.

'You're quiet,' he observed after a minute with a smile.

'Just thinking, I suppose,' I said.

'About what, may I ask?'

'Us,' I replied. He smiled, surprised. 'I mean I've been thinking back to when we were a couple.' I had been thinking about the memory Rory reminded me of, my first panic attack at the farm, that snowy night. And it had made me remember my first one at university. 'Do you remember when I was so panicked about a presentation I had to do, I had an anxiety attack in your room?' I remembered it vividly. The first few weeks of our relationship had been based around going out and having fun, spending nights together, and this was the first time he had seen me struggle.

'I know you worried a lot but...'

'We had gone out late. I wanted to come home early and rest before the presentation but you persuaded me to go dancing with you, we drunk a lot, and didn't get in until the early hours. I woke up exhausted and stressed, and hungover, and I broke down crying saying I couldn't do my presentation. And you said I just needed some breakfast so you left there in the room crying, and went to get us coffee and bacon sandwiches.' By the time he had returned, I had called my mother and she had calmed me down, with me pretending I was in my room and not with Stewart, and I'd brushed it off, leaving quickly for my lecture and somehow getting through it. We'd never discussed it and I'd learned to hide my worrying as much as I could from Stewart especially when I got really anxious over exam periods, sometimes making up lectures or meetings with tutors so I could study alone in the library, and not be persuaded by him to go out. A habit I still sometimes fell back into with my loved ones even now.

Stewart looked a little sheepish. 'I'm sorry. I never knew how to handle those kinds of situations. My family...' he trailed off for a moment then ploughed on. 'We've never been emotional with one another, or really talked about our feelings or anything, I hadn't ever had to deal with something like that before. So, yes, I didn't handle it well. I can see that now.'

'I know you had a different relationship with your family, compared to the one I had,' I said as we walked through the gate into the park. A hint of watery sunshine peeped through the leaves of the trees above us. 'I just worry though now. I have responsibilities.' I gestured to Harry. 'I would sometimes have to put those first, and not your hotel. I'm not sure that would work.' Stewart would put his all into this project, I knew that, and he'd expect the same of everyone else. He had always been someone who could be out all night but then still work well the next day, and he demanded that of everyone around him. I don't think he'd ever been sick, and that had stressed me out when we were together. I wouldn't want to feel the way I had felt after that panic attack again. Although the farm stressed me, Rory never did. He always understood if I needed to step back or work through something at my own speed, like learning to ride Prince, but I didn't think Stewart was capable of that.

'I understand,' he said quickly. 'I'm different now, I promise. I need you, Heather. In my life again. It has all fallen apart without you.' He stopped and turned to me. 'Are you really happy, Heather? Because I'm not and…'

My phone rang in my bag. 'I'd better get this.' I looked away, feeling awkward, as I answered the unknown caller. I wasn't sure I could handle Stewart like this. It was like my past and present had collided and I had no idea how to get out of the resulting mess. 'Hello?' As I listened, I met Stewart's eyes – mine widening as I listened to the woman on the phone, him watching, shifting his feet, looking impatient for me to finish. I hung up, still in shock. 'Blimey.'

'Who was that?' he asked, frowning at my stunned expression.

'That was *Countryside Watch*.'

'Who?'

'It's a programme on TV, all about people in the countryside, their work, and concerns, all about nature and they do a lot of farming segments… Anyway, they saw my post on Instagram. I can't believe it.'

'What post?'

Wordlessly, I handed him my phone to show him. 'They want to come to the farm and talk to me. To find out what it's really like to become a farmer's wife.'

'You're not married,' he said pointedly, handing my phone back.

'Well, you know what I mean. This could be such a great opportunity for the farm. I'll have to get back and talk to Rory…' I broke off at the hurt expression on his face. 'I'm sorry but this is huge for us. You understand that, don't you?'

'Huge for Rory. It's his farm. This isn't what you really want, is it?' He looked incredulous but I couldn't deny the burst of excitement that phone call had given me.

'I really don't know,' I admitted. It felt like finally things were clicking into place for me on the farm, like I was finding my place there. But here was Stewart offering me a way out. 'Let me think about it, okay? I need to get back...'

'I would be there for you now,' he said hurriedly. 'I promise you that. I made mistakes in the past, I know that.'

I turned to go but I couldn't not ask the question that had burned then simmered inside me since we broke up. I looked back at him. 'Why wouldn't you come to see me after my mum died? Just once? What you just said about not being able to deal with anything emotional... I know you said we were over on the phone but I still hoped, I still thought you might come to Glendale.'

'I couldn't bear the thought of seeing you so upset,' he half whispered. 'Can I ask you something I've always wondered about?' I nodded once. 'If I had come would you have changed your mind about not moving to Edinburgh?'

'I can't answer that,' I said. 'Because you didn't come, Stewart,' I replied and then I pushed Harry away, feeling Stewart's eyes on my back the whole way out of the park.

–

'I can't believe this,' Rory said with wide eyes as we watched the two large lorries drive into the farm. We stood outside with Dad and Harry, waiting for the *Countryside Watch* crew. They had only phoned the day before but they wanted to air our segment in next week's show while my Instagram post was still a hot topic so had wanted to come as soon as possible.

'They'll only be talking to me,' I reassured Rory. It was a turnaround for him to seem more nervous than me, but he wasn't good at small talk and was worried they might make him speak on camera. 'They just want to show you doing some farm chores. I already told them we don't want Harry on TV so you can hide with him and Dad if you need to. At least you didn't have to shave for it,' I added with a smile. The producer had expressly told me not to change a thing about us, that the viewers preferred authentic over everything else, and apparently my Instagram was the epitome of authentic. I think it was meant as a compliment, and not that I'm a hot mess or anything. So, I'd had to resist the urge to dress up and was wearing skinny jeans, my sparkly wellies as they were excited about them, a long jumper, my parka and a woolly scarf with gloves. I was wearing more make-up than usual though, and had styled my hair loose and curly.

'It's really exciting, I watch it every week,' Dad said, lifting his hand in a greeting wave as the first lorry parked in the yard. 'This will be great publicity for you.'

'It is the only show any farmer watches religiously,' Rory said. 'I've had messages all morning from people congratulating us. But let's just hope they don't stay all day, Angus is refusing to leave his cottage until they leave.' He grinned at me. 'Who knew Angus would be so camera shy?'

'He barely wants to talk to us so I can believe it,' I replied with a laugh. That didn't bother me today though, nothing could dampen my good mood. I was too proud that through me the farm was going to be on national TV.

'Heather?' A tall, pretty woman marched up to me from the lorry and stuck out her hand. 'I'm Wendy, the producer, we spoke on the phone? We'll get everything set up and then Julie, who's presenting this week, will join us for the filming.' She looked around. 'I can see why everyone online is raving about this place. I've never even heard of Glendale before, but it's beautiful out here.'

I could see both my dad and Rory swelling a little with pride as I smiled. 'Wait until you see the view from the top of the hill.'

'Lead the way!'

We set up filming on the hill so they could see the cows. Rory was told to be in the background tending to them for a few shots and they wanted to film us both doing chores, and then the presenter turned up and I was set up with a mic and we began the interview. It was surreal meeting someone I had seen on TV for years but she was very friendly, and great at putting me at ease.

'Your story really struck a chord with not only me but lots of our viewers,' Julie said as the producer fussed around getting the right position for the cameraman. 'I grew up in London and I still can't believe I get to live in the countryside now. I have a farm of my own in Yorkshire, and I really got what you said about it being such hard work, and how nervous I feel that I'm not doing things right, but then the rewards are amazing,' she said. 'It's a privilege living and working somewhere like this.'

As the interview started, it was strange talking about myself but it got easier the more we filmed.

'Tell me about why moving that cow out of the mud changed how you felt about your place on Fraser Farm?

On Instagram, you said you lacked self-belief about being out here...' Julie prompted me.

'Well, I have never done anything like this before. I used to be a librarian, and you really couldn't find a more different job, or workplace, could you? I have always struggled with anxiety,' I said, amazed at how easy it was to open up about something like that but it was because I'd had so much support for being honest. I had always thought I should hide my anxiety as much as I could but why when it was a part of who I was? 'And I have worried that I'm not capable of doing this, but that morning when I managed to pull the cow out of the mud, with Angus, it was almost a lightbulb moment – I thought well, actually, I can do it. I just need to believe in myself more.'

'Why do you think that has struck such a chord online?'

'I think more people suffer with anxiety than we realise. We all have moments when we lack self-belief, when we worry we're not good enough or capable enough or just not doing enough, there's so much to feel anxious about sometimes. I think people just understood that feeling, that they've felt like that at some point in their lives, and we all need a reminder sometimes that we *can* get through it. That we *are* capable. That we *are* good enough.'

Julie smiled. 'If only everyone could come for a visit here and experience that feeling; I think a lot of people would love to try this life even only for a few days.'

I thought about her words – it had been such a steep learning curve for me moving onto the farm that I hadn't appreciated that it was a life that many would love to live. That I should feel lucky, that I should feel blessed too.

As they changed camera angles again, I glanced over at Hilltop Farm below us, Stewart's words coming back to me that I didn't belong out here. I had worried for two years about that but all the TV crew here today thought I did, and their viewers too, and all the people still sharing my Instagram post, and I glanced at Rory who gave me a thumbs-up, and I knew he had always believed that I belonged here with him. Maybe I was starting to wonder whether they were all right.

But it had come at what felt the worst time possible – just as our future seemed in question thanks to the plans for Hilltop Farm. What if I had finally found my place here just to have it snatched from under me?

Chapter Eighteen

I was drying my hair the following morning when the hairdryer cut out halfway through. I tried switching it on and off again but nothing. I looked behind me and the clock on the bedside table was flashing midnight.

'Heather, is there something wrong with the power?' my dad called up the stairs.

That's just what we needed – a power cut. 'Looks like it but the weather is fine outside, I don't get why,' I said, coming onto the landing. 'I'll find Rory and get him to check the fuse box,' I said, walking down the stairs. I pulled on my boots and opened the front door, calling his name. The only power cuts we had had before had been in a storm or when we had been snowed in. At least it hadn't happened yesterday when we were filming, I supposed I should be thankful for that. I walked into the yard and saw Rory near the stables with Harry carrying a bucket of water. 'The power just cut out,' I said, going over to them.

'Seriously?' Rory asked, pouring the water into the trough for the pigs. 'I'll go and have a look. Can you feed the goats? That's the last of our jobs, isn't it, Harry?'

'Sure,' I said, although my hair was still half wet and I didn't have a coat on. 'Come on, Harry.' I led him around to the area where we kept the goats. There was a small barn for them and then a fenced-off grass area. Goats could be destructive and excellent escape artists so when I got there and spotted a hole in the fence, I groaned. I quickly did a head count and there was one missing. 'Oh, Harry, how did this happen? It was fine last night when we checked on them, wasn't it?' I pushed open the gate to carry the food in, trying to think back. It had been dark but I was sure I would have noticed the fence was damaged. It was such a small hole that thankfully only one goat had tried to get through it. I felt disappointed though that this had happened just the day after the *Countryside Watch* filming when things had looked so much brighter here. Now we had a new problem to deal with. But I was relieved not to be panicking about it, I knew we would sort it out somehow.

I gave them the hay, the goats all rushing up to me. They were a friendly bunch and Harry laughed as one of them tried to pull his jumper. I scooped him up and carried him out, not wanting to linger. I locked the gate and saw Angus coming over. 'The fence is damaged, and one of the goats has got out,' I told him.

'That explains the chewed wire Rory has just found,' he replied. 'I'll fix the fence, he's calling an electrician. I don't know if we'll get one today so close to Christmas though.' He sloped off, muttering under his breath.

I sighed. 'Shall we try to find our missing goat?' I asked, putting Harry down. 'Where do you think he is?'

'Horses,' he said, heading straight for their paddock. Well, it was as good a place as any to start the search. I hurried after him, always amazed at how quickly my son could move. 'Mummy, look,' he called, followed by a giggle. I saw our missing goat by the horse paddock munching on their hay through the fence, the two horses watching him with a look that seemed to say 'What do you think you're doing?'

'What a naughty goat,' I said. I saw Rory coming out of the house and I waved him over. 'We found the culprit,' I told him when he approached.

'Bloody nuisance, the electrician can't get to us until the morning so we'll be without power all night. How can one goat cause such chaos? I'll never know. How did the fence even get damaged?' he said crossly, pulling the goat away from the hay. 'You didn't notice it last night?'

I felt the accusation even if it was unsaid. 'No, I didn't, I would have said obviously.'

'Well, I'll take this guy back and help Angus with the fence. Are you okay to still drop supplies off at the shop?' He walked off with the goat before I could answer.

'Once I finish getting dressed,' I muttered to his retreating back. 'Come on then, more work to do as always,' I said to Harry, holding out my hand. I was not looking forward to a night without power so I was quite happy to get away from the farm for a bit and go into the village.

–

It was a relief to arrive at the farm shop and deliver the box of produce to Hattie. Until she told me her news.

'Those men I told you about who've been sniffing around the village… Well, I've found out why they're here! And can you believe it, they want to knock down Hilltop Farm and build a hotel and golf course there?! One of them is staying at the Glendale Arms and has had lots of meetings and phone calls, even had the council round, and in the end Malcolm asked him outright what was going on,' she said with a shake of her head. 'It'll be right on top of Fraser Farm. It'll be so disruptive and destroy the countryside. I don't know anyone who's keen for it.'

I was a little surprised it had taken Malcolm, the pub landlord, this long to work out what was going on. 'I suppose it will provide a lot of jobs locally though,' I said, trying to be diplomatic but also not let on my connection to Stewart. I was relieved it hadn't been found out as yet but I wasn't convinced it would stay that way however. Glendale had a way of finding things out. 'And bring in lots of guests who'll spend money in Glendale, I guess.' I adjusted Harry's hat in his pushchair, he was always trying to take it off.

'Well, I don't know about the jobs bit… Malcolm said that a big team will be coming in from Edinburgh to do the initial work on it. He heard the big hotshot talking about it on the phone. It's put a lot of backs up in the village, I can tell you.'

'Oh, really?' I realised then that Stewart had really only talked about me working on the project with him, telling me that he wanted a talented team working on it without saying who that team would be. I hadn't thought about who else would be part of the team with us if I agreed. If this didn't bring in local jobs then it would not be at all good for the village.

'Some people say change is good but when we don't ask for it, I can't see it myself,' she continued as though I hadn't spoken. 'And I'm surprised you're not up in arms about it yourself. Those cows of yours won't take too kindly to it, I bet, and you won't have that amazing view anymore. What about this one and his future? I bet it wouldn't be long until this developer turns his eye onto

Fraser farm. Mark my words. If he can push you out as well, I bet he will!'

I glanced down at Harry. 'Stewart is aware of the farm, and doesn't want to threaten it,' I said, hoping he was telling me the truth about that.

'I've never met a developer who cared about anything other than making money on a place,' she replied with a snort. She then realised what I had said. 'You've met him then? The developer?'

I supposed I had to tell her some of the truth, it would make it seem a much bigger thing if I kept quiet. 'Yes. Well, actually, I already know him. We were at university together,' I said, keeping our past relationship quiet knowing that would be all around the village in seconds if I mentioned it. I mean it had no bearing on things anyway. Did it?

'Well, then you can talk him out of it. I know how much you and Beth fought to keep our library, and all these shops are still here because of you, so you won't let him take over the countryside, will you?' she said confidently. 'I'll let everyone know you're on the case. Now then, I want to hear all about the filming. I'm so excited to watch it on Friday, everyone is. We've already had more people in just to ask me all about it!'

I was so taken aback by her certainty that I'd stop Stewart's development, I didn't know what to say so I jumped on the change in conversation and I told her all about the film crew at the farm. Then a family came into the shop so I was able to get away before she could say anything more about Stewart and Hilltop Farm. I thought about what she had said though as I walked mindlessly down the High Street. I had to admit that she was probably right that under any other circumstances, I would have been up in arms at such a development happening in our countryside. But if I did fight this one what would happen to our farm? Stewart was offering to protect it as much as possible so didn't that mean I should help him with it? Or was Hattie right and I should be trying to stop it at all costs?

Was my connection to Stewart clouding my judgement about the whole thing?

'Penny for your thoughts?'

I jumped as Stewart crossed the road to join me. 'Oh, hi,' I said, thinking it was better if I ignored that question right now. 'Out shopping?'

'Had to get some supplies, I need biscuits when I'm working. Walk with me back to the pub?'

'Okay,' I agreed, falling into step with him as we headed towards the Glendale Arms. 'I'll get a coffee afterwards, the power has gone out at the farm so I'm in no hurry to get back.'

'Seriously?' He raised an eyebrow. 'I couldn't function living somewhere the power goes out.'

'It's not a common occurrence or anything. One of our goats got out and chewed through some wires.'

'I'm trying not to laugh… It's so crazy you live out there with goats and all sorts.'

'What's worse is that I checked on the goats last night, and I didn't see the fence was damaged. Just when I think I'm getting a handle on everything there too. Yesterday was so great being filmed and everything.' I sighed. I felt like the farm was getting me back for feeling more confident, which was crazy.

'Well, surely, it's only natural that some things are going to slip, that you will miss something or make a mistake. I mean, you're not used to that kind of thing, are you?

And you have your hands full with this one too,' he said, pointing down to the pushchair where Harry had fallen asleep. 'I don't envy all you have to deal with. I'm surprised you're not tearing your hair out some days.'

'It's hard work and I have been on a steep learning curve but I do like doing things. You know I hate being idle. And Harry isn't hard work, unless I'm trying to make him do something he doesn't want to do.' I smiled ruefully. I thought then about what Hattie had said about protecting the farm for Harry. 'He'll be a farmer just like his father. Fraser Farm has been in the family for generations. It's important, you know?'

'Family businesses, eh?' he said, as we paused outside the pub. I wondered if he was thinking of his father. He was very successful and had always pushed Stewart to be as ambitious as him. Being honest, I hadn't warmed to him the few times we had met. Not that I'd ever tell Stewart that. 'It's admirable what you're doing on the farm for your family, but it shouldn't stop you from pursing your dreams, should it?' He turned to face me. 'I'm trying to keep quiet and let you think through my proposal, I know it's not easy for you but I can't help but think that you're selling yourself short in the farm. You need your own project, something you can see through from start to finish, something that's yours, and yours alone.'

I shifted my feet. 'I don't know, Stewart. Everyone is starting to hear about your plans for Hilltop, and people aren't happy about it. Everyone is worried about the impact on the countryside.'

Stewart sighed. 'Believe me, I know. People think it's acceptable to just come up to me and start attacking me about it. Now they know I'm staying here. I get the feeling though that people around here just hate newcomers and change, so they don't like that I'm about to launch both on them. They're a bit backward, aren't they? Can't they see what an opportunity it will be?'

'I mean, will it be an opportunity for them? Will there be jobs for locals, do you think?' I asked tentatively, hoping the village had got some of the news about the development twisted.

'Sure, down the line, we'll need staff in the hotel like cleaners, and so forth. But my partner is securing us a great building firm from Edinburgh, people we've worked with before on other projects, and our office staff will be joining us here once the council give us the go ahead. I need people I trust on this, like I said.'

'I suppose guests would come into the village though…' I said, worried he'd confirmed that for now, the hotel wouldn't be much of a benefit to Glendale at all. But if people were spending money here, that would be something.

He shrugged. 'I think there will be so much on offer at the hotel, I doubt many will want to leave. I want them spending money with us.' He saw my expression then. 'But this is why I need you, obviously. I haven't been thinking about the village, you're right. I do need the community on my side.' He touched my arm. 'If they knew you were going to work on it with me, I bet they'd change their minds. I could really do with your help, Heather.'

I felt a lot of pressure suddenly on me to make this work for Glendale, and I wasn't sure that was fair. 'I still need to think about all of it, Stewart.'

'I'm sorry, I shouldn't keep pressing you. I know you have a lot to consider. But when you get back to the farm and have to sit in the dark all evening though maybe you'll think more kindly about coming to work with me.' He grinned, letting me know he was joking.

'When I can't watch TV later, I think you might be right,' I replied just as lightly, but his earlier words swum through my mind. I didn't like how he talked about Glendale being backward, about how he'd have to get the community on side but didn't want his guests in the village, or people from the village working with him. Maybe he just saw us all as country bumpkins after all. I remembered then that he had said something similar before. When he first told me about his apprenticeship offer in Edinburgh, he'd laughed when I'd admitted to being unsure about leaving Glendale for good. He'd said there was no future for me here, and I had believed him at the time and agreed to move there with him. I still sometimes wondered if I hadn't lost my mum whether I would have been happy there or not.

'I hope you decide soon,' Stewart said then. 'I need you on this project. And I think you need it as much for yourself. I've got some calls to make but I'll see you soon, okay?' He leaned in and kissed me on the cheek, lingering a little to sweep a stray hair of mine back. I looked around, worried in case we'd been seen, now that I knew Malcolm was keeping an eye on Stewart. I didn't really want to be spotted with him too much. If Hattie was anything to go by, I'd be accosted by the whole village otherwise. Thankfully though, the coast was clear. 'And I hope your power comes back on soon, for your sake.' He gave me a look that I could only describe as a pitying one and walked off towards the pub.

Harry woke up then and I leaned down to tighten up his coat against the cold wind that was whipping up around us, smiling down at him.

Whatever Stewart thought about my choices since we broke up, Harry was the reason I would never regret staying in Glendale. And the choice I made next needed to be the best one for him, and no one else.

Chapter Nineteen

We ended up at Glendale Hall once it got dark. Rory had called Drew and he would brook no arguments about us spending the evening with them as we had no power and I had never been more grateful for our family and friends as I was huddled in the warm kitchen with them, along with pizza and wine. The evening turned into an impromptu party-like atmosphere. Along with us four, Beth, Drew, Izzy, Sally, Brodie, Emily and Iona were there too. Caroline and John had decided to eat out together. I think she wanted a quiet evening, which you definitely couldn't have when we were all at the Hall together.

'We didn't know if you'd still want to eat with us lowly types,' Drew said from across the table. 'Now that you're TV stars.'

I laughed. 'TV stars who have no electricity. Thank God it happened after they had gone.'

'I can't wait to watch on Friday,' Beth said, topping up my wine glass. 'We should all watch together, it's so exciting. Although I'm jealous – I've been on Instagram ages, and no one has come here to film me.' She pretended to sulk.

'What can I say? It's all about the cows apparently,' I replied, passing a piece of pizza to Harry whose eyes lit up.

166

'Everyone in the bakery has been talking about it,' Emily said, cuddling a sleeping Iona on her lap. 'Well, not just that. Have you heard about Hilltop?'

'I was just going to ask about that,' Beth said. 'Rachel at the shop told me about it.' She turned to me and Rory. 'You're not going to like this.'

'Actually, we already know,' Rory said, glancing at me. I felt my cheeks grow hot as my dad asked what was going on, and Beth told him everything she had heard. The whole village now knew what was going on, and I wished I could sink into my chair and become invisible as Beth turned to me. 'What are we going to do about it?' she demanded.

I had no idea what to say so I looked desperately at Rory who sighed, and then stepped in to answer her. 'They've already made a planning proposal to the council for a hotel and golf course on Hilltop. I've spoken to our solicitor and we actually don't own the lower field like we thought, which means if this sale of Hilltop goes through, they could build the hotel right on top of our farm,' Rory said.

'But Stewart said he wouldn't build that close to us,' I said before I could stop myself. I felt everyone's eyes turn to me.

'The company trying to buy Hilltop is owned by Stewart, Heather's ex-boyfriend,' Rory told the group, taking a long gulp from his beer.

'Stewart is in Glendale?' Dad asked next to me, his eyebrows almost reaching the top of his forehead. I knew he was wondering why I hadn't said anything to him, and my embarrassment deepened.

'He's staying at the Glendale Arms. When he realised I lived next door to Hilltop, he came to see me. He's promised to not threaten our farm with this project.'

'*If* Heather works with him,' Rory added, drinking more beer.

'He's offered me a designing job on the project, yes. I told him I'd think about it. But I'm sure he will try to protect our farm as much as he can,' I said, annoyed that he was telling them everything. I didn't miss the look that passed between Beth and Drew.

'You'd go to work with him, and leave the farm?' Emily asked, looking just as surprised as the others. 'You'd be helping to design this hotel?'

I wasn't sure why it sounded so bad coming from her lips. But it did. It suddenly felt too hot in the kitchen. 'You guys know I've always thought about doing some designing work, like I did for the bakery and our shops. This has come out of nowhere, I'm not sure what to do,' I said, sounding more defensive than I wanted to.

'Well, of course, you should do what will make you happy,' Emily said, giving me a supportive look, bless her. Beth frowned at her. It was clear she didn't agree with that at all.

I opened my mouth but Rory's phone rang, and I was saved from having to say anything more. 'Angus,' he said, picking it up immediately.

'You wouldn't really leave the farm, would you?' Beth asked me quietly as Rory spoke to Angus.

'I had always planned to set up my own business…' I said, picking at my pizza, my appetite fading.

'But I thought that was ages away when Harry goes to school? You'd miss him and Rory, and the farm, wouldn't you? And now that you've had all this publicity too. I guess I thought you had changed your mind as you enjoy working on the farm. And you get to be with your family every day. You are so much calmer now,' she said.

I glanced at her. She knew me so well, she had felt the change as I had lately. But was that enough to make me walk away from the opportunity Stewart was offering me?

Rory hung up then, saving me from responding to Beth. 'Angus has fixed the fence. He said he found a pair of pliers missing from the barn. They were thrown under a bush nearby,' he said, locking eyes with me. 'He thinks someone cut the fence deliberately.'

'I told you there wasn't a hole there last night,' I said, relieved I hadn't caused our power cut after all. But that relief was short-lived. Because I realised what that meant – someone had come to the farm to deliberately sabotage us. And that made me feel incredibly uneasy.

'Who would do that though?' Drew asked his brother.

Rory shrugged. 'No idea,' he replied, draining his beer dry. 'But I will find out.'

–

It was disconcerting to arrive home to the farm and see it completely in darkness. The only light flickered from Angus's cottage either from his log fire or candles, or both, as I carried a sleeping Harry inside the farmhouse.

Rory went into the kitchen, and Dad followed me up the stairs as I took Harry up to his room, walking slowly, my eyes trying to adjust to the darkness. Dad slipped into his room as I carried Harry into his cot. It was eerie here, no light to help from lampposts or cars, just the stars in the cold, clear sky, and the silvery light from the moon to allow me to see enough through Harry's window to place him down to sleep.

I left the curtains open as he couldn't have his usual night light on and watched as he slept peacefully, no idea that anything was out of the ordinary. I wondered what he was dreaming about. When I was pregnant I used to dream that I had lost my baby. I didn't even know what they would look like or if they would be a boy or a girl, but I was still worried about losing them. Working with Stewart would mean I couldn't be with Harry like I was now, and did I really want to be away from him every day? Then again, so many women worked, it wasn't like it was unusual to work away from home. Why did I feel then like I would be letting him down if I did accept Stewart's offer?

Slipping out of his room softly, I glanced at Dad's open door, and hovered in the doorway. 'I should have told you about Stewart,' I said softly. 'I was just confused about what to do.'

'You don't need to tell me anything but I'm always here if you want to,' Dad replied, coming over to kiss me gently on the forehead. Suddenly, I felt like I might cry. 'This isn't a right or wrong answer thing, love, it's about doing what you want, what will make you happy.'

'At the expense of others though?' Whatever decision I made, someone would be disappointed.

'No, not at the expense of people you love, and who love you. Those are the people who will always matter, but they will always support you.' He said goodnight, leaving me thinking he had given me some advice after all, but I wasn't quite sure what it was yet.

I went back downstairs thinking, to where Rory was sitting at the kitchen table, a hot drink in front of him, a candle burning on the counter. He gestured to the other mug so I sat down and took a sip of tea, which I was sure wouldn't do much to take away the cold I currently felt deep within my bones.

'Are you angry with me?' I asked Rory after a short silence.

He sighed. 'No. But I'm confused. I feel like you would have been completely against Hilltop being developed if it had been anyone else doing the developing but Stewart. And that makes me worry, I suppose.' He met my gaze. 'I know you're considering going to work with him but are you considering anything else?'

'What do you mean?' I asked warily.

'Do you miss him? Have you missed him?'

I thought for a moment. 'When I first moved back here and he told me he would be staying in Edinburgh, I was heartbroken. He was my first love. And we had planned a future together. I missed him a lot, especially that first year, and I was grieving for my mother so it was a pretty rubbish time. But I haven't thought about him for a long time. Him showing up here was a complete bolt from the blue.'

Rory nodded and was silent for a moment. 'I think you know that I don't trust him. It feels convenient to me that the site he finds for his hotel is right next door to his ex-girlfriend. I mean, what are the odds? I think he wants more from you than a working partnership.'

I bit my lip. Stewart had pretty much told me that but I, of course, hadn't told Rory. I didn't want to lie to him though, we had always tried to be honest with one another. 'He hasn't moved on like I have.'

'Have you really moved on though? You're still holding back from me even though we have Harry. I wish I knew why. But I know that I can't persuade you to want this.' He gestured around us. 'You need to choose the life you want, Heth. But I hope you choose us. Maybe we did fall in love really fast, maybe you didn't plan to be with a farmer or live this life, but I thought we were happy. I love how unexpected it was to fall for you. I just wish you felt the same.' He got up and I reached for his hand but he stepped back. He looked really hurt and I hated that I had made him feel that way. 'I know I don't always tell you how I feel, I'm not like that I suppose, but I thought I had shown you.'

'You have,' I whispered, my eyes filling up with tears as I wished I could reassure him more but the truth was that Stewart's appearance had made me question everything, and Rory had realised that too. I didn't know what to do. And then there were the words Rory wasn't saying – that he had proposed to me a year ago but I still hadn't said yes. How could I blame him for being hurt and angry, and confused about how I felt?

'Then I just have to hope you'll come back to me.' He reached down and kissed the top of my head before walking out quickly. I watched him go even as I wanted to cry out for him to stay.

Chapter Twenty

The following night I had promised Beth I would help out with the festive trail. Although it was free for villagers, and people who had started to come from afar to visit it, they needed someone there each night to make sure everything was okay and to hand out the hot chocolate and mulled wine. Sleet had started up again so we were wrapped up in lots of layers as we positioned ourselves at the entrance to the trail by the table with drinks and sweet treats donated by Emily from the bakery to welcome the visitors. Rory, Dad and Harry were back at the farm without me and I wondered what they were doing. The power was all back on now thankfully but there was definitely a strained atmosphere in the air between Rory and me so it had been a relief that I had already planned to be at Glendale Hall for the evening to be honest.

'Now that we're alone, do you want to talk?' Beth asked, handing me a cup of mulled wine as she poured one out for herself too.

'It's been a crazy week,' I admitted. 'Stewart turning up and everything with Hilltop, and then *Countryside Watch* coming to film. And dealing with the power cut at the farm too… I'm exhausted, to be honest,' I said, taking a long gulp of my mulled wine.

'You haven't told me much about Stewart,' she said, arching an eyebrow curiously.

When Beth arrived back in Glendale Hall after ten years, we had such a lot to catch up on but what with her burgeoning relationship with Drew, me and Rory getting together, and everything we did to save the High Street the past had been quickly laid to rest. 'I mean, I didn't think there was much to say. I thought I'd never see him again. It's so weird that he's right here in Glendale. He was my first love. Well, my only love besides Rory.'

'And you were together all through university?'

'We were. I thought he was The One. We had so much fun together, and had our future all mapped out until I had to come home for my mum. I can't help but think back, you know? When I was with him, I was young and had no responsibilities – it was fun and exciting. He was good-looking and charming, intelligent, and the life and soul of the party.'

'It's hard not to look back on the past fondly sometimes but I suppose there are reasons why he's in the past, why you're not together now,' she said.

I nodded. 'When my mum died, I couldn't even think about leaving my dad alone in Glendale. Stewart already had an apprenticeship lined up, he couldn't see what he'd do here, and I got it to a point. But I was heartbroken. And, it wasn't all perfect, of course not. I remember how he couldn't cope when I was worried or anxious…' I trailed off, wishing thinking about him didn't make me feel so confused.

'Why has he come back now? After all this time? I mean, he never tried to contact you before now did he?'

'No, not even a Facebook friend request. I think, like me, he thought we were done for good. But then Hilltop came up, and he couldn't believe it when he found out that I live next door.'

She thought about that. 'Are you sure he didn't know? It's a huge coincidence, isn't it?'

I sighed. 'You sound like Rory. Why bother lying about it though? If he did know, why not just tell me? Hilltop is a great opportunity, for him I mean, either way.'

'Well, perhaps it would reveal his hand too much. I mean if he chose Hilltop because it's close to you then you would have known that he was here just for you. You maybe wouldn't have even thought about working with him then. Your guard would have been up straight away, but this way he's spent time with you, hasn't he? Has he mentioned more than working with you?'

I had to admit that he had. More than once too. 'He has said that he misses me and regrets what happened between us but he knows I have Rory and Harry, he knew that straight away.' I felt guilty though that I had told him I found my life on the farm difficult at times. Maybe I had encouraged him more than I meant to. It was hard though not to be honest with him when we'd once been so close.

'Maybe he thinks all is fair in love and war and is prepared to fight for you. The question is whether you want to let him or not. And if it's a no, can you work together knowing he wants more?'

'I don't know but if I work with him then I can help protect our farm.'

'It sounds a bit like he's saying if you don't work with him then he'll disregard the farm. Seems a petty thing to imply, don't you think?' she raised an eyebrow, clearly full of distrust towards him, just like Rory. But I didn't know what to think. Beth had done all she could to keep Glendale as it had always been, it was natural she would be suspicious of change. As Stewart pointed out – the whole community here was like that.

'I'm just worried for you guys, and Drew too,' Beth continued. 'This will be such a big disruption right on your doorstep. And Rory and Drew promised each other they'd keep the farm going after their parents died so you can understand why they're freaking out somewhat. Can you really protect the farm even if you do go and work with Stewart, or should we be trying to stop it from happening all together?' She turned to greet an old lady walking in to the trail then, and I shrunk back, glad of the reprieve. Beth was hard to argue with at the best of times.

When she returned, my temper had become even more frayed. 'I don't know what I'm supposed to do. What you all expect me to do,' I said. 'This isn't my project. It will happen with or without my help.'

She didn't rise to my anger. 'Maybe,' she replied with a shrug. 'Then again, maybe not.'

'Beth, can you give me a hand?' John called over then, carrying a set of lights over his shoulder. Beth smiled at me before she went off to help him but I couldn't quite return it. What had she meant by that?

'Any chance of a mulled wine?'

I turned to see Stewart walking across the lawn towards the table, hands in his coat pocket, smiling at my surprised expression. 'What are you doing here?' I said, relieved he hadn't arrived in the middle of us talking about him.

'I heard this is Glendale's best evening entertainment so thought I'd better come and see it for myself.'

Seeing him made me feel more confused than ever. I had thought the time I had shared with him was long gone but here he was making me question everything.

Why did part of me want to tell him to leave me alone for good, but another part of me wished he would stay?

Chapter Twenty-One

I handed Stewart a cup of mulled wine. 'I help out every year, my best friend Beth is behind all of this. She owns Glendale Hall.'

'Wow,' Stewart said, looking at the house behind us lit up in all its grand glory. 'She's a lucky lady. So, how are things? Is your power back on?'

'It is, thank goodness,' I replied. 'And tomorrow they'll be showing our segment on TV. It was really nerve-wracking being on camera but hopefully, I'll come across okay. It should be a big boost for the farm.' I glanced at him, and he nodded once. I decided it was best to move the subject away from the farm. 'What about you? How long are you staying in Glendale?' Christmas was fast approaching and I assumed he would want to spend it with his family.

'I need to look at a few more things over at Hilltop, and then I'll head off to Edinburgh for Christmas. I'll come back when we hear from the council, hopefully soon in the New Year.' He crossed his fingers in the air. 'So, how about you show me this famous trail then? Or are you tied to the mulled wine?'

'I think it's safe to leave. Beth will be back in a minute,' I said, coming out from behind the table, eager to have some space from her. 'I think more snow is on the way,' I added as we walked into the trail, side-by-side. I could see my breath on the air. The stars above were hidden by the thickening cloud, and a few flurries floated around us. The fairy lights still shone brightly though, lighting our way. A family were in front of us so we slowed our pace.

'As long as I don't get snowed in in Glendale. I don't think my parents will be impressed if I miss Christmas.'

'Well, you can always have lunch here with us if you are,' I said, without thinking.

He raised an eyebrow. 'Are you sure that Rory would be okay with that?'

I gulped, and looked away. I knew he wouldn't. 'Can I ask you something?' I said, changing the subject.

'Of course.'

'What did you think when you found out I lived on Fraser Farm – really?' I looked up at the icicle lights above us as I waited for him to answer. Everyone seemed to think he had ulterior motives from the start, but I wanted to hear it from him.

Stewart glanced at me and smiled. 'I couldn't believe my luck. I was planning to look you up in Glendale, if you were still here. And I hoped you were when Hilltop came up – I told you, I thought maybe it was a sign.' He paused and turned to face me so I stopped too. 'Heather, I want us to work together and if that's all there ever is between us now, I'll be fine with that. But I can't stop thinking about you. I'll be honest – I heard someone in the pub mention you'd be here tonight. Helping out. Sally, I think her name is? And so, I decided to come and see you.'

I had no idea how to respond. How was I supposed to feel right now? Should I be angry with him for telling me that he couldn't stop thinking about me, for not respecting my relationship with Rory? Why did I also feel flattered though? Did I want him to think that there was a possibility of a second chance for him and me? I watched him gazing at me and despite these past years with Rory, my stomach did betray me by giving a little flip. I remembered all the times Stewart had held me and kissed me, and it was hard to tell my body to not want that again. My heart and my head were suddenly very much at war.

'Heather, is there any chance for me? For us?' he asked then as if he could read the confusion on my face. He stepped closer. *Too* close. We were only inches apart and all around us lights twinkled and sparkled like we were in the middle of a Christmas romance film.

As if they were willing us on.

'There you are!'

I jumped back as if I had been burned as Beth rounded the corner and saw us. Stewart frowned as I looked away, the spell between us broken in that moment.

'Oh hi, I'm Beth,' she said as she approached, looking curiously at Stewart.

'This is Stewart,' I introduced, feeling flustered. Stewart was trying to catch my eye but I couldn't look at him. He gave Beth a charming smile and they shook hands.

'What do you think of the trail then?'

'I can see why it's so popular,' he replied.

'Did you need me for something?' I asked Beth, wondering why she had been looking for me.

'Just to help me clear the trail. It's getting really cold, snow is apparently on the way, so I think it's a good idea to shut it off tonight and cover it in case it turns heavy. Could you check the grotto for me? It was nice to meet you, Stewart,' she said, waving as she left us again but only I caught the look she gave me as I left. I had no doubt she had seen how close we had been standing together.

'Let's look at the grotto then and see if anyone is still there,' I said in a falsely bright voice, trying to cover the sudden awkwardness. The fact that I hadn't given him an answer to his question before Beth interrupted us, and the fact that I had no idea what my answer would have been, scared me more than I cared to admit.

'So she really owns all this?' he asked as we walked down the rest of the trail to the grotto tent. The family that had been ahead of us were in there so I explained the trail was closing because of the weather.

'Beth inherited Glendale Hall from her grandmother,' I explained to Stewart when we were alone in the tent, and turned off the Christmas music.

'If only we all had such grandmothers,' he joked. 'How did Rory come to own his farm?'

'His parents died when he was eighteen in a car crash,' I said quietly. 'It means the world to him. You won't threaten his farm, will you? I mean, this resort could really disrupt the farm, the animals will be so close...' I trailed off, worriedly.

'I said I'd never do anything to hurt you.' Stewart reached out to brush a stray hair from my face. 'You call it his farm – not yours.'

'Well, I suppose it still feels that way sometimes,' I admitted. 'I fell head over heels for Rory. What we have was so unexpected, it took me completely by surprise. It's all been a whirlwind.'

'And now you're not so sure?'

'More like, I worry that this life I have right now, I'm not the right person for.' The words tumbled out, my biggest fears.

Stewart put his hand on my waist and pulled me closer to him. My breath hitched in my throat. 'I would never make you feel like you weren't the right person for me,' he whispered. I opened my mouth to tell him that wasn't what I meant. Rory had never made me feel that way, it all came from me I knew that. From my own insecurities. But Stewart took my silence as encouragement and brushed his lips against mine before I could stop him.

I jerked away in shock.

'Heather…' He tried to reach for me again, but I shook him off, horrified that I'd let him kiss me.

I turned and fled from the grotto without waiting to hear what he was going to say. His kiss had been like an electric shock waking me up. I rushed down the trail and out into the driveway.

I thought I heard footsteps behind me but I didn't turn around, I just jumped into my car and pulled away as fast as I could. I'd text Beth to explain when I got home. I just had to get away.

It wasn't until I was driving down the dark, twisting road towards the farm that I noticed a car was behind me. Rather unusual at this time of night on this road. I looked in my mirror but all I could see was headlights. The car behind me followed me closely, too closely, all the way until the hidden turn into our farm. It was unnerving.

I drove through the gates, opened the car door with the engine still running, and hopped out to shut the gate as fast as I could before jumping back in to the car, heart thumping as I drove down the drive up to our farmhouse. I looked in the mirror again but all was darkness behind me.

I let out a breath and told myself that I was crazy in more ways than one.

Chapter Twenty-Two

On Friday morning, I woke up in the dim light. I glanced beside me and saw Rory was already awake and lying on his back, eyes open, staring at the ceiling. I'd had a restless night after coming home and finding Rory already in bed, the house quiet and still, the guilt resting as heavy on my chest as a tractor. I rolled over on to my side, and he turned to look at me. 'I'm sorry,' I said in a soft voice. 'I never want you to think that I don't love you. My worries, my insecurities, my anxieties, I know that they all come from me. Not you.' I sighed. 'I'm letting you all down, I know that.'

'You've never let me down,' he said, his voice croaky from sleep. He rolled onto his side so we were face-to-face, separated only by our pillows.

'I have,' I whispered, knowing I needed to be completely honest with him even though I wasn't really sure quite where to start. I took a deep breath. 'Last night, Stewart came to Glendale Hall. He asked if me and him had any chance of being more than work partners, if we could get back together, I suppose,' I said, the words almost sticking in my throat but I forced them out. If we were going to move past this, I had to tell Rory everything. 'And then he kissed me.'

Rory closed his eyes. 'I knew it,' he muttered.

'It was only a second… and as soon as he did it, it was like I woke up from a dream.' I added quickly, reaching out to touch the side of his face. My heart raced inside my chest as I pleaded with him to believe in what I was telling him. 'I didn't feel anything for him, I swear it.'

He moved out of my reach and opened his eyes to look at me. 'How can I believe that? Ever since he came back, I've felt you slipping away from me.'

'I'm so sorry,' I said, my voice breaking at the end. 'I know that I haven't been fair to you. I've been so confused. I think because he reminded me of my past, and perhaps that made me question all of this.' I pointed between us. 'But when he kissed me, I knew instantly I didn't want to be with him like that. The only person I want to kiss is you.' I couldn't bear the hurt look on his face. I hated that I had hurt him.

'I want to trust you but…' He trailed off, the pain etched on his face.

'I'm so sorry, Rory. But I promise you that even though I am confused about what I want, and I'm scared about the future, I only want to be with you. I swear it. Only if you still want me, that is.' I bit my lip nervously.

'I'll never not want you but Heth, I need to know I'm not in this alone. You, Harry, this farm, our family – that's what I care about.'

'I know, and I do too. I'll prove it to you,' I told him fiercely.

'I don't need proof, I just want to know I'm not in this alone.'

I reached for him and we kissed. The way his kiss made me feel just cemented that whatever Stewart and I had had it was in the past. But even though I loved Rory, he was right – something was holding me back and I needed to know what that was, and to do something about it because I really didn't want to lose him. Or what we had. Stewart had at least shown me that.

'Mummy!'

We broke apart as Harry called out from his room. I smiled but Rory still looked uneasy, and how could I blame him? 'I'll go and get him and make us all a family breakfast.' I jumped out of bed and slid my feet into slippers. 'God, it's freezing.' As I passed the window, I looked outside. 'It's snowing again,' I said, with a sigh as I saw the farm was all covered in white.

'No rest for the wicked,' Rory replied, climbing out of bed too. He headed for the bathroom and I watched him go nervously. Rory was a better person than I'd ever be, but even he was reaching his limit, I could tell.

I had to save us somehow.

—

The gunshot echoed through the kitchen making my dad clatter his cutlery down on the plate, and causing me to slosh the coffee I was pouring over the table, and not into my cup. 'Oh my God,' I said, jumping up. I rushed out of the back door and saw Rory in the yard, airgun in hand.

'Dog,' Angus said, appearing at my side, making me jump all over again. 'Was trying to get in the horses' paddock.'

I watched as the dog ran down the driveway, Rory following it. Unknown dogs could cause a lot of problems on the farm worrying the animals. We waited, flakes drifting down on us, until Rory walked back. 'Chased him off. The gate was open,' he said, shaking his head.

'I definitely locked it,' I said, immediately. 'I…'

'What is it?' Rory asked as I trailed off.

'It sounds crazy but I thought someone was following me home last night. I don't know. What if they opened the gate after me? But why?'

'A lot going wrong around here lately,' Angus commented.

'I promise I locked it,' I repeated.

'I know.' Rory hooked the gun over his shoulder. 'It's okay.' He and Angus exchanged looks.

'What? Tell me,' I said, not wanting to be left out of whatever they were thinking, hoping it wasn't that I was a liability here or something.

'You don't think it's anything to do with Stewart, do you?' Rory said, running a hand through his hair.

My instinct was to say no but then I hesitated. Could it have been him trailing me from Glendale Hall after our kiss?

'Everything okay?' Dad said then, poking his head out of the back door. 'Harry's a bit upset in here...'

'I'm coming,' I said quickly, going inside, but Rory's question followed me all the way.

Chapter Twenty-Three

As the afternoon drew on, everyone began arriving at the farm ready for our episode of *Countryside Watch* to air. Things were still uneasy between me and Rory but I became caught up in everyone's excitement about the TV show. Pretty much everyone in the village was planning to watch, and our living room was filled up with friends and family who had wanted to come and see it with us. My dad had brought in lots of snacks, all now laid out on the coffee table, and Rory was passing out teas and coffees as I gave Harry to Izzy and tried to find seats for everyone. The room was full. As well as everyone from the Hall, Emily and Brodie and baby Iona had come, as had all the staff from our shops, everyone closing up an hour early to make it. I put the TV on ready, turning it on mute for now.

My phone buzzed in my pocket and when I looked, I saw it was Stewart again. He had tried to phone me four times today but I had ignored each call. A text came in then.

I'm sorry, Heather, if I overstepped last night. I'm not sorry that I wanted to kiss you, but I won't do it again if that's what you want. Please don't let this stop you working with me. I need you in my life now.

I quickly put the phone away; I had no idea what I would even reply to that. I glanced at Rory chatting to his brother, the room filled with people who were by our side day in and day out. That almost-kiss with Stewart felt like a dream, as if it had happened to someone else entirely.

It was becoming harder for me to see why I wanted to walk away from all of this. There was still an attraction in going back to how things were, perhaps we all felt like that sometimes – things always looked better in retrospect, but if I did then I could lose everything I had now.

Beth came over then. I hadn't seen her since I fled Glendale Hall after Stewart kissed me, although I'd messaged her to say I'd had to hurry back for Harry and hadn't been able to find her to say goodbye. 'Everything okay?' she asked me softly.

'I think so,' I said. 'It's been a strange few days but I think everything is getting back on track now.' I glanced at Rory, and smiled.

'Well, good,' she said, rubbing my arm. 'I've been worried. But this will be so great for you guys,' she said, gesturing to the TV. 'It's almost time, isn't it? I think you should make a speech,' she added more loudly, and the room grew quieter, everyone turning expectantly to me.

I looked around the room at my smiling and excited friends and family, and I knew that whatever happened, I was surrounded by people who loved and supported me. And that meant a lot to me.

Dad clinked his glass then. 'Heather has a few words to say everyone!'

'Thanks for putting me on the spot, guys,' I said, moving to the front of the room. 'Well, in a minute you'll see me chatting incoherently about posting on Instagram and somehow going viral. But, seriously, I think that people loved seeing our way of life out here, and the presenter said everyone wants to live in Glendale, and who can really blame them, huh?' There were claps and cheers then. 'I know that things feel a little uncertain around here,' I said then, more seriously, meeting Rory's eyes. 'But this farm has stood here for hundreds of years, and so has Hilltop, and so has Glendale village, and it will stand for hundreds more years especially if we can keep showing people that places like these need protecting.' I hadn't expected those words to come out of my mouth, but they had. And I believed them, and the response afterwards showed everyone in the room did too.

Beth sent me a photo she had taken of me making my speech so I posted it on Instagram asking my followers, which were steadily growing every day, to watch and tell me what they thought of my first ever TV appearance. It had become second nature to post updates online now, and I enjoyed reading people's comments, and I'd found a few other women in farming to follow, and they were lots of fun to chat to, and it was still a relief when they talked about finding our way of life hard sometimes too. I wasn't alone. And I needed to keep on remembering that.

I actually didn't feel nervous about watching myself on the TV show. I felt like it showed how far I had come. I still had far to go though, but so did everyone really. None of us were exactly where we wanted to be, but that was okay. Life was about the journey after all. I felt better about where I was on mine than I had in a long time, which was more than enough.

I went over to where Rory was sitting in one of our armchairs, and I perched on the arm, and he touched the small of my back as the programme started. 'Here we go,' I said as the titles came up. I put the sound on, and the room fell silent.

'Thank you,' Rory said, leaning closer to speak into my ear. 'I would never have thought of doing anything like this. I know you worry about what you bring to the farm sometimes but, Heth, you should never worry. You bring you. And that's exactly what this place needs.' He fell silent as *Countryside Watch* started, and I swallowed the lump in my throat as I leaned closer to him, and laughed as everyone cried out when they saw the first glimpse of the farm on TV. I smiled to see my sparkly wellies walking up the hill, Rory and the cows behind me, looking very much as if I was a farmer after all. Unexpectedly, and not at all a typical one.

But one all the same.

–

Thoughts of Stewart faded away as Christmas week arrived and with it, my mum's birthday. I had been dreading it for weeks. It was hard to believe that it had been eight years since I last heard her voice. So much time without her presence and support, and right now it felt like I needed her more than ever. The hole she had left in my life was bigger than ever, and I was scared it would never get any smaller.

'Are you okay, love?'

I turned around to see my dad walking towards me, holding hands with Harry. I wasn't sure how long I had been standing watching the horses in the paddock as I leaned against their fence. The sun was rising up in the sky, turning it pretty pastel shades of pink above us. 'I'm sorry, I was miles away.'

'It's a hard day,' he replied softly, coming over to squeeze my shoulder. 'Shall we head off? We said we'd drop Harry at the bakery on the way.'

'Okay.' I climbed off the fence. All the chores had been completed so I couldn't put it off any longer. It was the same every year – I wanted to mark her passing but I also wished I could forget all about it too. I looked up the hill and saw Rory walking up to see to the cows. I wished I could escape into his embrace, and never leave it, but I had to do this for my dad, and my mum too.

'Let's go then, bub,' I said, picking Harry up and carrying him to the car with us. Emily had kindly agreed to look after him this morning at the bakery and then take him to the vicarage for lunch with Brodie and baby Iona. We would join them there afterwards.

As we drove to the village, I looked out of the window watching the countryside roll by thinking back to eight years ago. I had rushed from university in shock to discover Mum was so ill, and I had only weeks with her in the end. She hadn't had that last birthday or Christmas with us as I'd hoped she might. My Dad and I had been stunned at her rapid decline in the end, and how quickly we had lost her after her diagnosis. It had been so shocking and devastating, but I had held on to the fact that I had at least been able to say goodbye to her.

I thought back to one of our last conversations, when she had been able to have a proper conversation with me still.

—

My dad went to get us a coffee so I was sat by her hospital bed alone. Outside, it was snowing and almost Christmas but it was as if time stood still on that ward, as if we were in this bubble where real life had been stopped – all we could think about was being there for Mum, the rest of the world forgotten. 'When will you go to Edinburgh?' she asked. 'With Stewart.'

'I can't think about that. I need to be here. He understands.'

'Does he? You know, I don't want you to stop your life because of me, I couldn't bear that…'

'You are my life,' I told her firmly. 'Mum, what do you really think of Stewart?' I reasoned that on her deathbed she would be honest. My parents hadn't spent much time with Stewart, only seeing him when they came to see me at university. He always had so much on in the holidays that he'd never stayed in Glendale with us.

'You know that if you're happy, I'm happy.' She squeezed my hand. 'He's handsome and charming and clever, but you know that. That's why you fell for him.' She hesitated and I nodded for her to continue. 'But is he kind? I never thought that mattered until I met your father, but I know now that it does. More than anything. I look up to your dad, I admire him both as a man and a person, and also as a father. He makes me a better person.

I hope he might say the same. That's the person you want to be with in life, I think. Don't you?'

—

Now I realised that at the time I had told myself that Stewart was that man, but I wondered if he had ever been. Rory was a better person than me, I knew that.

'Here we are,' my dad said then, pushing the memory of that conversation away. We had arrived in Glendale. He turned to me. 'I can take him in?'

'No, it's okay,' I reassured him, trying not to look as lost as I felt. I went to the back and lifted Harry out and put him in his pushchair. 'Let's go and see Auntie Emily, shall we?' I said, pushing him inside. Emily's bakery was one of those places that made you feel comforted as soon as you stepped through the door. It was cheerfully decorated in lemon and blue, the smell of delicious cakes and freshly baked bread making your stomach rumble on cue, the warmth from the coffee machine at odds with the crisp morning. Christmas music played quietly from the back and Jules who worked there was wiping down a table, a couple beside her tucking into coffee and croissants, and behind the long counter Emily, in her apron, was putting out a fresh batch of cupcakes. Beside her, Iona slept peacefully in her pushchair. She was just over a year old now, and had grown up used to noise and company, and was perfectly content accompanying her mother to work most days.

'Hello, you two!' Emily said cheerfully, when she looked up to see us enter, the bell on the door jingling merrily at our arrival. Her blonde hair was tied up, a streak of flour across her cheek, as she gave us a wave.

'It always smells so amazing in here,' I said, pushing Harry to the counter. 'Thank you for having him for me, I really appreciate it. I know you have your hands full.'

'It's no problem,' she said, coming round to kiss me on the cheek and to ruffle Harry's hair. 'Jules has it all covered here anyway, I'm like a spare part,' she said, smiling at the manager who grinned back. 'So, I can take these two home and then make some cakes with Harry's help there. I thought he might like to make some gingerbread with me. We have festive-d up our menu this week.'

'You'd love that, wouldn't you?' I said to Harry. 'I suspect it will get very messy, mind.' I leaned down to kiss him. 'I won't be long okay, love?'

'Bye,' he said cheerfully, waving. I smiled. Life didn't touch him much yet, it was a shame that it ever had to.

'Take as long as you need,' Emily said gently, when I stood up, touching my arm in support. 'We'll be just fine.'

'Thanks, Em,' I told her gratefully. Honestly, without the support I had in Glendale, there was no way I could get through Christmas. 'Save me a gingerbread man,' I added as I walked out, waving back to Harry as I left. It was always a pull to leave him but I knew he was in safe hands, and I didn't want him to see me cry, which I knew I would do. I always did.

Dad parked the car outside Glendale church and we set off arm-in-arm towards it. The sun was high in the sky now, the day cold and crisp, making the village look beautiful. The temperature was definitely dropping again. I wondered if it would be another white Christmas. I hoped so for Harry. As long as we could get to the Hall to celebrate then I wouldn't mind so much either. Perhaps the white stuff was finally growing on me. Or at least not worrying me as much as it had in the past.

'Heather, Don,' a voice said behind us. We turned to see Brodie coming out of the vicarage, giving us a nod in greeting. It was funny sometimes to see him in his dog-collar, performing his job, when I was more used to him at the Hall drinking and eating with us. I'd never met a more relaxed minister in my life but I knew he was an excellent one, everyone in the village spoke highly of him, and I could see how happy he made Emily. 'She brought the sun out for you,' he said, shaking my dad's hand, and giving mine a squeeze afterwards. He knew why we were here, of course.

'She was happiest on a sunny day,' my dad agreed with a smile.

'Well, I'll see you both later. I'm off to practise my sermon for Sunday,' Brodie said. 'I'll make sure you're on our prayer list too,' he added, and headed off into the church.

Neither Dad or I were believers really but the church formed a big part of our life anyway with all the family events we attended, and the fact Brodie was so close to us, so we appreciated his gesture.

We walked on together slowly around the back of the church and into the cemetery. It was a small cemetery and there was no longer burial space but Dad had paid for a bench with a plaque for my mother in there. It overlooked the village, which she had loved living in so it was a perfect memorial for her. She had been cremated, and her ashes scattered in the gardens of Broomwood Castle, a place she had loved to visit.

'Do you think she can see us here?' I asked when we had sat down on her bench. The cemetery was bare as it was winter, the trees empty of leaves, and the grass mixed with mud, but there was always a peace here that made it beautiful even at this time of the year, and with the sun shining down, there was warmth too. You could imagine that maybe she was here with us.

'I think she's always with us, I really do. Look at Harry – when he smiles, I can see her smile.'

'Me too,' I agreed. 'I miss her, Dad. I know that's obvious but it's the everyday, small things, that have hit me hard lately. Like with Harry, knowing what to do sometimes, I wish I could ask her. She always seemed to know the right thing to do.'

He nodded. 'I feel the same. I always went to her for advice, from when I first met her, right up to the end. There was no one's opinion I trusted more. But I don't think you need to worry. Everything she knew, and everything she was, she passed on to you. You're a wonderful mother, just as she was.'

I felt the tears rising up already. 'I wish I could feel that. I feel like I get it all wrong when I try so hard.'

'No one can possibly get everything right in life. I wish I could take some of your worries away. You've always taken so much onto yourself. When you really shouldn't. Harry has so many people who love him, there's nothing to worry about. He's so well looked after.'

'I worry about the future,' I admitted, looking down at my hands. 'About being there for him. I don't want him to ever go through what I did.'

'Well, that's understandable but none of us know what's going to happen in life. Surely worrying about things that haven't happened yet just robs you of the joy of today? We all need to plan ahead, of course, but not so much you don't enjoy what you have now. And you enjoy what you have now, don't you?'

I glanced at him, my eyes full of tears. 'Sometimes I feel like I can't let myself enjoy it. What if it all slips away from me?'

'Well, why will it?'

'I was so worried I wasn't suited to this life, to farming, all of it, and now it's being threatened by everything that might happen at Hilltop, by Stewart turning up too, and it's shaken me more than I thought it would. It feels like my fault. Like I need to stop it somehow.' I explained that Stewart seemed to think I was crazy to want the life I was living, that I should come and work with him, that if I did the farm would be protected, but if I didn't what would happen to it then? 'I'm stuck. There's no right choice to make, is there?'

Dad twisted to look at me, taking my hand in his. 'There is always a right choice to make, and it's the one that will make you and your family happy. Don't be pushed into something you aren't sure about because you think it's up to you to make it okay. You didn't ask Stewart to come here. It's not your fault.' He sighed. 'Perhaps this is a good time to tell you – I was never Stewart's biggest fan. Your mother told me to keep my opinion to myself in case we lost you, we could see how much you loved him. But I always thought he was rather… manipulative.'

'Really?' I raised an eyebrow in surprise.

'You changed so much when you met him. I don't think you realised. But a lot of your confidence seemed to go. You started seeking his opinion about everything. You were never the most decisive person but you always got there in the end, you just liked to take your time, and consider everything, but then you just let him decide for you. You're not like that with Rory. You seem… freer.'

'That's because he's so different from me, he's so laid-back, he doesn't worry, he just gets on with things.' I smiled a little through my tears. Rory could handle anything life threw at him, I was sure of it.

'But you've become like that too. You fell in love with him so quickly, and you just embraced it. Then you fell pregnant and you took that in your stride too, and moved into the farm and became this amazing woman building a family and a business. Look at how your posts about the farm have inspired people, you got the farm on national TV for goodness' sake. Who else could do that, love? Honestly, your mother would have been so proud of who you are now.'

My heart lifted for a moment. I wanted nothing more than for her to be looking down proud of me. 'I worry that I can't hold it all together though, Dad. Like it's all going to fall apart.'

'That's because you care so much, if you didn't love Rory and Harry and the farm then you wouldn't be worried about keeping it all together, right?'

I hadn't thought of it like that. I'd been so scared I was failing at all of it, I hadn't realised it was because I wanted it to work desperately. Because I did love it. Rory, Harry *and* the farm. And perhaps it had taken the past few days to really make me see that clearly. 'What if Stewart ruins it all?' I whispered, panic seizing me again.

My dad shook his head. 'Don't let him,' he said fiercely.

I sat back and wiped my eyes. We fell into silence as I processed his words. I had let Stewart voice my fears. That I'd never be good enough as a mother, and as a partner to Rory, but is anyone ever really good enough? All I could do was my best, right? 'Rory said something...' I said slowly. 'That maybe Stewart had chosen the farm next to ours because I lived there.'

Dad thought for a moment. 'It is a big coincidence, isn't it, that he would want to build a hotel on your doorstep? Did he know you lived there?'

'I'm not sure but I think I need to find out.' I turned to him. 'Stewart kissed me,' I admitted. 'I pulled away immediately but I feel so guilty. I'm not sure if Rory can forgive me. And I don't know what I will do if he doesn't.'

'Rory loves you, so much. If you love him just as much then you can work it out the two of you, I know that.' He pulled me into a hug. 'I'm always here for you, Heather. I hope you know that. I know I'm no substitute for your mum but I want to do the best I can.'

I pulled back to smile at him. 'You are the best,' I told him fiercely. 'Dad, I'd love you to come and live with us on the farm. Not just for Christmas, I mean. But forever. Rory does too. Will you consider it?' We didn't have my mother any longer to ask for advice, but we had each other.

He smiled. 'I will. Thank you.' I rested my head on his shoulder, as we looked out at Glendale, the place we called home. 'She will always be right here with us, won't she?'

'Always,' I agreed, another tear rolling down my cheek.

Chapter Twenty-Four

After we had lunch in the Glendale Arms, and raised a toast to my mum, I left Dad heading for the vicarage, promising to join him there shortly. There was something I needed to do first. If Rory and my dad were right that Stewart had chosen Glendale because of me, then both his job offer, and his behaviour around me since he arrived had indeed been manipulative.

My dad said he thought Stewart had always been like that towards me, and it got me thinking back over the course of our relationship. I thought about how he would push me to go clubbing even if I had to be up early for a lecture, how he got annoyed when I said I needed to study before an exam, that he always wanted me to do what he wanted to do. And how he had been so impatient if I felt anxious. And then there was the fact he had mapped out our whole future without even really asking me if it was what I actually wanted.

–

'I've applied for an apprenticeship at a firm in Edinburgh, my tutor recommended them because they'll pay me a decent amount to help me become a fully-fledged architect,' Stewart said in his room one night.

I was curled up against his chest and I propped myself up on my elbows. 'I haven't even thought about a job next year yet, we have months left of uni.'

'These things are really sought after, I had to get in there early. But my dad knows someone who works there so I think I've got a good shot. Grades depending obviously.' He shrugged – he was so confident he'd pass all his exams, he always had done.

I bit my lip and hesitated before saying. 'So, you'd be in Edinburgh next year then?'

He turned to face me. 'You mean, we will be in Edinburgh next year.'

'We will?'

Brushing back a hair from my face, he smiled. 'Well, I'm not going without you. You said it yourself, you don't know yet what you want to do but I have the perfect idea. We can set up our own design company. I'll do this apprenticeship and build a name for myself, and you can get any job you like in the city, and we can work towards setting up our own company. It'll be so great. You and me in the city having fun, we can rent a flat there, and it'll be just like it is here.'

'I don't know. I never really thought of living anywhere but Glendale, I suppose.'

Stewart snorted. 'What the hell will you do in that Godforsaken place? And you want to be with me, don't you?'

'Of course!'

'Well, then.' He kissed me. 'Let's celebrate…' he said, reaching for my pyjama top. I lifted my hands, feeling somewhat bulldozed but he was right that I wanted to be with him, and he was the one who knew what he wanted to do, so I should support that, right?

I shook my head at that memory. He hadn't asked me what I wanted. I had just gone along with what he wanted. And he was trying to do it all over again.

I thought about the problems at the farm – the power cut, the dog that had appeared, the cow getting stuck in the mud… things that had made me question even more whether I could handle life there. And Stewart had used them to suggest that I wasn't suited to being on the farm, that it was all too much for me. Rory even wondered whether he'd had something to do with those things.

And now I was worried that maybe he had.

I was furious that he thought he could threaten my family, and home, like he had been doing. I liked to see the best in people however, and I had loved him once, so much – surely if he still cared for me as he said he did then he wouldn't want to hurt the people that I loved? And for what ends – the chance to get me back? Or just to prove that he could?

Suddenly, I felt like I couldn't trust anything he said or did. And maybe I never should have.

As I walked to our farm shop, I thought about my dad telling me that he thought I had far more confidence now than I had back when I had been with Stewart. It was true that I had been intimidated on occasion by how ambitious and determined he was, how sure he was that he'd be successful, and how I had been nervous that he would leave me for someone better than me – someone prettier, more intelligent, more capable.

I compared that to Rory. I admired him so much for running the farm and I didn't want to let him down, but if I was really honest it was me who thought I wasn't capable, he had never once said or made me feel that way. He always wanted to show me things, to encourage me, to help me feel more confident. He treated me as his partner in everything, he never told me what to do, he always wanted my opinion even if it was on something I didn't have a clue about.

Stewart hadn't asked me if I was happy on the farm, he had assumed that I wasn't. Because it wasn't something that fitted the way he looked at the world. It didn't fit what he knew of me back when we'd been together, and what I had told him then that I wanted for my life.

It was completely true that my life hadn't turned out how I had planned it, or how Stewart had planned it for us back at university. Which had led to me worrying that meant I couldn't possibly be happy or content with what had happened. I worried it meant I'd taken a wrong turning somewhere along the way and got lost. But what if I had actually taken the path that I had always been meant to take? What if I was on the right journey *now*, and the one I had originally planned was actually the wrong one?

I really needed some sort of sign.

'I didn't expect you today, Heather,' Hattie said, looking at the door in surprise as I walked into our farm shop. 'How good was the *Countryside Watch*? People have been coming in all day today saying how much they enjoyed it, and we've made double already to what we did yesterday so it's already having an effect!'

'Oh, well, that's great,' I said, surprised and pleased to hear that. 'I'm actually making a flying visit, I'm afraid. I need some information,' I said, walking up to the counter. 'You remember when you first told me about the men who are trying to develop Hilltop? You said they'd been snooping about the village, asking questions... before we knew from Malcolm at the pub what they were here for. I need to know if they were asking anything about me, and the farm. Do you know who they spoke to?'

'Rachel at the Glendale Hall shop was the one who told me about them. She can tell you what they asked.'

'Got it, thanks.' I strode out before she could ask why I was so interested, and carried on walking along the High Street to the Glendale Hall shop. Rachel was behind the counter, and Beth was also in there, fiddling with the gardening display by the door. 'Hi, Rachel, Hattie said that the two men looking to buy Hilltop came in here when they first arrived in Glendale – and that you spoke to them? Can you remember what they asked you?' I said. Beth wandered over curiously.

'Only one of them came in. The good-looking one who's been staying over at the Arms. He said that he wanted to buy a property in Glendale. He asked a few questions about the village, and then he asked about your farm too.'

'What did he ask?' I prodded urgently.

'He said do you know a Heather Douglas – she lives out on Fraser Farm?' I sucked in a breath. 'He wanted to know if the farm was doing well, if you worked there too, and then he asked about Hilltop Farm – how long it had been empty, that kind of thing. I really didn't tell him much, I was suspicious why he was asking so much to be honest.'

'But he definitely knew I lived on Fraser Farm?'

She nodded. 'Definitely. And he frowned when I said you did work there, and I told him about the farm shop, and all I said about Hilltop was it had been empty for two years and it bordered your farm, which he didn't seem surprised to hear.' She looked worried. 'Did I say anything wrong?'

'Is this Stewart? Why did you want to know what he asked when he first got here?' Beth said to me, leaning on the counter.

'He told me he had no idea I lived next to the farm he wanted to buy but it sounds like he did know, and in advance of coming here. So maybe that means he did choose Hilltop because it was next door to me. That he came to Glendale because of me. All of it was to try and get me back,' I said, hating that I let him make me question my life with Rory, and my life on the farm. Him turning up hadn't been a sign of fate. He had tried to change my fate. Conscious of Rachel watching, I thanked her and asked Beth if I could have a word outside. She followed me readily. 'I've been really stupid, Beth,' I admitted as we faced each other on the pavement. 'I let Stewart make me think that I didn't belong on the farm, that I should help him turn Hilltop into a hotel, that I wasn't capable of living this life I've chosen. That maybe Rory wasn't the right man for me after all. God, I even let him kiss me.'

Beth's eyebrows flew so far up they almost disappeared into her hair then. 'Blimey,' she said, her years spent living in London making a reappearance.

'I know,' I agreed. 'You were right about him all along. We can't let him take over Hilltop and threaten our way of life. Especially not now when I know he's only here because of me. I don't want him in my life anymore.'

'What are you going to do?' she asked.

I hated being lied to. Dad was right – Stewart was manipulative. He had been all along. Trying to make me come and work with him because he knew I wanted to protect the farm, using that as a way to try to get me back. But why?

He hadn't tried to fight for me all those years ago. Why now? Was it just because I was happy with someone else, and he couldn't stand that? Well, there was no way I was going to let him destroy what I had now. 'I'm going to make sure he doesn't get what he wants,' I promised Beth fiercely. 'First things first, we need to ring your mum.'

—

Beth came with me to the vicarage where we sat around the table with Emily, Brodie and my dad, with Harry perched on my lap, over tea and cake to discuss the situation. Emily firmly believed that tea and cake could help in all situations, and I wasn't about to disagree with her. The sky had darkened as the afternoon drew on so they switched on the Christmas lights. I filled them in on what I had learned from Rachel.

'I never trusted him,' Dad said with a shake of his head. 'Far too charming for my liking. It never felt genuine. But I honestly didn't think he'd stoop to these levels.'

'Me neither. Especially because I haven't heard from him in five years!'

'He obviously can't bear to see you happy,' Beth said. 'What a dick.'

'Auntie Beth, I'm shocked,' I said with a smile as I handed Harry a piece of my muffin. 'But, seriously, have we got any hope of stopping this development? I wonder what the council are thinking about it. It will disrupt the countryside, won't it? And Stewart himself told me he was planning to bring in a team from Edinburgh to work on it so there won't be any local jobs created.'

'You stopped them from selling off the High Street, they did the right thing with that,' Brodie said.

'But that's because we had something else to offer instead,' I said with a sigh. 'And Hilltop has been empty for two years.'

'How much will it disrupt your farm?' Emily asked.

'Currently, Stewart is planning for the golf course to border our farm. It turns out, we don't own the land in the lower field like we thought. If we did then he'd have to move the golf course further away, and the hotel itself too, but all the plans say that it belongs to Hilltop.' I sighed, resigned. There didn't seem like any easy way to hold Stewart back from Hilltop, or from invading our lives.

'I know who would know what we should do,' my dad said then wistfully. When he saw me look at him, he continued, 'Your mother knew so much about Glendale. And all that research she had been doing before...' He trailed off, not wanting to finish the sentence. My mother had been a history teacher and she had a passion for local history. She had loved finding out as much as she could about Glendale. In fact, she was doing research to potentially write a book about it.

'That's it!' I cried, putting my mug of tea down on the table so hard everyone jumped, and my half-eaten muffin fell over on the plate. Harry reached for it eagerly.

'What?' Beth asked, exchanging a confused look with Emily.

'My mother's research! She did so much, about the Hall, about the surrounding farms, the village, she must have something on Fraser and Hilltop Farms. Right, Dad?' I looked at him, eagerly, hopefully. On her birthday, five years since she left us far, far too soon, perhaps she might still be able to help us through this.

'It could be worth a look,' he agreed. 'It's all up in the loft at home.'

'I'll dig it out. And once we have that, maybe I can find something that might prove that land is ours. Or something that might help us anyway.'

'In the meantime, what will you do about Stewart?' Beth asked.

I explained to the others that he'd asked me to work with him and would protect Fraser Farm if I accepted. 'My worry is if I turn down his job offer, he will do all he can to disrupt our lives. Especially when he realises I'll never leave Rory. In fact, he might have already started.' I told them about the things that had been going wrong at the farm and how Angus and Rory wondered if they had been done deliberately. 'I can't believe someone could be that vindictive but after all his lies, I think we have to assume the worst of him.'

'People like him definitely act out when they are denied what they want,' Brodie said. 'And it sounds like he very much wants you, Heather. But if that's the case, would he really want to hurt you like this? Maybe you can appeal to his conscience, make him realise how much Fraser Farm means to you.'

I thought that maybe Brodie was too used to seeing the good in people but I nodded. 'I can talk to him. The problem is I'm not sure anymore that he even has a conscience.' Brodie was right though about Fraser Farm meaning everything to me, and that was enough to try anything at this point.

Even if I really didn't want to have to see Stewart again.

Chapter Twenty-Five

Dad took Harry back home and I walked into the Glendale Arms to try to find Stewart. Malcolm, the landlord, was wiping glasses behind the bar. The pub was busier than usual for a Monday afternoon, people taking time off for Christmas already, I assumed. 'Is Stewart around?'

'In the corner,' he said, gesturing to the back of the room. I made my way over to the table where Stewart was bent over paperwork with a coffee cup beside him. As I approached, I saw that he was talking on his phone.

He was wearing a suit, looking out of place in the cosy pub. I realised then why I kept thinking that whenever I saw him. It was because he didn't belong in Glendale. But I did. And that thought spurred me onwards.

'I know what I'm doing,' he was saying when I moved into earshot. He sighed, frustrated. 'Yes, I told you I would,' he hissed down the phone. 'Please would you just trust me, for once?' He paused, listening. 'Fine, I'll conference you in. I said I would, okay? Talk to you later.' He half threw his phone down on to the table, leaning back in the chair.

I wondered who had got him so riled up. His business partner maybe? The one who came scouting around Glendale with him. It certainly didn't sound like they had a particularly good relationship to me. He looked up then and saw me, adjusting his expression quickly into a much calmer one. 'This is a nice surprise.'

I slid into the empty chair opposite him before he could get up. I didn't want him to touch me again. I had no idea where to start, and his hopeful expression wasn't helping either. 'Hotel planning?' I asked, looking at the sheets of paper in front of him. I didn't miss him sliding one paper underneath quickly although I tried not to show it.

'I was. I have a meeting with the council later,' he replied. I assumed that was the meeting his business partner wanted to be part of over the phone. 'I'm trying to sort out as much as I can before Christmas.' He looked at me. 'So, I didn't think you wanted to talk to me, you never phoned me back or replied to my text… I was worried.'

'You shouldn't have kissed me,' I said, leaning forward and lowering my voice just in case, I was well accustomed to the Glendale gossip machine and I did not want that to become part of it.

'I can't apologise for wanting to kiss you. You know how much I've missed you, but I'm sorry if it upset you. I thought you wanted me to though.'

'Why? You know I'm with Rory.'

'But you're not happy with him,' he said, trying to reach for my hand.

I folded my arms on the table out of his touch. 'That's not true!'

'Okay then, if you're so happy with Rory then why aren't the two of you married? Why hasn't he asked you yet?' Stewart asked, looking rather triumphant as he delivered what I assumed he imagined would be a fatal blow.

'He has actually, and it's none of your business why we're not married, is it? You made me a job offer and I said I'd consider it, that's it. I didn't say I would consider getting back with you,' I hissed. 'Rory and I have a son together. You know that. We are a family.'

Stewart sighed. 'Okay, okay, let's park the issue of us then. Have you thought any more about the job? Whatever you say about you and Rory, I know you can't enjoy being on that farm. God, you even lost power the other day. It's so backward there. Like you're living in the past.'

I resisted the urge to say the only one of us living in the past was him, not me. I wondered how I hadn't noticed just how derogatory he was when he spoke about the farm, and Rory, and our life. I could hear the scorn inside his voice, see it in the curl of his lip. And it made me furious. 'I have a couple of questions first…' I propped myself up by my elbows on the table. 'Why did you tell me that you didn't know I lived on Fraser Farm when I know you did? Glendale is a small town, people talk, Stewart.' I raised an eyebrow, waiting for his explanation.

'Fine.' He held his hands up. 'Yes, I knew.' He leaned forward, bringing us even closer. 'As soon as I saw Hilltop for sale, I knew it was the perfect opportunity for me to come here, and see you again. I knew you lived at Fraser Farm because I read that article. You remember? About how your friend had saved the shops in Glendale High Street. There was a photo of you and Rory outside of your farm shop. And I saw it in your eyes. That you had chosen the wrong life. I knew you'd never be happy with a farmer. I knew that you needed me.'

'To do what? Save me?' I asked him incredulously.

'Yes! To help you save yourself. It's a joke, Heather – you living on a farm with that scruffy cave man. Come on,' he scoffed. 'You belong somewhere so much better. You belong with a man like me.' He looked so sure, so confident, that he knew me and what I wanted. How could I ever have been charmed by this arrogance, I wondered?

I tried to stay calm. 'If you think I don't belong with him then why build a hotel here, we'd both have to stay if you do?'

'I know you wouldn't want to leave your father. And that's okay. We can stay in Inverness. Find a nice place while we work on it. We will make the hotel perfect, and then we'll move on to something else.' Stewart shrugged. 'You are bigger and better than Glendale.'

'It's a lot to think about,' I replied, my eyes glancing at the pile of papers in front of him. 'I could do with a coffee.'

'Me too. I'll get us some,' he agreed, getting up. I watched him walk towards the bar and couldn't believe that I had thought my future belonged to him once.

When his back was turned, I lifted the papers and looked at what he hadn't wanted me to see. It was a plan of his project, a large hotel and golf course as he had said. Scanning the layout, my eyes found the field he believed belonged to Hilltop Farm and I saw that he planned to build ten cottages there, up on the hill overlooking the hotel, priced at a premium no doubt as they looked like luxury spaces to stay. I shook my head. They would be right on the other side of the hill where our cows grazed, so close to our farm we would be able to see them from the house. There would need to be a huge fence between the two farms. The whole landscape would be disrupted. Surely the council wouldn't approve these plans? I wasn't sure I trusted them not to though.

I looked up as he returned with our coffees. 'When were you going to tell me about these?' I asked, jabbing the paper with my finger as he slid back into his chair.

Stewart sighed as if I was irritating. 'It was just one idea. My partner's idea. We haven't put that in our application to the council, it was just something we were considering. Obviously, if you came on board we could forget all about the holiday cottages. I would persuade him too.'

There was that ultimatum again. If I didn't work with him, he would do all he could to disrupt the farm and do whatever this partner of his wanted. 'You're unbelievable,' I hissed, trying to keep my voice down still. I could feel Malcolm looking over at us interestedly. I didn't want him to hear our conversation. 'You really think by threatening me you're making it at all desirable for me to come and work with you? Well, you're mistaken. I wouldn't want to be within six feet of this project now. I can't believe how manipulative and arrogant you've become. Or perhaps you always were but I was too young and naïve to see it, too blinded by falling in love with you, I don't know. But know this...' I stood up and leaned over the table, as close as I could get to him. 'You don't know who I am now or you wouldn't have tried to do this. This,' I said, gesturing to the paperwork, 'will never happen now. I will make sure of it.'

His eyes flashed with anger. 'Really? And just how will you do that? You could never make a decision, Heather, always so anxious and worrying, always so pathetic you let me decide everything. You did everything I wanted you to because you can't think, or do anything, for yourself. You want to fight over this, go ahead. Because I will enjoy watching you lose.' He was snarling at me now, his face turning red. Obviously talking back to him wasn't something he ever thought I would do. His words sliced through me like he was pressing a knife into my skin. He spoke aloud my biggest fears about the person I was, and he was enjoying hurting me. But I wasn't going to let him. I was going to fight for my life. He underestimated me, that was clear. I had underestimated myself plenty over the years. But I had to believe in myself now. For all our sakes.

'I feel sorry for you,' I told him, trying to keep my voice from shaking. 'You have no one who loves you or who you love, you're bitter and lonely, and full of anger at the world, but the only person you should be angry with is yourself. For becoming the man I see in front of me today. I am so disappointed that someone I used to love could treat people like this. Treat *me* like this.' He gaped at me, stunned by my words. And perhaps a little ashamed too? 'But you're mistaken if you think that I'm the same person I was back then. Because I'm not. And I'm going to show you exactly who I really am now.' He opened his mouth to say something but I swung my bag over my shoulder and walked away. I heard him calling after me but I carried on, hurrying outside of the pub, looking up at the sky as it started to rain.

I started walking, not really knowing in which direction, my eyes filling up with hot tears. I turned around and walked towards my old childhood home. I needed to do everything I could to try to stop Stewart now and I hoped that my mum might have found something all those years ago in her local research that might help me. Rain fell down on me but I paid it no attention, I was too angry to care that my hair was plastering itself to my face.

My phone rang then. It was the landline over at Glendale Hall. 'Hello?'

'It's Caroline,' Beth's mum answered. We had asked her to get on the phone with her contacts at the council, and find out what was happening with Stewart's planning proposal over there. There wasn't much Caroline couldn't find out if she set her mind to it. 'They emailed me over a copy of Stewart's plans. It's under a six-week consultation. As we thought, they believe that lower land belongs to Hilltop Farm, I'm afraid.'

'Has he proposed to build anything on that field? Holiday cottages?'

'Hang on…' She returned to the phone a minute later. 'Actually yes, I didn't see that before, I'm sorry. There are buildings proposed up there, yes.'

'The liar,' I hissed down the phone. Why was I not surprised that he was still trying to manipulate me with his lies? 'Okay, thank you. I'm going to collect my mum's research and see if there's anything we can use to stop this.'

'Good luck, Heather.'

I was definitely going to be needing it.

Chapter Twenty-Six

My childhood home stood in a non-descript road a few minutes from Glendale village, a three-bed semi with a small garden. It couldn't be more different to the farm. Even though you could easily drive past it and never notice it, to me it would always be special. I parked outside and looked at it through the rain that was turning into sleet falling down outside of my car.

Even though I moved out two years ago, and spent three years away from it when I studied at university, it still felt like home to me. The front garden where I sat in summer playing with Barbie dolls, the garage where I stored my beloved blue bike, the small back bedroom which I filled to the brim with books, and the tree out back that I would sit under and read until my mum would call me in for dinner. It had never felt the same after my mother died though. It felt bigger and emptier and less warm somehow. Gone were the wild flowers she would always have in a vase in the hallway, gone was the smell of her vanilla perfume floating around, and the kitchen which always had the radio playing loudly, her singing along cheerfully, was silent now.

But the memories remained and whenever I walked through the door, they would come flooding back. I braced myself as I jumped out of the car and went in, using the key I had never wanted to give back. I didn't want to dwell on melancholy thoughts, there was no time. I needed to get my mum's things and go back to the farm and try to find something that would send Stewart away. Because I had no doubt that if his plans were approved by the council, he would become a fixture in Glendale and our lives, and one that would be toxic to us all.

My eyes found the picture on the hall table that had been there for my whole life – Mum and Dad on their wedding day. They'd got married at Gretna Green with just a couple of witnesses, on a summer's afternoon, and I came along nine months later. Mum had my wild light brown hair and my hazel eyes. Sometimes when I saw a photograph of her at my age, we could almost be sisters. It was proving to be the same with Harry and Rory.

I thought of Rory as I went upstairs, he had worked so hard to keep his family business going when he lost his parents, he didn't deserve to have it threatened in this way. Nor did Harry. This was his future, and I needed to protect it. But also, having it threatened by Stewart, had made me see that I too loved the land that we lived and worked on. I hadn't realised that it had become part of me even if I had been scared of it, and still was. It was important to my family so it was important to me. Stewart couldn't take that from me. I wouldn't let him.

I climbed up the steep steps on the second floor that led up to the loft. Dad had said he thought Mum's boxes were in the back corner near to the pile of childhood books I couldn't bear to part with. I climbed up there and moved past old Christmas decorations and a dustbin bag filled with old teddy bears. I crouched down and moved a box out of the way spotting two plastic boxes each labelled 'research' on them. Next to them was a box of books. I couldn't help but grab all three. I would love to read Harry the books I had loved as a child.

I was exhausted by the time I had brought the boxes down from the loft, they were heavy and cumbersome. At the bottom of the stairs, I knelt on the carpet and opened the lid of one of the plastic boxes. Inside it were journals, books, typed sheets of paper with Mum's thoughts written on them, a box containing her passion for research. I picked up a journal and touched it. She had been determined to write a local history book, it was so tragic that she'd had to leave us before she had finished it.

Underneath the journal was a brown envelope. I picked it up, turning it over, and I let out a gasp when I saw who it was addressed to in my mother's handwriting.

For Heather. On your wedding day.

–

Rory met me by my car when I returned to the farm after having driven home from Glendale in a stunned state. He was in baggy jeans and a green jumper, boots on his feet, unshaven as always. Yes, it looked scruffy as Stewart had pointed out but it was practical for work, and it just suited him. 'I was getting worried,' he said when I got out.

'I'm sorry.' I reached for him and wrapped my arms around his neck. He held me by my waist, staggering a little in surprise. His jumper was soft and cosy, and his arms around me were strong. 'I'm so happy to be home.'

'Has something happened?'

I pulled back to see him frowning with concern. 'A lot. But I'm okay. Will you help me bring this stuff inside, and I'll tell you everything?' I let him go and opened the boot. We carried in the boxes between us, putting them on the table in the kitchen.

'Mummy!' Harry came in then, followed by my dad, holding a chocolate coin that appeared to be smeared over every inch of his face.

'Hi, darling,' I said, lifting him up on the table and holding his outstretched hand with mine. 'I missed you.'

'Look,' he said, holding up the half-eaten coin for me to see.

'What a treat,' I said with a laugh.

'Someone found the Christmas chocolate,' Rory explained dryly, grabbing a cloth to clean his face. 'What's all this then?' he asked as my dad peered in the boxes with interest.

'This is my mum's Glendale research. I'm hoping there's something in here that might help us push back on Stewart's plans, something about the land around here we can use. We have to stop him somehow,' I replied fiercely. I explained that he had proposed holiday cottages in the lower field. 'They would be right on top of our land.'

Rory sighed as he sat down. 'I was afraid of that. We'd have to put fences up otherwise the cows could wander into the hotel, or worse the guests onto our farm.' He shuddered at the idea of tourists on our farm, and I couldn't help but smile.

'The cows would hate it,' I said then, thinking about how I would feel if after roaming where I wanted, I was suddenly shut in.

'I'm still not used to you talking about cows,' my dad said with a chuckle. 'When you were a teenager, we were worried you'd get a Vitamin D deficiency with how long you spent reading in your bedroom.'

I smiled. 'My tan from this summer has still not fully faded, all the time I spent outside on the farm,' I said. 'Things have definitely changed.' I glanced at my son who was finishing his chocolate happily, and messily. 'I won't have to worry about Vitamin D with this one.'

'He's going to have such a lovely childhood growing up on a farm. I'm quite envious when I think about mine spent in Inverness. I don't think I even saw a cow until I was a teenager.'

'And Mum was the same, wasn't she?' I asked, looking at her boxes. I never tired of hearing about my mother's life. Now she wasn't around to ask things, I would always try to get Dad talking about her.

He nodded. 'Her family lived just around the corner, we went to the same school. She longed to live in the countryside though. That's why we came to Glendale after we got married. I always regretted not being able to give her a bigger home with more of a garden although you know your mum, she never complained.'

'I wonder what she would have made of this place,' I said.

'She would have loved it.' He opened one of the notebooks. 'Your mum went all out, didn't she? I remember how excited she used to get looking through the old history books, she was such a history buff.'

'Let's hope she found something that might help us,' Rory said.

'I think she will have done,' I said. I felt confident. There had to be a reason for all her work. It couldn't have all been in vain. I thought of the envelope I had found addressed to me, which was now tucked into my bag. I wasn't ready to tell anyone about it just yet. I needed to think about whether I wanted to read it or not. It was, after all, written for my wedding day, something I had been so against thinking about knowing she'd never be part of it. Now it seemed she had written me a letter so she could be part of it in some way. And I had no idea what to do. Should I open it now or not? It was too much to think about on top of everything going on at the farm so I tried to push it to the back of my mind. 'Caroline said the council have six weeks to make a decision on Stewart's plan so we have some time. He's leaving Glendale for Christmas so we need to come up with something while he's away.'

'I think we're going to need coffee,' Dad said, walking into the kitchen.

'Are you sure about not working with him, about staying on here?' Rory asked me casually then, wiping Harry again as he finished the chocolate. He didn't meet my eyes. I now realised that Rory did worry about things, maybe not as much as me, not many people did, but when things mattered to you then how could you not? I hadn't been very fair to him the past week.

Laying a hand on his arm, I said, 'The one good thing about him coming here is that he's made me see how much I have in my life that I love, and want to protect. I'm sorry that he's come here, and I'm going to do all I can to make him leave us alone again. Nothing is more important than you and this little one, and our home.'

'And you,' he added. He brushed my lips with his. 'We're a team. I want to support you in anything you want, you know that, right? We protect all of this together.'

'I know,' I assured him. 'I have been so anxious,' I said, feeling the tears rising up in my eyes then. 'I want to get everything right.' I looked at Harry, wishing that I could stop worrying that I would fail him.

Rory wrapped an arm around me. 'Loving us the way you do is getting it right. Nothing else matters but that.' His words broke me and despite never wanting to cry in front of them, I did. Instantly I felt relief from not holding back, from letting out how I was feeling. I couldn't be perfect, no one could, but I could love them, and they could love me back. 'It's all going to be okay,' he soothed me, pulling me close. I felt Harry's hand around my leg as he sat on the table watching us. I reached for him with my other arm, holding him against me. Turning, I saw my dad watching us with a smile, and through my tears, I smiled back.

Chapter Twenty-Seven

On Christmas Eve Eve, Beth, Drew and Izzy came out to the farm for dinner.

'It was like the apocalypse in the supermarket today,' Beth said when I passed her a glass of wine in the living room. Small, gentle snowflakes had begun to float down outside the window. 'We barely made it out alive.'

'Mum elbowed a woman out of the way to get to the last Christmas pudding,' Izzy said from her position cross-legged on the floor, stroking Tabby the cat who was asleep in front of the crackling fire.

'I'm shocked, Beth,' I said with a laugh. 'Where's your Christmas spirit?'

'It's fully intact here by the fire with my wine and my family but that place is enough to turn anyone into Scrooge. I went so crazy I bought five tubs of Quality Street. Five!' She shook her head, her long wavy hair bouncing. 'Thank goodness we have everyone coming for Christmas lunch because there's enough food for about fifty, I think.'

'We might get snowed in though so it was probably a good idea to stock up,' Drew said. The weather forecast was predicting a white Christmas and if it continued falling as it was now, I could well believe it would happen.

'As long as it lets us get to you and back on Christmas Day then I don't mind,' I said. I leaned back on the sofa.

I was tired. I had been reading Mum's notes until late last night after having made a supermarket run myself to stock up in case of heavy snow, and Harry had woken up early crying. He had already gone to bed as he had been so tired after I fed him before they got here.

'How's it all going?' Beth asked, nodding at the pile of books and paperwork on top of the armchair in the corner where I had been reading last night, only realising the time when the last embers of the fire had died out, and I had started shivering.

I had been spending every spare minute I had bent over my mother's research and I had found out more about Glendale than I had ever known but nothing so far that could prove useful to us. 'Mum focused on her research on historic buildings and landmarks in the area and she did a lot of looking into Glendale Hall, which you might want to read. I also found a book on Glendale Church, which I'm going to give to Brodie. It's all really interesting, but I haven't found anything to help with putting a stop to this hotel. Yet, anyway. I'm sure I remember her talking about the farmland around the village though.' I looked at my dad who thought about that.

'She was frustrated, I think, about the lack of information on the area,' Dad said. 'Farmers weren't the best at keeping detailed records, and there wasn't a lot of information on farm buildings in the library. A lot was passed on by mouth. Rather like you believing what land belongs to this farm, I suppose Rory,' he added.

'None of our barns have names listed on them or in the property plans but my dad told me they all had names, they were definitely just passed down through the generations,' Rory agreed from next to me on the sofa. 'It's very possible that there was an informal agreement made about the land at some point, but it doesn't help us if that was the case.' He glanced at his brother. 'Dad would have known.' I recognised that feeling well – needing the advice of a parent no longer here. It was so hard not having them here. I still hadn't decided whether to read my mother's letter or not although it was constantly at the back of my mind. I wanted to hear her voice again so badly but I was scared too to read it. It was a strange feeling of being both desperate to read it and wanted to hide it away forever. I rubbed Rory's arm in support, and he smiled at me.

'I feel so useless just sitting here,' Beth said. 'Can't we appeal to someone?'

'The council haven't approved the plans yet so there is a chance they will say no, isn't there?' Drew said, hopefully.

'I just wish Stewart didn't want to build so close to our land,' Rory said with a sigh.

'I don't think it's a good idea full stop, even if it wasn't bordering your farm,' Beth said. 'We will lose farmland and wildlife, the whole countryside will be affected, and it sounds like there will be no encouragement to support local businesses. It would be much better if Hilltop was developed into something of value to the community if it's not going to be a farm anymore. I just hope the council see that.' She didn't look as hopeful as Drew though that they would.

I didn't want us to become too maudlin – we were so close to Christmas after all. 'I've still got a box to go through,' I said brightly. 'I really think my mum will come through for us. But let's forget about it all for the evening, let's have something to eat, that'll cheer us up.' I didn't need to mention food twice, everyone got up eagerly.

'I'm sure there will be something in one of those books,' Izzy said to me as we walked into the kitchen. 'Books always hold the answer, don't they?'

'You're right,' I replied with a smile. 'They have never let me down yet.'

Rory hung back beside me then as everyone sat down at the table. 'If you can't find anything, we'll work it out. It's a long shot, after all,' he said softly, clearly concerned I was going to be upset if I didn't find anything. But my mum was a historian and I was a librarian. I might have been still trying to find my way as a farmer's partner, but I knew books, and so had she.

'Research takes time,' I said. 'You just have to have faith.'

'Brodie not rubbing off on you, is he?' he joked as we joined the others.

I laughed. 'You never know.'

I went to the Aga and pulled out the cottage pie I had made and carried it over to the table where Rory had put out the vegetables and crusty bread, and was handing out more drinks. The kitchen was lively and warm, just how it should be two days before Christmas.

'Hattie sent me our profits this week,' Rory said as everyone started to fill up their plates. 'And they have doubled since *Countryside Watch* aired. So, I think we need a toast…' He lifted his glass, and everyone did the same. 'To Heather for bringing us all this publicity, and for inspiring so many people with her honesty – not just strangers, but us too. To Heather!' I was embarrassed as everyone at the table cheered and toasted me, but pleased too that I'd made such a difference.

'I would never have thought of it without, Beth,' I said, over the noise.

'I hope I'm getting an extra Christmas present this year,' she joked.

'I'd like to make one more toast before we eat,' I said. 'At this time of the year, I can't help but think about people who are no longer with us.' We had each of us lost someone close to us. Rory and Drew their parents, me and Dad had lost my mother, and Beth had lost her grandmother. 'But we also should remember that we're here because of them and that means they are still with us, in the family we are today, and they always will be. So, here's to both absent and present friends – merry Christmas!' I raised my wine glass again, and everyone echoed my toast enthusiastically.

Rory reached across the table and gave my hand a squeeze.

I saw Drew and Beth exchange a smile when they saw him do that. When you loved someone, their happiness was also your happiness.

Chapter Twenty-Eight

I woke up before our alarm – the farmhouse quiet and still in darkness, a distinct chill in the air. Climbing softly out of bed, not wanting to disturb Rory, I crept out across the landing into Harry's room. He was still sleeping soundly, unaware of me in the doorway. I went downstairs into the kitchen where I put the coffee machine on and made a strong, black cup and carried it into the living room. Outside, the farm was still, and I could make out a crisp layer of frost over the ground when I looked out of the French doors.

Switching on the Christmas tree lights, I curled back up in the armchair and picked up my mum's books once again. One was photographs of rural Scotland and I flicked through it until I recognised a scene. It was taken at Fraser Farm – on top of the hill, the cows grazing on a summer's day, and in the background I could see Rory's father. Easily recognisable as he looked so much like Rory and Drew. There was a short history of the farm dating it back to the eighteenth century.

> *The surrounding land has been farmed since the seventeenth century. The oldest farm in Glendale is Hilltop Farm, dating back to 1700.*

Well, that was interesting. The farmhouse there was as old as I had thought it was when I looked around with Stewart.

My mum had written in her journal:

> Not all rural land has been investigated by the authorities. There are many buildings in Glendale that surely should be listed in addition to Glendale Hall.

I read those sentences twice. It was just a short post but the words stood out to me. If Hilltop Farm was as old as that book said then shouldn't it be conserved for the future? Surely the authorities wouldn't want it to be demolished to make way for a hotel?

'You're up early,' Rory said from the doorway, making me jump.

'I couldn't sleep. Come and look at this,' I said, waving him over. He came and perched on the arm of the chair as I showed him the picture of our farm. 'Look how old it says this farm is, and Hilltop.' And then I pointed to my mother's notes. 'What if both farms could become listed buildings?'

He traced his finger across the page, looking at his father, tragically taken from us too soon, and then he met my gaze. 'My father said that the main barn dated back even longer than this farmhouse, he always thought it should be protected but it was something we never really looked into. I mean, how do you even get buildings listed?' He tilted his head. 'You're thinking that if Hilltop was protected then the hotel wouldn't get planning permission?' he asked slowly, catching up to me.

'That's exactly what I'm thinking. I can look into listing, if we could get someone to investigate the farms, that would surely put Stewart's plans on hold at least, and if they agree with us, there's no way he'd be allowed to knock down the farmhouse. We could also protect this,' I said, gesturing around us. 'For the future too.' I smiled. 'And we thought that a librarian had no place on a farm.'

He leaned down and gave me a kiss. 'I want to show you something,' he said, climbing off the arm of the chair, and holding out his hand. I put the books down and let him pull me up.

I followed Rory out into hallway where he opened the front door and opened it up. 'You see that?' he asked, pointing to the wooden post by the door. There was a definite dent in it. 'When I was a teenager, my dad asked me to move the cows down the hill, so I got out the quad bike and was moving them when one of them got spooked by the bike, and started charging towards me,' he said with a wry smile. 'Well, I panicked. I was terrified so I turned the quad bike and started driving back towards the house. The cow kept on following, charging at me now, and I was so busy watching him that I didn't realise how close I was to the house. I swerved but I hit this post.'

'Oh my God,' I said with a shudder.

'I smashed up the bike and hurt my leg falling off it. The cow had followed me through the gate, which I had stupidly left open, and was happily eating my mother's plants by the house when my dad found us.' I smiled at that. Rory shook his head. 'He was furious but couldn't stop laughing at the sight. I had to work off the cost of fixing the bike, and wasn't allowed to move the cows without my dad for the next year.'

'I bet,' I replied with a chuckle. 'It must have hurt too.'

'Mostly my pride thankfully.' He turned to me and took both of my hands in his. 'I'm telling you this because you seem to think that no one has ever made a mistake around here. I was an idiot that day. I got too close to the cows, I drove too fast, I left the gate open… I thought I knew it all and I quite clearly didn't. And I still don't. None of us do. So, when you say you have no place here, it frustrates me. This is your home. Your place is here,' he said, firmly.

I reached for him, wrapping my arms around him. He hugged me tightly back, his face in my hair, his arms solid around my back as I hung off his neck. 'You, Rory Fraser, are incredible, you know that?' I asked, pulling back to look at him.

'Only because I have you,' he replied. 'I wish you could see how amazing you are.'

'God, you're going to make me cry,' I told him, kissing him quickly. 'Thank you for telling me that. I think I just always want to be perfect at everything, but you're right, that's impossible.'

He reached out to brush my hair from my face. 'I don't want you to change but if you are worried about something, just talk to me about it, okay? I will always try to help, I promise you.'

It was all I had ever wanted from a partner. 'I love you, Rory Fraser,' I replied. 'And we're going to stop this hotel. I want Harry to live here just like it is now – unspoilt.'

'What if he doesn't want to be a farmer though?' Rory asked with a grin.

'At least he will have the choice,' I replied. 'Now, go and have a shower, I need to do more research,' I said, extracting myself from his arms, and closing the front door behind us.

–

Once the office opened, I phoned the body responsible for looking after listed buildings in Scotland and the man I spoke to was really helpful and guided me through the online form I had to complete to propose both Fraser and Hilltop Farm as properties to be listed, detailing as much information as I had about their building dates. The man was very interested and seemed to agree that they were good candidates for listing based on their history. I asked about the planning proposals already submitted for Hilltop Farm and they said they would let the council know that they were investigating the property so no planning permission could be granted until they had come to a decision. Which meant nothing was going to happen before Christmas, and we could breathe a little easier and relax over the holiday.

I thought about what Rory had said. That my place was here. It felt good to be fighting for my home, that it really did feel like my home finally. I needed it to stay that way.

After the long phone call, I finished up some chores and then found Rory and Harry outside feeding the horses in the paddock. I went over to join them, pulling up the hood of my coat as a light drizzle had started. 'I think it might all be okay,' I said, smiling, as Harry wrapped his arms around my legs when I reached them in the paddock filling up the hay trough. 'All we can do now is wait for the decision.'

'I never would have thought of this, Heather,' Rory said, reaching up to pat Prince who had come straight over for hay. 'Your mummy is very clever,' he added to Harry. 'You'd better read lots of books like she did so you can be as clever, because I definitely didn't read growing up and look at me.'

I laughed. 'Luckily you have other qualities otherwise we'd be in trouble.' He flicked a piece of hay at me.

We all turned on hearing the sound of tyres on the gravel driveway announcing someone's arrival at the farm. My heart sank when the car turned the corner and came into view. I recognised the black car instantly.

'Who's that?' Rory asked, seeing my expression darken.

I reached down to pick Harry up. 'That's Stewart,' I said, exchanging a wary look with him. We moved out of the paddock, locking the gate, waiting as Stewart drove into the yard.

Chapter Twenty-Nine

'What the hell have you done?' Stewart called out angrily, as he slammed his car door shut and marched towards us, his face looking a lot like thunder.

Harry wriggled in my arms, frowning at his loud voice. 'It's okay, darling,' I soothed. 'Can you please calm down in front of my son?' I said to Stewart, holding Harry closer to me.

'I've just had the council on the phone,' he continued, ignoring me. 'Telling me that our planning proposal is on hold while the property is being investigated for grade listing.' He threw his hands up in the air. 'Why are you so bothered about me building on Hilltop?!'

'Heather asked you to speak civilly,' Rory said then, in a dangerously calm voice. 'You are at our home, you will not speak to us like this.'

'It's okay,' I said to Rory before turning to Stewart. 'The reason I am bothered, as you put it, is that you're planning to build right up to the boundary of our farm which will disrupt our animals, and you lied about that to me. I care about the land around here, and it needs to be protected. I will do all I can to achieve that. The farmhouse you want to demolish is hundreds of years old. It has been here forever. Future generations should be able to see it too.'

Stewart snorted. 'It's been empty for two years. Who is going to take it on? You're condemning it to be abandoned! I told you I'd protect your farm but now, I won't even think about it.'

'You only wanted to protect it if I came to work with you. You have an agenda here, Stewart, don't pretend otherwise. You came to Glendale because you knew I lived here – you wanted to disrupt my life. Well, I won't sit back and let you do that. You wanted a fight, so now you've got one.'

His eyes flashed. 'I can't believe I ever missed you. You are pathetic, Heather. Fighting for a life you never wanted, a life you'll never be good at, and I can tell you now it's a fight you're going to lose.'

Rory stepped in front of Harry and me then. 'If you think I'll stand back while you threaten my family, you're mistaken. I want you off my property right now. Or I'll be forced to defend it,' he told him.

Stewart scoffed. 'You think I'm scared of some country bumpkin in wellies?' But he did step back. I was certain Stewart had never got into any kind of fight before and I was equally certain that Rory could take him, not that he would in front of his son.

Rory didn't rise to the bait. He crossed his arms over his chest and stared Stewart down. 'I said I want you off my property right now,' he repeated.

'Oh, don't worry, I wouldn't want to stay in this place any longer than I had to,' Stewart replied, looking around him with distaste. 'You'll be hearing from my lawyer,' he added, before marching back to his car. We watched as he jumped in and roared away, tyres screeching as he left the farm.

Harry was wriggling, annoyed, so I put him down on the grass, stunned by Stewart's verbal attack on us. 'Have we done the wrong thing in provoking him?' I asked Rory quietly.

He sucked in a breath and then faced me. 'He wouldn't be so riled if we weren't doing the right thing. He knows we can win this, and that's annoyed him.' He shrugged. 'We're trying to protect our home and family, we've done nothing wrong.' He reached for me and gave my shoulder a squeeze.

I smiled gratefully. 'I am sorry though that he's here because of me.'

'It's not your fault.' He looked down at Harry. 'You know what I think we all need now? A mince pie!'

'Mince pie,' Harry repeated, enjoying the words. He reached for his dad's leg and held it. Any mention of food always caught his attention.

'Should we be worried now?' I asked, taking Harry's hand and leading him towards the house.

Rory followed with a sigh. 'You know him better than me.'

'I thought I did. Turns out, he's not the man I fell in love with.' It was hard to believe that I had thought my future was with him. For once, I was glad that life hadn't turned out the way I had planned.

'Let's try to put him out of our minds for Christmas,' Rory said firmly. I nodded in agreement although I was worried about his talk of lawyers, of fighting us, of how angry we had made him. I watched Rory lift Harry into his chair at the table. My dad came in to join us for hot chocolate and mince pies, as the rain outside turned to sleet again, and I tried to relax but Stewart's threats kept on replaying in my mind. I shivered as I watched my family, my heart full of love for all of them.

Perhaps it was only when you thought you might lose something that you realised quite how much it meant to you.

–

The snow began in earnest on Christmas Eve. Angus, Rory and I moved the animals inside, making sure they had extra food and water, and the cows were back in the lower field once again. My dad looked after Harry in the warm house as the snow drifted around the farm.

'I hope it doesn't get too thick tomorrow,' I said, as I shut Prince's stable door. 'And we can still get to the Hall.' Beth was doing Christmas there for everyone, and I really didn't want to miss it but if we were snowed in, there wasn't a lot we could do about it. 'Will you be able to get to your sister's?' I asked Angus who had led Duke into his stable.

'I'll be fine if not,' he replied, with a shrug, unfazed as ever. 'That lad has taken to you,' he added as Prince leaned down to nuzzle my hair.

'I think I might have taken to him too.'

'Rory said you're trying to stop that hotel over at Hilltop. This has been farming land for generations, I'm glad you're doing something about it,' he said, closing the stable door up. 'People always go on about change being good but sometimes things need to be protected.'

'I just hope we can stop it. I want Harry to have all this, one day, just as it is now.'

Angus nodded. 'When Rory's grandfather bought the farm, he did it for the generations after him. We all want to leave our mark on this world in some way, don't we? I know that old Sam would be gutted that his family didn't want Hilltop – the farm he had loved all his life. It's a damn shame that nephew of his can't see its potential.'

It was one of the longest speeches I'd ever heard from Angus since I had met him. 'Do you think anyone would buy it and continue it as a farm?'

'It's possible. It worked really well for sheep back in its day. I remember Sam's wife used to run a bed and breakfast there too when they were younger, it was really popular.'

'That's a good idea,' I said, reaching up to give Prince one last pat. 'Right, I need to get the stew on. You're coming in tonight, aren't you? Celebrate Christmas with us.' I glanced at him.

'Aye, I'll be in,' he replied gruffly, shuffling off, his big boots stomping across the yard.

I smiled as he left. 'I think he's warming up to me,' I confided in Prince. I thought about what he had said about Hilltop. It had made my mind start whirring with ideas, even though I wasn't supposed to be thinking about it until after Christmas. But what he had said about running a bed and breakfast, and about me getting used to Prince...

Snapping a photo of me with the horse for Instagram, I thought about the messages I still received each day from people struggling with everyday life, and wishing there was somewhere like our farm they could escape to. How people seemed to love hearing about the farm, and what the presenter of *Countryside Watch* said about us living a privileged life, how we were lucky even though it was such hard work.

And as I posted the photo online to my ten thousand plus followers now, and counting, I wondered if there was a money-making possibility in that for us somehow.

Chapter Thirty

With all the Stewart drama, and preparing the farm for a snowfall, I really hadn't had much time to think about the letter I had found in my mother's things. But it was Christmas Eve, and I always missed her the most at this time so when I found myself alone for a few moments in the early evening, I slipped into the living room to look at the envelope again. The stew for dinner was in the Aga and Harry was having a nap. My dad had popped out while the snow wasn't too bad, and Rory was finishing up the farm chores with Angus.

I stared at her handwriting, and was overwhelmed with wanting to hear her voice again. I was still stunned that she'd written this letter for me. For my wedding day. It brought back all my feelings of not wanting to get married without her. She had loved weddings so much that it made so much sense that the one letter she left for me would be for that. It made me smile through the pain that she would think of it. I wondered when she had decided to write it. It must have been when she had realised she was too sick to get better. When she had realised that she wouldn't be around to see me get married. My heart ached with how sad it was to know she had thought about that. And how upset she had clearly been.

But like my mother always had done, she had thought of a way to try to be there for me anyway. So I wouldn't have to try to get through it without her. The very thing I had dreaded for so long.

I thought about Rory proposing to me last New Year's Eve, it was almost a year ago and I hadn't been able to tell him yes still. I still just couldn't see the day without her, but perhaps this letter would give me some kind of sign as to what to do? But should I read it when it wasn't actually my wedding day? I hadn't told anyone yet about finding the letter, but I knew I needed some advice about what to do.

'What's that?' Rory asked, coming in to see me curled on the sofa holding the brown envelope.

I looked up at him in the doorway. I couldn't keep it to myself any longer. 'It's a letter. I found it with my mum's research.' I showed him the outside. 'It's for me. She must have written it before she died.'

'For your wedding day,' he said, reading her words aloud in a soft voice. 'You haven't opened it?'

'I'm scared to,' I admitted. 'I didn't even want to tell you I had found it because it made it real, do you know what I mean? And should I even open it when it isn't my wedding day?' I glanced at him. I knew he was still waiting for me to accept his proposal, and I felt so bad that I might be hurting him by my continued silence on the subject.

'Have you told your dad?'

I shook my head. 'Not yet.'

'See what he says, he might know about it, and be able to advise you. I think your mum would be happy for you to read it when you need to, even if it's not your wedding day, but only when you're ready.'

'What if I'm never ready?' I asked, unsure if I was only talking about the letter.

'It will wait until you are,' he promised. I hoped he meant both the letter, and him. 'Your dad is back by the way,' he added. 'I'll pour some drinks.'

'I'll get Harry,' I told him. He left me alone again and I tucked the envelope back into her journal, getting up to go upstairs. I wished I knew what my mum would want me to do.

I missed her so much. On Christmas Eve, growing up, my mum would make us a stew followed by her famous apple crumble and then we'd play a board game, and I wanted to continue that tradition on for Harry. There was something wonderfully comforting about stew and mash in a warm, cosy kitchen, the snow falling outside, the house sheltering us from it. I thought back to those happy Christmases of my childhood as I cooked, wanting to make sure that I gave Harry the same happiness. I hoped he'd love Christmas just as much as I had growing up.

'This looks delicious, love,' Dad said when I lifted the lid of the pot in the centre of the table and the smell of beef, garlic and red wine floated out.

'I used Mum's recipe,' I said, starting to spoon it out onto our plates.

'You know, that comes from her mother. When we got married, your mum had never really cooked before so her mum told her to make this as it was foolproof,' Dad said, remembering with a fond smile when I passed him his plate. He helped himself to mash and French beans. 'It went so well, we ate it every day for a month. No joke.'

'The things we do for love,' Angus said, having a sip of his beer. We all turned to him, unable to hide our surprise. He noticed. 'I was in love, a very long time ago, and we were about to get married... I was all set to leave the cottage and the farm, and move in to her parents' house.

They were wealthy, had a huge estate, I was ready to give up my life for hers,' he said gruffly. 'She became ill though. Didn't get to see her twenty-fifth birthday. Needless to say, I was never tempted to leave here again.'

My eyes filled with tears. 'Oh, Angus, I'm sorry,' I said, touched by the words he hadn't said – that he hadn't found anyone else. I, to be honest, had found it a tad strange moving into the farm with this older man living alone in the cottage at the edge of the grounds, only occasionally leaving to see his sister and nephew, but I understood him more than I ever had. I glanced at my dad – I knew he would never consider trying to find love again, and was reminded of Sally at Glendale Hall who had remained resolutely alone after the death of her husband. It was someone very special who made you unable to forget them after they had gone.

'It was a long time ago,' Angus replied, but I could tell it didn't seem that way to him sometimes. Perhaps Christmas reminded him of her as it reminded me of my mum.

After dinner, Rory said he would clear up and Angus said he needed to check on a few things but I knew he really just wanted to be alone in his cottage so I didn't press him. He had come for dinner, that was enough for him. I put on *Arthur Christmas* for Harry to watch while we waited for Rory to play a game, and then I showed my dad the letter I had found. 'I have been waiting for the right time to show you, I didn't want to upset you. It was such a shock finding it, and I haven't been able to open it…' I said while he stared at her handwriting.

'I had no idea she had written a letter for you,' he said finally. He looked up at me. 'But it doesn't surprise me either. You were what she worried about the most when she realised that she wouldn't get better. She said she wasn't scared for herself. She also said that I would be fine because she had taught me everything she knew,' he said with a smile. 'But she hated knowing she wouldn't be there for you in case you needed her one day. She said that sometimes you just needed your mum. She said she still missed her mother even though she had passed away when you were little.'

I sighed. 'It's true. Sometimes I just wish I could hear her voice or have a hug. I especially wish she could have met Harry.' I swallowed the lump that had lodged itself in my throat.

'I know, love. She would have loved to know him and Rory. And to have helped you with protecting the farm. She would have been so proud of you trying to save the land out here. She always said Glendale was the most beautiful place she had ever seen.' He passed the envelope back to me.

'It really is,' I agreed, looking at it. 'How did you know she was The One for you?'

'As you know, we lived close to one another but it wasn't until university that we really got to know one another. She was, of course, studying history, and I was doing engineering, we couldn't have been more different,' he remembered with a chuckle. 'I went into the library one evening and there she was sitting with a big pile of books, her long curly hair everywhere, and she looked up and saw me and said "Did you know that this library has been burned down twice? Once is bad luck but twice just seems like bad judgement to me," and I was hooked. She was beautiful, of course, but so bright and clever, she loved debating everything and anything, and she was so passionate about the things she loved.'

243

I loved seeing my mother through my father's eyes. It reassured me that I didn't have her on a pedestal because she was no longer with us, she really had been special, and we'd both been lucky to know her. 'I want to be as good a mother to Harry as she was to me.'

'Well, of course you will be. You already are. I wish you could see how much you are like her. Your passion, your loyalty, your love, your honesty, and your smile too.'

I smiled, pleased. 'But she was never as anxious as me.'

'You know what, she did used to be. When we met, she used to get really anxious about exams, worrying that she'd fail but she never did. After we moved to Glendale, when we were married, and then she fell pregnant, she told me that she really didn't have anything to be anxious about anymore. She had everything she had hoped for so nothing else really mattered.' He reached over to squeeze my hand. 'What's important is having people to love and who love you, everything else can be sorted out. As long as you have that, then you'll be just fine. You need to remember that more, that's all.'

He was right, of course. Rory and Harry were what mattered, and my dad, and our family and friends – the people we had in our lives were the ones who would carry us through everything. 'I will,' I promised. I turned to him then. 'Have you thought anymore about moving in here with us permanently?' I asked him. He belonged here with us, I knew my mum would have agreed with me.

'I wasn't sure about leaving the home that I built with Carol, leaving the memories we made there, but what I just said to you... being with family is the important thing, not where you are. My memories are in here,' he said, touching his chest. 'I would love to live here, if you're sure I won't cramp your style.'

I leaned my head on his shoulder and giggled. 'You always have but I wouldn't have it any other way,' I replied.

'The cheek of it,' he said but he kissed the top of my head, and my heart swelled.

Chapter Thirty-One

I opened my mother's letter on Christmas morning.

I had crept down to the kitchen to prepare a breakfast for everyone while the others still slept. A stocking waited for Harry at the end of his bed, and outside the snow had continued to fall during the night and now a thick layer of white was spread over the farm. I was less worried than I thought I'd be to see the blanket of snow covering everything when I looked out of the window because I knew Angus had salted the yard and Rory had parked the jeep at the end of the drive by the gate so we would be able to drive to Glendale Hall, and all the animals were safely under shelter. We also had enough supplies if we were stuck for a few days, and it really did look like a picture-perfect scene outside, like something lifted off of the front of a Christmas card.

After making myself a coffee, and putting the pastries in the oven to warm, I sat down at the table and with shaking hand, slit the envelope open. I pulled out the two sheets of paper inside, and let out a little gasp at the sight of my mother's neat, slanted handwriting. Smoothing the paper on the table, I had to take a deep breath before starting it. My heart was hammering inside my chest. I really hadn't thought I'd ever hear her voice again, but here I was eight years after her death about to read her last words, hearing her speaking them to me inside my head.

My darling Heather,

I have been thinking about writing this letter for a week now. I wasn't sure though if it was the right thing to do, or to be honest if I had the strength in me to be able to write it. You came home at the weekend, and the look in your eyes was more painful to me than this illness. The thought of not being with you anymore hurts so much sometimes I can't even breathe.

I've been so worried that I'll forget to tell you something important, that we won't know when our last conversation will be and miss telling one another something that we need to. So, I decided to write you this letter. Just in case.

Now though sitting here with blank paper and a pen in front of me, I am stuck. How can you even begin to tell someone you love as much as I love you everything you want to? I thought we'd have a lifetime together. How can I fit all those words into just one letter?

I had to look up then. My eyes were too blurry from tears to read her words. I wiped them and took a long gulp of my coffee. The thought of her writing this when she had just weeks left to live filled me with a stabbing pain as bad as when my father had called to tell me I should come home before it was too late. I had tried not to let her see my pain when I walked in through our front door but clearly I had failed miserably, she had seen it, as she had seen everything when it came to me.

Gathering myself, I read on.

But then I thought about all the times we watched a wedding on TV, or read about one in a maga-

zine, how much we enjoyed discussing the dresses,
the flowers, speculated on how funny the best
man's speech was… and I thought about our own
weddings.

My wedding day was the day I needed my
mother more than I would have guessed. It breaks
my heart to know that I won't be there for you on
your wedding day whenever that might be, but I
can try to help you in the same way that my mother
helped me.

The night before my wedding, I was gripped
by fear, panic and anxiety, and I sat in with my
mother in the kitchen I had grown up in while she
made us a cup of tea (what else?), and talked to
me. I want to pass on what she said to me that
night to you now.

I turned the paper over to continue reading. My grandmother was only a vague memory, she had died when I
was so young, I only really knew her from photographs
but my mother had always spoken of them being close,
as we had been. It made me feel better to know that
my mother had also been worried before her wedding,
even though I knew she had loved my dad with all her
heart, and she was right that her not being around for
mine would worry me. Enough that I hadn't been able to
accept Rory's proposal. My mum had known me better
than myself so much of the time. Sniffing loudly, I carried
on reading.

She said 'you've found someone you want to build
a life with and it won't be easy. Life never is. But as
long as you never lose sight of who you are, and the

love and admiration you feel right at this moment, there is nothing you can't get through together. I married someone who I thought had better qualities than I did and I spent my life trying to live up to them.'

When she said that, I thought, me too! I always thought your father was a better person than me. So sensible and calm, and so kind, so supportive of me, nothing has ever ruffled him, and he was an excellent father just as I knew he would be. I hope the man you're about to marry is someone you admire as much as I admire your father, and as much as my mother admired my father.

I was calm after our conversation. I knew I had picked the right man and even if life wasn't easy, we could get through it because of the people we were and the love we had for one another, just as my mother said we would.

Your father and I didn't have much money when we got married, we wanted to spend the money we had to buy our house in Glendale, so we had a small wedding. We got married at Gretna Green, as you know, and if there is one tiny regret I have, it's that I never got to wear a white dress. I dreamed of getting married at Broomwood Castle, and so I hope that whatever your dream is you can make it come true. I want all your dreams to come true. I want you to be happy and loved and feel special every day because you are special. So special.

Heather, you have been the great joy of my life. Growing up, I didn't dream of a husband and a baby. To be honest, my head was too stuck in books, and I was just focused on my career, but when they came along, they seemed even more special because they weren't planned. Don gave me more love than I could have ever imagined, and you made me happier than I could ever have thought was possible. I hope the same happens for you.

I know you worry. You always have. I know you're unsure of yourself and your place in the world sometimes but we all are. I also know that once you find your place, you will do everything you can not to lose it because you are someone who loves deeply and true, just like me.

It breaks my heart that I won't be there to help you find that place, but I know you will because no one deserves it more, and I'll be looking down on you and smiling with great joy when you do find it.

And it's okay if you find this letter and read it before your wedding day. Remember when you opened all your Christmas presents when I left you alone one afternoon? Or the fact that you always read the last page of a book before you reach the end? You have always wanted to know what was in store. Unfortunately, none of us really know. I never thought that my ending would come as soon as it's going to. But try not to worry, my darling. Because life really isn't about the ending, is it? It's about what you do, and who you meet, before you get there.

I'll always be with you, and you'll always be with me. I promise you that.

*So, be happy my darling, and be open to things
that come your way that are unexpected, they have
for me turned out to be the best things, and I'm
certain that they will for you too.*

*I can't put into words how much I love you, or
how much I'll miss you, but I can tell you that the
time we had together was the best time of my life.*

Mum xxx

I turned over the last page of the letter and read her last
words and then I put my head into my hands, and sobbed.

Chapter Thirty-Two

'Merry Christmas, darling,' I said when Harry stood up in his cot, yawning sleepily as he reached for me to pick him up. 'Guess what, it's snowing and Santa has been! Do you want to open your stocking downstairs with us?' I hugged him close to me, not wanting to let him go. I had stopped crying, put my mother's letter away carefully and prepared breakfast. Rory had headed outside to check on the animals, and my dad had shuffled in the kitchen for tea so I had come up to wake Harry.

I thought of my mother's words about how much I had meant to her. I hadn't realised that like me she hadn't planned for marriage and a baby, but both had brought her joy, and it was the same for me with Harry. I had fixated on the fact that I had things I hadn't planned for but what did that matter? I had them now, and they made me happy just as she had promised they would. I wondered if marriage would be the same. She had known I would need her on my wedding day. And, like always, she had found a way to be there for me, telling me exactly the words that I needed to hear.

Although her words had broken my heart, they had also healed it as well.

Picking up his stocking, I carried Harry down into the kitchen where my dad was tucking in to tea and croissants at the table, the radio playing Mariah Carey behind him.

'There he is! Merry Christmas, Harry. What have you got there?'

'Santa,' Harry said cheerfully, as I put him in his chair.

'That's right – presents from Santa because you've been a good boy, haven't you?' I sat down and opened up the stocking, handing it to him to reach into. Harry pulled out a toy truck with glee.

The back door burst open. 'We have a problem,' Rory said grimly. 'The cows have got out.'

'How?' I asked, startled.

'I don't know. The gate to their field was wide open when I went to feed them. We need to round them up before we lose any.'

'I'll come,' I said, scrambling to get up as he left as quickly as he had appeared. A sinking feeling settled in my chest as I pulled on my coat, boots and gloves.

'Can I help?' Dad asked me.

'It's okay, stay in the warm with Harry. I'll be back as soon as I can.' I glanced at Harry but he was playing with his new toys, oblivious, so I didn't feel too guilty about having to leave him on Christmas morning.

I hurried out and saw Angus leading a cow out of one of the barns. Rory was riding Duke out to the field. 'I'll get the ones who are out in the fields,' he called as he jumped into the saddle, the best way of getting up the hill in the snow. I saw two of the cows were by the horses' paddock so I went to get them. I didn't understand how they could have all escaped – there was no way Rory wouldn't have locked the gate last night.

I grabbed a handful of hay from the stables and went to the paddock, holding it out to the two cows there. They looked as stunned as we were to see them there, picking their legs through the snow, and clearly struggling. 'Come on boys,' I said, holding out the hay to lead them back towards the field. Once in the yard, we moved faster as it had been gritted but back on the snow-covered grass, we made slow progress. Angus joined me with the cow he had found in the barn and Rory was up the hill trying to lead the ones up there back to the lower field where there was a shelter and food and drink. Even though they were a hardy breed, it was too cold for them to be up on the hill today.

Angus shut the gate quickly when our cows had gone in, and I told him I'd check the driveway to make sure none had wandered that far. He spotted one standing by the farmhouse front door and hurried off.

I trudged through the snow to the yard and then onto the winding driveway, which was blanketed in snow. At the end was our car ready to take us to Beth's for Christmas lunch, covered over last night to protect it. Light snowflakes fell on top of me as I walked towards it.

The snow that had fallen on the driveway was pristine, my footsteps making the first prints into it after the night of snowfall but then I spotted something under one of the trees that reached over the driveway close to our front gate. I heard hooves behind me and turned to see Rory coming up behind me on the horse. 'Any cows this way?' he called out to me.

'Not that I can see, but look at this,' I said, gesturing for him to come over to me. He climbed out of the saddle and landed with a light thump in the snow, taking the reins and leading Duke over to me by our front gate. 'See that?' I asked, pointing to the distinct footprints I could see under the tree. 'The other footprints were covered by the snow but not those. You'd make them if you jumped the front gate.' I looked at him. 'Someone opened the gate in the field deliberately.'

'Someone?' He arched a brow. I sighed. Would Stewart really try to do us this much damage? Those cows were our livelihood. Rory touched my arm. 'It's okay, nothing bad has happened thankfully. We've found them all, and I think the snow stopped them wandering as far as they might have done, none came down here, and we always lock this gate so he wasn't able to let them out into the road. The ones that went up the hill are hungry and thirsty, but they'll be fine. We're lucky that Stewart knows nothing about farming life, I guess.'

I wrapped my arm around his waist and he slung an arm over my shoulders. 'Is he really that angry with us for the council putting his planning proposal on hold?' I smiled as Duke gave my hair a little nudge and with my free hand, I reached up to pat him. Thank goodness the animals were okay. I dreaded to think what could have happened to them.

'He was pretty pissed off when he turned up here shouting the odds. And from my limited knowledge, I'd say he's definitely the type to hold a grudge. Look at how low he's already stooped...'

'Why can't he just leave us alone? I really can't believe I ever thought he was the one for me. I really hope that I'm a better judge of character now.'

Rory grinned. 'I'd say so. Look at me.'

'Hmmm,' I replied with a smile. 'The jury's still out on that one.' He reached down to flick some snow at me, and I only just ducked out of the way. 'We'd better get back to the house, we've got Christmas to celebrate,' I reminded him. When he turned to climb back on the horse, I grabbed a handful of snow and sprinkled it on top of his head, making him swear loudly as I dissolved into giggles.

—

We begged Angus to join us as he didn't think he'd make it to his sister's in the snow, but he was determined to stay at home and keep an eye on the farm after what had happened in the morning. I felt bad leaving him but there was no arguing with the man. I promised to bring him back some goodies from the Hall, there was always far too much food so I knew we'd have lots left over, and made him agree to joining us over at the farmhouse when we got back later for a drink. He waved us off cheerfully, disappearing inside his cosy cottage, leaving Rory and I to look at one another with a smile. He was a curious character sometimes but it did make me feel better to know he was looking after things here, just in case.

We were only half an hour late to Glendale Hall for Christmas lunch in the end, which was pretty good for us, and we were enveloped immediately into the cosy, warm, merry atmosphere that Beth had created.

'Seriously?!' she cried as she stirred the gravy on the hob in the kitchen at the Hall, listening to me tell everyone about what had happened on the farm this morning as we prepared the lunch. I was drizzling honey over carrots as Rory carved the turkey, Drew was putting crispy roast potatoes into a dish, Sally was turning over the pigs in blankets, and Brodie was getting out the cranberry sauce from the fridge.

'I can't believe Stewart would do that,' Emily said over her shoulder as she carried in her Christmas cake to put on the side for later. She and Brodie were spending the day here and then her parents were coming up to stay with them until Hogmanay. Caroline and John were laying the dining room table as there were too many of us to eat in the kitchen, and keeping an eye on Harry and Iona along with my dad and Izzy. 'Mind you, when people are feeling desperate...' She trailed off and I guessed she was thinking about her ex, Greg, who had hurt her so much. They had come through that though, but I couldn't see a way forward for me and Stewart at all.

'Yes, hopefully it means he's realised how unlikely it is that he can build his hotel now,' Drew commented.

'Exactly. He's lashing out,' Beth agreed. 'I hope everyone will realise he's not someone we want in Glendale. That stupid nephew of old Sam should have known better than to sell to a developer like that, I've a mind to call him up myself about it. But if it becomes listed, he will have to think again about what he does with the place at least.' She stirred more vigorously as she became angry. 'It's a shame we can't all buy the farm ourselves,' she added.

I turned to smile at her. 'You can't save every building in Glendale, Beth.'

'We can try!' she protested with passion. After all, we stopped the library closing, and revived the High Street, so she might have been right that we could. I really hoped that we could save Hilltop Farm. 'Right, shall we start carrying things through?'

'Beth, Em,' I said when the others had left with their dishes, pausing before I followed them. 'Do you both fancy a little day trip with me, maybe on the 28th?'

'Where to?' Beth asked, pouring the gravy into a big bowl.

'Broomwood Castle, I'll explain why on the way.' I had been thinking about it since I read the letter. I had been there as a child and we had scattered my mother's ashes there but I hadn't been back there since, and my mum mentioning it in her letter made me feel like I wanted to go there, and feel close to her, and see the place where she had dreamed of getting married. And I really didn't want to go alone.

'I'm up for it,' Emily said. 'I've never been there. Brodie has a service that day. Mum and Dad will be fine on their own for a bit, they want to go into Inverness to hit the sales anyway I think.'

'Count me in,' Beth agreed. 'Izzy would love it there if we can bring her?'

'Of course,' I replied. A trip for mothers and children seemed fitting to me. 'Right, we've got enough food to feed an army, let's go,' I said, picking up the dish of carrots and leaving the kitchen, trying not to trip over Izzy's cat Ginny who could smell the turkey and had decided to follow me all the way into the dining room.

Chapter Thirty-Three

After we finished our huge and delicious feast, Brodie, Drew and Rory went into the kitchen to clear up and make coffees, and Emily took Iona upstairs for a nap while the rest of us went into the living room where a log fire was roaring, and flickering candles filled the air with the scent of frankincense and myrrh. Beth put on a Christmas CD and handed out the remaining presents under the tree while we all complained about eating far too much as we did every year.

I sat on the floor with Harry to help him open his presents from his Auntie Beth and Uncle Drew, my jeans uncomfortably tight after all the turkey. Beth sat in the armchair with a glass of wine, John and Caroline were on the sofa sipping the family whisky, my dad was perched on the end, and Sally curled up in the other armchair hunting through a tin of Quality Street for a sweet that she liked. Izzy was cross-legged on the floor by us two unwrapping presents, which were mainly books that she held up for me to ask if I had read or not (almost always yes), her Christmas jumper glittering in the light from the fire. Both she and Beth always wore the tackiest ones they could find each year, much to our amusement, and Caroline's despair.

'It feels strange not to be helping to clear up,' Sally said. It had been a while now since she had been the housekeeper at the Hall although she still tried to help out as much Beth would let her. The Hall's housekeeper positon had been vacant since Sally retired, although as she now lived in the old gardener's cottage in the grounds she still helped out when needed, and worked a few hours a week in their shop in the High Street to keep herself occupied. I knew Beth struggled to keep up with the house upkeep even with everyone pitching in though.

'You have done enough Christmases to earn the break,' Beth told her. She sighed. 'I still can't find anyone who could live up to your standards.' She had met with a few housekeepers but no one she could imagine living with the family.

Emily re-joined us then, easing into a chair. 'Well, Iona is zonked out, and I know the feeling,' Emily said, her velvet dress fitting her hourglass figure like a glove.

'I'd quite happily have a nap,' I agreed. There was something about eating that much at lunch time that made you very sleepy. I glanced at Dad and John who looked like they might nod off any second.

Emily's phone vibrated with a message then. 'Merry Christmas from Brodie's sister, that's sweet. I kept trying to get Anna to join us but she's been working in a bar in Glasgow and couldn't get any time off. His parents came for a meal with us last night and then are going to see her, and have lunch at her pub.'

'She went through five jobs last year Brodie said, I think?' Beth asked her.

Emily agreed with a nod. 'Brodie gets worried about her. She's always moving to new places and trying new jobs, and then getting fired or getting bored. She can't seem to settle,' she said. 'I don't understand why. She's a lovely girl.'

'Shame she can't come to Glendale, we'd soon sort her out,' Caroline said, firmly. I suspected Caroline could sort most people out if they let her.

'That's an idea,' Emily said, brightening up. 'Maybe she could come and stay with us for a while. I don't have any work at the bakery though but I'm sure we could find her something.'

'She could help out around here while you're still without a housekeeper,' I suggested to Beth. I could see Emily was worried and desperate to help as she always tried to do for people, it seemed like a win-win to me.

'I'm always in need of help,' Beth agreed. 'If she's not happy in Glasgow…'

'I'll talk to Brodie,' Emily said. 'We can ask her. Thanks, guys!'

Brodie, Rory and Drew joined us then with our hot drinks. 'Have you all seen what's happening outside?' Brodie asked us, nodding at the window.

Izzy jumped up to open the curtains that covered the large, front-facing window, and we all stared at the thick sheets of snow falling down outside.

'We'd better not stay too late,' Rory commented. 'We might not make it down the drive otherwise.'

'Well, I hope you've got enough toilet rolls in,' Beth said with a laugh.

'We're well-stocked,' I replied, smiling.

After coffee and once all the presents were opened, we played a couple of board games before I said we should get going, getting nervous about Rory having to drive through the snow in the dark. It took another half an hour to actually leave what with all the hugging and kissing that accompanied our leaving, Beth pressing as much food as she could into our hands and Harry crying after all the excitement, but we finally all got into the jeep and set off slowly for the farm, unsure if we'd be back at Glendale Hall for any more celebrations over the next few days.

'You have to make it for Hogmanay,' Izzy pleaded when we said goodbye. We always attended the fireworks party at the Hall.

'Even if we have to come on horseback,' Rory told her, making my dad look at me in horror. 'Heather is quite the horsewoman now.'

'Around the farm maybe,' I said dryly. I hadn't made it off our land on Prince yet and wasn't exactly eager to either. 'I hope we can still get to Broomwood,' I added quietly, worried about the snow.

'Me too,' Beth said. 'Call me tomorrow, okay? Let me know you guys are coping all right. If you need us...'

'It goes without saying,' I promised, but if the snow became too bad, I knew they wouldn't be able to get to the farm.

The farm came into view finally and I relaxed a little that we'd made it home at last. We drove slowly up the driveway, snow covering everything as far as the eye could see. As we parked in the yard, I saw Angus's cottage light was on, and I was relieved that he was safe and well. I hoped he hadn't been too lonely today. I glanced at my dad who was helping Harry out of his car seat, happy that he'd agreed to come and live with us, not wanting him to be like Angus on his own, and knowing my mother wouldn't have wanted that for him either.

I had promised her that I would look after my dad, and even though at the time it had felt like I was giving up on something, I realised as we made a run for it through the snow to the farmhouse, it had actually turned out to be quite the opposite.

Chapter Thirty-Four

'What was that?' Rory asked as he stood by the back door early on December 27th, shaking the snow off his boots all over the tiled floor.

'What was what?' I asked from my crouched position, helping Harry into a second jumper. It was freezing. The snow had continued all through Boxing Day confining us to the house save for essential farm chores, and we'd had a cosy evening in by the fire with party food and sweets, a few bottles of wine and catching up on all the Christmas TV specials. Angus had even joined us, and it had been lots of fun. This morning, it was easing off a little although the snow was piled up inches high everywhere and there was a fierce wind blowing around the hill, howling around the house.

'It sounds like the quad bike,' he said, listening.

'What's wrong?' Dad asked when he walked in to see us standing in silence looking at one another.

'I heard that!' I cried, the definite sounds of an engine revving coming to my ears.

'Angus is up the hill,' he said with a frown. 'Oh, God!' he cried, rushing for the door.

'Stay with Grandad,' I said to Harry and tore after him, realising a second after Rory what was happening. We raced to the barn to see someone on our quad bike coming out of it. Rory jumped in front of him and he swerved the bike to a stop.

'Luke?' I asked as the teenage boy looked up to see us, panic registering on his face. I recognised him from the village – he was often hanging around the shops with his mates. I knew that Brodie had tried to encourage them to join the church youth club but had been rebuffed.

'Get off my bike now,' Rory roared, coming towards him. He grabbed the handle as Luke reluctantly slid off. He made to run but Rory grabbed his collar of his coat. 'Give me one reason I shouldn't call the police on you.'

'I was paid to steal it!' he cried in a panic. 'Please,' he added, looking at me. 'I needed the money, I didn't want to do it.'

'Paid?' I asked, exchanging a puzzled look with Rory. 'By who? Tell us, Luke.'

He hung his head. 'Some guy in a suit staying at the pub. He's been paying me to do things around here. Said you were meddling in his business. That you needed teaching a lesson.'

There was no one else that it could be. 'Stewart?'

'Jesus, that man,' Rory said, still holding Luke's coat. 'What else? What else did he pay you to do for him?' he demanded.

'Just some silly things. Said he wanted you to feel like things were going wrong...' he said, glancing at me. 'That you didn't belong here. And you needed to realise it.'

'What did he get you to do?' I asked, the past couple of weeks clicking to place. I knew that Stewart had been desperate for me to work with him, and to take him back, and that he was furious I wouldn't do either and had tried to stop his development, so he had clearly decided to make as much go wrong on the farm as possible to try to persuade me that I didn't want to be here anymore.

'I led one of the cows down to the mud, and let out a pig from the barn, I left the gate to the field open too, and I made a hole in the fence to the goats' paddock. He asked me to steal this today… paid me double to do it too.'

'I thought he was leaving for Christmas?' All the things I had worried I had caused, it turned out that Stewart had been behind them all. To try to make me feel like I couldn't make a success of this life, to try to manipulate me to come and work with him. I really had been as naïve as Stewart had accused me of being.

'He said he was staying until this was all sorted,' Luke said with a shrug.

'Sorted?' Rory snorted. 'Bloody cheek of the man.'

I was seething with anger. 'I can't believe he would do this.' I remembered him threatening us after finding out we'd proposed Hilltop be listed. He had escalated things from minor annoyances to theft to teach us a lesson. Well, me anyway.

'Right, Luke, clear off now. I'm calling your parents about this. And if I see you on my property again, I will call the police,' Rory said, letting Luke go. Luke's eyes widened in fear. 'Do you understand?'

'Yes, sir,' he stuttered. 'I'm sorry,' he said, breaking into a run, hightailing it down the driveway and off the farm.

'I'm sorry,' I said to Rory when we were alone.

'For what?' he asked, surprised.

'For Stewart. I had no idea he would stoop as low as this.' I shook my head, furious. He really thought that making me feel useless on the farm would push me into his arms. And as that hadn't worked, he was now trying to scare us into backing down over Hilltop. 'Well, there is no way he's getting away with this!'

'What can we do? We have no proof for the police…'

'We can't just let him carry on doing things like this. What if it gets worse? Who does he think he is?' He had no right to do this. I had realised how manipulative and controlling he had been with me, and I now knew he was not only ambitious but ruthless too. He had no idea though how different I was to the woman he had loved years ago. I had Rory and Harry now, and they meant the world to me and I was not going to let him hurt either of them. 'This is our home, we have to protect it,' I said firmly, stalking back into the farmhouse where I pulled my coat off the hook. My dad and Harry were at the table, and looked up as I slammed the door open.

'Heather, what are you doing?' Rory said, coming in after me.

'I'm going to have it out with him,' I replied, pulling my coat on. 'I'll ride into Glendale.'

'By yourself?' he asked, taken aback.

I hesitated for a moment but I pushed my anxiety away. 'I have to do this, Rory. He's messing with my family and that is not okay.'

'I really don't think…' he began, coming towards me but I had yanked the door back open already. 'Let me come with you at least!'

'No, you stay here and call Luke's parents. And let the police know even though I doubt they'll do anything. And maybe find a lock for our barn. I need to do this by myself, okay?' I reached up to kiss him quickly and then I went over to give Harry a kiss too. 'I love you guys.'

'Heather,' my dad began, looking concerned.

'I'll be fine,' I promised them, hoping that I was telling the truth.

'Please be careful,' Rory called after me as I went back out into the snow. 'Your mummy is both stubborn and incredible,' I heard him say to Harry, which made me smile as I went to the stables. I thought about my mother's letter then, which I had pretty much memorised now.

I also know that once you find your place, you will do everything you can not to lose it – she had written.

And she couldn't have been more right.

The snow had eased into gentle flakes drifting on the breeze as I rode into Glendale village. I had been too nervous to go faster than a walk on Prince, but the roads had thankfully been empty as everyone stayed at home to wait out the snowfall. It being the holidays, even fewer people were in the mood to brave the weather than usual, and everyone was well stocked on supplies for the season anyway. So, I didn't pass anyone as I took the shorter way on horseback over our hill and then through the small wood at the edge of the farm, which led out onto the road to the High Street. I could see Glendale Hall in the distance as I rode past but I didn't stop off, I was too eager to confront Stewart. I was amazed at how comfortable I felt on Prince now, and Rory had been right about being able to ride being a blessing in such weather. Although he had assumed I'd stick to our land when it happened I think.

The village had been ploughed and gritted so once I made it there, riding was easier. The snow was pushed back to the edges of the road; there were even a few signs of life with a couple of cars parked on the High Street, and a family walking into the pub.

'Heather!'

I turned around surprised to see Emily standing by the gate to the vicarage, waving at me. I rode over to her.

'Rory called us to watch out for you,' she said as I approached. She was wearing a fake fur coat, polo neck jumper, jeans and boots, her arms wrapped around across her chest. 'We could look after the horse?'

'That would be great,' I replied, sliding out of the saddle, lifting the reins over and leading Prince up to her. I guessed Rory had been more concerned about me riding alone than he'd let on and had called Emily and Brodie to make sure I was okay. 'Did he tell you what's been going on?' I asked as she opened up the gate to let us inside their front garden, which was carpeted in white.

'I can't believe what your ex has been doing, I'm so sorry. Are you sure you're okay to go and see him alone, I could come or Brodie would?'

'I'll be fine,' I reassured her as I tied up Prince around her fence. 'I promise,' I added seeing her bite her lip anxiously.

'Well if you're sure… knock as soon as you come back, you'll need a hot drink and something to eat before you ride back. Shall I get him some water? I have carrots and apples too.' Smiling, I told her what to give Prince, thanked her for her help and headed out of the gate, walking towards Glendale Arms, feeling forever grateful that I had friends like Emily.

The pub was a haven from the cold weather, the warmth and merry noise welcome signs as I walked through the door.

'Hi, Heather,' the landlord said cheerfully from behind the bar when he spotted me. 'No Rory with you today?'

'No, I've come to see one of your guests actually,' I replied. 'Stewart. Is he upstairs?'

'No, actually, he's in the back room having breakfast. You can go through,' Malcolm added with a wave.

'Thanks,' I replied, slipping through behind the bar. The pub was small but had some bed and breakfast rooms although they were usually empty this time of year, most visitors only coming in summer for walking the Highlands. So Stewart was, as I expected, alone in the small dining room, sat at a table with a plate of eggs and bacon, sipping a coffee.

He looked up, startled to see me, but broke into a smile. He wore a cashmere jumper, dark jeans, his shoes polished and his face clean shaven. It was annoying how well put together he looked when I could tell my hair was frizzy from the weather, my nose felt red raw, and my boots were caked with mud. 'I would have thought you were snowed in at the farm, the landlord said most of Glendale is stuck inside,' he added conversationally, gesturing for me to sit down, as if the last time I had seen him he hadn't come to the farm to yell at Rory and me, not to mention doing everything Luke had told us he had done to us. He really was shameless.

I sat down, folding my arms on the table. 'Well, you would know what the snow is like at the farm, wouldn't you? Considering your lackey has been there so often.'

Stewart frowned. 'What lackey?'

I leaned forward. 'Luke.'

His face turned pale but he tried to front it out. 'I have no idea who you're talking about.'

'Oh, really? Well let me refresh your memory then. Luke is the kid from the village who you've been paying to sabotage my farm, and I'm here to tell you I won't let you do this anymore. This stops right now.'

Chapter Thirty-Five

'Look, whatever this boy has told you...'

'Enough lies!' I snapped, my patience completely evaporated. 'We just caught him red-handed trying to steal our quad bike. He told us everything. If you're going to do petty things like you've been doing, you could at least have the decency to own up to them.'

Stewart dropped his gaze from mine. 'I promise you it wasn't me. I knew about it and I didn't stop it okay, but this... all of it, it was all my father.'

I stared at him. 'What's your father got to do with this?'

'Everything! He's my business partner.'

'He is?' I thought about the elusive business partner of his, the other man in the suit that people had seen around Glendale. I shook my head. It was all starting to make sense. I thought about how I had felt like I'd failed when I first saw Stewart again, all his talk of success, and now it appeared he hadn't done it by himself after all.

He looked rather sheepish. 'Yes, and when he found out you'd made the listing proposal, he frankly hit the roof. I am sorry for coming to the farm and talking to you like I did but I'd had him on the phone for almost an hour ranting and raving at me, calling in our lawyer, and I took it out on you. You know he's never been easy to deal with, he expects so much, and he is furious that the site I proposed for our hotel is causing us so many problems.

That's why he got Luke involved. To encourage you to listen to me, to come on board and not get in our way. He was furious when he saw you on *Countryside Watch*. Told me I'd let our plan get away from me. That you were becoming too successful to want to work with me, and I knew he was right.' He hung his head. 'And when he found out our proposal was on hold, it was the last straw. He said he was going to sabotage your farm. So he told Luke to steal the bike, and he had a whole list of things he wanted him to do. He thought he could threaten you into changing your mind and supporting our development.'

I had certainly not warmed to Stewart's father when we had met back at university but I hadn't thought he could be this nasty. 'Why would you run a business with this man?' I asked incredulously.

He looked down at the table. 'Because I couldn't get a loan from the bank without him on board, he has a lot of sway, sway that I just don't have. I should have tried to stop him, I know that. But I was selfish... I wanted you to come and work with me so I turned a blind eye to it. I really am sorry, Heather.'

I leaned back, watching him. He seemed sincere with his apology. 'I'll have to go to the police if he does anything again, and tell them who's responsible, you know that, right? You're trying to buy a piece of land, but you're threatening my home in the process. I can't just let that happen, Stewart.'

He met my gaze. 'I know, I'll talk to him, I promise. He's so focused on money, he has these blinkers on, and thinks he can do whatever he likes to get what he wants. He was the one who came up with the idea for the holiday cottages, I told him it was too close to your land but he didn't listen. I was too... proud to tell you that when you came here that day and saw the plans. God, he always gets his own way! Look at what he did to you and me.'

'What do you mean?' I asked.

'I wanted to come here, to be with you, when you asked me to but he told me he'd disown me if I did. He told me to stay in Edinburgh, to do my apprenticeship, to forget you. Otherwise he would cut me off. And I was weak and did what he asked. I suppose that's why when I saw Hilltop for sale, I persuaded him that it was the perfect site for us. I wanted to have a second chance with you. I've always missed you, and regretted walking away from you. But I know now that I destroyed any chance of that happening.' He looked down at the table, and I thought back to the last conversation we had had. It suddenly made a whole lot more sense.

—

'I told you, I can't leave my dad,' I said, tearfully on the phone. I sat in my bedroom in Glendale, the rain pouring down outside, as I explained again why I felt I had to stay at home. We'd spoken the day before, and it had ended in an argument, but I hoped he would change his mind about coming to be with me.

'I can't give up this opportunity here,' Stewart said, his voice low. 'What would I even do in Glendale? I love you so much but this was what we had planned.'

'Plans change!' I cried. 'You could find something here, you have a first-class degree.'

'You don't understand the pressure I'm under. I have to succeed, Heather. I can't walk away from this apprenticeship.' He sounded weary.

Tears rolled down my cheeks. 'But you're happy to walk away from me?'

Stewart sighed. 'Not happy. Of course I'm not happy! Maybe in a few weeks you'll feel like coming to Edinburgh. Your dad needs you right now but he won't forever.'

'Everything has changed,' I whispered, my heart breaking all over again.

'I wish it hadn't.' There was a voice in the background. 'Look, I have to go.'

'What? But we haven't sorted this out, Stewart. You can't just end it like this.'

There was a short silence before he spoke again. 'I have to,' he said firmly. 'I can't come to Glendale. I need to follow my plans through. I'm sorry, Heather but I think this is for the best.'

'But you said we were soul mates.'

'Honestly, I'm not sure I believe in soul mates now.' He hung up, and I cried for what seemed like hours.

–

I always thought it had been easy for him to say goodbye whereas I had grieved all over again losing him from my life so soon after my mother. Now I realised that his father had been in the background telling him that he had to let me go.

I found myself feeling more sympathy for Stewart than I had since he'd arrived in Glendale. What must it be like to have such a domineering presence in your life? I was thankful once again for the support of my own parents, and was determined to be like them with Harry, and not like Stewart's father. 'It sounds to me like you need to cut ties with him but that's something you need to decide for yourself. Just please stop him from trying to hurt us, okay?'

'Whatever else, my dad puts reputation above everything, so now you've found out what he's been doing, he will back off. He won't want you telling anyone, he will lose investors if they know the kind of tactics he's willing to use in business. Trust me. I know I haven't given you any cause to but I'll make sure he doesn't try to hurt your farm again. I promise.'

I nodded. 'Do you think he can walk away from Hilltop though?'

'I hope I can persuade him to. I've lost all interest in this venture. Now that I know you won't be part of it…' He trailed off. 'And I don't think the council will approve it now anyway, not when it might be listed. My dad knows that buildings under conservation are too much of a headache for a project like this. I suppose I'd better start looking for a new site for us.' He didn't look happy about the prospect.

'Maybe you need to re-think working with him,' I suggested. It was funny how you could have this picture of someone but then discover that underneath, they were very different. I always thought that Stewart was far more confident than I was, that he was my superior to be honest, but now I understood that he had his own issues. We all had things that people didn't know about going on, and just because someone showed you something on the surface, it didn't mean that was what was happening below it too. For a moment, my heart did go out to him. He looked so lost, and lonely. Even though I struggled sometimes, I wasn't alone. Far from it. And I needed to make sure that I remembered that.

'Maybe.' He sighed. 'I really am sorry for everything, Heather.'

I stood up, feeling weary. I knew he meant his apology but it would take a long time to forgive him for what he'd tried to do to us. 'Goodbye, Stewart,' I said, walking out of the room and heading back to Emily's, my heart heavy.

—

After a cup of tea and slice of cake with Emily, I felt a little bit better and began my ride back to the farm. The snow had ceased but Glendale was still quiet, carpeted in white, and from my seat up high on Prince I took a photo of the village for Instagram, telling my followers I'd ridden alone for the first time. Even though it hadn't been for an enjoyable reason, I had to mark the moment for myself. And now I had confronted Stewart, I could enjoy the ride back home.

When I reached the gate at the bottom of our field, Rory, Angus, my dad and Harry all appeared to greet me, and opened it up to let me through. I was touched to see them all there, and I gave them a cheerful wave as I approached.

'Thank God you're back in one piece,' Rory said, taking Prince's reins to hold him steady as I climbed out of the saddle.

'I told you she'd be fine,' Angus grunted at him, giving me a nod. I smiled at him, appreciating his support.

'Hi, darling,' I said as Harry ran to hug me when I hit the ground. I was proud of myself I thought as we walked into the yard, not only for riding into the village alone, but for talking to Stewart. I'd often shied away from difficult conversations in the past. Now I felt like I could face them head on. 'That was actually kind of fun,' I said, patting Prince grateful that he had looked after me. 'Well, not seeing Stewart but the ride.'

'What happened?' Rory asked, touching the small of my back as we walked towards the stables. I held Harry's hand tightly, making sure that he wouldn't slip on the snow.

'Well, Stewart told me that his father is his business partner, and that he's the one who has behind everything that's been going on around here. He was furious about us putting a pause on their plans, so he paid Luke to try to sabotage us, hoping he would make us back off. To be honest, his dad sounds pretty terrible,' I replied. 'Stewart told me now we know the truth, his father will be worried about us exposing his tactics so will leave us alone. I think Stewart realises that they should walk away. Let's hope he can persuade his father to realise the same thing.'

'Sounds like his father has been calling all the shots then. Stewart needs to man up by the sounds of it,' Rory replied, handing Prince's reins to Angus when we reached the stables. 'Caroline called while you were out. Her council contact told her that Stewart and his dad offered William £250,000 to buy Hilltop.'

'If only we had that kind of money,' I mused. 'You know what I was thinking when I was riding Prince? About what Julie the presenter of *Countryside Watch* said – that so many people would love to live in a place like this. That people have connected with my Instagram photos because they too have struggles in their life. I thought about how far I've come living here, I mean I never thought I could be a farmer, yet here I am. Maybe Julie is right. Maybe there are others who would like to try this life out, you know? Escape the city, and come here,' I said, gesturing around us. 'Get back to nature. To leave their problems for a few days. Recharge. Get some good Scottish air in their lungs,' I added with a smile.

'It's idyllic out here,' my dad agreed. 'I honestly think my back is better from all the walking I've been doing since I came to stay too.'

'Exactly. I think people would pay to come on a farm retreat, I'm sure of it,' I said, watching Angus take the saddle off Prince. 'Especially stressed-out mothers in need of some self-care,' I added with a wry smile, knowing from the messages on social media I now received every day that there were a lot of women living with the same anxiety and worries as me.

'If you owned Hilltop, people could hire the farm-house out,' Angus said a minute later, as I had turned to go into our house. I paused to look at him as he led Prince into his stable. 'It would be ideal for a retreat. And if you brought sheep back there, then it would be a working farm too. A real money-maker I think, with you in charge of it, Heather.'

I gaped at him. I couldn't deny that the idea did excite me. It might not be the design business I had thought of but I could still use my design skills, and I really believed it could help people too. I breathed in the fresh air around me, and knew that people would love to get away from their lives to a place like this.

'If only we had the money to buy it, huh?' Rory said. 'Come on, I need a strong cuppa,' he added.

'And cake!' Harry said, clapping his hands. He was my son, after all.

'What is it with you lot and cake?' my dad asked with a laugh, following Rory into the farmhouse. I trailed after them, thinking about what Angus had said, and wishing that I could make it happen somehow.

Chapter Thirty-Six

The snow had cleared away enough for me to be able to get our jeep out of the driveway the following day so our planned trip to Broomwood Castle could go ahead. I drove to Glendale Hall with Harry to pick up Beth and Izzy, and Emily met us there with Iona. It was a grey day, still bitterly cold, snow still lining surfaces, but we were used to this weather and were all bundled up in layers, and carried thermoses of hot coffee and tea in our bags. We piled into my car and set off, music and heating on, for the drive through the countryside.

I remembered the first time I had gone to the castle with my parents, I had been really young and it had been a hot summer's day, and I remembered running through the grass, my mum helping me to make a daisy chain, the castle rising up in the background behind us. And then came the less pleasant memory of being there on a rainy day with my father to scatter my mother's ashes in the rose garden, her favourite spot, feeling like the sun would never come out again.

As we approached, I could see the grey tower rising up above the sloping hills. It was a place straight out of a fairy-tale, you could imagine a princess up there looking out for her prince charming, knights on their white horses patrolling the gardens below. 'Right out of a book, Iz,' I said, glancing back at her watching out of the car window as I pulled into the car park. Broomwood dated back to the seventeenth century and stood in a national park with stunning views all around. 'This was my mum's favourite place in Scotland.'

'I feel like I'm in *I Capture the Castle*,' Izzy replied as she climbed out of the car, looking up at it in awe. That was one of our favourite books, and my mother had loved it too. I had been so pleased when Izzy had loved it after I recommended it to her.

'This was one of my mother's favourite places, which is why I wanted to come here today. She wrote me a letter,' I said to Beth and Emily as we walked towards the entrance, Izzy taking Harry's hand in front, Emily pushing Iona in her pushchair. 'I found it when I went to get her Glendale research. It had been in a box up in the loft for all this time.'

'Wow, Heather, that must have been so emotional,' Emily said, looking across at me.

'I could barely read it through the tears,' I agreed. 'She somehow knew I needed her advice, that I might be feeling unsure, and honestly what she said was exactly what I needed to hear.'

'How is it mothers always seem to know how to do that?'

'I'm not sure mine always does,' Beth said with a shrug. 'Often I did the opposite of what she said. God, I hope Izzy doesn't do the same thing.'

'You guys are too close for that,' I told her, hoping Harry and I would be also. We paid and walked through into the courtyard. It was quiet today thanks to the chilly weather so we strolled around peacefully. 'One of the things my mum said in her letter was that she had regretted only having a small wedding to my dad, that her heart had always hoped to get married right here,' I said as we walked inside the grand hall, my voice echoing in the large space.

'I can see why, it's beautiful,' Emily said as we went into the grand function room. 'She didn't have a big white wedding then?'

'No, they went to Gretna Green.'

'It's funny – I had always thought I would have had a big church wedding but I knew that wasn't right for me and Drew. I loved getting married at home.'

'Glendale Hall is really special,' Emily agreed with Beth. 'I wanted to have our wedding there, after the church, because it meant so much. It was my sanctuary when I needed it. And it feels like my second home. I think getting married somewhere that has a special meaning is the icing on the cake, so to speak.' She turned to me. 'I understand why your mum missed out on doing that although I'm sure she was really happy marrying your dad that day regardless.'

'Exactly,' I agreed as we found ourselves in the pretty chapel. I imagined her at the altar in a white dress with my father, and I was sorry she had never got to do that. 'I have been so unsure about getting married to Rory because she can't be with me,' I said, my voice cracking a little as I thought about it. 'In her letter, she said she had never planned on getting married and having a family but they had almost been even sweeter because they had been so unexpected, and I realised that that's how I feel about Rory and Harry. It's all happened so quickly that I've been trying to get my head around it all, and worrying that I might lose them somehow but I don't know, reading her letter made me realise that all you can do is treasure the things you love while you have them, none of us know the future but we do know what we have today. Does that make sense?'

'Yes, and you're going to make me cry,' Emily said. 'It's been exactly the same for me! I met Brodie when I was still with Greg, and I was pregnant with his baby, I never expected any of that to happen. And I'm glad I didn't because I think I would have run in the opposite direction,' she said, shaking her head. 'But somehow, it all worked out. I have Brodie and Iona, Greg is doing really well, and I'm happy. Really happy.'

'Heather, there's no way I would have planned to get pregnant at sixteen, or lose Drew for ten years, but I feel like I needed that to happen to bring me to this point today,' Beth said, reaching out to give my hand a squeeze. 'Look at them,' she said, pointing to Izzy helping Harry to climb onto a pew, Iona sleeping peacefully in her pushchair next to them. 'No matter what, we did something pretty good with our lives, right?'

I wiped a stray tear that had fallen down my cheek. 'When Rory proposed to me at New Year, I was terrified. I told him I needed time, but it was like my mum gave us her blessing in that letter. She said that you should marry someone you admire, who you feel is a better person than you, so you can be a better person because of them. That's exactly how I feel about Rory!'

'Let's face it, Drew is a far better person than me,' Beth said with a laugh. 'He's patient and kind, he saves people's lives for a living, and he forgave me for not telling him about Izzy for ten years. I mean, I lucked out with him, I really did.'

'And I married a vicar!' Emily said, still surprised by this. 'He was so understanding about Greg, and he treats Iona like his own. I am really blessed too.'

'Why are you all crying?' Izzy asked then, looking up at us with a frown.

'Because we're happy,' her mother replied. 'It really would be beautiful to get married here,' Beth said, looking around. 'It's such a shame your mum didn't get to have her dream wedding.'

'Oh my God,' Emily cried, startling us all. 'Oops, sorry, about the God word here,' she added, glancing at the altar. 'But you know you've been holding back from saying yes to Rory because you'll miss your mother?' she said, turning to me. 'What better way to have her with you on the day than if you got married right here? Like she wanted to do!'

'That would be amazing,' Beth cried. 'She would look down on you and feel so proud, I'm sure of it. If she can't be with you then marrying in the place she wished she had, is the next best thing. Rory is your One, isn't he?'

I thought about Stewart and how the person I was back when I loved him was a completely different person to who I was now. Rory had helped me become more confident in myself, he supported me, looked after me, loved me, had given me Harry, a home that challenged me but one that I loved and wanted to protect so fiercely, and he made me laugh, and just wanted me to be myself. He wanted me to be happy, I knew. And the fire I had felt when I had first kissed him still burned brightly. He was my One, I knew it. And it both thrilled and terrified me to know that. 'Forever,' I told her. I looked up to the altar. 'You're right, getting married here would be the perfect way to have my mother be part of the day,' I said.

'Are we going to have another wedding?' Izzy asked. 'I might start charging for my bridesmaid services, I've been asked so many times now.'

We laughed. 'We do seem to love weddings as a group,' Beth said. 'I'll be sad not to arrange this one though if you have it here. Maybe I need to start up that wedding business at the Hall…' she mused.

'Unless Rory has changed his mind,' I said, suddenly nervous. I had kept him waiting for almost a year, after all.

'Absolutely not,' Emily said firmly. 'He adores you.'

'I'm never getting married,' Izzy said then. 'Boys are gross and besides, I just want to write books.'

'You can still be a writer and be in love,' Beth said with a smile. 'If you find the right man then they will never hold you back, they will want you to be successful, and will support you all the way.' Emily nodded in agreement, and I smiled, thinking of how Rory had been there for me these past years. I wanted him to know how much I appreciated him.

'We'll remind you of this when you come to us head over heels in a few years' time,' Beth warned Izzy as we left the chapel and went in search of the café.

'Not going to happen,' Izzy protested. 'I have all the romance I need in books. Real life could never compare.'

I had thought exactly like her when I was her age. But now I knew when you found the right person then it could compare.

And it was time that I went after my own happy ending.

Chapter Thirty-Seven

In the castle café, we found a corner table, and sat down with drinks and sandwiches, peeling off our coats, soon getting warm and cosy. Izzy pulled out her book to which her mum rolled her eyes. I handed Harry pieces of a ham sandwich, and Beth put Iona into the highchair we had found while Emily bought her food.

'Em, what are you doing with tea?' Beth asked in mock horror as Emily sat down with her tray. Like me and Beth, Emily was usually a coffee drinker.

'I just didn't fancy coffee. I don't know the past couple of mornings, I haven't enjoyed it…' She trailed off, her cheeks turning bright pink.

'Oh my God,' Beth said slowly, catching on to something.

'What?' I asked, none the wiser to what was passing between them. Even Izzy looked up from her book, interested.

'When Emily was expecting Iona, she went right off coffee, remember?' Beth asked me. 'Are you feeling well?'

'Yes,' Emily said quickly, then paused to consider. 'I have been pretty tired but I put that down to all the wedding preparations and then it's been so busy at the bakery in the run up to Christmas, you know?'

'Could you be?' I asked her, taking a bite of my tuna melt.

'Could you be what?' Izzy asked, frowning, still confused.

'Pregnant,' Beth said. She didn't really keep much from Izzy.

'I suppose I could be, I mean we haven't been trying or anything but I never went back on the pill after having Iona,' Emily said, looking at her little girl. She smiled. 'Brodie will be thrilled.' Then her face dropped. 'But how am I going to cope?' She looked at us, suddenly panicked.

I knew that feeling well. 'Of course you will cope,' I said immediately. 'Didn't we just say that the most unexpected things have been our favourite ones?' I reminded her, passing Harry a crisp as he held out his hand to me. 'You're always terrified when things are about to change, that's only natural, but this change will be a good thing, won't it?'

'Why are you so good at advising other people but not yourself?' Beth asked me suddenly. I felt all their eyes on me and I had no idea how to respond. It was true that my advice to Emily came easily but if I was the one who thought she might be pregnant again, I would have reacted just the same way as she had.

'Because you see things more clearly when they're not happening to you,' I replied.

'Well, that's true,' Beth said. 'Listen, you're both going to be fine. Heather, you're going to get married, and Em, you're going to be a mother again, and I'll be right here on hand to help you guys, we all will so there's nothing to worry about.'

'What about you?' Emily asked, clearly wishing Beth was going through some change of her own to make us feel better still.

Beth thought for a moment. 'I'm going to start a wedding business and I'm going to hire Brodie's sister as our new housekeeper.' She shrugged. 'I think that's more than enough for all of us to be starting the New Year with, don't you think?' She held up her coffee cup. 'We've said it before but I think it needs saying again, we can get through anything together, right?' Emily and I exchanged a look before we clinked our mugs against hers, Izzy joining in, and Harry holding up his plastic beaker trying to reach across the table. I clinked my cup against his, his little smile more than enough reassurance that Beth was right – we were a tight group, and we were all that we needed as we moved to not only another year, but more change on the horizon.

'Actually, I already know how you can all help,' I said as I gulped down the rest of my coffee. 'I've had an idea…'

–

Rory and I were mucking out the stables the day before Hogmanay. The snow had almost all cleared away now, instead a light drizzle floated down from the dark sky. Rory sprayed his hose at my wellies. 'Missed a bit,' he said with a grin when I yelped in protest.

I lifted my pitchfork with hay stuck to it and brandished it at him. 'You want this over your head? It's dirty hay, by the way,' I threatened.

He held up his hands in peace. 'That rhymed,' he said with a laugh. I couldn't help but smile. 'So, you were telling me about this retreat idea?'

'I was,' I said, dumping the hay off the pitchfork. 'I keep thinking how stressful it can be, just modern life, and that being outside really does help. The animals, they take you out of your own head, don't they? Look at how I couldn't even go near a horse and now I ride Prince. I used to sometimes have panic attacks too but I realised today, I haven't had one since Harry was born. I mean, I still worry all the time but I know now that I am capable, I'm learning to believe in myself more. And maybe other people can do that here too.'

'It's a good idea,' Rory agreed, filling up the water trough. 'Whenever I've had something on my mind, it's helped being out here with the animals and the open air, for sure. Like when I thought you thought us sleeping together was a huge mistake, I rode Duke all over the farm, and I realised that if I didn't ask you then I'd never know, and that was better than torturing myself with possible outcomes.' He shrugged when I turned to look at him, surprised. It was rare that he admitted to worrying, and I didn't know he had felt that way about us at the start of our relationship. 'But I just don't think we could get a loan to not only buy Hilltop but also set up another business.'

'What if you had help?'

We both jumped as Angus seem to float in from the shadows. For someone as big as him, he managed to go unnoticed a lot of the time. 'Help?' I repeated.

'To buy Hilltop.' He leaned against a pole and regarded us both. 'I was thinking… I want to keep it as farmland as much as you do. We keep talking about bringing back sheep and they can graze over there plus Heather you could set up these retreats you mentioned. And I can help across both farms, wherever I'm needed. I could give you money towards a deposit, I have a fair bit and it's just sitting in the bank.' He shrugged.

Rory looked at me and I stared back, stunned. He cleared his throat. 'Angus, mate, that's very generous—'

'I don't have a family to leave it to. My sister doesn't need my money, and I'd rather see it put to use before I go anyhow,' he said.

Rory was stumped into silence again. 'I mean, that's not true,' I said, touched. 'You are family to us, Angus.' Oh, God, he looked like he might cry after I said that.

'Speaking of family,' my dad said, walking into the stables with Harry. They'd popped into Glendale with supplies for the shop now that it was open again after the heavy snowfall. We all turned to him this time. 'Did you think I would just sell our house and not give you any of the money?' he asked me. 'Half of it is yours anyway, from your mother, and you can have it as soon as we sell it. I can have the other half, not that I need all of that living here… And I can help out at Hilltop too, with Angus. We should keep these farms for the future. For this little one, and whoever comes after him,' he said, pointing to Harry who had rushed over to see the horses. I loved seeing how his face lit up in their presence, it confirmed once again that growing up here made him happy.

'Are you sure, Dad?' I asked, marvelling at these two men offering us so much.

'Of course!'

'Wow…' I turned to Rory. 'You know what else? I've had a few companies reach out to me on Instagram about doing some sort of collaboration, we could probably get one of them to sponsor the retreat or give us equipment… I mean, it's a definite possibility.' I was starting to feel excited by this idea. It was hard not to.

'Are you sure we can take this on though?' Rory asked me. 'You said yourself that we have so much going on already – another farm would be a lot of work even if we hired more staff, I don't want you to be stressed.'

It was strange but I felt more eager than nervous about it. Maybe because I felt like these retreats could really help people, especially women like me, and that the past few weeks had shown me how much I loved this farm even if it was hard work, and even if I was still learning how everything should work. And most of all, I wanted to protect it for Harry and our future as a family. Rory had been amazing taking it all on as a teenager, he couldn't lose it now. 'I can do it if I have you all with me,' I said. 'I thought I needed to have all the answers but I don't, I just need people that I can ask questions of, if I need to. But do you think that William would sell us Hilltop?'

'If he knows what's good for him,' Angus said. 'His uncle would turn in his grave if he doesn't.'

'If we match Stewart's offer then why wouldn't he? Plus, we're happy to buy it even if it is listed.' Rory said. 'We want to keep it as a farm, and conserve the house as it is, whereas they want to tear it down. I know he lives in London but even he has a heart, surely?'

I smiled at his view of city dwellers. 'I suppose all we can do is ask,' I replied.

Chapter Thirty-Eight

Hogmanay dawned clear and crisp, the sky turning a bright blue once the sun finally rose up in the sky – perfect for the night's celebrations to see in the New Year. I felt jittery but in a good way for what I had planned for the night.

I was walking around the farmhouse with Harry, carrying a bucket of water to refresh the chickens' supplies, when I looked up to see a car coming down the drive. Harry walked beside me, both of us in wellies and thick coats. I squinted and let out a sigh when I recognised Stewart's car coming down the track. I wasn't sure I could take any more arguments. 'Come on, Harry, he can come and find us in the chicken shed,' I said, carrying on. The water sloshed out of the bucket as I went down the two steps and walked into the shed.

'Chickens, come here!' Harry said, cheerfully, when we entered. They did not helpfully 'come here' but scattered instead as we walked in.

'Naughty chickens,' I said. 'Let's fill up their water, will you hold this steady for me?' We went to the water trough and he held it as I smashed some of the ice on top and re-filled it with fresh water. 'Good job,' I told him. 'Now they won't be thirsty, will they? Shall we check on the horses?' We left the chicken shed, and I paused as Stewart rounded the corner and stopped abruptly. He wore a dark overcoat, a scarf wrapped tightly around his neck, his shiny shoes already getting muddy. 'What are you doing here?' I asked, putting the empty bucket down. Harry reached for my free hand, looking a little warily at him, no doubt remembering the last time he had been here. I didn't blame him, I felt the same way.

Stewart looked down at Harry. 'I never asked – did you name him after Harry Potter?'

I raised a small smile. 'I did. We need to check the horses,' I added, setting off again. I needed to get the chores out of the way quickly today and wasn't about to let Stewart slow us down. I led Harry to the stables, Stewart trailing behind. Harry went to stand on the bricks Rory had put out for him so he could reach Prince. The horse leaned over the stable door and Harry reached out to stroke his nose. I pulled out two carrots from the bag hanging by the door and gave one to Prince and Duke. 'So, why did you come?' I asked Stewart as the horses munched on them, Harry fascinated as always by them eating. Stewart stood in the doorway, just as fascinated by what we were doing.

'I don't think I realised…' he said. 'What your life was like out here.' I glanced at him but he seemed more surprised than derogatory this time.

I leaned against the stable door. 'I know you think that somehow I haven't lived up to my potential being here, but you're wrong. I have a man who loves me, a son who I adore, and family and friends who are there for us. This place, it's not what I pictured that's for sure, but it makes you feel important. These animals, they need us, this land, it needs us, and it's hard bloody work, but it's so rewarding.'

'Carrot,' Harry said hopefully.

'They can have one more,' I told him, bringing them over. 'That's it though. Like chocolate for you, it's a treat.' I reached up to Prince and patted him as I gave him the carrot. I wasn't sure when I had fully turned the corner but I wasn't scared of him now. Maybe I realised that he trusted me, so I trusted him in turn. 'I thought I had to carry on with what I had always planned on doing in my life, but I know now that I don't have to force myself to do something just because I wanted to do it once. You can change your mind, you can find things you love without even realising it, without even thinking that you would love them. Maybe I will do more design work in the future, maybe I won't, but I'm not worried now either way. You've made me see that what's really important is being here for my family.'

'I didn't mean to be disparaging about your life, I really didn't,' he insisted. 'I was just so surprised. When I saw you in that newspaper, I think I was jealous.'

'Jealous?' I repeated, unable to believe that he could be jealous of me.

'You had this life that I knew nothing about, that I wasn't part of, you had someone special, and a child, and so maybe I fixated on the fact that you were doing something completely different to what you had said you wanted to, I don't know, to make me feel a little bit better for having none of what you have. Especially when you started getting all this publicity online, and then that TV show. I felt like such a failure compared to you. I haven't loved anyone else the way I loved you but you moved on, you found someone else, someone you clearly love and who makes you happy, and so I clung to what I did have – my business. And I think I hoped I could make you feel… less somehow for not having the same thing.' He shook his head. 'That was wrong of me. I'm sorry.'

'It's weird, isn't it? I've spent the past two years telling myself that I needed to do better, that I wasn't good enough. Of a partner to Rory, of a mother to Harry, that I was failing because I hadn't set up my own business like I said I would, so when you came and basically said all those things, I thought you were right. I've never been confident. I've always been too anxious, too much of a worrier, but I know it and I try really hard to not let it stop me from living my life.' I sucked in a breath, feeling emotional again. 'But I realise now I've been too hard on myself. I kept seeing the things I hadn't done, and not what I *have* done. And now I see you doing exactly the same thing. We're not the same people we were, we haven't done everything we wanted to, but who has? You've got a really successful business, and I've got a family. If you're happy then that's all that matters, surely?'

'It is. But I'm not happy. That's why I came here. I took my unhappiness out on you, and tried to make you feel like a failure. But out of the two of us, it's me who has failed. I was so focused on my business that I let you go and the only person to blame is me.' He sighed. 'I can blame my father, and he hasn't made things easy at all, but I know that I should have stood up to him sooner. I should have done all of it differently. And I can't blame him for that. I can only blame myself. I really am sorry, Heather. Do you think you could ever forgive me?'

'I just wish you could have talked to me instead of trying to disrupt my life here like you have done. I'm scared of losing all of this, you don't even know how scared I am. And you tried to take it from me.' Harry came to me then and I wrapped my arms around him as he leaned against my legs. I was still terrified of not being there for him in the future but I needed to make sure that it didn't stop me from being here for him now.

'I don't think anyone could ever take this from you,' Stewart said. 'I've never seen anyone try so hard to protect something like you have. I wish I cared about something as much.'

'You will,' I promised him. 'If you're open to it coming into your life. What will you do now?'

'I'm going back to Edinburgh with my parents for Hogmanay. I'll talk to my father. Tell him that none of this is what I want. And I'm ready now to go out on my own. I need to. I've let him have too much control over me for too long. I can see that now.'

I smiled. 'I think that sounds like a good plan. Especially today. A fresh start for a new year.'

'What about you? What will this new year bring for you?'

I looked down at Harry. 'I have a few ideas,' I said, not about to tell Stewart what was on the cards tonight. 'But as long as we're healthy and happy then I will call it a successful year.' I met his gaze again. 'Good luck, Stewart. I hope you find happiness.'

He hesitated for a moment before nodding, recognising my words for the goodbye they were. 'Take care, Heather,' he said, turning and walking out of the stables, his head low. I watched him go, amazed that the life I thought he had was so very different in reality. But then it was the same for me too. The difference was that mine had brought me happiness. And I did hope that he found that one day too.

'I'm hungry,' Harry said then, breaking through my thoughts.

'Come on then,' I said, holding out my hand. 'I think we have some muffins from Emily left.' As we walked back to the farmhouse, I saw Stewart's car driving away and it felt as if our past together had been finally laid to rest.

Chapter Thirty-Nine

It was our tradition now to celebrate Hogmanay at Glendale Hall. Beth and her family held an annual party to coincide with the Christmas trail being switched off, ending in a spectacular firework display at the stroke of midnight.

The first time they had held the party was when Beth had returned after ten years living in London, and that had been the night I had slept with Rory for the first time.

And then after last year's party, Rory had proposed to me when we got home. So, the night was definitely always memorable. I hoped that tonight would be no exception.

'Where is everybody?' Rory called upstairs as I put on red lipstick in front of the mirror in our bedroom. It was dark outside, the sky still clear and twinkling with stars, a perfect night for fireworks. 'We passed the ten-minute warning ages ago!' he added.

I glanced at the clock on our bedside table – we were indeed running late as was, let's face it, also our tradition. 'Five minutes!' I called back. 'Right, let's get our shoes and coats on,' I said to Harry who was cross-legged on my bed playing with a teddy. I knew it was crazy to be nervous for tonight but I couldn't help it, I just hoped everything went to plan okay. I helped Harry into his shoes and coat then slipped on my boots, no heels unfortunately as we'd be standing on the grass later, and pulled on my coat. 'How does Mummy look?' I asked as I helped him off the bed. I was wearing dark skinny jeans with a long jumper, my boots, coat and a red scarf to match my lipstick. It was the best I could do trying to keep warm as we'd be outside all night.

'Pretty,' he said. 'Bring lamb?'

'Of course you can.' We went downstairs where Rory was waiting by the door with my dad. 'Is Angus coming?'

'He said he'd better stay here,' Rory replied, opening up the door. 'He really hates parties.' He shrugged with an 'I tried' expression. 'All ready to see the New Year in then?'

'I think it's going to be a good one,' my dad said, throwing me a wink behind Rory's back. I grinned as we filed out of the house into the car. I glanced back at the farm before we set off. I had fought a lot against it these past two years but it was home. And soon it would be home for my father too. Everyone I cared about under one roof. I really hoped my mum was looking down on us proudly.

Glendale Hall was lit up in full splendour when we arrived, the driveway crammed with cars. They welcomed anyone in the village who wanted to join us, and it was a popular night out. We walked around into the grounds where the trail was glittering and people were milling around with drinks, some holding sparklers, kids running around the lawn, others sipping drinks in front of the bonfire John had lit in the centre of the garden.

'You made it,' Beth said, coming over with Drew. 'It's our busiest Hogmanay so far, I think. Most of the village seems to be here. My mum is stressing we don't have enough mulled wine or popcorn, and our lit-up reindeer fell over and broke, but other than that we're okay.'

I smiled. 'Something always has to go wrong but as long as it's not the fireworks not working, we'll be fine.'

'Or any ambulance trips,' she added with a sigh. At the first display, her grandmother had been taken ill and we always had some nerves about anything going wrong like that again. 'Right, Harry, do you want to come and see the bonfire with me?' She held out her hand for him.

'Don, I could do with a hand carrying a barrel of beer out, would you mind?' Drew asked my dad. I hid a smile at how they were trying to be subtle but really failing.

Rory raised an eyebrow at me when we were suddenly alone. 'Something I should know about?'

I feigned innocence. 'No idea. Let's get a drink, shall we?' I needed some Dutch courage to be honest. We went over to the drinks table and Rory got a beer, and I picked up a mulled wine. 'Why don't we walk the trail one last time?' I suggested. We walked in silence, the lights as dazzling as ever, the trail quiet as everyone gathered around the bonfire waiting for the fireworks. 'So, I didn't tell you about my mum's letter. I read it on Christmas morning. And it was as emotional as I thought it would be but it was so wonderful to hear her voice again even though it was only through words.'

'I can imagine.' He took my gloved hand in his.

'She talked about how she knew my dad was the man for her, and a lot of what she said rang true for me. That she admired him as a person, and that's how I feel about you.' I kept my eyes ahead, knowing that if he looked at me I would cry and not be able to tell him what I wanted to. 'She said that once I found my place in the world that I would do everything not to lose it, and she was right. I've found my place with you and Harry, and I have been terrified that I'll lose you and that's made me push you away sometimes when I should have been doing the opposite. I should have pulled you even closer.' I stopped then and finally faced him. 'It was like somehow she knew I would end up falling in love unexpectedly, that I'd find myself somewhere I wasn't expecting to, and that I would be worried about it. What she said made so much sense. That things you don't plan are even more special because of exactly that. And you should treasure them.' I dropped to my knees. Rory's mouth fell open in shock. 'I didn't plan on falling in love with you or having Harry so quickly but you two mean the world to me. I'm sorry that I ever made you unsure about how I feel about you. I should have said yes when you asked me last year but I wasn't ready. I am now though. So, a year later, it's my turn to ask you instead.' I looked up at him, and my voice broke to see the tears glistening in his eyes. I reached for his hand. 'Rory Fraser, will you marry me?'

Chapter Forty

He grasped my hand in his. 'You are the only woman I have ever loved, and you are the only woman I will ever love,' he said, choking a little on the words.

'Is that a yes?' I asked, smiling as a tear rolled down my cheek.

Rory got down on his knees too then. 'Of course it's a yes.' He kissed me and I threw my arms around his neck, pulling him closer. The kiss was deep and lingering and I felt it travelling through my body sending warmth right down to the tips of my toes. 'I don't want to ruin this romantic moment but I'm losing all feeling in my knees,' he said when we broke apart.

'Me too,' I agreed. He helped me up, our jeans wet, our skin cold, and our knees aching but the smiles wide on our faces.

We walked on hand-in-hand, passing all the fairy lights but not really noticing them. 'She said something else in her letter,' I began when I was able to speak again.

'Your mum can tell me anything at this point, and I would do it,' he replied.

'She said one thing she regretted about marrying my dad was that they had such a small wedding. They couldn't afford anything else. They got married at Gretna Green but she wished she'd had a big, white wedding at Broomwood Castle. I was thinking as she can't be with us on our wedding day that we could have the wedding she always wanted. Like in memory of her?'

Rory lifted our joined hands and kissed the back of mine. 'That sounds perfect.'

'It might be expensive but Broomwood said they'd happily work something out with us if we publicise it on my Instagram. Who would have thought Stewart's dad trying to sabotage us would make me social media famous!' I shook my head. It was all very surreal.

'We should do it this summer,' Rory said. 'We'll make it work. We'll always make things work.'

I smiled, trusting his words for the first time. 'Always.'

'Oh, wait,' he said then, stopping. I turned to watch as he fumbled in his jacket pocket. 'We need this,' he said, pulling out a small velvet box.

'You have a ring?' I asked, surprised.

'I've had this ring for a year. I've been waiting for you to be ready. I'll be honest, these past couple of weeks what with Stewart turning up, and everything that's been going on, I wondered if I was starting to lose you. But Brodie told me to not lose hope, that I should believe in us, and that man is always right.' He grinned as he opened up the box. I gasped at the ring in there because I recognised it immediately. He smiled at my reaction. 'I got it from your dad last Christmas, and I've been holding on to it since. Your mum's engagement ring. I couldn't think of anything more suitable to put on your finger, can you?'

I shook my head, finding it hard to speak again as my eyes filled with tears. 'No,' I said, staring at the antique gold and sapphire ring. It was understated but beautiful, and I had always admired it on my mum. I had wondered if one day my dad would pass it on to me but I'd never have guessed Rory had gone to him for it, that he even remembered me mentioning it to him. I was so touched. Rory picked it up and I held out my hand for him to slide it onto my ring finger. 'A perfect fit.'

'Just like us,' Rory whispered. 'It's almost midnight, we should find Harry,' he said, giving me another kiss.

Reader, we were going to get married, and I felt like finally everything was going to be okay.

We walked slowly back down the trail and I looked up at the stars above us, and I was sure that one twinkled up there just for us.

—

Rory paused as we approached the bonfire to see our friends and family waiting in a circle watching us walk back towards them from the trail with big smiles on their faces. 'They all knew?' he asked me as I pulled him to keep walking with me.

'They were all in on it. Didn't you wonder why the trail was empty?' I laughed as he shrugged, evidently having been none the wiser. Honestly, men. 'We're engaged,' I said when we reached the group, their expectant faces lit up by the flickering flames behind them. I waved the ring on my hand for them all to see. 'Thank you, Dad,' I said, going to him, Harry in his hands. I folded them into a hug with me. 'Having her ring is so special.'

'She told me to give it to the right man for you,' he said, looking as if he might join me in crying too. 'When Rory asked for my blessing, I knew it was him.' I kissed him on the cheek.

'I'm so happy for you!' Beth threw her arms around my neck, squeezing me so tightly I had to tell her to stop. 'We are now basically sisters, you know,' she added, picking up my hand to show Emily the ring as she came over to look too.

'Congratulations, big brother,' Drew said to Rory behind us, thumping him on the back. 'Finally going to make an honest man out of you.'

'Took her long enough,' Rory said, wrapping his arms around my waist with a grin.

I rolled my eyes. 'The best things are worth waiting for,' I said. And I saw Beth and Drew, and Emily and Brodie, exchange looks. They all knew what I meant.

'It's time,' Caroline said then, quietly to us and then louder to the rest of the people around the bonfire. Rory took my hand and we all turned to the end of the lawn where John was ready with the fireworks. Beth and Drew hastily handed around paper cups of champagne.

'It's definitely going to be a good year,' Rory said into my hair as my dad and Harry joined us. Our friends and family surrounded us as we all waited for the countdown. I smiled back at him. I couldn't believe what a crazy time it had been since he first kissed me.

Thank goodness life didn't turn out the way you planned.

'Okay, everyone,' Beth called for quiet then. 'I just want to say thank you for coming to spend Hogmanay with us here at Glendale Hall. I hope that the New Year will be wonderful for each and every one of you. Right, here we go. Ten...'

We all joined in then with her counting down to the stroke of midnight. I leaned closer to Rory and Harry stood between us, Rory's hands on his shoulders, my dad beside him, all of us shouting louder as we got closer to midnight. I hoped my mum could see us now. And that she knew what a big difference she had made in my life, and would always make even though she was no longer here.

'Three, two, one!' We all chorused in unison, and then we watched as the sky above us exploded into a volley of colour, light and sound.

Chapter Forty-One

After the fireworks were over and the village dispersed, we congregated in the kitchen of the Hall for Sally's famous hot chocolate and a selection of cakes made by Emily. The warm and cosy atmosphere was just what we needed after standing out in the brisk night air. Harry and Iona both fell asleep in their pushchairs as we sat around the table, each of us telling the group our resolutions for the year ahead.

'I think we all know what Rory and Heather's resolution is,' Emily said with a smile.

'And to take over Hilltop,' I added, holding up my crossed fingers.

'I want to read every single Agatha Christie novel,' Izzy said.

'I'm moving onto Fraser Farm,' my dad said, holding up his mug of hot chocolate in our direction. 'That'll be a huge change.'

'I think we need a dog on the farm,' I said, turning to Rory. 'Especially if we might have sheep again.'

Rory opened his mouth to respond but then his phone vibrated on the table where he'd left it. 'It's Angus,' he said before answering with a frown because Angus would never call just for a chat. I immediately felt on edge, worried that something was wrong at the farm. 'What's up?' he asked, urgently, as Angus spoke into his ear. 'Oh my God, have you called 999?' Rory jumped up. We looked at one another, worried. I got up too, automatically. 'We'll be there as soon as we can. Priority is the animals, okay?' He hung up and met my eyes. 'There's a fire at the farm.'

'Oh my God,' I said, pulling on my coat quickly.

'Angus has called the fire department but who knows how quickly they can get to us. We need to get back as soon as we can.'

'How can we help?' Beth asked, hurrying to grab her coat, handing Drew who had joined her his. Emily and Brodie followed us too.

'I'll stay here with the kids,' Dad said, quickly. I gave him and Harry a quick kiss and followed Rory out, leaving Caroline, Sally and my dad looking after the children. We piled into two cars and roared away from the Hall towards the farm.

'Did he say what happened?' I asked Rory as he drove as fast as he dared home.

'Just that the barn was smoking. He's moving the horses, we need to start extinguishing it if we can before the firefighters get here.'

'I'll call Greg for advice,' Emily said from the back. Her ex-boyfriend Greg was a fireman in Inverness.

I glanced behind me and gave her a grateful nod. I saw Brodie mouthing something and I turned back, realising he was uttering a silent prayer. I'd take all the help we would get right now.

'No answer,' Emily said with a sigh. 'He might be working tonight.'

I hoped he was a good firefighter if that was the case.

As we approached the farm, I could see a thin wisp of smoke coming from the barn. Angus was leading Duke and Prince to the paddock, ushering them in as we drove into the yard, Drew's car right behind us. I looked out of the window and saw there was someone else with Angus. I jumped out of the car and Emily and Brodie climbed out too. And then I paused. I looked back and Rory was still in the car, hands gripping the steering wheel.

'Give us a sec,' I said to the others who went to greet the other car, and I opened the driver's door. 'Rory, what are you doing?'

His face had become deathly white. 'We'll lose it all,' he said as he looked out of the window.

'We won't,' I said firmly, shocked that he was the one gripped by panic right now, and not me. I leaned in closer and touched his shoulder. 'Listen to me, there are no flames yet, only some smoke. Look. That gives us a chance. But the longer we sit here, the more time we lose. We need to get out and save our home right now,' I said urgently. I touched his face and turned it to me. 'Everything is going to be okay, I promise.' Then I raised my voice. 'Now get your bum out of the car, and let's stop this before it's too late.'

He blinked then nodded. 'Okay.'

'Okay.' I clicked his seatbelt open and then held out my hand. He hesitated for a second before gripping it and getting out of the car. I breathed a sigh of relief that he was moving. 'Let's talk to Angus, find out what we can do,' I said, taking his hand and pulling him with me. I could feel the fear radiating off him that he might lose his farm, and I was determined to not let that happen without a fight.

'Angus!' I cried as we approached, the others joining us. 'What happened?'

'I found him trying to take the quad bike again,' Angus said, through gritted teeth. I looked and saw it was Luke with him. 'It's okay boy,' he soothed Prince. 'He had lit a match to see in the barn, dropped it when it burnt down into some hay. It hasn't caught alight yet but the hay is smouldering.'

'I didn't mean…' Luke began, his face ashen.

'We'll talk later,' I cut him off. 'Right, Rory and Drew we need to see if we can get the smoke under control. Maybe we can move the bales away from the ones smoking, so they don't all catch alight, and then try the fire extinguishers on it? Anything to stop flames starting and the whole barn going up,' I said. Thankfully, Rory nodded, relieved he had been given directions, and they hurried off for the barn.

A fire in the barn would do devastating damage. All I could hope was because it was winter and cold that the hay hadn't been as warm as it could get, so we might be able to stop it all from burning.

'What can we do?' Beth asked, from behind, bringing me back to the moment. I thought about what else we could do to prevent this turning into an utter disaster.

'Okay, while they try to tackle it, we need to move anything out of the way in case it doesn't work,' I said, after a moment. I couldn't let panic set in. We had to keep as calm as possible. 'Brodie and Emily, can you do a perimeter check of the barn and move anything that could catch alight, Beth – can you help me move as many animals as possible into the paddock?'

As Drew and Rory tried to stop the smoking hay in the barn, I took Beth into the barn next door where the chickens and pigs were. They could sense the tense atmosphere and were awake already, making a lot of noise. 'Grab that bucket of feed, and use it to lead the pigs out,' I said to Beth, flinging open the gate to the pig pen. I ran to the chicken coop and opened it up, and they headed straight for their outside pen. It was on the other side to the smoking barn so I would leave them there for now. If the barn did catch alight, I'd have to move them too.

As Beth tried to coax the pigs to follow her, I ran out and over to the goats where I opened the gate and basically chased them out of the barn towards Angus who had led the horses safely into the paddock, and then came out to help Beth round up the pigs. Thankfully, the cows were back up on the hill as the snow had cleared so they were out of danger. I glanced at the farmhouse though, panicked the fire could destroy our home if the barn did start burning.

'Stray pig!' Beth suddenly cried. One of the pigs was heading back towards the barn. I ran after it and clapped my hands so it turned and then I practically pushed it after the others.

'I'll get the hose and help Rory,' Angus said as he locked the paddock, which was now full of animals.

'Everything is clear,' Emily said when she and Brodie joined us.

'Thank you,' I said gratefully. 'Can you please stay here and try to keep the animals calm, and I'll see what's happening in the barn?' I glanced at Luke sat on the grass, his knees up, head buried on his elbows. When Rory had rung his parents after we found him trying to steal the quad bike on Stewart's dad's orders, they hadn't been all that bothered. I wondered at his home life that he was here on Hogmanay and not celebrating with his family. Their neglect, if that's what it was, could cause us to lose our livelihood and home. I took off back to the barn, parking those thoughts until after we saved it, and got there at the same time as Angus who started hosing around the edge of the barn and walls to keep it all cool.

'How's it looking?' I had to shout to Rory over the noise of the water and the extinguishers, which were almost all out. He and Drew put them down and we watched the bales of hay. The smoking hadn't ignited into flames yet, which was a good sign but I could still feel the heat radiating off them. They had managed to move some of the surrounding bales but I knew if a fire got out of control, we would lose them all.

Angus came in, washing the floor with cooling water. 'It looks under control.'

'Look at that bale!' I cried, pointing to one of the ones they had moved. It was starting to smoulder. Angus immediately turned the hose on it.

'I think this one is dying out,' Rory said, reaching out to touch the one that Luke had ignited. 'It's cooler than it was. At least we learned from that hay bale fire that summer when we were kids, do you remember?' he asked Drew.

'The whole barn went up,' Drew explained to my questioning raised eyebrow. 'We had no extinguishers in here, and we stored double the amount back then too. We ended up losing all the hay, and the barn roof was badly damaged. It cost a lot of money to sort it out and Dad needed a bank loan to buy enough hay for feed for the next year.' No wonder Rory had freaked out. He didn't want history repeating itself, or something even worse to happen this time. I glanced at him; he was focused on the task but was still pale. 'What was that boy even doing here?' Drew asked then.

'Trying to have a ride on our quad bike,' I said. I turned around. 'Is that...?' My chest sagged with relief as we heard the unmistakable signs of sirens approaching.

Chapter Forty-Two

Greg indeed jumped off the fire engine with his colleagues and approached us standing outside the barn. 'What happened?' he asked me. He had been to the farm a couple of times when we'd had the whole group together. I told him what had happened and what we had done to try and stop the fire, then he followed the others inside with hoses.

I wrapped an arm around Rory's waist. He was watching the barn silently. 'It's going to be okay,' I repeated to him. There were no flames. Even though we would lose two bales of hay, things could have been so much worse.

'We've done all we can,' Angus agreed with a decisive nod. I felt better. No one could argue with Angus.

'Let's check on the animals,' I suggested. 'They need us.' I didn't think just staring at the barn was doing any of us any good.

'Come on,' Beth agreed, putting her arm through Drew's. We all wandered over to the paddock. The horses had moved well back and seemed to be okay. The pigs were happily eating, as were the goats. They looked remarkably unfazed by the whole thing. I supposed with food and water and at a calm distance, they had all they needed. Angus went in to see the horses and Beth and Drew carried some more hay in to the paddock.

Luke was still there, evidently too terrified of Angus to move, his face red and tear-stained as he sat with his knees up to his chest. 'Is it destroyed?' He asked, fearfully, looking up when I went to stand over him. 'Did I...?'

I crouched down so we were face-to-face. 'Why did you do it, Luke?' I needed to know. I thought we had treated him leniently after catching him trying to steal it last time, why had he come back?

'I was bored. There's nothing to do. My mum tells me to stay out of our flat as I get under her feet. And I like seeing the animals here. And I thought it would be fun to try riding the quad bike. I wasn't gonna take it this time, I swear. Just drive it around for a bit.'

'Quad bikes can be really dangerous. And you broke in. You do get that what you did was wrong, don't you, Luke?' He nodded miserably.

'Heather,' Emily said, from behind me then. I looked to where she was pointing and saw Greg walking over to us. I stood up hurriedly and went to meet him with Rory by my side, my heart in my throat.

'How bad?' Rory asked without pre-amble. I knew he didn't mean to be sharp with Greg, he was just braced for bad news. I wasn't sure how we seemed to have swapped roles with him being the pessimistic one, but we had tonight.

'No sign of any more smoke,' Greg said, equally briskly. 'We've taken the two damaged bales out of the barn just in case though. There is some smoke damage in there but structurally, it's sound. But you, young man,' he said, turning to Luke, 'you cannot light matches in areas like that. The whole barn could have gone up and spread to the farmhouse. This could have been extremely serious, do you understand?'

Luke was crying again. 'Yes… yes, sir,' he stammered, unable to meet any of our eyes.

'Thank you, Greg, so much,' I said, reaching for him and giving the surprised man a swift hug.

Rory shook his hand energetically afterwards, some colour returning to his cheeks. 'We cannot thank you enough.'

'You did good work before we got here,' Greg said, waving our praise aside. 'It was good to see you all albeit under these circumstances. We'll head back. We're bound to get more call outs tonight with fireworks and bonfires.' He nodded at Emily and Brodie. 'Happy Hogmanay all.'

In the drama, the fact that it was now the first day of the New Year had escaped me. What a dramatic start! I hoped the rest of the year would be more peaceful. As the fire engine left, Beth and Emily went inside to make us all coffee and ring to check on everyone back at the Hall, Drew helped Angus take the animals back into their shelter, and Rory and I spoke to Luke.

'I think you'll agree you did some serious damage tonight,' Rory said after asking Luke to stand up to speak to us. I couldn't help but feel some sympathy for the kid, he looked so shattered, and was clearly having a tough time at home. 'Damage that needs to be paid for.' Luke opened his mouth but Rory held up a hand to silence him. 'You'll work here to pay us back for tonight. For one hour every day after school and on Saturdays. Once it's been paid off, you can stay on for money but only if you work hard and keep out of trouble.' Luke looked at me, taken aback. I was so proud of Rory. I gave Luke a reassuring nod. 'Is that something you can do?'

'Yes! Yes, sir,' he replied, quickly. 'Can I help with the animals?'

'Only if you do a good job. Most of the work will be menial and it'll be hard, and you have to do it in all weathers but if you prove to us that you can do it then you can help with the animals. Now, Drew has offered to drop you home when they go back to the Hall. As school doesn't start up until Wednesday, I want you here all day on Monday, okay?'

'I'll be here,' he promised. 'I'll see if Angus needs help now.' He turned to go then paused and glanced at us shyly. 'Thank you,' he added before running off.

I wrapped an arm around Rory's waist. 'You big softie,' I said as we watched him head into the stables to find Angus.

'I think he's a good kid but he needs guidance. To be honest if I hadn't had the farm, I might have gone off the rails when I was younger. I wasn't like you and Drew, all studious and focused, I needed a firm hand sometimes from my dad. I don't think Luke has anyone at home to help him so we might as well try, right?'

'I think you're doing a wonderful thing.' I gave him a quick kiss. 'Are you okay? You worried me back there,' I asked then, gently.

'Yeah, I'm sorry,' he said. 'I think I panicked, thinking the whole thing was going to burn. Sometimes it feels like a huge responsibility owning all this, isn't it? Like I want my parents to think I'm doing a good job, and I want to secure it for the future for Harry and his children too. I'm so glad you were here. You took control and got everyone doing what they needed to.' He pulled me closer. 'You just swept into action. If I had hesitated for longer… what I'm saying is thank you, you saved us.'

It was certainly a change to hear Rory thanking me and not me thanking him. I smiled. 'You don't need to thank me. We were a team back there. All of us saved it.' I couldn't help but feel proud of myself though. I felt like a few months ago I would have been panicked too, certain that I couldn't have helped, but tonight I knew I was capable, and that had made me capable somehow. Like a self-fulfilling prophecy or something. I also was no longer unsure about being here on the farm. I felt as passionate about it as Rory now, and equally determined to protect it as far as I could.

I decided then to take a photo of the burned hay bales. Earlier, I had shown off my ring to my Instagram followers. This would be a very different post. But I was determined to keep being honest on there. This was my life. Warts and all.

It was scary how often we had come close to losing everything this Christmas, but we had pulled through, and I believed that whatever the future held, we would be okay.

'Let's find the others,' Rory said then. 'See if Harry is all right.'

'He'll have slept through it all I bet,' I said as we walked towards the farmhouse. I was so pleased he was safe and sound, and that he'd have his home intact to come back to. 'We won't forget how this year started, that's for sure.'

'It can only get better from here. Especially with our wedding to look forward to,' he said, glancing down at the ring on my finger. 'I still can't believe you proposed to me. And on the same night, the farm almost burned down.' He shook his head.

'We don't do things by halves around here,' I replied with a laugh.

'I'll never be bored married to you, that's for sure. You've always kept me on my toes since that first night we spent together. Never change Heather Douglas.'

'I won't,' I promised. 'Even when I become Heather Fraser.'

Chapter Forty-Three

Once the Christmas holidays were all over and the decorations had come down, life slowly returned to normality. My dad, however, didn't move back home as originally planned. I went with him to our old house to collect more things and start sorting through it all. The estate agent had valued it and we'd put it on the market, hoping it wouldn't be too long as Glendale was a sought-after place to live.

'How are you feeling about leaving here, really?' I asked after a few minutes of silence as I folded shirts into a suitcase on the floor in the living room while he sorted through the desk. Harry was on the floor beside me playing with his new train set. I had indeed got him far too much for Christmas, he only wanted the train and his lamb toy from Granddad. I looked around the room. Everything was the same as it had been while my mum was alive, Dad hadn't changed anything and I knew he must be thinking of her as I always did when I came back here.

'I think our drama at Hogmanay confirmed I'm doing the right thing,' Dad replied, looking up from a mountain of paperwork. You only realise when you need to clear out quite how much of a hoarder of unnecessary things you are. 'I like being there for you and Harry and it can get lonely here especially of an evening, there won't be a minute to myself when I move into the farm.' He smiled, thankfully happy with that.

'I'm not sure if you know what you've let yourself in for,' I said. 'But I'm really pleased you're staying. I miss you when you're not with us, and I hate thinking of you lonely here. I think Mum would be pleased too.' My voice caught a little when I said that and I looked quickly down at the shirts, worried I might cry if I carried on looking at him.

'She would,' he agreed. 'And she would be proud of you marrying Rory at Broomwood Castle. Thank you for letting me read her letter. Hearing her voice through her words was wonderful, if difficult. She seemed to have known somehow what you needed to hear, didn't she? But that was your mother all over. I have never met, before or since, anyone who was always right like she was. Not that I ever told her that though.'

'She really was. I certainly didn't inherit that from her but I'm trying to work on my anxiety and worry. I think Stewart turning up actually helped in that way. He showed me how much I loved my life even if I was terrified about it, and even if it was unexpected, and all happened so quickly, and I needed that. It's helped me to not be so scared, but to embrace it and try to enjoy it more. I think I will still always worry, it's just who I am, but I'll count my blessings more now.'

'I think you were scared that things you hadn't planned for had happened but now you can see they were always meant to happen. I think seeing Stewart showed you that what you have now is so much better for you than what you might have had with him.'

It was true. My life was unexpected in every way and it had made me happier than I thought possible. Just as my mother had predicted. Seeing how unhappy Stewart was made me realise how differently my life could have turned out. I reached out to brush Harry's hair off his face as he chatted to his trains, and I felt a burst of joy. I was determined to hang on to that joy and not let myself self-sabotage as I had done in the past. My phone rang then. 'Hey,' I said, smiling when I realised it was Rory. 'Missing me already?' I saw my dad roll his eyes.

'Well, yes. But also, I have news,' he replied, the smile clear in his voice. 'William just rung, he's officially accepted our offer on Hilltop. I've booked a meeting at the bank to get a loan before the house sale goes through so we can go ahead.'

'That is very good news.' I gave my dad a thumbs-up, and he looked confused. 'We've got Hilltop,' I explained to him. 'Well, life is about to get even busier for us,' I said to Rory. 'Are you sure we're up to this?'

'Hilltop will be a top, working sheep farm, and will offer retreats to people looking for an authentic farming experience. It will soon be the best retreat in Scotland, I have no doubt. Oh, better go, Luke is giving the pigs way too much food, I can see.' He hung up abruptly. Luke had become a fixture around the farm helping out as much as he could, and I could see he was blossoming from the work, Rory and Angus's guidance, and all the fresh air too. 'Last chance to change your mind,' I said to Dad then. 'I so appreciate the money you're giving us but I want to make sure you really want to do this.'

'That money is yours from your mother. She would love to see you helping people like you will with this new venture, and I can see you're loving working on it. I loved this house, it's true, but only because you two were here.

Now that your mother has gone, my home is with you guys on the farm. This is just a house now.'

'I don't think Mum was the only one to have a way with words,' I told him, welling up again. I looked around. It was true that this place reminded me of her, but she was no longer here, and it was no longer our home. But I would cherish the memories we shared here and carry them in my heart always as I hopefully made many more memories with my family.

–

I took Emily and the kids along with me to see Hilltop Farm the following day. I wanted to get a feel for the grounds. I hadn't really explored the area properly and now that the sale was going through, there was no time like the present to start planning exactly what we wanted to do with the land once it was ours.

'This place is even more remote than Fraser Farm,' Emily said as we bumped along the gravel track that led up to the farmhouse. It was a crisp, sunny January morning and the blue sky and sunshine showed off the rustic farmhouse beautifully. As we got out of the car, I had to agree with Emily. It was so peaceful here. Set back miles from the road, all we could hear was birdsong. 'That's why I thought it would be perfect for retreats, you can totally get away from everything here. There isn't even a phone signal. And I doubt we'd get Wi-Fi. Guests would be deep in the countryside, and I think it would be perfect for people looking for time to just be with nature, away from their life for a few days, you know?'

Emily put Iona in her pushchair as I let Harry out, him running towards the field, obviously not in the mood for his own pushchair. 'I know my old friends in London would have paid a fortune for that so I think you will have no shortage of takers. I'd be interested myself,' she added with a laugh. 'So, shall we take a walk around?' We set off after Harry. 'Have you heard about the listing yet?'

'We have people coming out here and to our farm next week, but it looks like both properties will be listed. I think that will be a selling point to visitors. We'll try to keep it as closely as we can to how it's always been. Obviously, some of the electrics need looking at, and the heating and water, but the property is all intact, it just needs decorating. There are five bedrooms, which could all be hired out either together or individually. And we realised there's a small property near the woods that could be used for a live-in manager. Which I think we'll need as I can't be here all the time, and Angus wants to help but I don't think he'd be great with the guests to be honest.' We shared a grin. 'He can be more of the groundsman here. And my dad likes the idea of offering some classes like in woodwork or something. I thought I could run an art class. And as we said, if you wanted to do any bakery ones…'

We walked towards the woodland area side-by-side, Harry in front of us skipping along cheerfully. Iona was sleeping peacefully. She was almost ready to walk and then I thought the two of them would likely cause all sorts of chaos for us.

'Well,' Emily began, glancing at me rather coyly, 'I'm not sure if I'll have the time for a while. I took a test and I am pregnant. It's really early though so I'm only telling you and Beth because you both got me wondering if I was, and Brodie of course, who was right there with me when I took it!'

'Oh, wow, congratulations. How do you feel?' I asked, but I could sense the happiness radiating out from her.

'Surprised,' she said with a laugh. 'It took so long to get pregnant with Greg, Iona felt like a miracle baby especially after everything we went through, I honestly thought if it ever happened again, it might take years or I'd need help. I can't believe I'll be having a honeymoon baby.' She shook her head. 'I feel like I still can't take it in, do you know what I mean?'

'Definitely. I was in shock when I realised I was pregnant with Harry.' I thought back as we walked into the woodland, the sun turning into a trickle through the leaves. 'He wasn't planned and I had always planned everything. But as you know with Iona often the best things are the ones we don't plan.'

'That's true. I never thought I'd have a baby and then leave the father. Mind you, Brodie would say that unexpected things are planned – just not by us.' She smiled. I knew she wasn't religious like her husband but she supported it and tried to find her own faith, seeing how much happiness it brought to him. She once said that Brodie's opinion was the one she trusted most in life, and that had been the case before they had even kissed, and I wondered if it was because of his faith. 'But the thought of having two young children and running the bakery...' She shrugged. 'I might not sleep for like ten years!'

'I'll be honest, that's why I worried about having a second baby, it seemed so much to even have Harry but I think I'd be less scared now. Don't get me wrong, I want to wait before we try, but I guess if something unexpected happens again I could cope better this time around.' I watched Harry find a log and I hurried forwards to help him up on it, holding his hand so he wouldn't fall. Before,

I would have just told him no and pulled him away but Rory was right – he needed to explore and discover the world for himself. I just needed to lend a helping hand when he needed me too.

'Why, do you think?' Emily asked as she stopped to watch us.

'Honestly, these past few weeks have shown me that I can deal with so much more than I thought I could. First my ex came and tried to sabotage the farm and take me away from it, and then we had that fire… It's been a crazy Christmas but I feel like we've come out of it stronger, especially me. And then I read my mum's letter. She made me see that you need to fight for what you love.'

Emily leaned down to check on Iona. 'I couldn't agree more.' She looked up. 'This place is wonderful. If we can show more people how good Glendale is for your health and happiness then all the better. If only we could bottle it like water, right?'

I glanced back to see the farmhouse through a gap in the trees. I felt like this project could be something special, and something that would secure us financially in the future. Emily was right – if we could give others a taste of Glendale, the untouched countryside, and our warm community, they would feel so much better, I was sure of it. 'We'd make a fortune,' I agreed, laughing.

Chapter Forty-Four

I offered to take Luke home after a day's work on the farm as I needed to drop off a few things at the farm shop. It was growing dark outside although it was only late afternoon, the sky threatening rain. Luke's boots were covered in mud and there was a smear of it on his cheek. 'Is your mum going to let you in the house like that?' I asked as he directed me to his road. It was a few miles away from the High Street and he lived in a block of flats at the end. It was strange. Glendale was such a pretty place that to be honest I hadn't realised that this estate sat just outside it. It proved that I led a very entitled life, one that I failed to appreciate sometimes but I supposed we were all guilty of that.

'She probably won't be in, she works two jobs. My dad is out of work right now so he's always there.'

'I'm sorry.'

'It was his own fault,' he muttered. I raised an eyebrow but he didn't elaborate.

As I pulled up, I saw a group of boys on the corner, a few kicking a ball, a couple smoking, leaning against the railings, watching my car with interest.

'It's pretty rough here,' Luke said apologetically, when he saw me looking at them.

'Are they your friends?'

He shrugged. 'We hang out sometimes. But now I'm at the farm most days, not so much.'

'What about a girlfriend?'

He gave me a look. 'As if I'd tell you.' But he was grinning.

'Are you enjoying working with us?' I asked. Although it had begun as Luke paying off his 'debt' to us, Rory had quickly started giving him a small wage, and he always had lunch with us while he was working – he had felt too guilty making him work for free. We hadn't lost too much over the barn fire and hearing about Luke's home life, I was glad Rory had done that.

That brightened him up. 'I love it. I hope I can stay on. Like for the summer too?'

'Of course you can.' I nodded. 'Go on then, you'd better get inside. See you after school tomorrow.'

'Bye, Heather!' He ran inside the block of flats ignoring the jeers from the boys trying to get his attention. I pulled away and drove back towards the village, looking in my rear-view mirror to watch as he disappeared inside. He was a good kid and I was pleased that we could offer him a helping hand. We'd need more local help as well with Hilltop to manage as well as Fraser Farm, and I wondered if we'd have work for some of Luke's friends too. As I arrived in the High Street, I passed by the farm shop, and had a sudden urge to sit on my mum's bench. Perhaps it was Luke speaking about his parents and realising how different his upbringing was to the one I had.

Parking outside the church, I walked into the cemetery, the air brisk around me. I pulled my red scarf tighter around my neck as I sat down on my mum's bench to try to keep the wind away from my face. The cemetery was empty but not lonely. As always, I felt close to her here. I wasn't sure if I really believed that she was looking down on me but I did feel as if she was always with me, even if it was just the memory of her love, and the fact that my heart would also be full of it. 'Well, Mum, a lot has happened since I came here with Dad,' I said softly, my voice mingling with the breeze. I felt self-conscious speaking aloud but if there was any possibility that she could hear me then I wanted her to. 'I read your letter. And wow, what a letter. I wonder if you ever realised the mark you left on my life. I know that all mothers leave a mark on their daughters. Good and bad for some too, of course. But you really have helped me be both a better mother and a woman. Thanks to you I was able to let go of my fears, and I actually proposed to Rory.' I smiled, rubbing the ring on my left hand, which I was still getting used to feeling against my skin.

'He said yes, in case you weren't sure. It's funny but you were right. I didn't end up with the handsome, charming, ambitious businessman I thought I loved but I actually found my perfect partner in a rough and ready farmer who is kind and loyal and who, despite his teasing, is my biggest supporter in life. I'm so happy that you were right – the unexpected things in life really are the best ones. And I think I'll always worry when things don't go to plan but I know now that if that happens, I can handle it because I have Rory, and my dad, Harry, all our family and friends...' I looked up as a burst of light streamed in through a gap in the trees above me. And I smiled. 'And you, right by my side.'

'Talking to yourself again.'

I turned and smiled to see Brodie walking behind me on the path.

'Want me to keep on walking?' he checked.

'No, come and sit,' I said. He was in jeans and a thick jumper today but still seeming very much at one with his surroundings of the church. 'I was just talking to my mum. I felt like I needed to tell her what's been going on.' I glanced across at him shyly when he sat down beside me. 'Is that mad?'

'If it was mad then most of the population would be crazy. I think it helps to talk to the people you miss. And, hey, I talk to someone not beside me all the time.' He pointed up to the sky. 'I caught Em talking to her non-existent bump earlier too. Perhaps we all need the comfort of saying things to people who we hope can hear but who can't say anything back. Maybe it lets us be honest in a way we can't be sometimes with people who *can* say something back.'

'I did tell her that it's thanks to her that I'm the mother and woman that I am. I can imagine her actually saying "don't be silly" if I had been able to say it to her face-to-face so you might be right. Do you ever wonder if God can really hear you though?' I asked curiously.

'I do think He has better things to do than to listen to me rambling on sometimes,' he replied with an easy laugh. 'But no, I think He's always there with a listening ear if you want to talk. Much like your mother is too, I'm sure.'

I smiled. 'It makes me feel better to know that she's around, so I understand what you mean about God. It's going to be another year of big events, isn't it? Mine and Rory's wedding, you and Emily having a baby...'

Brodie tilted his face towards the sun. 'There is always something to look forward to.'

I knew we all needed to remember that.

Chapter Forty-Five

The cold, crisp weather continued so I suggested that Rory and I took the horses for a ride while Harry was having an afternoon nap and Dad was content watching a film inside.

'From someone who was too scared to even get on Prince, you look very comfortable now,' Rory said with a grin as I climbed into the saddle, reaching out to pat the horse as I gathered up the reins.

'I have got over my fear,' I agreed. 'Somehow, I trust him,' I said, setting off across the field side-by-side with Rory on Duke.

'And he trusts you. So, I just booked an appointment with our solicitor next week to get the ball rolling on the Hilltop sale,' he said as we walked steadily up the hill. The wind was brisk as we moved higher, blowing any cobwebs away. I looked out at the countryside stretching for as far as my eye could see and felt relief all over again that there wouldn't be a huge hotel to take that away from us.

'I can't believe we're soon going to own two farms,' I said, shaking my head. My dad had had a couple of viewings on his house already so we hoped it would sell soon. 'I used to be petrified by change but I'm so excited.' We moved towards the cows grazing in the cool sunshine and my phone buzzed in my pocket. I stopped Prince to answer it in case it was Dad but I was startled to see

Stewart's name on the screen instead. 'It's Stewart,' I said to Rory, who paused Duke and watched as I answered his call.

'Hi, Heather,' he replied. 'I just wanted to ring and say congratulations on buying Hilltop, I heard it's all going through now.'

He sounded genuine. 'Thanks, Stewart.'

'You're right that what you have planned suits Glendale more than what I had pictured. I think I'm still learning that buildings need to work with their surroundings. Listen, I wanted to tell you that I've moved down to London. I've just got the keys to my new flat. I decided I needed a fresh start. I'm working for an architecture firm down here now, instead of with my father.' He sounded so much brighter than he had done before he had left Glendale.

'That's really good news, Stewart,' I said sincerely. 'I do wish you the best.'

'Thanks, Heather. You too. Take care, okay?' He hung up quickly, and I knew that would be the last time I heard from him.

'He's moved to London,' I said to Rory as I put my phone back in my pocket. 'I'm glad he's away from his dad. Isn't it strange how people come and go from your life?' We set off walking again.

'But I think they all teach us something.'

I raised an eyebrow. 'That's pretty wise, Mr Fraser,' I joked. But it was true. Stewart had taught me to realise what I had. I looked around at the beauty surrounding us and I was so relieved I hadn't lost it. He'd taught me that I was someone who would fight for what I loved, and that I was stronger and braver than I could have imagined. He'd also taught me about the kind of partner I needed by my side in life. 'You're right though.' The sun shone down on us as we reached the peak of the hill, the cows looking up at us as we approached. I thought of how much my mother had taught me too. I hoped I brought something to the lives of the people I loved, and who loved me, too.

'When my mum and dad died...' Rory began then paused. I turned to him. He didn't talk about them much. And I understood better than anyone that it was to spare himself from pain. 'I raged against the world. I couldn't see any way of making things work here without them, especially as Drew wanted to be a doctor and didn't want to work here with me. I almost gave up. More than once, to be honest. But I'm so glad I didn't. It feels like all of it had to happen in a way to bring me right here, right now. Do you know what I mean?'

'I do,' I replied. 'I don't think there's a big master plan for us but I do think that we often underestimate how we can cope and adapt to things, that often afterwards you can see there's a reason why something has happened. We've both lost such special people but they've given us so much, and they're always with us. So even though we will always miss them, we are still blessed.'

Rory brought Duke over to me and leaned over. I reached for him and we managed to share a kiss across our horses, smiling at the awkwardness. 'I'm definitely blessed with you and Harry.'

'Me too,' I agreed. 'And we have a whole lifetime together.' I doubted I would ever completely not worry that Harry could lose me, but I was determined to be the best mother I could be while I was around. And I really hoped that would be for many, many years. 'So, want to race me back to see our boy?'

Rory grinned. 'What do I win when I beat you?'

'The winner makes breakfast for the next week,' I said, ignoring the dig.

'Deal!' He took off so fast, I took a second to catch up. I cried out and urged Prince on. What a cheater.

We cantered down the hill, my hair blowing out behind me, my breath catching in the wind, laughing at how exhilarating it felt as we raced towards the farmhouse. It felt as if I was leaving my worries behind me. Although they were bound to reappear at some point, I would try to think of them as still up on that hill, small and too far away to hurt me.

–

That evening, Rory, Angus, Dad, Harry and I settled around the kitchen table together for dinner.

'Here's to the victor,' I said, raising my glass of wine. I couldn't believe I had beaten Rory back to the farmhouse, and I wasn't about to let him forget it any time soon.

He rolled his eyes but joined in with our clinking glasses good-naturedly. 'I'm not sure if I didn't prefer it when you weren't confident with things around here,' Rory said after he had had a sip of his beer. 'It seemed more peaceful here before Heather, didn't it, Angus?'

'It was quieter,' Angus said, his eyes twinkling in the candlelight. It had been easier than I expected to get him in here tonight, he was slowly coming around to being more sociable with us. 'But there is more than enough quiet out here. This place needs a family in it.'

I gave Rory a pointed 'see' look, pleased that Angus hadn't joined in his teasing of me. I would feel bad forever that I had in the past hoped Angus would leave us. He had helped us more than I could ever thank him for, he really was part of the family now even if he would never accept me saying that. 'And as if you didn't find all that peace boring,' I added. I watched Angus cut up Harry's roast beef for him with a smile.

'There won't be much peace around here tomorrow,' Dad commented with wide eyes. I smiled. It was Harry's second birthday tomorrow, and I still couldn't believe my baby was officially a toddler. I really hoped the years would go more slowly than they were, I wanted to hang on as tightly as I could to all the memories we were making together.

'I'll be hiding in my cottage, don't worry,' Angus said. 'Harry understands don't you, boy?'

'I'm sure he does,' I said although I thought Harry would ask for him, he loved it when Angus carried him on his shoulders, I think Angus seemed like a big bear to him. I wasn't about to force Angus into a party though. I understood he liked to be on his own. Everyone found their contentment in different ways. There was no reason to try to force them to do things that you wanted to do. 'To be fair he probably won't remember the party but we do it for us, don't we?'

'Your mum was ill when you turned two,' Dad remembered then. 'A really nasty cold. So, we had your birthday the following week. She felt so guilty even though you had no idea of dates or anything.'

I chuckled, knowing I would have felt the same way if I'd had to postpone Harry's. It was hard to always be rational as a parent, as I knew better than anyone. 'I think that probably did scar me, you know.'

Dad snorted. 'Actually, I think it's the reason why you're always late everywhere.'

He had a point. I wondered if I'd be responsible for something in Harry's nature down the line. Harry held out his hand then and dropped a pea into my palm. I wasn't sure what that could symbolise. The fact that he would be a giving person?

Or maybe he just didn't like peas.

Chapter Forty-Six

Harry's second birthday was welcomed in by another snowfall. We hadn't had a significant one so far in January but when we woke up, we saw that the weather reports had been right that the cold front would bring with it snow. Rory had moved the animals with Angus the night before so everyone was sheltered and the farm was blanketed with two inches by the time the afternoon arrived, and with it our guests.

Luckily, only gentle flakes floated down and it wasn't deep enough yet to stop anyone getting to us, but the forecast was that we might very well have enough overnight to cut us off for a couple of days. I was far more relaxed about the idea now. I had my dad with me so we wouldn't be trapped from him, and we had all the food and supplies we needed ready. I was learning to go with the flow more with things on the farm. I couldn't control the snow, could I? But I could control how it made me feel.

'Hi, guys!' I said when I opened the door to Beth, Drew, Izzy, Sally, Caroline and John, and showed them into the living room. They were soon followed by Brodie, Emily and Iona, and Luke followed, looking rather uncomfortable in the shirt and jeans he had donned for the occasion. 'Come on through.'

I paused as I saw Angus walking over from his cottage.

He shrugged. 'Couldn't disappoint the wee lad, could I?' he said as he shuffled past me sheepishly. I grinned at his retreating back.

Rory had brought in a long table which we laid a buffet out on, and we'd added some extra chairs, and tied balloons to everywhere we could. The birthday boy was wearing dungarees and hadn't stopped grinning all day.

'Where shall I put this?' Emily asked, carrying the cake she had kindly baked for the occasion. It was in the shape of a lamb to match his favourite teddy and looked almost too adorable to eat. But obviously we still would. I found an empty spot and helped her put it down.

'Luke,' I said, noticing him hovering in the doorway. He wasn't shy exactly, more awkward at social occasions as he really hadn't been to all that many. 'This is Izzy,' I said, leading him into the room where Izzy sat on a chair, a book poking out of her bag. 'Luke helps out around here now,' I added to her. Luke was a couple of years older than her but I hoped they might become friends. I glanced at Beth who smiled as Luke sat down beside Izzy and looked rather stumped for something to say. I was about to help them out when he noticed her book.

'You reading that?' he asked, nodding at *The Catcher in the Rye*.

'I am. I'm really enjoying it. Have you read it?'

'It's my favourite,' he said, brightening visibly. 'I've read it, like, ten times.'

'I don't think I've read anything other than *Harry Potter* that much,' she replied, looking surprised.

'Well, my teacher gave it to me. I guess I don't have many books at home.'

'Really? Well, I have loads you can borrow…'

I walked away, smiling. I didn't even know Luke was a reader. I was pleased. There was nothing Izzy liked better so now they were bound to become friends, and maybe she'd pull him away from the group he still hung around with sometimes. Brodie told me they caused trouble in the pub at the weekend trying to buy alcohol even though they were underage. Beth had once commented she might have got in with the wrong crowd at school if it hadn't been for me, trying to rebel against her home life. Maybe Izzy could be Luke's Heather. I liked the idea of that.

'I hope you're not trying to corrupt my daughter,' Beth said with a laugh, handing me a drink. 'I don't want her to have a boyfriend until she's like twenty. Maybe not even then.'

'She still says boys are gross, don't worry. I think she could be good for him. And maybe he'll bring her to the farm more too,' I said, taking a sip of wine. 'I don't think she'll end up like you, don't worry.'

'Hey!' She nudged me, making me nearly spill my drink. 'I could have been a lot worse.'

'You were a bad enough influence as it was. All those nights we drank whisky stolen from your dad's drinks cabinet for a start.' Drew and Rory joined us then. 'Remember when Drew took Rory's car to drive us to the pub. On your request obviously, Beth,' I added. Drew only ever got in trouble over Beth. She had always been, and always would be, his weakness. 'He hit that tree and we had to call him for help.'

'Rory was terrifying that night,' Beth said, shuddering.

'Well, Drew hadn't even got his licence,' Rory said, shaking his head. 'You lot caused me a lot of grief, you know, back then.'

I slipped an arm through this. 'I'm sorry. It was all Beth's fault though. God, what do you think our kids will be like when they hit that age?' We glanced at Izzy and Luke looking at her book together, and Harry playing with Emily and Iona on the floor. I wondered how many of the things we had done would come back to haunt us when they did the same thing.

'I dread to think,' Drew said, wrapping an arm around Beth's waist.

'It's lucky we don't have grey hair in our family or these luscious red locks of ours wouldn't last long,' Rory joked to his brother.

'Heather and I remember you both being called carrot-tops at school, don't forget,' Beth replied.

'We've known each other too long,' Rory complained but he smiled at me. I knew he loved our lifetime bond as much as I did.

'I think it's time,' I said, going over to the cake and adding candles, lighting them up. Rory hushed the room and we all started to sing happy birthday to Harry sat on his knees, grinning as I carried over the cake to him.

'Blow the candles out and make a wish,' I said, smiling as he tried and only managed to blow a couple out. Rory crouched with me and together we all blew them out. I assumed that meant I could have a wish too, so I wished that my family would be healthy and happy for as long as possible.

Everyone dived into the buffet then and we all sat down to eat. 'Brodie just said he had a long chat with his sister, Anna, about coming to work at the Hall. I really need someone this spring, what with starting this wedding business, I'll need all the help I can get. I really need the house taken care of while I'm doing that. But I'm not sure if she'll agree as she's working at a pub in Glasgow right now,' Beth said next to me as she munched on a sausage roll.

'If anyone can persuade someone to do something then Brodie can,' I replied. 'How will you feel seeing someone else taking on the Hall though, Sally?'

Sally, sat in the armchair, paused in eating her pasta salad. 'It will be about time. You need someone full-time. The place is going to rack and ruin with you in charge and not letting me help,' she replied with a smile but I had no doubt that Beth's standards were not as high as they needed to be in Sally's opinion. She had run the Hall like a navy ship, and more than deserved her retirement.

'It's your fault I haven't found anyone I like enough to take on the job permanently. No one can ever replace you, Sally,' Beth said, good-naturedly. 'Anyway, this time it's not me being too picky. Apparently Anna has never stayed anywhere for more than six months so it can only be temporary.'

'I hope she does agree to come and help you,' I said. 'It sounds like she might shake up Glendale a little bit.'

'Brodie did want to check that I realised Anna is quite a free spirit,' Beth said. She shrugged. 'I just hope my mother will be able to handle her,' she added, leaning in closer to prevent Caroline on the other side of the room hearing our conversation. We all had a chuckle about that.

'Sounds like she's rather like you were as a teenager,' Sally remarked. 'So, it sounds like we might all be kept on our toes.'

'Honestly, I wasn't *that* bad!' Beth protested. 'You all like to re-write history sometimes.'

Before I could respond, Izzy came over to us then. 'Heather, we're going to give Luke a lift home and stop off at the Hall on the way so I can get a few books for him. Can you believe he's never read *Harry Potter*? He thought it was just for kids.' She looked so outraged, it was difficult not to laugh.

'I'm shocked, Izzy, but if anyone can educate him then you can,' I said. I looked at Luke who had a mountain of food on his plate. He always ate everything in sight here, I wasn't sure if he ever got a proper meal at home so I didn't mind. 'I hope you know what you've let yourself in for,' I said to him. He just shrugged but I saw the smile he hid behind his chicken drumstick. So sweet.

'Why does being pregnant make me so hungry?' Emily complained as she brought over her second helping from the buffet. 'I'm just so relieved we all like to eat here.'

'Have as much as you like,' I assured her. Rory had told me I'd bought far too much food but I was glad I always over did it at the supermarket – this lot really could pack it away. I looked at Harry on his dad's lap having another sausage roll. He was already very much part of the Glendale fold in that respect. 'But save room for cake, everyone,' I added, louder. There was a chorus of groans and tummy pats but I also caught quite a few pairs of eyes lighting up too. I shook my head with a smile. Shameless, the lot of them.

'I think we should play a game after lunch,' Izzy said then. 'I think Harry would like that.' There followed a lively debate about what should be played. Even Angus joined in with a suggestion.

I found myself watching and listening, marvelling that I had such a lovely group of family and friends to spend time with. And we weren't a conventional bunch. Single teenage mothers, caring for children that weren't biologically ours, second marriages, people whose partners had long left them, and were still longed for, but the type of family we had just didn't matter. We were still family.

All that did matter was that we loved one another, and were there for one another. Through thick and thin. Through the good times and the not so good times. And I had never felt more grateful to have these people in my life. And my son's life. Because if Harry ever did lose me, I knew I wasn't as worried anymore. Because he had this lot to look out for him, just like they had all looked out for me.

And if that wasn't something to celebrate then I didn't know what was.

'Heth, can you please decide?' Rory pleaded then. 'They will never agree otherwise.'

'Harry Potter Trivial Pursuit,' I said, trying not to laugh as my suggestion was greeted with loud roars of disapproval because everyone knew that only me and Izzy would have a chance of winning.

Epilogue

Rory and I arrived at Hilltop Farm with the keys for the first time. With us was Harry, who bounded out the car running for the field, followed by my dad, Angus, and our new sheepdog puppy Darcy who I, of course, named after *Pride and Prejudice*. It was a sunny February morning, much needed after such a snowy January, and it felt like possibility was in the air as we went inside the farmhouse as its official owners.

'It's just how I remember it,' Angus said, looking around. 'Your dad and I used to play cards with old Sam in the winter sometimes, he liked his whisky, and he always won – the shark,' he said to Rory with a shake of his head.

'I really want to keep it as close to the original farm-house as possible,' I said. We had just received official grade listing for both Hilltop and Fraser farm so any modifications we made had to keep within tight guide-lines but I wasn't concerned, I wanted it to be exactly as it was when it was first built, and would publicise that fact to future guests. 'Look at those beams,' I said in wonder, looking up at the ceiling.

'And this fireplace,' my dad said, gesturing to it. 'When it's working, it will be so cosy in here.' He walked through into the kitchen and to the back door, which he flung open. We followed him outside and looked out across the fields, which rose high up to the hill that stood between our two properties. We were planning to farm sheep again here, and were trying to train Darcy. He ran off towards the grass, followed by a skipping and laughing Harry. We had some way to go with that training obviously.

'The first thing we need to do is get the old game-keeper cottage up to scratch,' I said, looking over at where it stood close to the woodland area.

'Cameron can't wait to get stuck in,' Angus said with a proud look. His sister's son, who often helped out on our farm during summer, had agreed to take on the role as Hilltop manager. He'd be moving into the cottage as soon as we could get it ready for him, and would help us with our renovation project ready for our first guests to arrive in the summer we hoped.

'Have you heard back from that company you've been talking to?' my dad asked as we walked across the field. A farming supplies company had approached me about doing some social media work together, and we were discussing them potentially sponsoring our retreat here, providing equipment we needed, and doing some mutually beneficial publicity.

'We have a meeting booked next week but they are really excited. I think it could work really well. And would mean the pressure would be off to be profitable in the first year with them backing us. So, we can really focus on creating the best retreat we can, and getting the farm working alongside Fraser.'

'And I love the new logo you showed me last night,' Rory said as he swung Harry up on his shoulders. I thought it was a good opportunity to refresh our logo to include both farms, new signage for both, and to create new things to sell in the farm shop. It meant I was using my creative side too, which I was really enjoying. He looked around. 'Honestly, my dad would be thrilled to see us taking on Hilltop.'

'I'm so proud of you both,' my dad said. 'You are giving Beth a run for her money in taking over Glendale.'

'I told her to watch out,' I agreed, laughing. 'But with her new wedding business, I think she still has us beat.' I gazed around at our new land – the opportunities here were so exciting. I didn't feel overwhelmed though, I was just looking forward to seeing what we could do here. I really had come a long way these past three months. I looked at Rory. 'She's already told me she has to be our wedding planner, whether we like it or not. I think as we're not getting married at the Hall, we'll have to let her, we'll never hear the end of it otherwise.'

He grinned. 'You know, she's more like her mother than she'd ever admit.'

'She'd kill you for saying that,' I said. 'Only four months until we'll be at Broomwood Castle…'

'I can't wait,' he said. 'About bloody time, don't you think, guys?'

I rolled my eyes as my dad and Angus let out roaring laughs. Even Harry clapped, wanting to join in. I looked at Darcy for some support but the puppy had spotted a rabbit and had run off, barking at full volume. I sighed. 'Still outnumbered by men,' I muttered under my breath.

'You wouldn't have it any other way,' Rory said, putting Harry down, and leaning over to kiss me. 'Let's walk up the hill and tire these two out,' he said, pointing to Darcy who was now running after Harry. We set off across our land, a merry party of five humans, and one dog, the sun beating down on us from a clear, blue sky, and I sent up a silent thank you to my mum for helping me to see just what a blessing my life was, and how much I loved the people in it.

And for showing me that life doesn't have to turn out the way you plan, and thank goodness for that.

A Letter from Victoria

Dear readers,

I started this book at the start of 2020 and had to finish writing it during the UK Coronavirus lockdown in March. It was a surreal time to be writing but I was grateful to have the lovely world of Glendale to escape to.

This time, Heather is the main character and I was eager to show that the Heather we had seen in the first two books wasn't always the whole truth, that sometimes she felt the need to show everyone just how capable she was even if underneath, she was struggling. I think we all do that sometimes. Heather is a worrier, just like me, and her anxiety sometimes stops her from enjoying her life as much as she should. It was interesting to climb inside Heather's head during such an anxious time for the world, and even though I decided not to mention the virus and keep Glendale as the escape we all need it to be, I felt like I understood Heather's mindset even more. I hope that Heather finds a place in your hearts like she has in mine, and that if you are a worrier like us you know that you are also a warrior, and you are capable of anything you want to do.

I want to take this opportunity to thank you all so much for your wonderful messages about the Glendale books. Honestly, it's amazing to know that so many of you love reading these stories as much as I love writing them. Writing is such a solitary profession, and I decided to write full-time just as we went into lockdown, so it's been such a support knowing there are so many of you out there waiting to read this third Glendale story. Thank you so much to anyone who has contacted me this year, or followed me on social media – your messages have brightened my day so many times, and your support really does mean the world to me.

I hope you stay safe and well, and that you enjoy escaping to Glendale once again. Glendale welcomes you back with open arms to a snowy Scottish Christmas with a cup of hot chocolate and a slice of cake so please curl up, read, and enjoy! And please do pop a review up on Amazon if you can, and come and say hello to me on social media too.

Lots of love,
Victoria

Instagram: @vickywalters
Twitter: @vicky_walters
Facebook: VictoriaWaltersAuthor
Blog: www.victoria-writes.com

Biography and List of Books

Victoria Walters writes uplifting and inspiring stories. She's the author of the bestselling GLENDALE HALL series, which continues with its third book *HOPEFUL HEARTS AT GLENDALE HALL* in Autumn 2020, as well as two other standalone novels – *SUMMER AT THE KINDNESS CAFE*, and *THE SECOND LOVE OF MY LIFE*. She has been chosen for WHSmith Fresh Talent and shortlisted for two RNA awards. Victoria was also picked as an Amazon Rising Star, and her books have won wide reader acclaim. Victoria is a full-time author who lives in Surrey with her cat Harry.

Glendale Hall series:
Coming Home to Glendale Hall
New Beginnings at Glendale Hall
Hopeful Hearts at Glendale Hall

Standalone novels:
The Second Love of my Life
Summer at the Kindness Cafe

eBook short stories:
Dancing in the Fire
The Summer I Met You

Acknowledgments

Thank you to my editor Keshini Naidoo for all your guidance on this book and the whole Glendale series, for sharing my enthusiasm and love of these characters, and for all your helpful notes and phone calls! I couldn't have written this one without you. Thank you so much Lindsey Mooney for all your hard work in getting the Glendale books into readers' hands, and for the cheering Zoom chats too! Thanks, as always, to my agent Hannah Ferguson for your support and encouragement.

A big thank you to all at Hera and the team at Hardman and Swainson for all the work you do behind the scenes for my books, I really appreciate it all! Special thanks to copy editor Dushi Horti, Vicki Vrint for proofreading, and Cherie Chapman for all the gorgeous Glendale covers.

During lockdown, I was lucky to be able to chat with lots of authors and readers, more than I ever have done before, and 'meet' some via Zoom too, which was lots of fun. Special thanks to Kim Nash, Kiley Dunbar, Lisa Swift, George Lester, Anna Bell, Cressida McLaughlin, Heidi Swain, Lisa Dickenson, Isabelle Broom, the Doomsday Writers, and Laura, Hayley, Rachel, Jenn for all brightening up my days! Thank you so much to my Facebook Book Squad, and all the book bloggers and reviewers who have shown so much support and love for the Glendale series.

I really do appreciate every message I receive from readers of my books, and I was so honoured to hear that my books helped cheer some of you up during lockdown. It's such a pleasure to write for you all! I hope Glendale continues to be a lovely escape for us all for a long time to come.

Lots of love to my family and friends too, especially to my mum and Harry, my lockdown companions, for helping me through writing this book.